WOMEN OF THE UNITED FEDERATION MARINES

SNIPER

Colonel Jonathan P. Brazee
USMCR (Ret)

Semper Fi Press

A Semper Fi Press Book

Copyright © 2016 Jonathan Brazee

Illustration © 2016 Jessica TC Lee

ISBN-13: 978-0692729380 (Semper Fi Press)
ISBN-10: 0692729380

Printed in the United States of America

Acknowledgements:

I want to thank all those who took the time to pre-read this book, catching my mistakes in both content and typing. I'd like to thank Jonathan and Creativo1 for their editing and proofreading. Any remaining typos and inaccuracies are solely my fault. Another shout-out goes to my cover artist, Jessica Tung Chi Lee. I love her work, and I think she nailed this cover as well. You can see more of her work at:

http://www.jessicatcl.com/news.html.

Original Art by Jessica TC Lee

Cover Layout by Steven Novak

Dedicated to:

Joseph Medicine Crow-High Bird
(October 27, 1913 – April 3, 2016)
Last War Chief of the Apsáalooke
Author, Historian, WWII Army Veteran

Major Megan Malia Leilani McClung, USMCR
USNA Class of 1995
KIA 6 December 2006
Ramadi, Iraq
A bright star extinguished too soon.

RIP

BOOK 1

Jonathan P. Brazee

KULISHA

Chapter 1

Lance Corporal Gracie Medicine Crow pulled herself forward a few centimeters, then slowly reached under her body with her right hand and grasped the barrel of her Windmoeller, pulling it forward as well. Centimeter by centimeter, she crept through the low scrub. Gracie had been in her stalk for over six hours, and she'd barely advanced 200 meters. She was running out of time, she knew, but she refused to panic and rush. Just another five or six meters, and she should have eyes on her target—if she'd read the map app correctly.

Gracie was in her stalk naked—not literally naked, but without a tarnkappe,[1] fractured array,[2] or any other hi-tech method for remaining unseen. A tarnkappe was a passive piece of gear, but it could hook on a plant as she advanced, making it move unnaturally, and she thought the fractured array could subconsciously grate on an observer. He might not be able to see her, but something would tell him that someone was out there.

No, Gracie had chosen to go natural, using the local vegetation, her ghillie, and very controlled and thought-out movement to escape detection. Others thought she was a throwback, an anachronism, but it was her ass on the line, and so it was her choice to make.

---

[1] Tarnkappe: a piece of cloaking that bends light waves around an object, making it very difficult to visually detect.

[2] Fractured Array: A method of bending and "fracturing" light waves that throws off an observer's ability to pinpoint a position.

Jonathan P. Brazee

She resisted uncovering the scout-sniper wrist PA she was wearing. She knew time was running out, but she was most vulnerable at the end of a stalk, and she could fail her mission with an untimely mistake, such as taking the camo covering off the PA (even if only for a moment).

With her eye on the slight rise in front of her, she edged forward, first her body, then sliding her weapon up underneath her. It would be easier and a heck of a lot more comfortable pulling her Windmoeller alongside instead of under her, but even when camouflaged, even if it was designed with calculated angles to throw off observation, the weapon still had an unnatural shape, so she lay on top of it as she moved.

"Comfortable" was all relative, however. She was acutely aware of her sore knees and elbows and of the rash of bites from every insect that inhabited the last 200 meters. One particular welt along her belly ached to be scratched, but she would not allow herself any movement except to advance her stalk.

Come-on, Crow. Focus!

She'd planned her route carefully, but the ground truth was never the exact same as in a map app. For the last 50 meters, she'd been creeping up a small, almost unnoticeable swale. Right in front of her, a meter away now, was the crest of the shallow slope. Clearing that, the top of her head should be in line-of-sight to her target. With the stress of the stalk, she had a sudden urge to pop up and spot her target, to engage as quickly as possible and just get it over with.

Calm, calm, she repeated to herself. *Don't blow it now.*

Slower than she thought possible, she raised her head until her eyes cleared the edge of the higher ground. For a moment, she thought she'd calculated incorrectly, that she'd failed. It would be too late, she knew, to move to her alternate FFP.[3] But as she rose just a centimeter or two higher, she saw the enemy party some 800 meters ahead, under a huge umbrella thorn.

Just as slowly as she had risen, she lowered herself back down. Cautiously, ever so cautiously, she pulled up her

---

[3] FFP: Final Firing Point

Windmoeller, running a finger over the muzzle to make sure the frac-tape hadn't come off during the stalk before pushing forward once more. Even moving less than a meter, it took almost ten minutes for Gracie to be in position, her rifle trained on the group below.

She scanned the seven men, trying to pick out her targets. Her secondary target was easy. The big man was facing her, talking to another man. But she couldn't spot her primary target. She had a grainy image of him displayed on the left side of her scope, but no one in the group seemed to match it. A sinking feeling threatened to take over her. If she couldn't find her primary, she'd take out the secondary, but her mission would be a failure. She raised herself a few more centimeters to get a better view

There! Could that be him? she wondered, spotting a prone body at the base of the tree.

Her scope AI tried to use facial recognition to confirm the target, but the man had a hat over his face as he snoozed. It couldn't even come up with a probability that the man was him.

Gracie was stymied. She'd known she could be spotted. That came with the territory. But she never considered completing the stalk but being unable to identify her target. Her ROE[4] required a positive ID to take the shot. She wondered if she should just take out her secondary target and hope for the best.

She knew the range to the tree should be 816 meters from her location. She could laze it, of course, but even with her Miller Scope's cloaked rangefinder, there was always a chance that the enemy would have detection equipment that could pick it up. She was confident that she was where she thought she was, so she entered the range into her scope AI. She'd already entered the Coriolis numbers for Kulisha, and her Windmoeller had automatically uploaded her round type into the AI so it could plug in gyroscopic drift into the firing solution. Gracie had never heard of the wrong round type being uploaded, but still, she toggled the data screen to confirm the info as it was projected onto her scope display. As expected, her PGI .308, 172-grain, tef-sleeved round was

---

[4] ROE: Rules of Engagement

confirmed. With her Windmoeller's 1:10 twist rate entered, her scope AI had all the internal numbers needed for the firing solution.

Externals were always more problematic. Her Miller was far more advanced than the Roeniger Scopes that had been the Marine Corps standard for decades until being phased out five years earlier, and it did a better job at analyzing the temperature, air density, and humidity for various terrain points along the bullet's flight and then uploading that data into the firing solution. The results would be pretty accurate, but as derived from active methods, they created a huge risk of detection, so Gracie chose to use her passive systems.

Wind was light-to-moderate, about eight or nine KPH coming from her two o'clock, but she could see swirls in the grass that indicated it was not steady. This was where the firing AI was weakest and where sniping became more art than science. Gracie had to look at the patterns and try to figure out what the wind would be doing over the entire 800 meters during the flight of the round.

Most laymen seemed to think that with modern firing AI's, anyone could be a sniper. To them, it was basically just point and shoot, something far from the truth. A poor position, poor trigger control, poor breath control, and unlucky externals such as a gust of wind were just a few of the problems that could ruin a shot. Gracie was damned determined that she would not fall into any of those traps. She would make the kill.

It was time. She took five deep breaths, then exhaled half-way out, settling herself. She centered the crosshairs of her scope mid-chest of her secondary target, just below the base of his neck. A gust of breeze tilted the grass halfway to the target, and that made Gracie hesitate. Some snipers clicked in windage, but Gracie preferred a quicker solution. She held five centimeters off her target's left and started to squeeze the trigger. . .

. . .and stopped dead. Something was trying to break free from her subconscious, and she couldn't get a hold of it. She shifted her scope back to the prone man. He hadn't moved. He was still on his back, hat covering his face, hands interlocked over his chest.

What is it? she wondered, refusing to rush despite the ticking clock.

In a flash, it came to her. *The ring!*

The prone man had a largish ring with what looked to be a green stone of some sort. She'd seen it before, she was sure. She toggled her AI, and the lone image she had of her primary appeared on the left side of the display. It was somewhat grainy, and his face was not terribly clear, but on his left hand was a coal black ring with a large green oval stone setting. It looked exactly like the ring on the prone figure.

She slowly reached forward to her scope screen, framed the ring, and hit the interrogatory. Within five seconds, the results flashed on the screen: there was an 86% probability that the rings were one and the same.

She only needed a 75% to take the shot. But that was on the target himself, not a ring. What if her primary had simply given the ring to someone else? But in her heart, she knew that was him. The prone man had the same general build as her primary, and if it wasn't him, then where was he?

Screw it, I'm taking the shot.

She shifted her point of aim, and before she could second guess herself, she squeezed the trigger. The Windmoeller bucked against her shoulder, and without pausing, she cycled in a new round and shifted her aim to her secondary. The enemy were not amateurs. Before she could acquire her target, the men were diving for the ground. All the better, Gracie thought. As with her primary, when prone, windage becomes less in play. Her AI's weakness was in lateral targeting, not vertical, and she trusted it to get her on target.

There was a limit to that, though. She could only see the top few centimeters of her target as he lay prone, trying to spot her. He turkey-peeked a few times, only popping up for an instant, not staying exposed long enough for her to fire. Several of the other men jumped up and moved to get better cover, but they weren't her target.

Finally, she could see her secondary's butt bunch up. She knew he was going to make a dash.

Lead or ambush?

If he was going to run, she couldn't hold her crosshairs on him. At over 800 meters, he would run past the round's trajectory by the time it reached him. She had to fire where he would be, not where he was at the moment. If she led him and squeezed the trigger, the muzzle of her Windmoeller would be tracking him, and that movement could be picked up. By ambushing him, the muzzle would not be moving, but she wouldn't be able to squeeze the trigger slowly—she had to send the round downrange on command.

Gracie was pretty confident that she had better-than-average trigger control, though. So ambush it was. She picked a spot a few meters to her secondary's front and waited.

But not for long. Within five seconds, her secondary rose up, and while crouching, started to run to Gracie's left. With a minute adjustment to take into account his crouching position, Gracie pulled the trigger. Again the Windmoeller bucked against her shoulder. She froze in place, not moving a muscle. The recoil knocked her off her sight picture, but she could still see through part of her scope. She thought she caught a glimpse of her secondary disappearing behind the cut bank of the creek behind their position, but she couldn't be sure.

"Cease fire, cease fire," came over her ear buds. A few moments later, "Two kills confirmed."

Gracie tried not to let out a sigh of relief. She'd been sure of her shots, but it wasn't until the powerful exercise AI calculated all factors that a kill could be confirmed.

Her test wasn't over yet. In the raised platform to the right of her targets, five instructors were sitting, glassing the area. She'd gotten the kills, but if she'd been spotted, she'd have failed. She'd have one more chance, and if she failed that one, the last nine months of school would have been a colossal waste of time. Gracie didn't want to have to try her final stalk again with all of that added extra pressure.

During her sniper history classes back in Phase 1, she'd learned that in centuries past, the instructors would hold up a number that she'd have to identify to prove she had eyes on her target. With modern AI's determining her shot had been good, there was no need for that, to Gracie's relief. She didn't want to move her weapon even a millimeter to pick out some stupid number.

With her naked eye, she saw a walker, one of three instructors who were wandering the range, start towards her.

Shit! she thought, trying to will the man to stop.

It must have worked because he turned into a large acacia bush 20 meters away.

"Here?" she heard him pass on his comms, then, "That's a negative. No student-sniper within 10."

I wasn't born yesterday, she thought despite telling herself not to be too cocky.

The acacia offered perhaps the best FFP in this section of the range—which was why she hadn't chosen it. She was pretty sure the spotters hadn't seen anything and were trying to pull her location out of their collective asses. She hadn't been a favorite of any of them, and she knew they wanted to drop her. She just couldn't give them the excuse to do so.

Gracie had never been anyone's favorite. When people first saw her, most men and more than a few women's eyes lit up as they approached to chat her up. Her cold exterior was her shield to keep them at bay, and that usually translated into antipathy towards her at best, downright hostility at worst. She knew most other Marines called her the Ice Princess, but that didn't bother her. It wasn't as bad as what she'd been called at St. Labre back in Ashland.

"Exercise is terminated. Go ahead and get up, Lance Corporal Crow," Master Guns Masterson, the chief instructor passed on the comms.

Gracie felt a thrill run through her. She'd done it!

She stood up and was thrilled to see Sergeant Kilkelly startle from where he was standing only 20 meters away. She realized that even while walking the course, he hadn't spotted her.

"Cutting it close, there, Crow. You fired with less than two minutes left."

"Two minutes or two hours doesn't make much difference, right Sergeant?" she said, unable to help herself. "I passed."

His eyes seemed to cloud over for a moment, and Gracie mentally kicked herself. She knew she could be prickly, but did she have to make it worse? Sergeant Kilkelly wasn't a bad guy.

"Yeah, Crow, you passed. So congrats."

He safety-checked her weapon (which Gracie thought was a joke as they'd never been issued live ammo) and said, "Now get back to the bleachers for the debrief."

"Yes, Sergeant. And thank you," she said, trying to sooth him.

"Thanks? For what?"

"You know, Sergeant. For training me."

"Shit, Crow, you passed. No need to suck up to me. Graduation's on Friday, and you'll be out of here."

Gracie could almost hear the "and good riddance" in his voice. She didn't let it bother her, though. She was just proud of what's she'd accomplished. She slung her Windmoeller over her shoulder and started to march across the training range to the bleachers.

"Double time, Lance Corporal Crow! I'd like to get home to my wife sometime tonight."

She broke into a jog, willing to do whatever was necessary. Sergeant Kilkelly had been right. As of Friday, she'd be an official Marine Corps scout-sniper and on her way to her new unit!

TARAWA

Chapter 2

Gracie stood in the main passage of the battalion CP, waiting for the sergeant major. On the wall in front of her was a plaque with all of the commanding officers of the Second Battalion, Third Marines, stretching back almost 400 years. There were a few notable names on the list, not the least being that of Lieutenant Colonel Ryck Lysander, who'd commanded the battalion twenty years earlier. That was when Gracie had been born. Lysander was famous for his role in both coming to terms with the Klethos and in leading the Evolution, but that didn't have much of an emotional impact on her. She'd been in sixth grade at St. Labre during the Evolution, and in the windswept Montana plains, far from the fighting off-world, not much had changed in her life. Still, it was sort of interesting seeing his name engraved on the plaque. Two-three was proud of its long history. Facing the commanding officer plaque on the opposite bulkhead was another plaque with all of the battalion's sergeants major, and on the bulkhead by the entrance into the CP, Gracie had seen individual plaques honoring battalion notables such as Federation Nova holders and commandants.

"Lance Corporal Medicine Crow, come on in," Sergeant Major al Boudrey shouted out from his office.

"Take a seat," he said as she entered, pointing at a well-worn couch along the bulkhead. "Welcome to the Fuzos. You do know our patron unit, right?"

"Yes, Sergeant Major. The Corpo de Fuzileiros. From Portugal."

Upon the formation of the United Federation Marine Corps, all of the new infantry battalions had adopted as their patron unit one of the 48 extant national or planetary Marine Corps at the time, absorbing their history and traditions. In addition to celebrating the two UFMC birthdays, each battalion celebrated its patron unit's birthday as well. Gracie had known that 2/3 was known as the Fuzos, but she had to look up just what that meant. The Marine Corps loved traditions and history, but Gracie was more of a here-and-now girl. She'd known, however, that she'd better be well-versed in the battalion's history before she reported aboard.

"So you knows our history. I can gives you the long speech about what that means, and how you needs to honor and uphold all of that, but if you don't already feels that in your bones, nothing saying will change that.

"Before you meets the CO, I want to clear the air and gives you the lay of the land."

Gracie said nothing, waiting for whatever the sergeant major had to say. She'd had more than a few such conversations in her short career so far, and whichever way it went, she'd just react.

"Major Cranston, our Three, he pulled some strings to gets you assigned to us. The Scout-Sniper Platoon is his baby, and he does what he can to gets the best. You had the highest final score in your class, so as far as he was concerned, that means the best was you."

Gracie sat there, looking at the sergeant major with what she hoped was a respectful demeanor.

"But you didn't gets the Takahara Award, and that's a red flag to me."

Gracie had received the highest score of any of her classmates, both in class scores as well as marksmanship and field scores. The Takahara Award, which was given to the Honor Graduate, had gone to someone else. She'd been pissed when she'd first found out, but like so much else in her life, she'd just let it slide off her.

"So I calls me my good friend, Master Guns Masterson."

Gracie's heart fell just the tiniest bit. The master guns had not been a big fan of hers.

"Here's what the master guns tells me. From all accounts, you're a kick-ass Marine. You can do everything thrown at you, every task, every mission. That's good, right?"

He seemed to be waiting for a response, so Gracie said, "Yes, Sergeant Major."

"But, he says, you're not a team player. You thinks of yourself and not of the rest. He says he thinks that's why you volunteered for the school, 'cause you think you'll be working alone."

Gracie thought that was unfair. She never shirked from her duties, and she didn't create any conflict. If she didn't socialize with too many others while off-duty, if she didn't share in the grab-ass with the other Marines, that shouldn't matter.

"And there was the incident with a certain corporal, one that could have gotten you dropped from the course," the sergeant major continued.

Gracie felt the familiar surge of anger start to boil. That wasn't her fault. Corporal Weintrub had been drunk, and he'd come on to her at the E-Club. She'd been sitting alone, nursing a beer, when he'd taken it upon himself to "give her some company," was how he'd put it later. What he'd neglected to mention was that his "company" had included a hand on her thigh. So she'd stood up and punched him in the chin before stalking off.

She'd not gotten into any official trouble, and Weintrub had barely escaped harassment charges, but the incident had soured her relationship with most of her fellow students. The master guns had kept it an enlisted problem, not involving official action from the officers, but he had lectured her on "diffusing" such a situation instead of escalating it. Which was exactly what she'd thought she'd done. She'd put a quick end to Weintrub's advances before they could have gotten any further.

"I knows you had provocation, but the corporal was drunk as I hears it, and you didn't have to go all physical on him."

As if drunk is an excuse.

"Look, I'm not saying you were wrong, but we are a team here, and we needs to know how to work together. We needs to know everyone has each other's back.

"I also knows your nic: 'Ice Princess.' That's not so good, and it worries me.

"Look, I'm out of here in a month. I'm being bumped up to be the regimental sergeant major. But until then, unit morale's my responsibility. You're going to one of the best, if not the best, scout-sniper platoon in the Corps. I told you the platoon is Major Cranston's baby, and he pulled one of our best lieutenants, Lieutenant Wadden, from the line companies to be the platoon commander. The platoon is tight, really tight. I wants to keep it that way. I don't care if you are Annie Oakley reincarnated, if you creates a diversion, if you creates a rift, then I'll yank you so fast that you won't know what hit you. Capisce?"

Gracie had no idea how to respond. Her hope of a clean slate had rapidly flown out the window.

"Capisce, Sergeant Major. I understand."

"OK, good," he said, standing up and offering his hand. "You've got the skills, Lance Corporal, so with only a little effort here," he said, pointing at his heart, "you can be one of the best. Master Guns Masterson thinks so, and I've known him my whole career, so I trust his opinions on things like this."

That took Gracie a bit by surprise. If the master guns had thought that, he'd never let on.

"Let me see if the CO's ready for you," he said to her before lifting his head and speaking out, "Connect with the CO."

After the soft chime, he said, "Colonel, you ready for Lance Corporal Medicine Crow?"

There was a pause, and Gracie could hear what sounded like papers being shuffled before, "Sure. Give me a second and bring her over."

"Remember, the colonel's busy, so this is an in-and-out. If she asks if you have any questions, no, you don't. Understand?"

"Yes, Sergeant Major."

"She doesn't usually welcome every non-rate to the battalion, but she does for the scout-snipers since you works for her, so we goes in, she says 'welcome aboard,' and we goes out."

Technically, the Scout Sniper Platoon worked directly under the S2,[5] but Gracie didn't think she should mention that. Besides, when you got down to it, everyone in the battalion worked for the commanding officer.

She acknowledged the order and followed the sergeant major out of his office and across the passage to the CO's office. The sergeant major nodded at the duty clerk, then rapped on the door jamb of the open hatch.

"Ma'am, Lance Corporal Medicine Crow."

"Come on in, Sergeant Major," the CO's voice projected out of the hatch and reached her.

"Report to the CO."

Gracie marched in, centered herself in front of the CO's desk, and while staring a meter above her head, announced, "Lance Corporal Gracie Medicine Crow, reporting as ordered, ma'am!"

"Stand at ease," the CO said. "I've only had a chance now to look at your records, Lance Corporal Medicine Crow. I can see now why Major Cranston pulled strings to get you here. Very impressive."

"Thank you, ma'am," Gracie said, risking a glance down to look at the CO in the eyes.

And she was surprised. Lieutenant Colonel Rhonendren was short, almost as short as Gracie. Gracie hadn't expected that. She knew that the CO was one of the first women to take command of an infantry battalion, and she'd pictured some hulking Valkryie of a woman, a street-brawler. But facing her was a petite, very attractive woman. She'd obviously never let her size or appearance get in the way of her military advancement. And if the CO could succeed in what was still for all practical purposes a boys' club, then why couldn't she succeed as well?

Women had only been allowed into the Federation armed forces after the Evolution, and while the integration was now a fact of life, a much lower percentage of women than men qualified for recruit training and then completed boot camp. The pool of women selected for the officer ranks was therefore smaller, and it had taken this long for the first of those female enlisted Marines selected for officer school to reach lieutenant colonel.

---

[5] S2: Intel. The term can be used for the entire intelligence staff or the specific intelligence officer.

Gracie realized her mind had wandered, and she snapped her gaze up.

". . .good training during workups," the CO was saying. "So unless you have any questions, I'll let the sergeant major point out the way to the Scout-Sniper Platoon. I think they're coming in from the field this afternoon."

"No ma'am, no questions," she said, very conscious of the sergeant major hovering just off her shoulder.

"Sergeant Major, Lance Corporal Medicine Crow's all checked in with admin?"

"Yes, ma'am. Sergeant Ruskin's standing by at the Pig Shack to get her locked on."

"OK, then. Welcome to the Fuzos, Lance Corporal Medicine Crow."

Gracie recognized a dismissal, so she came to attention, did an about face, and marched out of the office.

"Wait here," the sergeant major said, pointing to the bulkhead outside his office. "I'll get Sergeant Ruskin to come fetch you."

Gracie stood at an easy parade rest, back against the bulkhead, as the sergeant major disappeared into his office. It had been an interesting check-in. She hadn't been pleased when she found out the sergeant major had done his sleuthing about her time at the sniper course, but seeing the CO, who could have been an older version of her, lifted her spirits.

If the CO could succeed in the Corps, then why not her?

Chapter 3

Gracie sucked in her gut, slipped past Staff Sergeant Riopel, and plopped into the vacant seat. The PIG Shack's "briefing room" had once been a storage locker, and the bolt holes from the shelving that had been removed gave the briefing room a rather makeshift feel. More Marines wandered in, taking seats where they could.

The room was tight and the rows of folding chairs close together, and Corporal Pure Presence made a show of trying to slide past Sergeant Win, then "accidently" fall to sit on the smaller Marine. Gracie couldn't see exactly what the sergeant did to Pure Presence, but it made the corporal jump up with a yell, much to the delight of the other Marines.

Gracie had been with the platoon for over a week, and she thought she had meshed well with the others. She was one of only three "lance coolies"[6] and the only female in the nineteen-man platoon, but she had felt welcomed enough, or at least not rejected. The platoon had returned from a two-week training exercise the day Gracie had arrived and had immediately gone on a 96,[7] so her first four days had been spent either on duty or drawing her gear. Consequently, she hadn't had too much interaction with the others in the platoon, but still, even after everyone got back, they seemed to accept her. The lieutenant had given her the usual ooh-rah welcome aboard, and the gunny had painted a demanding, but entirely reasonable view of what he expected of her. The rest of the platoon hadn't exactly embraced her, but no one had expressed anything negative about her, either. That was a win in Gracie's book.

Some people seemed to elicit an immediate impression of themselves. Gracie was one of them. With her striking appearance, people usually took an instant liking or disliking of her. With the

---

[6] Lance Coolie: slang for lance corporal
[7] 96: Four days of liberty, as in 96 hours.

platoon, there was a casual acceptance, but it seemed like they were delaying developing an opinion of her until after she proved herself as a sniper—and that was exactly as Gracie wanted it.

Gunny Buttle entered the briefing room with two Marines in tow. The casual jaw-jacking ceased as he walked behind the podium. Toby Buttle was the senior HOG,[8] or Hunter of Gunman, in the platoon. He'd gotten his first kill on First Step during the Evolution, and he'd added 26 more to his tally since then. Gracie was a little in awe of the man, and she hoped she could hone her craft with his guidance. She knew she was probably a better shot than anyone else in the platoon, but that was on the range, not in a field environment, and Gracie was not arrogant enough to think she was anything but a crass newbie as a sniper. If she wanted to succeed, she needed to absorb everything she could from the other HOGs.

Of the nineteen Marines in the platoon, twelve were HOGs. The rest, including the lieutenant, were PIGs, or Professionally Trained Gunmen. The PIGs would remain PIGs until they shot and killed an enemy.

Gracie glanced up at the stuffed head of a mean-looking boar that hung high on the bulkhead behind the podium. She had no idea where the tradition of HOGs and PIGs originated, but the boar's head was a decent-enough mascot/logo, even if it was probably a fabricated fake.

Under the boar's head was a sign that read:

Snipers aren't deadly because they carry the biggest rifles; they're deadly because they've learned how to weaponized math.[9]

You've got that right, she thought to herself, remembering the hours upon hours of high-level physics she'd endured at sniper school.

---

[8] HOG: Hunter of Gunman, a term for a sniper who has killed in battle. Pronounced "hog."

[9] Attributed to Robert Evans, Chris Radomile, and Emir Hadzimuhamedovic: *Cracked.com*, October 14, 2012

"Ok, listen up," the gunny said. "The lieutenant's ordered a stand-down of all personal weapons. We've been pretty up-tempo, and he wants everything re-calibrated. Sergeant Irvash, coordinate with Staff Sergeant Holleran for a schedule. I'm locking on R102 for zeroing in on Friday."

Gracie's ears perked up at that. She'd been issued all of her field gear, but without the lieutenant around until yesterday, she hadn't been issued any of her weapons. A Marine without a weapon, much less a scout-sniper, wasn't much of a Marine, after all.

"Section leaders, we've still got the 5500 checklist, so unless someone is physically in the armory for the recal, I want them working on getting that thing out of the way."

There was a collective groan among the platoon. The 5500 checklist was an inordinately long, detailed, and excruciatingly boring admin requirement that had to be updated every three years. Gracie had gone through a 5500 twice: once at boot camp, then another a year later with 3/12. The general theory was that headquarters required it only to make Marines so sick of the process that any mission, no matter how onerous or dangerous, would be heaven-sent in comparison. Gracie tended to accept that theory.

"And as you can see, we've got new meat. Lance Corporals Oesper and Gittens have just completed the division school. Kierk, you've got Oesper as your new spotter, and Crow, you've got Gittens."

Gracie sat up quickly and turned to look at the two newbies in shock. She'd just been assigned to Corporal Kierkegaard as his spotter, and now she was a sniper? As a graduate of the top-level Marine Corps Scout Sniper School, she knew that she'd probably be assigned as a sniper sooner rather than later, but within a week, and a week in which there had been no real training?

"Section leaders, meet me in five in the lieutenant's office. The rest of you, get your asses moving. I want the 5500 done and out of our hair by COB Thursday."

Which one is Gittens? she wondered for a moment as she stood up.

The larger of the two newbies looked around, spotted her, and stepped over the row of chairs to stand in front of her, hand out.

He was tall, at least 2.2 meters, and probably hit 110 kgs. His square jaw and rather handsome face beamed with a confidence with which some people were born. He was probably his school Alpha, the star jock, the one who dated anyone he wanted, the kind of man who thought he controlled not only his destiny but the destiny of all those around him.

Gracie always seemed to attract the attention of his type. But she was not some sort of arm-candy, and it took the cold and down-right rude face she exhibited to them to quench their interest in her. She wanted to become the best sniper in the Corps, and dealing with some hormone-filled hulk was not in her plans.

"Hi. I'm Eli. I'm your new spotter," he said, holding out a massive hand.

This is not going to be good, not at all.

Chapter 4

"Work it out," Gracie told Eli.

"I know what you said, but I don't quite get it," Eli said, frustration evident in his voice.

"Work it out again," she told him. "You need to understand this."

"Not that I'll ever have to use iron sights," he muttered, but he dutifully looked down at the pad of plastisheet and tried to make the calculations.

Gracie didn't try to correct him. "Iron sights" were not actually old-fashioned post and aperture sights, but were the slang for what was merely a simple scope without an internal AI. The scope provided a reticle and magnification, but nothing else. He was right in that he most likely would never have to fire without a normal AI-powered scope, but Eli was her spotter, and it was up to her to make sure he was trained. If they were in a hide for any length of time, she couldn't be on the glass 24/7, and he'd have to spell her. Since it could be her ass on the line, she wanted him trained up.

The Miller sniper scopes were all pretty well shielded, and the likelihood of them being compromised was slim. It had happened before, however. Anything from a virulent virus to a powerful, directed EMP could knock them out. Every sniper rifle in the Marine Corps' inventory was fitted for iron sights for a reason.

She heard another batch of chuckling to her right where Staff Sergeant Riopel and his spotter, Creach "Possum" Khalil occupied the next firing position. She knew they thought it was ridiculous that she was making Eli fire without a fully-operational scope, and they hadn't held back from expressing their opinions. But Gracie was in charge of her team, and unless she were doing something illegal or dangerous, not even her section leader would interfere.

The platoon was on R505, Known Distance Range. Targets were scattered from 350 to 2,000 meters out from the firing positions. R505 was a kinetic small arms range, and along with R506, the Unknown Distance Range, was one of the more frequented firing ranges for the platoon. While scout-snipers had a few energy weapons in their arsenal, the very nature of their missions—long range sharpshooting—and the physics of energy weapons with regards to ablation, meant that they almost exclusively used their kinetics.

Today, Gracie and Eli were on their Kyoceras. The slug-throwing Windmoellers were the weapon of choice for most missions, but the inducted-coilgun had its place in their arsenal. While the Windmoeller was not too terribly different from a conceptual standpoint from the early British Enfields and American Springfields of the 19th Century, the Kyoceras were a far cry from 21st Century Gaus guns. Using finely tuned arrayed coils, nitrogen cooling, and rotational power feeds, the Kyoceras could impart spin on the round as well as control the muzzle velocity. Dial down the power and the round would be sub-sonic, exiting the muzzle with barely a whisper. Dial it up and the round became super-sonic, up to 800 meters per second. While more maintenance-hungry than the Windmoeller, not as reliable, and much more of a complicated system, it never-the-less offered some distinctive advantages in the right situation.

"Uh, I think I have it," Eli said at last.

"OK, engage your target."

Eli settled into his firing position. Gracie looked at him with a critical eye and thought his feet were not spread far enough apart, but she let it slide. She turned her eye to the truthteller. The tripod mounted ME2003 Ballistic Tracker, Small Arms, would analyze and display the trajectory of the round from the moment it exited the muzzle to the moment of impact.

Eli took in a deep breath, let out half, then squeezed the trigger. The 162-grain round exited the barrel with a crack as it broke the sound barrier, and an instant later, impacted the dirt well short and to the right of the target.

"Hell, Gittens, what were you aiming at?" Gracie asked as she looked at the truthteller. "You're 20 centimeters to the right and 32 low."

"I thought I had it right," Eli protested.

"I thought I had it right." Gracie mimicked in a child's voice.

"Nice shooting," Staff Sergeant Riopel called over to them. "I'm sure you scared him to death."

"Give me your numbers," Gracie said, ignoring her section leader.

"What's this? Twenty KPH of crosswind? Where did you get that?"

"From the range flag. Look at it. It's at about a 45-degree angle."

"And where is that, Gittens? That flag's 20 meters in the air. Look down on the deck. Does it look like the wind is that strong down there?"

Eli looked back downrange and seemed to consider that for a moment before admitting, "Well, maybe not. But I can't tell how strong it is with just my eyes."

He glanced at the Miller Scope that had been detached and was sitting back on the shooter's bench.

Gracie caught that and said, "And so if your scope is dead-lined, you can't perform your mission? Why don't you just join the Navy? You can sit there in your comfy seat and let the ship's AI calculate the firing solution, so all you have to do is push the button."

"Ooh, man that's cold," Staff Sergeant Riopel said while Possum laughed.

Another figure scribbled on the piece of plastisheet caught her attention. She looked back at the truthteller to see the actual velocity of the round.

"What was your N-setting?" she asked, already knowing the answer.

"Uh, five-point-three."

"Check your weapon."

"It's five-point-three, I told you. See. . .uh, wait a minute. I know I set it. But now it's—"

"It's four-point-five. I can see the muzzle velocity from the truthteller, and that means you had a four-point-five. Are you that much of an idiot, Gittens? You can't even set the power on your weapon?

"Get up," she told him.

He sheepishly stood until he was towering over his shorter team leader.

"Give me your weapon," she demanded.

"What? Why?" he said as he pulled back his rifle and twisted so it was farther away from her.

She understood his reluctance. Every weapon was customized for each sniper to take into account body size and structure and everything from cheek-welds to trigger-pull preferences. Marine scout-snipers became extremely possessive of their weapons, and many resorted to naming each one.

"I said give it to me."

Both Marines were the same rank, but Gracie was the scout-sniper and team leader, so after a moment, he hesitantly handed her his Kyocera.

She didn't even glance at the control panel but flopped down to the prone position instead. Without changing the settings, she sighted at Eli's target 874 meters downrange.

Crack, crack, crack; she whipped off three shots in less than two seconds. The Kyocera, unlike the Windmoeller, was semi-automatic, so there was no need to feed in each individual round to fire again. She also didn't need the soft chimes from the truthteller behind her to confirm the hits.

She shifted her target, and immediately engaged the "Head Shot" target, a small, round target 14 centimeters in diameter at 1,240 meters downrange. Three more shots, three more hits.

Without hesitation, she shifted her target to the "Old Man," the silhouette at 2200 meters. She almost fired, then slowed down for an instant as she noted the far range flag was hanging limp. She adjusted her hold about half a meter to the left, and with a quick mental calculation of the drop at an N of four-point-five, raised the hold almost two meters. She squeezed off two quick rounds, emptying the magazine.

She thought she was on target, but she held her breath for the moment it took the round to reach the old man and for the truthteller to confirm two hits. After the two welcomed chimes, she lay there for a moment, breathing a sigh of relief. That had been pretty stupid. Knowing what Eli had on his weapon and seeing his failed shot, she'd been sure she'd be able to hit his target. The Head Shot had been a little riskier, but using pure Kentucky windage for the Old Man had been taking a huge leap of faith. She'd let her arrogance get the better of her, something she couldn't afford. She'd pulled it off, thank goodness. But if she'd missed even one shot, it could have backfired on her. Even so, she realized that her overreaction to Eli would be noted, and her "bitch" reputation would only be strengthened. At least, by making the shots, hopefully her competence would counterbalance anything else.

She stood up, dropped the Kyocera's magazine, and showed the empty chamber to Eli before wordlessly handing him his weapon. He accepted it, his mouth hanging open in surprise (Shock? Embarrassment?)

"The capy," she said, indicating the small, roundish target at 575 meters. "Start working on it."

"Damn!" she heard from Staff Sergeant Riopel.

Whether that was because of her shooting or her treatment of Eli, she didn't know.

Chapter 5

"Gittens, let me out," Gracie told Eli. "I need to use the head."

She waited for him to scoot out of the booth, then followed him out. He almost jumped back into the booth in his eagerness to catch the rest of Zach's, or now she should say Corporal Pure Presence's story of one of his high school exploits. Zach's adventures, which he was always eager to share, usually disgusted her. He was a Torritite, and she'd always thought they were a conservative sect, but he'd led a pretty wild life before enlisting—even if only half of what he said could be believed. Gracie's school life paled in comparison. Granted, St. Labre was a conservative Roman Catholic school, and the tribal elders frowned upon alcohol use, but even considering her somewhat limited experiences of party life, she thought Zach's self-professed exploits pushed any reasonable envelope.

The party was for Zach's promotion to corporal, however, so it was his stage. The entire platoon had shown up to help him celebrate the promotion. Even the lieutenant had made an appearance in the E-Club before he and Gunny Buttle left the rest to enjoy the party without adult supervision. Gracie wondered when it would be OK for her to leave. Not yet, she knew—which was why she made her excuse to use the head when Zach was reaching the climax of his adventure with an evidently morally-handicapped young lady named Ruth.

Gracie made her way through the crowded E-Club. Most of the Marines would start to filter out to the clubs out in town, but the E-Club was significantly cheaper than those bars. Credit-pinching junior Marines tried to get their Friday night drinking started at the E-Club, saving their cha-ching for later on in the evening.

She slipped inside the head. She didn't need to use it, but it had been an excuse. She walked up to the sink and ran some water over her hands, then splashed it on her face. That done, she looked at her reflection in the mirror-screen above the sink. She put both hands on the sink and leaned in closer, taking in her aquiline nose and deep, almost green eyes. Most of her tribe had brown eyes; the dark green was a rarity. The Crow prided themselves as being one of the last "pure" First Peoples, but retro-DNA mapping showed that a few Europeans, probably of Irish or Scottish descent, had managed to contribute their genes to the tribe. Her eyes were probably a vestige of one of those deeply hidden recessive genes.

She leaned back and turned her head slightly to the left. Gracie knew she was beautiful from the perspective of most others. Intellectually, that was evident from how people, mostly men, treated her ever since she was 12 or 13. It was attention Gracie did not seek nor appreciate. Emotionally, though, she really couldn't see it. She was just herself, Gracie Medicine Crow of the Apsaalooké, Children of the Beaked Bird.

She knew she should get back out there. Gracie did not enjoy socializing. Everything felt awkward to her, and she frankly distrusted the motives of those who were overtly friendly to her. She wondered if Zach had finished his story yet and it was safe to come back out.

Am I really that much of a prude? she wondered, looking straight into the mirror-screen again.

She didn't think so, but she was smart enough to realize she could be simply fooling herself. She thought about men; she thought about sex, but more as general concepts. Within the Crow, families were matriarchal, and husbands came to live with their wives' families. The Crow were a warrior people, from back in the time of their wars against the Sioux, Cheyenne, Kiowa, Shoshone, and other plains peoples, to their service with the US Army—Gracie's namesake, the War Chief Joseph Medicine Crow, was a decorated Army veteran—and on into the Federation Marines or the FCDC.[10] Her family approved of her service, but they expected her to come back after her enlistment and bring a man into the family. Gracie was not against this, but she was happy to put that off onto the distant future.

---

[10] FCDC: The Federation Civil Defense Corps: part police, part army, the FCDC's focus was on domestic security.

She sighed, turned off the water, and left the head. If anything, more Marines had crowded inside the club, and her way to her table was blocked. She had to make a detour, coming around to it from behind.

". . . let the Ice Bitch crush your balls, man," Zach was saying.

She stopped dead and took a step back behind the half-wall between her and her table. She'd known some people referred to her as the "Ice Princess." Was she the "Ice Bitch" too, or was that someone else?

When she heard Eli say, "Nah, it ain't like that," her heart fell. It was her.

"Bullshit. She rides you like a witch on a broom. Only she's cut your dick off to keep you in line."

"But what does she do with it?" someone, maybe Possum, asked while the table erupted into laughter.

Mortified, Gracie started to step back so she could leave unnoticed, but Eli's comment stopped her.

"Eat me, all of you. Yeah, she's hard, and yeah, she can be a bit of a bitch, but she knows her shit. I'd rather be her spotter than any of you roos, 'cause she can make me a better sniper."

"Holy shit, he's in love!" Staff Sergeant Riopel said to the enjoyment of the rest of table.

"With all due respect, Staff Sergeant, you can eat me, too. I don't think that woman knows the meaning of love, but she's a hell of a Marine, and even as a PIG, she's a better sniper than any of you HOGs."

Gracie edged back again, and the protests about who was a better sniper became too muddled for her to make out. She turned and almost ran out of the E-Club and into the welcoming embrace of the night.

WYXY

Chapter 6

Corporal Gracie Medicine Crow sat in her seat, head back and eyes closed, as the Stork juked and jived to the LZ.[11] She looked every bit the calm and collected Marine, but inside, she was about ready to burst with excitement.

This is it—first combat as a sniper!

The Stork flared into the stadium that was serving as the LZ and settled down with barely a bump. Gracie felt her excitement level rise a notch.

Exiting the Stork was somewhat of a madhouse with Marines running helter-skelter while getting organized. The battalion was employing the asinine MEEP, or Minimal Electronics Emissions Protocol, where the new upgraded PCS, the latest and greatest version of the Personal Combat System, was turned off, and Marines were back to simple hand-and-arm signals. Pretty much everyone hated MEEP, but orders were orders, and the battalion was thrown back into the Dark Ages. Guides were being employed to get the Stork sticks out of transport mode and into combat mode, but still, it was pretty much a clusterfuck. Gracie and Eli were directed to their left after getting off the Stork's ramp, but that got them into the middle of Fox Company.

They were supposed to move with Golf, and finally, an exasperated sergeant ignored the hand-and-arm to tell them, "Golf's over there, under the press box."

The two Marines cut across the playing field, ducking around another Stork coming in for a landing and ignoring two LST[12]

---

[11] LZ: Landing Zone

Marines trying to wave them around. They married up with Golf, and much to Gracie's surprise, the company was already moving out.

Wyxy was a friendly planet, and their landing had been unopposed. This was a rescue mission, not an assault on enemy territory. The SevRevs, the Seventh Revelationists, had invaded the small city of Serenity, executed hundreds of citizens, and were now holding 500 hostages in a farmer's market in a neighboring village. The SevRevs were just the latest in a string of apocalyptic groups, but instead of merely waiting for the End of Days, they thought it their holy duty to bring the End of Days about. They'd done some pretty horrific things in the past, all recorded and broadcast to the rest of humanity, and the Federation was bound and determined that they didn't succeed in promulgating their perverse message as they had on several other worlds.

This operation might be relatively small scale, but it was being taken very seriously. It was a righteous mission, and everyone wanted it to succeed, but from a professional standpoint, the mission could turn to shit quickly. The fifty or so SevRevs could not hope to stand up to a Marine battalion, but the fanatics welcomed their death, and they had the ability to take the hostages and possibly more than a few Marines with them.

Golf Company started snaking its way out of the stadium in a modified arrow with one platoon in a wedge and the remaining Marines in two columns in trace. Gracie and Eli, along with one other team, were moving with Golf, but they were not attached to the company. They were in general support of the battalion, and as such, were still under the lieutenant's command and not Golf's Captain Mueller's. Two teams were with each of the line companies. Fox Company, which was the assault element, was moving in trace of Golf, and Echo and Hotel were on the other side of the farmers' market to provide both support and to keep any SevRevs from escaping.

As the sergeant major briefed them aboard the *FS Klipspringer* before debarking, this was a kill mission. The goal was

---

[12] LST: Landing Support Team: personnel whose mission it is to control an LZ or beach landing.

to rescue as many hostages as possible, but each and every SevRev was to be eliminated. The message had to be sent that if you join the SevRevs, you will die without advancing your cause. The End of Days will be no nearer.

The Scout-Sniper Platoon's mission was vital to the overall mission. The SevRevs welcomed death, and the snipers were to assist them in reaching that goal. Once the PsychOps team issued their ultimatum, it was weapons free. Any SevRev was a target of opportunity. If the past SevRev operations were any indication, these terrorists probably had something planned, something spectacular. Taking out any one of them might delay that surprise until Fox Company could defuse it. Gracie was pretty sure that a year after becoming a PIG, she was finally going to fire a shot in anger this afternoon.

She should feel something more about that, she thought. She could be killing a human being in an hour, a person with parents who loved and raised him, a person who might have a wife and kids. But she felt no remorse. She only felt excited.

There was a quote from a 21st Century US Marine general named "Mad Dog" Mattis that she had saved on her PA:

The first time you blow someone away is not an insignificant event. That said, there are some assholes in the world that just need to be shot.

That pretty much summed up her viewpoint. These terrorists might be someone's sons, but they had long ago ceded their right to be considered part of humanity. Gracie was determined to remove as many of them from the gene pool as she could.

Wyxy was not known to be a hotbed of Federation loyalty, but the 30,000 or so citizens of Serenity had been traumatized. Several hundred in the city had been killed and an even greater number taken hostage. The survivors turned out in numbers to watch the Marines move through the city. Many watched in shocked silence, but some cheered. A father and daughter leaned out a window over a Federation flag they'd hung, calling out encouragement to the Marines below.

The stadium was located near the edge of the city, and after a klick-and-a-half, the column was moving into agricultural fields. Even before leaving the city proper, a few soft breezes had hinted at what was ahead. Once into the fields, the stench became overwhelming.

One of the Golf Marines in front of Gracie asked, "What the hell is that smell?"

Gracie almost laughed. Montana was a hotbed of back-to-nature agriculture, and she sure recognized the smell.

"It's chicken shit, Lance Corporal! You never smelt it before?" another Marine said.

"Geez!" Eli muttered to no one in particular. "Who cares what it is?"

Gracie had to agree with her spotter. They were moving into combat, and this bozo was all up in arms because of the smell?

"Why would I ever smell chicken shit? What, they can't get rid of it? And I don't see no chickens here nowhere," the first Marine said, looking around the fields.

"They use it for fertilizer. See those plants? They're strawberries. They use the shit as organic fertilizer."

"Bullshit, Korf! No one uses shit on food. It'd be unsanitary; that's what it'd be!"

The two went on in this vein for a few moments without regards to security. The fields were probably clear of hiding SevRevs, but "probably" did not mean "certainly." Gracie shifted her grip on her M99 and intensified her scanning of the area as that thought came to her mind.

Finally, Sergeant Vinter, one of the Golf squad leaders said, "Keep it moving, Wythe. We haven't stopped."

"About time," Eli muttered to himself again.

After another klick and crossing Renter's Creek, the strawberry fields gave way to knee-high sweet corn, which was far more benign. Either that or their noses were becoming smell-blind. Still, it was a welcome relief.

It took the company another 25 minutes to move through the corn fields and into the assembly area. The press was already there in full force, eager-beaver reporters and camcorder crews searching the Marines for interviews. A dozen cam-drones flitted overhead like dragonflies, ready to pounce.

The Rose Garden Farmers' Market, where the SevRevs were holed up, was a mere 600 meters away, well within small arms fire. The Marines were all in their skins and bones, which should be protection enough against most kinetic small arms. The reporters in this backwater corner of the Federation had a hodgepodge of protective gear thrown together, but only a few had a decent degree of protection. Most any Marine had the ability to reach out 600 meters with his or her M99, so if it had been the Marines in the market instead of the terrorists, all of the reporters would have been at risk given their lack of appropriate gear. Gracie didn't know the capabilities of individual SevRevs, but some had to be from planets that hunted for sport, and some of them had to be able to make that kind of shot as well.

Assembly areas should be covered and concealed from an objective, and 600 meters was simply too close. Staff Sergeant Riopel felt the government types thought that the mere sight of a battalion could make the SevRevs give up. He could be right, Gracie thought, not that any Marine gave any credence that their mere presence would cause a surrender. Regardless, she was sure there was no way that the CO would have approved this assembly area, and that it had to have been forced upon her.

"What a circus," one of the Marines said.

That was something upon which Gracie could totally agree. But that was beyond her control. She had to get her mind in the zone.

"Over there," she told Eli, moving to the public toilet she'd selected as her FFP.

The toilet was small, about five meters by five. It had looked good from the aerial survey, but she couldn't know for sure until she could see it up close. It was immediately obvious that it would do. Made from concrete, it was in good shape and could easily hold their weight.

"Give me a boost," she said.

Eli placed the sniper case on the ground, bent over, and cupped his hands. Gracie stepped into his hands, and with barely an effort, he raised her to where she could pull herself on top of the building. She got down on her stomach to take the sniper case and his M99 before offering him her arm. He grasped it, and with his legs on the building wall, scrambled up. Eli was a big man, and he was quite a load for Gracie, but she managed to give him enough support so he could grab the edge of the roof and haul himself up as well.

Both Marines walked to the edge of the roof facing the farmers' market. Their vantage point, a mere 2-and-a-half meters up, let them look over the approach to the market, giving her clear fields of fire. With Fox Marines going to be between her and the market, she'd be able to fire over the Marines' heads until the Marines actually reached it.

The market was quiet, with only the slightest movement visible inside a few of the windows. A newsdrone buzzed the two Marines, an annoying gnat, but seeing nothing interesting, the operator or AI sent it on its way to bother someone else. Below them, Golf was falling into position and Fox was passing through to the LOD.[13]

Above them, a Wasp overflew the assembly area and the market. Air couldn't engage the SevRevs with the hostages at risk, but this was all part of the psychological plan. A Wasp was a pretty nasty warbird, and if any of the SevRevs were having second thoughts, they might be rattled.

An amplified voice sounded out from where the psych team had assembled. "Inside the market, we are the United Federation Marines. You are trapped where you are. If you want to live, release the hostages. If you comply, you will not be harmed.

"If you do not release the hostages and resist us, you are inviting a certain destruction. It is up to you. Surrender and live or resist and die."

---

[13] LOD: Line of Departure

No one expected the SevRevs to surrender as easy as that, but especially with all the press, the forms had to be followed.

"OK, this will do, and we need to get ready. Let's get set up. Give me the Kyocera."

She slung her M99 as Eli opened the weapons case. Most snipers would have carried his or her own case, but Gracie was much better with the M99 than Eli was, and even surrounded by Golf Marines and passing through supposedly safe terrain, she'd felt better with the M99 to quickly deal with any surprises. Snipers prayed to the gods of war with their liturgy of "one shot, one kill," but for immediate action in close quarters, that wasn't always the best course of action. The M99 threw out a shitload of small 8mm darts at hypervelocity speeds, and that could make hamburger out of any enemy who managed to get close.

Gracie liked the M99, and it was a fun toy, but her heart purred as she took her Kyocera in her arms. She still wasn't too sure which weapon she liked better, this or the Windmoeller. The slug-thrower was basic, strong, and reliable, and that had its own allure. It was the workhorse, the pick-up that everyone wanted. The Kyocera, though, was sleek and sexy. It was the sportshover, the 0-100-in-four-seconds wonder.

From the target's standpoint, either was bad news. The Windmoeller's PGI .308, 172-grain, tef-sleeved round was bigger than the Kyocera's Western polymer-cased 162-grain round. On the other hand, the Western round could be fired at much higher velocities. The round was pulled rather than pushed, so it didn't have to obturate, and by goosing up the N's, it could reach hypersonic speeds. Either round, though, would certainly mess up someone's day.

For this mission, Gracie had chosen the Kyocera. The Kyocera was slightly more accurate up to 2,000 meters, but at 600 meters, she was confident that she could hit anything with either weapon. Something told her, however, that she might need to fire quickly, and as a semi-automatic with almost no recoil, the Kyocera had a quicker rate of fire. Gracie not only had to fire quickly, but the round had to get there quickly. If a target was running across an opening, she'd only have a second or two in which to acquire the target, snap off the shot, and have the round reach her intended victim. The Kyocera's round could be over twice as quick in its trajectory than the Windmoeller's.

Bill Kierkegaard, the other sniper with her in Golf's position, had chosen his Windmoeller, and Gracie thought that balanced the two of them. She glanced over to where he and Dave Oesper, his spotter, were setting up almost 150 meters away, right at the edge of the road leading to the market. She wasn't sure how effective he'd be, but with her grabbing the toilet building, he might not have had much of a choice.

"Give me the readings," she told Eli as she attached her bipod to the barrel clip.

Her Miller Scope was capable of them, but Eli had a truthteller, which was more accurate.

"Twenty-eight-point-three degrees, humidity seventy-two percent. Uh, I'm getting between eight and ten KPH on the wind, coming from your one-thirty."

Gracie was on active-mode with her Miller, and the smaller scope's data matched what he was telling her. She didn't tell Eli, though, that she was checking his numbers.

"Range the front door."

"Wait one. . .I've got 635 to the left jamb."

"Roger that."

The Miller had uploaded the atmospherics and would update them as necessary, but she manually entered the range if for no other reason than to let Eli see she was accepting his input. Since she was letting the Miller do the firing solution, the rounds' velocity would be automatically entered into the calculations. Still, she couldn't resist checking. It was still on 6.3, which converted to a muzzle velocity of 573 meters per second.

"Now we wait," she told Eli as she settled into a good solid prone position.

She started glassing the market with her scope, planning shots. She lingered on an armed man who was on the roof of the market, looking back at the Marines, but until she was weapons free, she could not engage.

"Fox is moving," Eli said beside her.

Gracie looked away from her scope and saw that the lead elements from Fox had stepped past the LOD.

"Any moment now, then. I want you to map and mark any target you can spot."

"Roger that."

She could feel Eli moving around the truthteller. The instrument was designed to track trajectories. In this type of scenario, Gracie thought she wouldn't need it for that purpose. She had to be on target the first time. If she had to adjust and fire again, she'd have failed. However, the truthteller also had the ability to mark targets and then upload those targets to her Miller. If the targets moved, the mark would move, too. All Gracie would have to do would be to click her zoom out, select a mark, and then click the zoom back to her standard magnification. It was designed as a teaching tool, to enable an instructor to identify a target for the student to engage, but Gracie thought it would be a slick way to engage multiple targets in a short amount of time in a real combat situation. She'd told the gunny she wanted to do it, and he shrugged, said others had tried it, but if she wanted to, it was her choice.

When Fox started moving, her friend on top of the market ducked down below the low wall along the edge of the roof. He had his UKI-52, the ubiquitous general-purpose rifle that Gentry made in the billions and distributed to every second-rate military in the galaxy, at the ready as he watched Fox company advance. The weapon was old and only had a maximum effective range of 400 meters, but it was relatively idiot-proof, and a head shot could kill a Marine. Weapons free or not, if he took aim at the Marines, Gracie was going to take him out and worry about the ROEs after the fact.

"How we doing on the targets, Gittens?"

"I've got eight so far."

Gracie took a second to hit the slide on the side of her Miller Scope to zoom out. Red target dots filled her scope display. She had a veritable cornucopia of potential kills just waiting for her. Her scope AI tried to prioritize them, but the flashing dots indicated that it was confused. Gracie zoomed in on three, but none seemed any more dangerous than the terrorist on the roof. She zoomed back in on him. He was getting antsy, and Gracie knew he was about to break.

"I'm going to take him out," she told Eli.

"But we haven't been given weapons free."

"Screw that!"

The SevRev started to rise as he put the UKI-52 to his shoulder. Gracie began to squeeze the trigger.

The Kyocera had an almost negligible kick, but at such a high velocity, the round broke through the sound barrier with an extremely sharp crack.

"Hit," Eli said.

Gracie reached up to zoom out. She'd picked the Kyocera because it was semi-automatic, and she wouldn't have to waste time cycling in a new round. But using the zoom in and zoom out to acquire targets took two moves, and the motion was almost the same as working the bolt to eject and chamber the next round on the Windmoeller.

"Weapons free," Lieutenant Wadden passed on the platoon net, breaking MEEP.

Within a couple of seconds, Gracie was back on the next target, a SevRev, who was using the butt of an ancient energy weapon of some sort to break a window.

Stupid, Gracie thought as she aimed and fired through the half-broken window.

Plastiglass, especially when used as hover windshields, could partially deflect rounds, particularly the lighter Western rounds used in a Kyocera, but with him only centimeters behind the window, her round took him in the chest.

"Hit!" Eli said unnecessarily.

Heavy fire broke out from the market, immediately answered by the Fox Company Marines.

Gracie zoomed out, then back in, but that target disappeared behind the walls of the market. Zoom out; zoom in. A SevRev was rushing out the main entrance. Sight, trigger, crack. The SevRev's head exploded into a pink mist. The tiniest motion at the side of the door caught her attention. It was the muzzle of another weapon, and just barely, the fingers of the man holding it. This would be a difficult shot, but she took it.

Her round struck the handguard of the rifle, sending it spinning to the floor. She'd hit a couple of centimeters high, she thought. She missed the fingers, but it had to have hurt. To her surprise, she saw a hand snake out along the floor to the rifle which remained just out of reach.

Come on, do it! she implored her unseen target.

Sure enough, she saw the top of a head. Just as it gave a flinch, she fired between the head and the rifle. The round took less than a second to reach the doorway, but that was enough time for the SevRev to dart forward to recover his rifle. He recovered a bullet to the neck instead and instantly collapsed.

"Target 6!" Eli told her.

She zoomed out, acquired it, and zoomed back in. Deep within the second floor, almost in the shadows, a figure stood, his hands holding what looked like a detonator against his chest. Gracie could only see his torso, but his posture was that he was watching Fox get ever closer.

With the sturdy plastiglass between them, and with him so far back, the shot was easier contemplated than actually doing. Gracie did some quick mental calculations. She'd fired through windshields on the Moving Vehicle Range back on Tarawa, but not with the Kyocera. She'd used the heavy Barrett for that. Still, it gave her some basic comparisons.

"I'm taking the shot," she said as she aimed right by almost a meter.

Mother of All, let me be right.

She squeezed the trigger, and a moment later, the window shattered. The body in the background stumbled and went to his knees, clutching his left shoulder. With an expression that almost looked like rhapsody, he reached for something on the floor, and Gracie's next round took him high in the chest. Another man rushed into the scope's field of view, and Gracie dropped him as well.

Whether someone else reached what Gracie was sure was a detonator or if the SevRevs had backups, she never knew, but the market erupted into a huge fireball. Gracie flinched as the light flared in her scope. A moment later, the shockwave hit.

"Holy shit," Eli murmured.

Flames and smoke climbed into the air.

Gracie jumped back onto her scope, searching the maelstrom for targets.

"No one's surviving that," Eli said.

But people had. Bodies rushed out of the rubble. Gracie almost blew the first person away, but she was sure the man was a hostage, not a SevRev. She held her crosshairs on him for a few more moments before a woman stumbled out of the ruins, her shirt in tatters. More and more people appeared, most looking to be in pretty bad shape. Only a few seemed to be OK. Others stumbled around due to injury and probably shock.

Gracie glassed each one, conscious that a SevRev could be using the hostages as cover.

The first Fox Marines reached them and started funneling them back. They would be isolated and interviewed at the collection points, but Fox had to clear the ruins before the area was declared secure. Gracie's mission was still in place—she had to support Fox as they entered the ruins.

The stream of hostages escaping the flames petered out, but Gracie ignored them. Golf Company would deal with the people. But after a few brief firefights, things had quieted in the rubble of the market. Flames were still roaring, but anyone that deep into the rubble was most likely dead. It would take a while for the all-clear to be sounded, but it looked as if the Battle for Rose Garden was, for all intents and purposes, over.

Gracie finally allowed herself start to relax and wind down. She'd been keyed up, and it was only now beginning to dawn on her that she'd just killed, four, no, five men. She'd snuffed them out like candles. She felt empowered.

She just started to turn to Eli to see if he'd captured each kill on his truthteller—she'd got probably two on her Miller scope, but she'd shifted too quickly for the others—when shouting erupted below them. She looked down and saw two Marines on the ground, one wrestling with a civilian. The Marine had his hands locked around one of the civilian's while the civilian pounded away with his free hand at the head of the Marine.

Something told Gracie that this was serious, more than just a panicked hostage being subdued. A Marine was in trouble, and that was enough for her. She pulled down her weapon, but immediately realized the distance was too close for the scope to be of any use. She should drop it and grab her M99, but her instincts told her that delay, as short as it would be, would have drastic consequences. Instead, she released the rail lock and her 28,000-credit Miller Scope fell to the concrete roof where Gracie could hear it shatter. With a naked weapon, she sighted down the small nub of a front site at the struggling pair. The back of the Marine's head was between Gracie and the civilian, but the slightest twist as they fought gave Gracie all the target she needed. She snapped the trigger instead of squeezing, and an instant later, her round punched a hole clean through the civilian's head.

Curiously, to Gracie, at least, the head hadn't exploded into the proverbial pink mist. Maybe her round had just been moving too quickly to start to tumble after it hit.

Why am I worrying about that? she asked herself as she stood up to get a better view.

One of the Golf Company Marines—it looked like Sergeant Priest—walked up to the pair, leveled her massive Piedmaster handgun, and simply blew the civilian's head completely off his shoulders.

"He was already dead," Gracie protested to Eli as if she was afraid of not getting credit for the kill.

"Don't let go, Marine!" a voice called out from below them.

Priest, First Sergeant Pele, and two more Marines surrounded the pair and yet another Marine reached over to cover the Marine's hands, which were still clutching the dead man's hand.

"We've got it now," the first sergeant said calmly, but loud enough for Gracie to hear from 15 meters away. "Keep holding it, and we'll get someone here to disarm this guy."

The Marine looked up in a daze, and Gracie realized that the big Marine was female, not male. The SevRev, because that's who the man had to be, was quite a big man himself. Gracie was impressed that the Marine had been able to keep him from detonating whatever bomb he had on him. And now she was in it deep. The first sergeant was zip-tying her hands and that of two more Marines around the dead body's hand. They weren't going anywhere until EOD diffused the situation.

Man, sucks to be you, she thought with more than a little admiration.

"Did he say disarm?" Eli asked.

"Yeah, and I think we'd better get down like now!"

Eli started to climb down right from where they were, but Gracie grabbed him and pulled him to the other side, away from the potential bomb blast. She didn't wait for help but jumped down. Eli tossed her the sniper case and the broken scope and jumped down after her.

An EOD Marine, in his bulky blast suit, came jogging up as the area was being cleared of all Marines and hostages. After a hundred meters, Gracie looked back. The EOD Marine was bending over the four people—well, three Marines and a hunk of dead meat.

"Hang in there, Marines," she muttered before turning to follow Eli out of the blast area.

Chapter 8

"And that's about it from the CO. She's pretty pleased with us," Lieutenant Wadden said. "So, that's about it for now, unless there are any saved rounds?"

No one had anything, so he continued with, "Gunny, I'll leave the retrograde in your hands. Top Della Corte will let you know when we're up. Other than that, relax the best you can, and I'll see you back aboard the *Klipspringer*."

The fact that the S4 Chief had somehow scrounged up trucks to take them back to the stadium had been welcomed news. A couple of klicks wasn't much, but the general consensus was why walk when you could ride?

Gracie thought the ship's shuttles could have landed right there at the assembly area, but with hostages still being processed, maybe the stadium was more secure. She looked over at the pile of rubble that had been the Rose Garden Farmer's Market. Smoke still rose from several sources within the pile of rocks. Under that rubble were the bodies of upwards of 450 citizens, people who'd done nothing wrong, but two days ago found themselves on the slippery slope to their demise. The local volunteer fire department had arrived on the scene, and with an FCDC rescue team, was just starting the long recovery process.

It wasn't just hostages under the rubble; there were from 30 to 40 SevRevs in there as well. Gracie had zeroed five of them before the market went up, and a few minutes later, she'd killed another not 30 meters from where she now stood. And she felt. . .fine. Nothing different. She thought she would have felt something significant one way or the other. But other than pride as doing her job, she didn't feel much, and certainly no regret.

Gracie thought she was a normal human being, whatever "normal" was. She liked puppies and babies. She'd help a little old lady across the street if needed. In high school, she'd been a volunteer tutor for the primary students. She was a nice person. But she'd just killed five human beings, and she was fine with it. They deserved to die, and she'd just been the instrument.

"Righteous job, Crow," Staff Sergeant Riopel said. "No, not just righteous. That was fucking premier."

"You zeroed six of them, right?" Zach said from beside the section leader.

Most of the platoon had arrived just as the lieutenant had started his brief, and this was the first time they'd had a chance to speak with her. More than a few had been shocked when the lieutenant had mentioned her tally. Brick Liogeni, in Bravo Section, had nailed two SevRevs, and only two others had even gotten one kill.

Gracie involuntarily backed up a step as 16 of her fellow Marines crowded close.

"Uh, yeah. It looks like six," she admitted, almost warily.

"You could have at least left some for the rest of us," Sergeant Manuel Chun said.

For a moment, Gracie thought the sergeant was serious, but when Zach laughed and said, "Not that it would have done you any good, Manny. You need to be able to hit something, first," and the rest of the platoon broke into laughter, she knew he'd been joking.

"Can I, I mean we, can we see the spool?" Staff Sergeant Riopel asked.

She understood his hesitancy in asking. Technically, the recording made by her scope would go to the S2 first, and only then be disseminated to the rest of the staff and back to the platoon. But Gracie wasn't so hide-bound to proper procedures that she wouldn't have shown her section leader it if she could.

She sheepishly pulled the mangled body of the scope out of her cargo pocket and held it up.

"I kinda broke it."

"Hell, Crow, that'll cost you ten month's salary to pay that back," Zach said to more laughter. "What'd you do to it?"

"I've got it here!" Eli interrupted. "I've got every shot on the truthteller."

"Well don't stand there, my lad. Let's get it up and running," Staff Sergeant Kwami, the Bravo section leader said. "We want to see that shit."

Eli snapped down the tripod legs, turned the unit on, and reversed it to just before Gracie took out the SevRev on the roof. The other Marines crowded around like lions on a kill. Gracie was almost pushed back out of the way, but that was okay with her.

The next several minutes were punctuated with "damns," "shit-hots," and "ooh-rahs" as the recording related what happened.

There was a pause then some said, "I only counted five!"

"Wait," Eli said. "I'll fast forward."

A moment later, there was a collective mumble of exclamations, with a single "No fucking way" breaking through the rumble of noise to reach her.

"Run it again," someone else said while the rest jumped in to agree.

Gracie stood back, almost as if she wasn't part of the platoon. She was human, so she liked the comments being made as the rest watched the recording for the fourth and fifth times, but she felt a little apprehensive for some unknown reason. In ones and twos, Marine turned from the truthteller and congratulated her. Everyone seemed happy for her.

Zach, when he shook her hand, turned back to the rest, put his arm around her shoulder, and loudly announced, "I taught her everything she knows!"

Gracie flinched when he put his arm around her, but with the others throwing covers and ration packages at Zach, she didn't think he noticed.

As Eli started to stow his truthteller, Marines went back to their field rations. Gracie pulled out her own Meatballs with Penne in Sauce, one of the more palatable meals, and sat down to eat. Three of her platoon mates sat down around her and started asking her questions about her engagement. In her enthusiasm for the art of being a sniper, she forgot her social reticence and delved right into the hows and wherefores of each shot.

Time flew by, and she was surprised when gunny came back and said, "OK, up and at 'em. We've got the next truck. Section leaders, get your people ready.

Gracie crammed the empty ration package in her cargo pocket and stood up. Tradition had it that the ship's company put on a feast for returning Marines, and she was looking forward to that.

"Crow, where's your sidekick?" Staff Sergeant Riopel asked.

Gracie looked around. Eli had dropped off the sniper case a while back and walked off. Gracie thought he'd been going to use the head, which had some long lines around it. She couldn't see him, though.

"I'm not sure," she said.

"Well, you'd better find him."

She picked up the case and walked to the restroom. Two Marines were waiting in the men's line.

"Gittens, you in there?" she shouted into the entrance.

There was no response.

"Gittens!"

The two waiting Marines looked at her curiously. Gracie waited a moment more before turning and striding off.

Where the hell is he? she wondered. *If he's slacking off, I'll have his balls.*

She'd felt pretty good discussing the action with the other three Marines, but now she felt a rise of anger spoil her mood. Eli was her charge, her only charge, and if she couldn't control him, she didn't deserve to be an NCO.

She returned to the platoon, who were all mounted up and ready to move out. She was about to tell Staff Sergeant Riopel when she caught sight of someone running from the direction of the market towards them. She stared for a moment before recognizing the figure as Eli. She felt both relief and anger.

She moved forward to the edge of the assembly area and waited while a slow burn took over her.

"Gittens! We're moving out, and you decide to go sightseeing? Riopel's on my ass, and you're just gone?"

"Sorry," he managed to get out as he panted for breath.

"Sorry? What kind of answer is that? You screwed up big time, and you're going to pay. And just what the hell were you doing?" she asked, hands on her hips as she glared at the junior Marine.

Instead of answering, Eli slowly held out a clenched hand and opened it, exposing a stubby rifle round.

"What's that? You were souvenir hunting?"

"I saw the 52, you know, the one your first kill had. I saw it when I was slow-moing the spool for the rest of the guys. When the market blew, it flew up and landed over there," he said, cocking a thumb back over his shoulder and towards the market. "I figured I could find it, so I went looking. I got this out of the mag."

And it hit Gracie.

She'd become a HOG today, a Hunter of Gunmen, and there was a tradition with that, or maybe a superstition. It was accepted that every sniper had a bullet with his or her name on it. If you could take that round and keep it, it could never be used against you. All HOGs kept a round on a chord around his or her neck

When a sniper first killed someone, the strongest juju was to take a round from that dead enemy and make that the charm. The problem with that was that snipers often took extremely long-distance shots, and the target could be in the midst of the enemy positions and could not be recovered, so it was rare when that happened.

Eli had gone out into there and found her first kill's weapon and retrieved a round from it. He'd recovered the bullet with her name on it.

She reached out and took the round from his hand. The UKI-52 fired a short-chambered .308 jacketed round. It had to be the ugliest round in use, but it had taken its toll over the years. It felt heavy in her hand.

Her throat choked up. Many men had tried to give her presents over her short years, and she'd refused each one. This, however, was different. Eli had given it to her as one Marine to another. He knew the significance of it, and he'd risked a boatload of trouble to retrieve it.

Jonathan P. Brazee

She slipped the round into her breast pocket and said, "Well, thank you. But Riopel's going to have our ass, so we've got to move it."

She turned and started jogging down the gentle slope to where the platoon was lined up, the first of them already clambering into the bed of a dump truck. With each step, the round inside the pocket bounced against her breast.

It felt good.

TARAWA

Chapter 9
6

Gracie increased the resistance and leaned into the bike. Her thighs were burning, but she had two minutes at this level, and she wasn't going to back down. The time seemed to creep, each second taking an eternity to wind down.

Most of the others on the bikes had the VR helmets on. The helmets lowered around the shoulders and formed a half-sphere a meter in diameter. Any number of scenarios were displayed on the inner surface of the sphere, and by linking up, a riding partner's image could be displayed as well, allowing two people to ride up Kilimanjaro on Earth or through the Canyon of Kings on Century 2, chatting with each other as if on a leisurely jaunt. Gracie had tried the VRs, and she had to admit that the tech was amazing. It really was as if the rider was transported to some exotic location. But Gracie wasn't riding for fun. It was her job to remain in good physical condition, and she biked as part of her exercise regime. Using the VR helmets made it too much of a carnival ride for her, and that took away from her intent.

Finally, the last second ticked away, and she entered her cool-down. She took a quick glance at the clock on the bike display. If she were going to make it to the Down 'N Out, she'd have to quit pretty soon and shower. Tamara Veal, the lance corporal who'd gotten into the wrestling match with the SevRev on Wyxy had tracked her down as the one who'd taken the terrorist out, and she'd invited Gracie for a beer at the bar out in town.

Barely pedaling the bike as she cooled off, she looked around the gym. It was pretty full as Marines got in their workouts. Many of the Marines were exercising together. For some of the groups, it seemed more of a social occasion than PT. That was a foreign concept for her. She sometimes asked others for a spot while lifting, but exercise was an individual effort as far as she was concerned. The only thing that worked was what each person put into the session, not gabbing about the latest flick or who won the latest football tournament.

That's what she told herself, at least. Intellectually, that was true, but she had to admit that it would be nice sometimes to have a workout partner. She and Eli had gone to the gym a few times to exercise together, but when on the free weights, he lifted so much heavier than her to make them lifting together more of a hassle than anything else.

Across from the cardio deck, she watched two female Marines lift. It looked like they were more in her range. They were standing side-by-side, egging each other on with their curls until one of them dropped her dumbbells with a laugh. The other managed two more curls before dropping hers and punching her friend in the biceps.

She fleetingly wondered what it would be like to have a friend in the unit. She thought a female Marine might be a better fit, but she was the only female in the platoon. Things were better with the platoon ever since Wyxy, but there was still somewhat of a distance between the other snipers and her. She wasn't sure if that was because of them or her.

Probably me, she thought sourly.

On one hand, she'd proven that she had the goods. No one doubted that she'd earned her place in the platoon. On the other hand, though, no one was particularly friendly with her. It seemed that whenever someone initiated a conversation with her, it was only about shooting, nothing else.

Back in Montana, the Billings Bisons Specball team had a center-major named Diego Nolan. For his year with the team, before he was called, up, he pretty much carried the Bisons on his shoulders all the way to the Mountain League championship. The thing is, from all reports, he was a total asshole, both to fans and to his teammates. No one liked him as a person. He didn't get sponsorships or advertising gigs, and fans didn't wait after the games for his autograph. Everyone was glad he was on the team, glad that he set the league record for goals scored, glad that because of him, the team had the championship banner hanging in the stadium. But no one liked him, and when he was called up, no one shed a tear.

Gracie could see a similarity here. Every one of the others treated her professionally, and they seemed to respect her. She wasn't sure that anyone *liked* her, though, not even Eli.

She realized that she'd pretty much slammed the door on socializing early on when Zach asked her out, and that had to have affected how others related to her. But she was not looking to hook up with anyone, at least anyone in her platoon. It would be nice, however, to be able to be friends as well as co-workers.

She stopped her pedaling. The two Marines across the gym were now on the bench, the one spotting shouting to encourage the other to get the bar up. She watched for a moment, then shrugged.

Gracie knew she had to leave if she was going to meet Lance Corporal Veal out in town for that beer, and wasn't that what she'd just been contemplating? Being more social?

Screw it, she thought. *I don't need that.*

She set her timer for another 45 minutes and started pedaling again.

Chapter 10

6

"I'm serious about that. You all are spotters now for the duration. I want all of you to back off and let the sniper take over," Gunny Buttle told the platoon. "They need to be ready to step up, but they won't be able to unless they've had the experience."

"Yeah, remember that, spotter," Dave Oesper said to Kierk. "I'm in charge now."

"Yahs suh, Sniper, suh!" Kierk said, snapping an exaggerated salute.

Gracie stole a glance at Eli. He was excited. For three days, he would be in charge, from conducting the infiltration to selecting the site to taking out the target. The platoon had the entire R505b range to themselves, over 25,000 hectares of wilderness in which to work. Each team was being assigned their individual target, a level 3 simulacrum that moved pretty much like a real human.

Better yet, this was a live fire exercise. They would be using live rounds. It wouldn't totally be the same as an actual op, though. Each of them would be wearing no shoot me's, the small electronic beacons that would shut down any scope trained on them. Gracie thought that was stupid. It might be OK for regular infantry who might have to react quickly, but snipers identified each target before engaging. But the safety-conscious Corps didn't make exceptions to range rules.

Gracie was surprisingly a little jealous. They hadn't had any live-fire exercises in the almost three weeks since they'd been back from Wyxy, and now that the S3 had scored one of the best ranges in the camp complex for them, it was the spotters who were getting the slots.

As the Marines started getting up, Eli stood and looked at her expectantly. Gracie made an effort to say nothing.

"Uh, should we start our route recon?" Eli asked.

"Up to you, Scout-Sniper Gittens. I'm your spotter, not your leader."

"Oh, yeah, right. OK then. Yeah, let's go do our route recon then."

Gracie stood, and the two of them started to leave the briefing room when Gunny Buttle called out, "Corporal Crow, I need to see you for a moment."

"Go pull the app and start your recon," Gracie said, taking charge by force of habit. "I'll be there in a sec."

"Yes, Gunny. What's up?"

"I've got some gouge for you, Crow. The CG's[14] approved your BC3.[15] You'll be getting it at the next battalion formation."

"What?" she asked stupidly.

She'd heard the words, but they took her by surprise.

"Your BC3. It's been approved."

"I didn't know anything about that. What for?"

"What for? Come-on, Crow. You've been in combat with us exactly once, and you tallied six kills. What do you think it's for?"

"But no one said anything about that."

"The lieutenant didn't want anyone to know he'd put you up for it, you know, in case it got downgraded. The CO could have approved a Navy Achievement, but the CG has to approve the BC's. Anyway, congrats. It's well deserved."

Gracie was rather stunned. She'd always considered herself beyond ribbons and commendations. But hearing she was getting a BC3 filled her with pride. It wasn't a particularly high award, but she didn't care at the moment.

"Well, you'd better get going. The lift will be here at 0400, and you and Gittens, Well, Gittens and you, have a lot of planning to finish."

"Thanks, Gunny. And tell the lieutenant thanks, too, if you see him before I do."

Just as Gracie turned to leave, the gunny said, "No, wait a moment."

---

[14] CG: Commanding General

[15] BC3: Battlefield Commendation 3. This is the second-lowest medal given for meritorious service or valor in a combat situation.

She turned back, and the gunny looked at her as if marshaling his thoughts.

"Uh, look. You're turning into a first-rate sniper. And you're riding Gittens hard, teaching him. That's a good thing, as far as the craft. But remember, you're also his NCO, and there's more to a Marine than pulling a trigger. Gittens is a good kid, and I can see he looks up to you, so remember that. A slight word of encouragement every now and then might do him a world of good."

The euphoria Gracie had been feeling vanished like a Montana prairie dog down his hole.

"Do you think I've been too tough on him? Am I screwing up?"

"No. Well, maybe. Not the screwing up part. If you were, I'd officially step in. And I think the technical skills you're teaching him are worthwhile. But, and this is off the record, as someone whose been in the uniform for 19 years now, being a leader does not always mean developing warfighting skills. You're doing great at that. But Gittens is a person, too. Did you know his brother died last month?"

That floored her. *His brother?*

"No Gunny, I. . .he never told me."

"I thought not. I didn't know either until the chaplain told the lieutenant yesterday."

"He never asked for leave."

"No, he didn't. But of all the Marines in the Federation, don't you think you should have been the one to know first? You're his NCO, and it's your job to know everything about your men."

Gracie thought back for a moment. About two weeks before Wyxy, Eli had been acting rather distant. He kept having stupid brain-farts, and finally Gracie had exploded on him. Maybe she should have realized that something was wrong and dug to find out what it was.

"You're a kick-ass sniper, Corporal. But you need to grow into those stripes. OK?"

"OK, Gunny. I understand."

"You'd better go get your sniper now and get on your planning. And while you're up all night, I'll be home and up all night with my grandkid, so I need to get going, too."

"Grandkid, Gunny? You've got a grandkid?"

"Don't sound so surprised, there, Corporal. Toby Junior's a new papa, and he and his soon-to-be wife don't have two sticks to rub together, so they're all camping out with us for now."

As the gunny left the briefing room, Gracie realized she knew virtually nothing about any of her platoon-mates. That was something she needed to rectify.

Chapter 11

6

Gracie lay prone in the grass, her Zeis Commandos trained on the target 1,225 meters away. This was a live fire exercise, so she couldn't have lugged around a truthteller. But the Zeis binos were pretty high-speed, low drag.

She'd have moved up another 200 meters or so—there was a relatively easy stalk route they could have used where they could make time closing the distance without being within view. But this was Eli's call, and so she'd kept her mouth shut and played the good spotter.

The simulacrum was only a level 3, so it didn't do much more than walk back and forth along a programmed path. The range operators had dressed it in fluid camo, which threw a slight wrinkle in things, but it was not a game-changer. Fluid camo was used by small corporate security teams and militias where funds were tight. It consisted of small capsules that were embedded in cloth that collected light and refracted the waves back out. It could be fairly effective, but there had to be full coverage. The uniform the range operators had used had more of a haphazard coverage, and there was none on the head at all. It might make holding the crosshairs on the target a little more annoying, but any sniper should be able to do it.

Gracie ached to ask Eli his firing solution, and she nearly had to bite her tongue to keep quiet. She heard him take in a deep breath, then let half of it out. A long moment later—too long—the crack of Eli's Windmoeller went off beside her. Another long moment later, and a ripple in the leaves just beyond the simulacrum's head gave her the point of impact.

"Miss. High 20 centimeters, right four centimeters," she said.

"Shit," Eli whispered beside her as he cycled in another round.

Gracie tried to keep quiet, to let him figure out what he'd done wrong, but she just didn't have it in her.

"Try and fire sooner. Don't hold your breath so long," she said, trying to keep any criticism out of her tone.

Eli didn't say anything but settled back into his position. He took two quick breaths, then a deeper one. He let it half out again, and this time, within three seconds, he fired.

Please hit, she prayed and was rewarded when the simulacrum went down.

"Hit!" she said, louder than she'd intended.

"I'm sorry, Corporal, about that first one. I don't know—"

"Nice shot," she interrupted him. "Give me five."

Snipers don't give each other high fives in enemy territory, and Gracie had never instigated anything so familiar with him before. That caught him off-guard, she knew, and he instinctively reached over to return it.

"You nailed the sucker," she added. "So what now?"

"Well, I guess we need to exfiltrate, right?"

"Roger that."

Gracie didn't know if she'd ever felt as awkward in her entire time as a Marine as she'd just felt over the last 30 seconds. But she'd taken the gunny's lecture to heart, and she was trying.

She knew she'd never be the life of the party, but like anything else worth doing, practice made a person better at it. And being a Marine noncommissioned officer was definitely something worth doing.

Chapter 12

6

Gracie handed her M99 to the H&S Company armorer. She'd never fired it during the exercise, so it had been a quick clean. As expected, the armorer looked it over, then keyed the turn-in into her PA.

She returned to the cleaning tables where Eli had his Windmoeller apart. He'd fired it, and it was his weapon, so he had to clean it. But Gracie could at least hang around awhile. Most of the other spotters were hanging around as well. Both Staff Sergeant Riopel and Sergeant Glastonary were arguing about whose spotter had made the toughest shot during the exercise.

Gracie stole a glance at her watch. The chow hall would be closing in 45 minutes, and after three days of field rats, she was ready for some real food. Looking at Eli's weapon in pieces, she wasn't sure he'd get done in time. With a sigh, she picked up one of his handguard halves and started cleaning. Eli looked up, then went back to his trigger housing.

"Hey, did you guys hear?" Sergeant Dillimouse, the S2 clerk, said as he came into the armory.

"Hear what, Mouse?" Staff Sergeant Riopel said. "We've been in the field for three days, something rather foreign to you."

Dillimouse and the platoon were all part of the S2 shop, and the eager sergeant liked to think he was a sniper, too, but Riopel and some of the others usually just gave him a ration of shit.

The sergeant brushed off the insult and excitedly said, "One of us is going to be a gladiator."

"No shit?" Riopel said as every one of them stopped what they were doing to hear more.

"Yeah, no shit. Lance Corporal Veal, the one who stopped that suicide bomber, she's got orders to Malibu. I saw them myself!"

Gracie put down Eli's handguard as that hit her.

A gladiator?

Before enlisting, when the shift was made from male to female gladiators, Gracie had thought she wanted to become a gladiator. The Crow prided themselves on their warrior heritage, and what better way to prove the bloodlines than by becoming the ultimate warrior. However, that was before she found out she was too small and more importantly, not that great of an athlete.

Then, her cousin, Falcon Coups became a gladiator. Gracie had initially felt a surge of jealousy. She'd felt it was her idea. She hadn't been close to Falcon, who'd lived over 70 klicks away from her, and she'd illogically felt that Falcon had somehow taken her spot.

She knew that was foolish, and she'd let the jealousy burn out. If she wasn't qualified, then at least the Apsaalooké, as small as they were, had a gladiator. Falcon had finished her genetic modification a few months ago and had come back to Montana where she been named an honorary War Chief by the tribe and a Montana Governor of the Day. Even the US vice-president had made the trip to see her.

There were billions and billions of humans in the galaxy, but there were only something like 400 or so gladiators. And beating the odds, Gracie knew two of them. One was her cousin, and she'd probably saved the life of the other.

Gracie was proud of being a sniper, and she knew she was serving the Federation. But maybe, just maybe, she'd served all of humanity when she'd nailed that SevRev in the head.

Chapter 13

6

"How're you getting on, Corporal Medicine Crow?" Staff Sergeant Megan Holleran asked, coming to the back of the armory. "I've got Hotel out there waiting to get their embark done."

The staff sergeant, beside one of the few people who used Gracie's full last name, was the battalion armory chief. With the sudden orders to Jericho, the battalion was in surge mode rushing to make the embark.

"Almost, Staff Sergeant. But you can send them in. There's room here."

"You've obviously never done a mount-out before. No, I don't need your and Hotel's mount-out boxes getting mixed up. You finish, and then I'll let Hotel in."

No, I've never done a mount-out before, Gracie thought. *I'm a grunt, not a pogue.*[16]

All Marines were riflemen, as the saying went, but the converse of that was that all riflemen were also a jack-of-all-trades. The Marines relied heavily on the Navy and civilians for their support functions, and there just weren't that many warm bodies around to get things done. The gunny has assigned Eli, Dave Oesper, and Lance Corporal Demetrious "Suggs" Rustan to her to get the platoon's weapons crated and ready for embark. Over the last six months, she's been assigned more than a few of these "special tasks," all in a supervisory mode. She knew this was his way to develop her as an NCO, and while she understood his reasons, it was beginning to become a royal pain in the ass. Right now, when the rest of the platoon was taking care of personal business, she was stuck in the armory. They were embarking the day after tomorrow, and there was still lots to be done before she was ready.

---

[16] Pouge: Slang for someone who is has a job that is not directly combat-related.

A Marine battalion was technically able to embark on a mission within 24 hours, but that was more theory than fact. Sure, they could get aboard ships with their weapons and enough supplies to fight for ten days of sustained ops, but this deployment to Jericho would be at least six months, and that took more planning and preparation.

"Come on, you heard the staff sergeant. Let's get this done," she told her working party.

Twenty minutes later, she scanned the last weapon, checked the scan against her master list, and called over one of the armorers to bulk scan the last box, seal it, and slap on the shipping chip. Hopefully, the platoon's weapons would arrive safe and sound when and where they were needed.

"It's too late for the chow hall," she said, checking her PA. "Just go back to the barracks. Formation's at 0630, so do what you have to do before then. We've got just one more night here after that."

Eli hung back a moment as the other two left. Nervously, he approached her.

What now? she wondered.

Instead of saying anything, he slipped her an envelope, then turned and hurried out. Curious, she opened it and took out the plastisheet inside.

Corporal Medicine Crow,

Please meet me at Chicos Noodle House at 2130 tonite. Its vary important. Dont tell anyone. Pleese. Thank you.

Oh, shit! was her first thought

Following the gunny's advice, she'd tried to get to know Eli better, asking him about his home, his family, and his background. He'd certainly opened up, and he seemed to be getting closer to her—and that concerned her. She'd hoped he wasn't getting the idea that she was interested in him on a personal level, but only as one Marine to another, as an NCO to one of her subordinates. As he'd gotten more, well, friendly, she'd pulled back, erecting her protective wall once again.

And now she was sure he was about to express his undying love or some sort of romantic bull-crap. She took some guff from the others in the platoon about having a love-struck puppy dog mooning after her, but she'd thought it was just the usual razzing that went on, even if she half-suspected it might be true. And now she feared that was the case.

Gracie wondered if she should tell the gunny and ask his opinion. She wavered for a moment, looking over to the PIG Shack. He'd probably still be there, knee-deep in paperwork. But she knew he'd expect her to deal with the problem. She took a deep breath and calmed herself before continuing on the barracks.

Gracie had her own room, one of the advantages of being the only female in the platoon. It would have been nice to have a roommate for once, though, to get her advice. Actually, she knew what she had to do, but it would have been comforting to have someone else confirm that. She had to tell Eli that there was no room for romance, and then she had to get him assigned to another sniper. Gracie had spent a lot of energy training him up, and he'd been progressing. He knew what she expected. Now, right before a deployment, she'd have someone new, which was not desirable. But keeping him would be even less desirable.

For a moment, Gracie considered not showing up. She was sure he'd get the message then. But she knew that was taking the coward's way out. She had to confront the situation and take care of it.

She took a quick shower and then grabbed some clothes. She started to put on the new turquoise Benny Blouse she'd bought at the PX,[17] then shook her head and put it back. She didn't want to look cute or anything else for this. She rummaged around, and from her dirty clothes hamper, pulled out an old, shapeless black T-shirt. She gave it the sniff test. It failed, so she that was the one she wanted, and she put it on.

---

[17] PX: Short for Post Exchange, it is a generic term for stores on military bases.

Gracie opened her hatch just a crack and looked out. The platoon occupied one-half of the passage, all the way to the center ladderwell. With the upcoming embark, she didn't want anyone to see her sneaking out in civvies and have to explain why.

The coast was clear, so she slipped out and hurried to the ladderwell, then taking two steps at a time, ran down to the first deck and out the entrance. Gracie didn't have a hover; she relied on an old second-hand Patterson MX-90 road bike. It was about two klicks to the main gate, then another three or four to the small, out-of-the-way restaurant Eli had chosen. It was a small, somewhat dingy place, which Eli probably thought was romantic given the low lighting inside. It would probably be empty, though, at least of 2/3 Marines, so there was that.

Five or six klicks wasn't much, but she'd work up a little sweat, she knew. All the better, she thought. She'd be even riper by the time she arrived. She unlocked her bike and pedaled out of the battalion area.

Gracie realized she could have waited. She'd get there before 2130. She slowed down and even stopped for a passionfruit smoothie, one of her weaknesses, but she still arrived at 2110 and decided just to go on in and wait for him.

But Eli was already there. He was in the first booth, facing the door. As soon as he saw her, he jumped up and waited until she slipped into her seat before he sat down again.

"Thank you for coming, Corporal."

He's coming on to me, and he's still calling me corporal, she thought, almost smiling despite the gravity of the situation.

Most of the two-man sniper teams were on a first-name basis, especially when the ranks were close to each other, but between them, it had been "Gittens" and "Corporal."

"What do you want to say to me that you had to drag me all the way out here?"

The waitbox chimed, and the voice asked, "Would you like to order now?"

"I already ordered a cherry slushiemax," Eli said. "Do you want anything to drink?"

Yeah, a shot of Jack might be good.

"No. I want to hear what you have to say," she answered, keeping her voice steady but firm.

"OK. I, well. . .oh, lizards, this is hard to say."

"Just say it. I don't have all night."

"OK, right Corporal. Well, here it goes," he said before taking a deep breath, then letting half out sniper-style as if he was preparing for a 2,000-meter shot. "Do you think, I mean, do you believe in marriage?"

Oh, hell! It's worse than I thought.

"No!" she blurted out. "I mean, of course, I believe in marriage, but not now, and only if there is love between the two people."

A huge smile broke out over his face as he leaned forward and said, "So if two people love each other, then you think it's OK? To get married, no matter the regulations?"

Suddenly she understood. E3's and below were generally prohibited from getting married. There were exceptions, and married people could technically enlist, but that was rare. For a lance corporal to get married took a lot of paperwork and time.

She could use that as an easy out, she realized. But that would only delay the problem. Eli would probably pick up corporal within a year, and this would surface again.

"Love is the most important thing, I think. Not that I understand love. I've never been in love, and I'm not in love now."

Get the hint, Gittens?

He didn't seem fazed. "But if two people are really in love, do you think it's OK?"

She wanted to say no just to get it over with. But she couldn't lie.

"Of course it's OK. That's what marriage is about."

"You don't know how happy that makes me, to hear you say that," he said before motioning over to someone behind her.

Curious, Gracie turned around as a young woman got out of an adjoining booth and hurried over to slide into Eli's seat and up against him, her arms wrapped possessively around his right bicep.

Gracie stared at the two beaming people in confusion, then shock as it all became clear.

How friggin' conceited, she admitted to herself. *It was never me!*

"This is Antigone, I presume," she said.

"Yes, this is Tiggs," Eli said, positively beaming.

Eli had told her about his high school sweetheart, but he'd never seem to put much emphasis on her, and Gracie figured that was ancient history. Evidently, it wasn't, and he'd brought her to Tarawa. How he'd managed to support her out in town on a lance corporal's salary, she had no idea.

"Hi, Corporal Medicine Crow," Tiggs said. "I'm so happy to meet you, ma'am. Eli's told me all about you."

She held out a dainty hand for Gracie to shake.

Tiggs was almost exactly as Gracie had imagined. Almost as short as Gracie, she was curvy and had pale blonde hair cut in a bob. Her cheeks were honest-to-goodness rosy, and her smile had to be the best that modern orthodontic medicine could create. She'd been a spirit leader at their school, exactly as Gracie had surmised when she first saw Eli. The jock and the spirit leader, the classic Hollybolly young couple.

Gracie shook her hand, then asked, "So you two want to get married?"

"Yes," they both answered in unison.

"You know the regulations, right?" she asked Eli.

"Yes, but like you said, love is what matters. Besides, it's not illegal."

Which was true. Both of them were adults, and they could marry if they wished. The regulations were only for Marines, and it wasn't as if the Corps would even do anything about it. That fact that some non-rates were married was not a big secret. Married non-rates and their spouses could not get any of the benefits married Marines received, however, so that usually meant the spouses stayed on their home planets until the Marine made E4, and considering a corporal's salary, maybe even not then.

"True. But why now? What's the rush?"

Tiggs looked up at Eli, squeezing his arm tighter as the smile faded from her face.

"Well, Tiggs came over for two weeks to visit. . ."

Which explains how you could afford it. She's not living here.

". . .and we got the call-out. We don't know what's going to happen there, but if, you know, if something happens to me, I want Tiggs taken care of."

Geeze Gittens! Don't you know what happens in every Hollybolly flick when someone says that? They're a goner for sure!

Gracie wasn't particularly superstitious, but there were some things which you just did not challenge.

"Nothing's going to happen. The fighting's died down, and we're just there to keep the peace until they can sort things out."

"I know, but still."

And he's breaking all sorts of regs by letting his girlfriend know we're deploying, too, she thought, before letting that slide for the moment.

"OK, you want to get married. But I don't understand. Why are you asking me?"

"You're my team leader, so we wanted to know what you think. Besides, if something does happen, I want you to let the Marine Corps know about Tiggs so she's taken care of."

If getting married while still only a lance corporal was against regulations, that would have no impact on survivors' benefits. They would go as by law, and in most jurisdictions that was to the spouse.

"Nothing's going to happen to you."

"I know. But if it does?"

"If it does, I'll make sure they know you're married."

As soon as Gracie said that, she realized she'd not only given her blessing, but she'd become complicit in it. The gunny had told her to get to know her subordinates and express an interest in their lives, but she was sure he didn't mean this.

"Thank you so much, ma'am," Tiggs said. "I knew we could ask you."

"Don't call me ma'am, Antigone. I mean, I'd appreciate it if you didn't."

"You mean I can call you Gracie?" she asked, surprised.

"That's my name. I feel old with you calling me ma'am."

"Sure, uh, Gracie. But please, call me Tiggs. And there's one more thing we'd like to ask, though."

"What? I really don't see anything I can do for you."

"We want you to be a witness," Tiggs said.

"Really?" Gracie asked, surprised.

She'd attended weddings before, and she'd even been a bridesmaid for her sister's wedding. But no one not of her family had ever asked her to be an actual part of a ceremony. She was surprised to find out that she welcomed the offer. She felt honored.

"When? We're embarking soon."

"Right now," Eli said.

"What? But it's. . .it's 2125."

"They have a kiosk at the county center," Tiggs said.

Gracie immediately felt deflated. A wedding should be a grand affair. Back with the tribe, a wedding might take all weekend, with both a traditional Crow ceremony and a modern ceremony, each planned out in exquisite detail. If Gracie ever did get married herself, she wanted all of that.

But this wasn't about her, she realized, looking at their eager faces. This was about them, and if a kiosk marriage was good enough for them, then who was she to feel disappointed?

"I'd be happy to."

"Then maybe we should go. We don't have much time," Eli said, swiping his card to pay for the cherry drink still sitting untouched in front of him.

The county center was about 500 meters away, and with those two walking, Gracie pushed her bike along to walk with them. She could have ridden, she thought without rancor. Those two were so enthralled with the moment that she doubted they even knew she was there.

The county center was in Lysander Plaza, along with city hall and the Federation's administrative center. Tarawa was a federally mandated district, so it did not have its own government. The planet was carved up into 23 counties and the vast unincorporated areas. All of the major cities were located in counties, and the counties answered to the Federation governor. As such, there were limited regulations when compared to other planets and nations and even fewer restrictions. Getting married on Tarawa was a simple process. There was no license, no blood testing. During working hours, a marriage could take place with a county clerk, and a holographer was available to immortalize the moment. However, there was no need for the clerk to conduct the process. A kiosk could be used. The couple submitted to a retinal scan, affirmed their intent, and paid the 500 credit fee. That was it.

The three of them walked across the plaza center, past the Lyre Fountain, and up to the county center. The kiosk was empty, so there was no waiting. Feeling kind of foolish in her smelly black t-shirt and holding her bike, Gracie stood back and watched Eli entered their names and ID's, Tiggs holding onto his left arm, looking almost enraptured as the screen gave them their prompts. They both leaned forward in turn for the scans, then Eli turned back to Gracie.

"It's asking for witnesses."

There was no requirement for a witness, but it was an option. Gracie knocked down the kickstand, stood the bike, and then stepped up to the kiosk. She entered her information, and then leaned in to be scanned, too. The light flashed green, and Gracie started to step back as the prompt asked for payment. She fumbled out her PA and held it up to transfer the funds.

"Hey, I'll get that," Eli protested.

She held up a hand, palm facing him, and said, "Call it my wedding present."

"I didn't want that," he protested.

She figured he might protest, but she was a corporal who didn't spend much, and he was a lance corporal who'd probably spent more than a few credits to bring Tiggs to Tarawa for the visit. She could afford it.

"Too late, now," she said as the green light lit once again to indicate the funds went through.

There was one more thing for them to do. Gracie stepped back as the two read the final screen. It was the affirmation that they wanted to be married. Without hesitation, the two reached out, their hands clasped together, and hit the accept button as one.

Mr. and Ms. Gittens turned around together, wonder in their eyes as they realized that they were joined.

Gracie felt a lump in her throat. This wasn't in any way the kind of wedding she would have wanted, but it was the end result that mattered, not the ceremony.

"Congratulations," she told them.

She knew they wanted to be alone, so she said, "Formation's at 0630. You've got about eight-and-a-half hours, so I'd suggest you two get back to whatever room you've got and, uh, celebrate your marriage."

She'd almost said "consummate," but that would have felt too weird.

"Thanks so much, Corporal," Eli said. "I really appreciate it."

For some unknown reason, going completely against character, Gracie stepped up to her spotter, arms out. It was an awkward hug, but still, a hug nonetheless. They broke quickly, and Tiggs stepped up and gave Gracie a much stronger, more heartfelt hug.

"You bring him back, Gracie," she whispered into her ear. "Promise me that."

"I will. I promise," she whispered back.

And it wasn't an empty promise. Gracie would do everything in her power to bring Eli back safe and sound; not because of their marriage, not because Tiggs asked her, but because they were Marines, and she was Eli's leader. And that's what NCOs did.

JERICHO

Chapter 14

6

Gracie followed in trace of Lance Corporal Britta Harrison. She scanned the buildings on either side of the road, mentally picking out hides—and where enemy snipers might be right now observing them.

The problem with that was that she didn't know who the enemy was. No one knew that yet, or even if there really was an enemy. The Fuzos had been sent in as a neutral force of peacekeepers. This should have been entirely an FCDC mission, and there were two of their regiments on the planet, but the fact that the Marines had been sent in as well was a pretty good indication that the Federation Council thought the situation was teetering on war breaking out again.

Marines were trained to attack and destroy the enemy or defend Federation citizens from foreign attack. In this case, both sides of the conflict were Federation citizens.

With 217 planets and stations and another 87 nations in the Federation, it was probably inevitable that mini-wars would break out between Federation worlds. On Jericho, the war had been over resource rights, with the northern continent's population revolting over what it saw as the western and eastern continent's control over its resources. When they shut down the mines, the government had sent militia to reopen them, and fighting had broken out. The militia was driven back, and a state of war was declared.

It wasn't so cut-and-dried, though. Svealand, the northern continent, was controlled by the Opal Party, which was the minority party on the planet as a whole. The PRP (the People's Rights Party, which had members spread over half of the Federation) and the local Republic First Party were the major political powers in the two southern continents. All three parties were spread throughout Jericho, however, and between them, controlled more than three-quarters of the planetary parliament, with the remaining seats belonging to independents and minor parties. So when war broke out, 40% of Kaglsand were self-declared loyalists and almost 15% of the southlands supported the north.

One FCDC regiment had been sent to Nya Asgard, the main city of Svealand, and the other regiment was at the planetary administrative center of San Martin. The Second Battalion, Third Marines had been sent to Skagerrak Point, the 300,000-person city on the isthmus connecting Svealand with the eastern continent of Gran Chaco. Skagerrak Point, besides have a protected deep-water harbor, was the nexus for the roads and maglev lines between the two continents. While within the borders of Svealand, the population was pretty evenly divided between those supporting the north and those supporting the southlands. The war's worst fighting had been in the city, both sides had committed atrocities, and now the Marines had been plopped down right in the middle of it.

The signs of the fighting were evident. The patrol had just passed a Svea neighborhood where an entire block had been reduced beyond mere rubble to almost gravel. Gracie wasn't sure just what had the power for such absolute destruction. Most of the buildings showed at least some signs of fighting, even if nothing so severe. As they crossed Drottninggatan, which the Marines designated Route Gazelle, and into Barrio Blanca, a Tino neighborhood, the signs of war were even more pronounced. The streets within the barrio were small and winding, and almost every building showed signs of damage.

Gracie felt positively claustrophobic inside the barrio. She was a scout-sniper, using long fields of fire to reach out and touch the enemy, and within the neighborhood, she couldn't see more than 20 or 30 meters in any direction. She was armed with her M99, but she was glad that she was surrounded by regular infantry who continually trained in combat in a built-up area.

Thank goodness the ill-advised MEEP was not in play and the Marines had their full command and control systems. The patrol was preceded by hummingbirds, dragonflies, high-altitude drones, and the new nano-drones which when combined gathered terabyte's worth of data that were fed into one of the *FS Joshua Hope of Life's* CIC AI's and then downloaded back down to the battalion's PCS. Gracie's helmet display sparkled with possibles, people who may or may not wish the Marines harm.

With the bulk of the Tinos supportive of the PRP, and the PRP being a Federation-wide party, logic would dictate that here in the barrio, the citizens would welcome the Marines. Logic was not a universal trait, however. Gracie's Uncle Jason was a tribal cop, and he'd said time and time again that domestic disputes were the worst calls—both spouses often turned from fighting each other to fighting with the cops.

Gracie hadn't marked very many potential hides as they wound through the narrow streets. She asked her AI to piggyback Eli's display, but his was not much better, with only one more potential hide within the barrio. She zoomed out and was pleasantly surprised that his overlay pretty much matched hers in the Svea area they'd first patrolled.

Maybe that's not so good, she thought after a moment's contemplation. *If we've both got the same hides, then maybe others might, too?*

She decided she'd discuss that with the gunny. With 26 confirmed kills, the gunny was one of the top HOGs on active duty, and she valued his opinions on the art of sniping more than anyone else's.

The patrol wound its way through the barrio and emerged back on Route Gazelle, only 800 meters from where they crossed it on the way out. Gracie felt the weight lift off her shoulders. She knew that if she now had the fields of fire she wanted, so would an enemy sniper observing them. But within the barrio, it would only take a disgruntled teen dropping a grenade over the edge of a building to cause some damage.

It took more than two more hours before the patrol returned to the battalion's camp in the port's bonded cargo facility. The two scout-sniper teams broke away from Hotel to go back to the container that was serving as the platoon's CP. There was a lot of planning to be done. Things were quiet now, but Gracie had the feeling that things might get hot any moment.

Chapter 15

6

"Any moment" happened to be that evening.

"India just got hit," Staff Sergeant Riopel said, walking into the corner of the warehouse that the platoon had claimed.

"What happened?" Zach asked, and the eleven Marines there put their chow down to listen.

"One of their platoons was inbound, just 400 meters out, when they got hit with some sort of rocket. The Quick Reaction Force deployed and brought them back in."

"Anyone hurt?" Gracie asked.

"First Sergeant D-ski had his leg taken off at the knee, from what we've been told. We'll know more after they get him to the aid station."

That got their attention. First Sergeant Dzieduszycki was the very popular India Company first sergeant. There would have been no tactical reason for him to be on a patrol, but it hadn't surprised any of them that he would have wanted his Marines to know he was there for them. And to hear that he'd lost a leg hit them hard.

"Mother-fucking svermin," Possum said, using their newly minted derogatory slang for the Svea.

"We don't know it's them," the staff sergeant said. "And you heard the sergeant major about how we refer to everyone here. Jerichites for all of them, Svealanders and Argentines, or even Svea and Tino are OK, but not that other shit."

"Who else would it be if not the *Svea*," Possum said, drawing out the word, his opinion of PC-speak more than clear.

"We don't know. The *Porto* tracked the rocket and took out the launcher, but it looked like a remote-control setup. No signs of anyone actually on the site."

"So what now?" Sergeant Muad asked.

"Now we get to play in the sandbox. This planet has just gone hot."

Chapter 16

6

Two weeks later, and the city hadn't erupted into violence. Gracie and Eli had been out in the ville almost the entire time, tagging along with patrols, then slipping out and into buildings. The first one, the night after First Sergeant D-ski had been hit, was abandoned but had been used before. Gracie had selected a ninth-floor room, facing away from the port and with decent fields of fire, but upon entering the room, the used stim-tabs and coffee packs that littered the deck were evidence that others had spent time in this room as well. Whoever that was would know that the Marines would probably use it, too.

She spent a nervous night and next day, knowing that it was just Eli and her against anyone trying to take them out. The following night, she discussed the issue with Gunny Buttle, and he agreed with her thought process. After that, she selected decent, but not great hides.

It didn't matter as neither of the two Marines saw anything that could be considered a target. Three patrols were hit, but far from their little AO.[18] Sergeant Muad, from Bravo Section, had a kill when a patrol from Golf got hit, but other than that, not a single scout-sniper had fired a shot in anger.

The fact that the city had not erupted into an orgy of violence was a good thing, but still, it made for some intense boredom. Gracie felt guilty for wishing for some action—but only a little.

Tonight, they were in the port control tower. With eight teams, they were out for three nights, in for one. One of the nights in would be a complete stand-down, and the other one would be in the control tower overwatching the port. Even with the control tower mission, it was good to get a couple of hot meals, hot showers,

---

[18] AO, Area of Operations

and simple down time to decompress. Kierk and Oesper had the stand-down this rotation, and Gracie and Eli had settled into the cushy seats favored by the VTCs.[19] With a curfew still in effect, and with most seaborne traffic curtailed, the port was quiet after dark, and the VTCs were all home. This gave the entire tower over to the team. The last time they'd taken the "Tower," as they had started calling the duty, one of the H&S cooks had brought up midrats[20] for them just after midnight. Midrats were normally leftovers, but Gunny Coventry, the battalion head cook, had baked up some amazing chocolate chip cookies to go with the leftovers.

"Think gunny will send them up again?" Eli asked after checking the time five minutes after he'd checked last.

"I hope so," Gracie said, knowing that he was asking about the cookies.

Gracie didn't think she was too motivated by food. She wasn't a die-hard foodie. Eating was primarily just fuel for the body. But when eating field rats every day, real food became more and more alluring, and the thought of the cookies made her mouth start to water. She cocked an ear to listen for footsteps coming up the ladder hoping for a treat.

"Corporal, we've got an alert," Eli said, snapping her back to the mission at hand.

Gracie and Eli had been alternating wearing the helmets, and for the moment, she was bareheaded. Scout-snipers also had the same monocles used by recon, but the PCS helmets had a much bigger display which could show much, much more information being fed to it.

She grabbed hers and put it on. Immediately, she saw the alert. It was a Marine feed, not from the *Josh* in orbit above them. She oriented herself and peered down to the corresponding spot on the ground, beyond the F-line of warehouses.

"Hornet-Four, are you picking up the alert at 447832-slash-797919?" came over Gracie's comms.

"Roger that. We are trying to get eyeballs on it now."

---

[19] VTC: Vessel Traffic Controller, personnel who control the movement of ships.
[20] Midrats: Midnight Rations, a meal cooked and given out to those on duty during the night.

She ran her face shield to max, and she thought she could see a low-lying lump on the ground just outside the fence, but the magnification coupled with light amplification resulted in a pretty blurry image.

"We've got the QRF[21] ready and awaiting your visuals."

Gracie whipped off her helmet, pulling out and inserting the remote earbud, and brought up her Windmoeller. She could fire any of her weapons in full battle rattle, to include the helmet, but like almost all snipers, she preferred to take off the helmet when firing. At the moment, she was not going to engage, but the Miller had much more advanced optics than the PCS helmet.

It took her a second to locate the spot. A man lay prone on the ground, cutting away at the links. There were what looked to be extra wires attached to various parts of the fencing around him. He had to be using them to bypass the sensors embedded in the fence wire itself.

"I've got him," she told Eli, before passing "I've got one male in the process of cutting through the fence," on her comms.

She waited a moment while the duty comms in the CP passed the word up.

In a moment, her comms crackled again with, "Are there any signs of arms?"

Gracie had been searching for that, but despite the Miller's superb tech, it was still over 900 meters to the man, it was dark as Hades out there, and the man was in a shallow depression on the ground. She just couldn't tell.

"Nothing in sight, but that is not confirmed. I say again; that is not confirmed."

"Roger. Wait one."

Another moment later, the voice said, "We are deploying the QRF. Do not engage the target unless you elevate to orange."

Orange was the second highest threat alert, where there was a "high" risk of danger to Marine or civilians. Only red was higher, and that was reserved for actual combat taking place. Gracie, as part of the scout side of scout-sniper, had been drilled incessantly on

---

[21] QRF: Quick Reaction Force

both the legal and practical ramifications of the alert tree, and she could place the entire battalion in that status on her call.

"Roger that. I've got angel-watch," she passed before settling into a good firing position.

The VTC chairs were very comfortable, but that made them poor supports. She pulled down her bipod, placed the legs on the control counter with the barrel of her rifle extending past the window, and leaned up against the counter with her waist. She was standing, but the counter provided her with a solid support.

"Anything else showing up?" she asked Eli, who still had his helmet on.

"Negative. Just the one, but I'm monitoring."

Infiltrators didn't always work alone. If this guy was attempting the Marines harm, it could be just a diversion for something bigger. She knew the CP would be all over it, but Eli was right there with her, and their view of the port compound was excellent.

The guy trying to get in might not present a threat, Gracie knew. There were millions if not billions of credits in goods in the port's warehouses, stuck there due to the situation. This guy could just be a thief, and if so, the QRF would sweep him up and turn him over to the local authorities.

Still, he could be intent on killing Marines, and Gracie was going to be prepared.

"What does the *Josh* have our range as?" she asked Eli.

The ship had both their and the infiltrator's position. She hadn't received any comms from the ship as to who or what the guy was, but range was an automatic function that was continuously downloaded and didn't need a human interface to request it.

"She's got it at nine-two-nine meters."

Gracie's Miller marked it at 928. The ship's measurements would be more accurate, but the exact range depended on just what the ship was using for both the man and them. One meter, either way, was not going to change the firing solution.

What she didn't like was the fact that she was 92 meters above ground. If anything, elevation had been her weakness at school. She'd always done the math correctly, but still, somehow her accuracy had suffered, and she'd missed the shot more than she'd care to admit. It had to be in her cheek weld and body position, but it was something with which she sometimes struggled.

As she stood in the tower, she focused on those two things. Her AI had the calculations for the high angle, and now it was just up to her to execute the shot.

The other thing that concerned her was the fact that the man was still behind the fence. The Windmoeller threw out a relatively heavy round, but it could be deflected off the target if it hit a metal fence strand just right (or wrong, from her perspective). She was glad she had the Windy over the Kyocera, but the Barrett would have been an even better choice.

"I've got the QRF on the move, six pax, about 400 meters and closing from your eight o'clock," Eli said.

"Roger," she acknowledged.

She was tempted to swing about to spot them, but they weren't her target. She stayed on the man, who had already cut away a decent-sized piece of fencing.

Just as Eli said, "100 meters," the man stopped cutting and sat up, looking in the direction from which the QRF would be approaching him. Gracie fully expected him to bolt away from the fence and try to escape into the city. Instead, he pulled up something from his far side, something that his body had hidden from Gracie's view. Gracie didn't exactly recognize what it was, but it looked like a projector of some sort, and the man's body language said he was going to attack.

When he'd sat up, his head and chest were in back of the fence, and only his legs and groin were uncovered by the hole he'd cut out. As he started to swing the projector around, Gracie reacted.

She dropped her aim on the first shot, aiming at his groin, not willing to take the chance on the fence deflecting her round. She fired and immediately chambered another round, regained her sight picture, this time aiming higher, and firing just as the first round hit the man in the crotch.

"Hit, low, in the balls," Eli said as Gracie chambered the next round. He followed that with, "Hit, center mass," as the next round reached the target.

The man was still sitting, though. The second round should have dropped him, but with one hand cupping his crotch, he reached for his side. Just as Gracie fired the third round, a huge blinding flash of light filled her view. The Miller immediately compensated, but not before enough light got through to give Gracie stars. She jumped back, hands to her eyes.

"Great green lizards! He just blew up!" Eli said.

Ignoring the eruption of comms through her earbud, Gracie peered forward to where small fires lit the area where the infiltrator had been. A huge 30-meter gap had appeared in the fenceline. Lights appeared, probably from the QRF, and it was only then that she picked up the comms reporting two men down.

She pulled out her HOG's tooth—the round the Eli had recovered on Wyxy and which was now mounted on a necklace made from polychord—from under her cammie blouse, gave it a kiss, then slipped it back. She wasn't superstitious, she told herself as usual, but it cost her nothing, and better safe than sorry.

She watched for a few minutes as a platoon-sized QRF rushed to the scene. The two Marines down were WIA, not KIA, she heard, and the hole in the fence was soon filled with armed Marines. The Marines would probably keep the gap covered, not trusting the local police, until a work crew could erect something to close it.

"Where's the midrats?" she asked.

Eli looked at her in surprise.

"What? I'm hungry."

"You're not, well, excited by what just happened," he said, obviously hyped.

"Just our job, Gittens. Nothing more."

Chapter 17
7

The recording showed that Gracie's first round had hit the man in the crotch which elicited laughter and shouts of "ball buster" and "dick-dicer" from the other four teams at the debrief.

"As you can see," Staff Sergeant Riopel said, nonplussed from the general levity, "the second round hit right here."

He highlighted an area right in front of the man's chest.

"The round deflected on the fencing, ripping through his sleeve, but otherwise missing him. The third shot probably hit him just as he detonated the pyrostene."

Gracie studied the recording. To her, she thought she could see the impact of the round a split second before the screen went white.

"If he blew himself up, does Crow still get credit for the kill?" Zach asked.

Gracie wheeled around to stare at him, wishing she could slap the smirk off his face.

"Yes, she gets the kill. That's our SOP. So if you want to catch up to her, Sergeant One-Kill-To-His-Name," the staff sergeant continued, "you'd better get off your ass and do something about it."

There was more laughter, and Possum said, "Bam, Sergeant. Staff Sergeant's got you painted!"

Only slightly mollified, Gracie turned back to the staff sergeant and the paused display on the screen. She hadn't been sure she'd get the kill, and this was a relief to her. Despite that she'd told Eli she'd just done her job, she'd realized that numbers mattered to her, even numbers as anathematic to "civilized society" as killing another human being. But numbers didn't lie. She could be dinged because she was not overly friendly. She could be dinged for being a weaker NCO than the others. But no one could argue kill numbers, and she had more since she'd joined the platoon than everyone else combined.

"So, to get back to the question on whether Corporal Crow should have shifted her point of aim to part of the body that was not lethal and wouldn't kill the target—"

"Speak for yourself, Staff Sergeant. I'd die without mine!" Sergeant Glastonary said, barely getting out the words through his laughter.

". . .instead of going for a kill shot," the staff sergeant continued as if he hadn't heard, even if he let his lips curve up into a slight smile. "As we can see from the recording, her hunch was right. The, well, not-immediately-lethal shot, I'll call it, did immobilize him, while going for the kill shot and having the round deflected might have let him fire his beam-thrower and possibly taken out the six-man QRF."

The Intel types had identified what Gracie had termed as a projector as a Vassily Mining Knife, a 12-mega-joule disrupter. It was designed for short-range work, but even at 100 meters out, if he'd been able to fire it, enough energy would have made it that far without ablating to jeopardize the QRF squad.

"Our take-away from this is a simple reminder that it is the Marine in back of the weapon that makes a scout-sniper so deadly. Number-crunchers can calculate firing solutions, but they can't take in all the inputs and make the same decisions that we can. Remember that.

"Corporal Crow, do you have anything to add to that?"

"No, Staff Sergeant."

"OK, then. We've got 55 minutes before Fox's first patrol brief, so get some chow if you want. We'll be out there for 72 this time, so keep your heads on straight."

Chapter 18

7

"And those are the best ones," Eli said. "The sweetest honeyberries known to man. You need to try them sometime, only I guess you got to come to Taggert to get them right off the vine."

Gracie listened with only half an ear as she scanned the area along Route Gazelle below them. They'd been on the roof of the building for a day-and-a-half, and except for a mortar attack on the port, quickly suppressed by the *Josh*, it had had been a quiet mission. For thirty minutes, Eli had been waxing poetic about the various foods back in his home country. Gracie had never met anyone from Taggert, a small nation on Lister 4, but if she listened to Eli, it had to be the garden of the heavens, the best gosh-darned spot in the universe.

Eli had hinted more than once that she should visit him and Tiggs during their post-deployment leave, but she knew that wasn't going to happen. She ached for home, for the wide-open prairies surrounding Lodge Grass. Her family had lived there for hundreds of years, always returning home no matter how far into the stars they roamed.

They had adapted over time, as the Crow always had. Lodge Grass wasn't even the original name of the town. It was named after the creek that ran through it, but the Crow called the creek the "Greasy Creek." The Crow word for "greasy" is *tah-shay*, and the word for "lodge" is *ah-shay*, so when the white men came and misheard the word, the new name stuck.

The prairies were somewhat desolate, according to most people, but that might explain how in the middle of the modern universe, Lodge Grass would have still been recognizable to War Chief Joseph Medicine Crow from back in the 21st Century. They had all the modern conveniences, but there was a feeling in the town of the old ways of life.

Eli was still going on about the honeyberries, which had become quite popular since they were developed by Propitious Interstellar 20 or 30 years ago, but for Gracie, nothing could beat the sour taste of wild buffaloberries she and her sister Dana found in the grasses outside of town. The small, red berries, famed as a source of lycopene, were farmed as well—no food conglomerate was going to allow that opportunity to slip away, even with fabricators providing the bulk of humanity's food resources. However, for Gracie, the wild berries, found by her sister and her (with help from grandma), were always the best.

Gracie felt that she was born to be a Marine. The life suited her, especially the life as a scout-sniper. But she was still a tribal girl, and home was home. When she retired, she knew to where she was headed.

Retire?

And it struck her. That was the first time she'd ever assumed that she would retire as a Marine, that she'd make it a career. A smile came over her as that realization sunk in.

Me, a career Marine!

That thought also got her mind off home and back to the job at hand. She'd been glassing up and down Gazelle, watching the comings and goings of the citizens. It had been a quiet day so far. They'd heard firing early in the morning off to the north, but no Marines had been involved, and they hadn't heard what that was. People had to live, and with a beautiful sunny day, without any strife, it looked like most of the people who hadn't fled the city were out shopping and running errands. It looked peaceful, and if a person could discount the ruined and damaged buildings, the scene could be anywhere in human space.

She watched a portly man with a teal scarf standing in front of a heavily damaged storefront, guessing he was the owner and wanting to see what he'd have to do to repair it. With the Marines in town, normal commerce could get back on track.

On the west side of Gazelle, about 450 meters to the north of Gracie's position, someone had cleared out part of the rubble from a destroyed building. A dozen or so kids were playing football in the cleared area. Gracie watched as an errant kick sent the ball out into

Gazelle and down the road, two kids in hot pursuit. An older woman stopped the ball with her foot, then kicked it back onto the pitch with a high, arching trajectory.

Yes, life was emerging from the war.

A young man approached the man with the teal scarf, said something, and both turned to enter the ruined shop.

Probably the contractor.

Eli was enjoying his break, lying on his back, now nattering on about some sort of bread—and of course, the best bread in the galaxy—that his mother made. Gracie shook her head, but with a smile on her face. She'd turn the glasses over to him in another 15 minutes, but for now, let him natter.

The teal scarf guy reappeared in front of his store, simply standing and watching the crowd. Gracie thought it must be hard to see your livelihood destroyed and have to start from scratch.

Gracie was scanning further up the road when a man caught her attention. He looked like anyone else, but there was an air about him, not nervousness, but something else upon which she couldn't put her finger. He suddenly seemed to spot something and started crossing the street. Gracie zoomed in on him, following him as the man pushed past other pedestrians. To her surprise, he walked up to Teal Scarf. Zoomed in as she was, she saw the man make a strange motion with one hand. Teal Scarf lifted a finger, then tilted his head towards the door of the shop.

What the. . .?

Without having been zoomed in, she would have probably missed the hand signal, which she was sure it had been. But why?

"Gittens," she said over her shoulder.

"What? Am I up already?"

"No. But call the CP," she said as she range-shot the building with her binos. "I want a scan of 447638-slash-797801."

She continued to watch, and another man came forward. He made the same weird flick of the wrist, fingers apart, that the previous man had made. He went inside, and after a slow scan of the area, Teal Scarf turned and entered as well.

About three minutes later, Eli said, "The *Josh* says there are seven adults in the building, clustered together. Battalion wants to know who you think they are."

During the current state of martial law, gatherings of more than four people were prohibited. That was hard to control in reality. More people than that went to a market or were in a family. It was more of a tool for law enforcement when needed.

Gracie keyed her comms. "Coyote-Three, this is Hornet-Four. Get me the whiskey-oscar, over."

A moment later, Captain Giardino, the S3-A, came on the hook. "Hornet-Four, what do you have there?"

"We've got seven inside a destroyed building at coordinates—"

"We've got a feed on the building now. What did you see inside?"

"We do not have eyes inside. We did see the last four. They exchanged what looked like hand signals for recognition. I think the ones joining were looking for someone with a teal scarf, which is what the man just outside the front of the building was wearing, over."

"Do they look Svealander or Argentine?" the watch officer asked.

There wasn't a clear-cut difference in how the two groups looked. Sveas might tend more to the old Nordic genotype, and the Tinos could tend a little darker, but that could hardly be assumed from one or a few individuals.

"The building is in the Svea side of Route Gazelle, but I can't say more."

"Wait one. I'm going to bring it up with the six."[22]

Less than a minute later, the captain was back on the hook with, "Hornet-Four, keep your eyes on the building. Do not, I say again, do not engage. You are not cleared hot unless to protect lives. We are sending a patrol to the location."

"Roger, over."

---

[22] Six: Military slang for the commanding officer, from the old designation, S6.

It took almost 20 minutes, which was far too long, as far as Gracie was concerned. She first noticed people looking down one of the side streets, then scattering. Teal Scarf made a quick appearance, looked down Gazelle, then disappeared back inside. A moment later, the first Marines appeared. It looked like an entire platoon started back along Gazelle, appearing as if they were on a routine patrol.

Gracie reached down for her helmet and slipped it on. She powered up the display on the face shield, and as the avatars appeared, she realized why the delay. A squad of Marines had snuck in behind the building, there to scoop up anyone who might want to flee. Gracie hadn't seen them as buildings had blocked her vision.

The street below, which had been bustling with people only a few minutes before, was now mostly deserted. Only a few people were still in view, scurrying to get off the road.

The first couple of fire teams in the platoon went past the building as if it were of no interest to them. By the time the third fire team walked abreast, all of that changed. With a well-concerted swoop, the first squad turned and disappeared inside. Gracie had her Windmoeller ready for action, but there was no sign of fighting. The second squad followed the first one side, leaving a fire team on Gazelle for security.

"Who do you think they are?" Eli asked.

"Haven't a clue."

"Then why did you call in battalion?"

Gracie started to snap at Eli, but when she turned to address him, the look on his face was curiosity with a hint of confusion, not derision.

"There was something about them that struck a chord, and not a good one. Then there were the hand signals. They were amateurish, but that really has no relevance. It was just how they were projecting themselves, I'd say."

"But what if they're innocent? I mean of doing anything wrong?"

"They're breaking the rules by having seven of them meeting at once. If that's all they're doing wrong, then they'll get their wrists slapped. No harm done."

"I guess so. I just, well, I don't know. It doesn't seem as if that's our job, you know, being the police in case someone is breaking the temporary rules of this place."

"Gittens, what's the name of our platoon?"

"We're 2/3's Scout-Sniper Platoon."

"And what's the first word in that, 'Scout,' right?"

"Well, yeah. I know that. We're supposed to go out and find the enemy and take them out."

How the hell haven't I realized until now that he doesn't have a clue? she wondered. *And what are they teaching at the division school?*

"Look, you and I are going to have a talk about this later. But we aren't just snipers. We're the eyes and ears of the battalion. Why do you think we did those bridge and route recons back Camp Anderson?"

"I thought that was cross-training with recon."

"We are the battalion's in-house recon, Gittens. Don't forget that. And that's just as important a mission as shooting the enemy."

"Yeah, of course, I know that. Sorry. I just, well, I don't think I would have noticed anything about those guys down there."

"Look," Gracie said, interrupting him. "They're coming out."

Both Marines watched as one-by-one, each civilian was led out, blindfolded and hands zip-tied behind them. A 7-ton drove up, and the men were bodily lifted into the cargo bed and driven off. The platoon formed up and started to move back to wherever they'd been before.

"I guess they really were bad guys," Eli said.

"You're up," Gracie told him, handing him the binos. "Remember, though, you're not just looking for the obvious threat. Anything out of place, you tell me, and we'll let battalion decide what to do about it."

"Aye-aye, Corporal," Eli said, accepting the binos.

Gracie watched him settle in, elbows on the edge of the retaining wall as he started glassing the area. She realized she'd been at fault. She'd been so intent on making Eli a better technical sniper that she'd forgotten to stress the other side of the mission.

Gracie only had one subordinate. If she were in a rifle company, she'd have three other Marines under her. If she wanted a career as a Marine, she'd have more junior Marines under her, and if she wanted that opportunity, she knew she'd better figure out how to lead.

Chapter 19

7

Over the next three weeks, the city was getting hotter. Clashes between the Svea and the Tinos were becoming more common, and the Marines had been targeted as well. Incoming mortars were a daily occurrence. The *Josh* immediately destroyed the firing sites, but the mortars were all remotely operated. As both sides had the same weapons, the CDAs, the Combat Data Analysts, couldn't determine which side emplaced and fired the mortars.

IEDs had become a problem, both to the local populace and the Marines. Four Marines had been WIA when their hover hit one, and even a PICs had been damaged when the Marine had stepped on a mine. No one had been killed yet, but a feeling of apprehension had settled over the battalion that it was only a matter of time.

Staff Sergeant Riopel thought the morale problem was not so much that some of them would be killed, but that the Marines were out of their element. Marines closed with and destroyed the enemy. That was embedded in their DNA. The same Marines who would charge 100 Klethos armed with just a combat knife sunk into a sulk on Jericho.

The officers and SNCOs were not blind to this, and they were doing their best to counter it with increased access to calls home and keeping the Marines busy, but it was hard just to sit and wait for incoming. Gracie found that on her down days, she joined the others off duty in the make-shift gym or binge watched the latest and greatest holo series. She began to detest those days. At least when she was out in the ville, she had to keep alert, and that occupied her thoughts.

Today was better for her. She and Eli had the northern checkpoint angel mission. To try and stop the flow of weapons into the city, the Marines, augmented by the local police, had set up a roadblock along Route Wildebeest, the main—and only—highway into the city from the north. Just two days prior, Falino Getty, one of the snipers in Bravo Section, had taken out a gunman who had strafed the checkpoint with an energy weapon. The area around the checkpoint had been cleared past 200 meters, and the idiot had lost his nerve, firing as soon as he emerged from the bushes alongside the drainage canal. Two police and one Marine received the tingles, but nothing strong enough to hospitalize any of them. Falino, who was on the roof of the Jasper Motor Inn 400 meters behind the checkpoint, had nailed the man with the Barrett as he turned to run. A 665-grain round, traveling at over 850 meters-per-second, packed a big punch, and it had almost torn the man in two.

Fal was actually Staff Sergeant Kwami's spotter, but he'd been on the Barrett when the guy came out firing, and he'd taken the shot. This had been Fal's first kill. The fighter had been using a UKI Series B beam projector and therefore hadn't had a round for Fal to take, so Staff Sergeant Kwami scrounged up one of the cop's .357 rounds as his HOG's tooth.

Like every Marine, Gracie loved the Barrett. The rifle had been around in various permutations for hundreds of years. This one was a fantastic piece of gear, but it wasn't that much different in concept from the first Barretts introduced back in the 20th Century, Old Reckoning. A sniper from back then, plucked from his world and plopped into the modern Marine Corps, wouldn't have a problem figuring out the M6B4 Barrett, and within an hour, be reasonably proficient with it.

While Fal made his kill with the Barrett, it was generally not the weapon of choice against personnel unless at extreme (1,800 and longer) ranges or when firing the CDR, the Counter Defilade Round. It could stop most civilian hovers or ground cars with one shot, however, so with the checkpoint angel mission, it was the right weapon.

"Look at those cops," Gracie remarked to Eli as she surveyed the manned checkpoint.

Four Marines and twelve cops, six from each side of the conflict, were at the primary point. A hundred meters in front, a lone civilian tech in a blast-booth monitored the vehicle detection system (which used X-rays, Gamma Rays, and a magnetic scan to check the commercial cargo vehicles), and various sensors stretched out another 300 meters past him.

"They're not too happy to be together, are they?" Eli noted. "Like as not, as soon as they're off-duty, half of them are going to be carrying on their little spat."

Six of the cops were on one side of the road, the other six on the opposite side, with the four Marines in the middle. Gracie couldn't tell which six were Tinos and which six were Svea. They had on the same uniforms even if they were on opposite sides of the conflict.

"Could very well be. Someone's doing the killings, and these guys have the weapons."

"Seems sort of stupid. I mean, us here, trying to keep them apart. They have to play nice like this, but as soon as we leave, they're going to try and kill each other. I don't like this."

"You're preaching to the choir, Gittens, preaching to the choir."

The traffic was light, and during the first hour, only one truck and a handful of hovers passed through the checkpoint. Four more Marines relieved the first section. The local sun beat down on the two Marines on the hotel roof. The day dragged on.

Gracie sucked on her camelback, then made a face. The heat exchanger wasn't working well, and the water was warm.

"I saw Sergeant Winston bring a field chiller. Why don't you head below and see if you can get her to give up a couple of cold ones."

"Really? She's got a chiller? Sure, I'd kill for something cold. I swear my camelback's heating my water. What do you want? And you like it at a 17, right?"

"Anything she's got. And if that little portable unit can hit a 17, great. If not, anything colder than a 10's OK."

The older camelbacks, the ones made by GE, had pretty good temperature capability, able to heat or chill water within seconds. The new contracted camelbacks, fulfilled by Hargrove Industries, were supposed to be lighter and more convenient, but the chillers were crap.

Gracie didn't watch Eli go down the roof access but focused on the area in front of the checkpoint. Two sets of eyes reduced the stress, but that wasn't always possible. From sleep requirements to simply taking a dump, much of the time only one of them was observing at any given moment.

Of course, the gods of perversity decreed that two minutes after Eli left, a late model hover slowed to a stop 600 meters in front of the roadblock. Add the 400 meters from Gracie to the roadblock, and it was 1,000 meters from her. Just shy of 1,027, to be more specific. Gracie had previously ranged a more than a dozen landmarks, and the hover was a few meters closer than the half-buried tire at the side of the road that she'd ranged at 1,027. The landmarks were for quick reaction; through her scope, Gracie could see that he was merely staring ahead. She hit the targeting laser, and the range immediately came back as 1,024 meters. An easy shot with the Barrett.

What are you doing, buddy?

"Hornet-Four, do you have a visual on our friend?" one of the Marines at the checkpoint asked.

"Roger that. He's just sitting there looking. I think he's deciding if he wants to come and play with you."

Gracie lightly stroked her trigger. She knew she had the firing solution nailed. Just a gentle pull and their friend out there would be dead.

She was almost disappointed when he rotated and took off back north on Wildebeest.

"Checkpoint 2, the Papa-Oscar-India is retreating," she passed.

Gracie thought that "Papa-Oscar-India," or "Person of Interest," was an awkward phrase to use when referring to a potential threat, but ever wary of the PC crowd, the battalion had been ordered to avoid terms or derogatory slang that could be construed as taking sides.

"What do we got?" Eli asked, bursting out of the roof access.

He rushed across the roof to where they had set up.

"Just some asswipe coming down the pike, then deciding he didn't want to come and say hello."

She wasn't on the net, so she thought "asswipe" was OK to use.

"So what now? If he's running, he's got to have something to hide, right?"

"I'd guess so. But it's out of our hands. I'm sure we've got drones on him now, tracking him back to wherever. And the *Josh* will be backtracking his route here. I don't think I'd want to be in his shoes right now."

"What I do want is whatever you've got for me there. I'm parched."

"Oh, here," Eli said, handing her a pouch.

It was cool to the touch, which was always a good sign. Without reading the label, she popped up the straw and took a deep draft. It was Krystal Kola, which was not Gracie's favorite. She was a Coke girl, through and through. But it was cold, possibly at the 17 she preferred, and that was what was important. She knew she owed Sergeant Winston now, but it was worth it.

"Here, take the B," she said. "You've got it for a while."

Unlike the Windmoellers and Kyoceras, each sniper did not have his or her own Barrett. With only four in the platoon, they had to share the weapons. Eli took the rifle and punched in his personal code. There was a slight whirring sound as the Barrett modified its configuration to match Eli's preferences. The stock extended itself by close to three centimeters, and the scope rails raised, bringing the scope higher. The transfiguration took three or four seconds, and when Eli brought the weapon to his shoulder, it was basically fitted to his personal firing profile.

Gracie leaned back and took another swallow of her drink. This was not a round-the-clock post. They would be relieved at curfew, so there wasn't any reason to take a nap, but still, she had to blank out her mind for 15 or 20 minutes. Staying on the scope or binos too long at a time messed up the mind and could even lead to hallucinations.

She let Eli remain on the Barrett for an hour before asking for it back. She could see Eli was disappointed. She knew he was very aware that he was still a PIG, and he wanted to prove himself. She almost let him stay on the gun, but the mission came first, and now rested, she knew, without hubris, that she was the better choice to be back as the designated shooter. Vehicle shots could be tricky, and she had spent far more time on the moving target ranges than Eli and was a far better shot.

She settled in behind the Barrett in a relaxed position, not looking through the scope but over it. She knew she could lay there like this for hours unless she had to take a shit. Her piss-snake was connected, so that was not a problem, but unlike Marines in PICS or HEDs, the hazardous environmental suits, the Corps had not come up with an effective way for grunts to deal with the big Number 2 except in the same way as the Romans and soldiers before them did—simply dropping trou and having at it.

The sun was getting low on the horizon when a glint of light caught Gracie's eye.

"What do you see over there, a finger to the right of Eveline's Bed?" she asked Eli as she brought up the Barrett and looked through the scope.

All of the major landmarks in view had been named for easy reference. She wasn't sure who had named Eveline's Bed (probably some love struck fan of the HollyBolly star), but it had a flat roof and a raised wall that could be a headboard, so it kind of fit.

There was another flash, and Eli said, "Just looks like the sun hitting a broken window. Do you want me to call for a scan?"

She looked a little closer. The flash had come from the window, and she could see inside the building. There didn't look to be anything there. She could call for a scan, but she didn't know how busy the ship was, and she didn't want to call in too many false alerts.

"No, I don't think it's anything," she said, her momentary flash of excitement settling back into the routine boredom.

The raucous blare of the alarms at the checkpoint made her jump. She swung around from Eveline's Bed. Out at the leading edge of the sensor field, a beat-up hover was barreling down Wildebeest. Gracie took in the civilian at the scan station baling out and running, the hover sliding back and forth on its cushion of air as it tried to accelerate, and the scramble of cops and Marines at the checkpoint as they turned to face the oncoming vehicle.

Gracie brought the crosshairs of her scope on the driver, a young man; she could see the determination on his face as he held the wheel in a death grip. There wasn't a shadow of a doubt in her mind that he was a suicider.

The hover was picking up speed as a burst of fire from at least one Marine below peppered it without effect. Gracie was tempted to snap off a shot, but the window of opportunity was short, and she knew she had to make good.

She noted the pothole in the road, the one she'd ranged at 662 meters. Wind had been light at almost 90 degrees from her right, something she subconsciously considered as her brain went into overdrive. At 662 meters, the flight time of the round would be about half a second, during which time the hover would travel about five meters. She was 40 meters high, and that meant the angle of declination was about 3.5 degrees.

All of this gelled in her mind within two seconds, and with the hover approaching the pothole, she didn't have time to enter the data into the AI. She had to go with her gut.

Aiming high and slightly to the right, she pulled the trigger as the hover was just short of the pothole. With the Barrett's superb recoil system, she was able to adjust for the closing speed and send off another round before the first one hit.

The windshield in front of the driver exploded into a mass of pulverized crystal-matrix. Gracie thought the first round hit dead center of the man's upper chest. The second one hit the steering wheel, and probably continued on, so even if the first merely cleared out the windshield and was deflected away, it didn't matter. The hover started to veer off the road when it exploded into a fireball. The concussion knocked the civilian scan tech to his feet, and a moment later, the much-dissipated wave hit Gracie and Eli.

"Great Green Lizards, Corporal! Does that happen every time you shoot someone?"

Gracie sat up and scanned the area. Insurgents often used a suicider or some sort of indirect-fire weapon to hit a target, then assault it with massed direct fire. Below her, the scanner tech was getting to his feet, and at the checkpoint, the Marines were alert and ready for anything. All four Marines had stepped up to the road, ready to shoot down the hover despite the danger that put them in. Five cops were still at the checkpoint, standing and looking around, weapons at the ready. Seven more cops were either on the ground and scrambling for cover or were just now stopping from running away.

"Looks like whoever that suicider was, he didn't tell the cops on his side," Gracie noted. "Looks like two of one side and three of the other stood to fight."

"Not like the Marines. Look at them. All four ready to take down that fucker," Eli said, a note of pride in his voice.

Gracie felt the same way. She might have recorded the kill, but neither she nor Eli had been in any danger. Those four Marines down there had been, though, and with a suicide bomber like that, there wouldn't have been enough left of any of them to fill a sandwich bag, much less enough for a resurrection.

Gracie slowly stood up. One of the Marines turned around, spotted her, and raised a hand in a salute.

Gracie came to attention and returned it.

Chapter 20

8

"Well, here comes the Mad Bomber," Zach said as Gracie and Eli walked into the cargo container that was serving as the platoon headquarters.

"Mad Bomber?" Muad asked.

"Yeah, like all her kills blow themselves up. Boom!" he said, making two fists, then expanding his hands to imitate a blast.

"Not bad, but not good, either. Back to the drawing board," Muad said.

"I don't know. How about it, Mad Bomber? Or maybe 'MB.' What do you think?"

"Eat me, Sergeant," Gracie replied.

"Eat me she says? Eat me? I'm not the one blowing people up right and left. It's 'one round, one kill,' not 'one round and a freaking bomb!'"

Gracie ignored him as she checked the board. She saw that she and Eli were going out again tonight, but their mission brief wouldn't be for another two hours.

"Let's go," she told Eli as she turned and walked out, but making sure her knee hit Zach's legs as he sat on the chair, almost blocking the way.

"Boom!" the sergeant said as she exited the container.

Gracie was steaming, but she was keeping it contained. She thought Sergeant Pure Presence was a flaming asshole; it was really starting to wear on her. As she and Eli made their way back to the company CP, she spotted Staff Sergeant Riopel heading their way.

"Gittens, you go ahead. Draw me my chow, too, and then I'll see you at the brief."

She waited alone until the staff sergeant reached her.

"You got something for me, Crow?" he asked as he noticed her waiting.

"Yeah, Staff Sergeant. I was wondering if I could talk to you for a sec."

"We can talk in the shack," he said as he came abreast.

"I'd really like this to be private, if I could."

The section leader stopped, waited a moment, then said "OK. Shoot."

"It's about Sergeant Pure Pleasance," she said, then hesitated.

"OK," he said after she didn't go any further.

She started having second thoughts. Marines didn't go crying to teacher when they had a problem. A hard-charging Marine took care of her own issues. But she was still steaming, and if she tried to take care of things, she thought she would end up slugging the man.

"It's just that. . .he's, you know, he's been on my ass." When the staff sergeant said nothing, she added, "Like all the time."

"And your point is?"

She hadn't expected that reaction.

"I mean, I think he goes over the line. And I think my being the only woman in the platoon might have something to do with it. I think he resents that."

"You think that, do you?"

"Well, yes. I don't want to pull the woman's card, but when his actions support it. . ."

Staff Sergeant Riopel slowly shook his head, then said, "Let me tell you something, Crow. Yeah, some people don't like others based on some sort of categorization. They probably have since we were still in the trees and looking down at the ground in fear of the leopard. Some people don't like Earthers, some don't like redheads, some don't like Torritites—like Sergeant Pure Pleasance—some don't like you-fill-in-the-blank. And yes, some don't think women should be Marines. Women have only been in the Corps again since the Evolution, and it's still mostly a boy's club. Our own CO is the first female battalion commanding officer the Corps' ever had since women were allowed back into the ranks. And as you know, there are only a handful of female scout-snipers in the Corps right now.

When we received your advanced orders, a few of the Marines expressed some reservations about you joining the platoon."

"And that's my point. I think that Sergeant—"

"Hold on, I'm not done. When that came up, it was Sergeant Pure Presence who was one of the guys who said your sex didn't matter. He said snipers are like Wasp pilots; no one cares if pilots or snipers piss standing or sitting, but how many of the bad guys they can kill."

"Sergeant Pure Presence said that?"

"Roger that. Crude, in his way, but he was sticking up for you even before you came. And after you zeroed those six SevRevs on Wyxy, he was running around bragging that he'd called it, that he was right."

"But I don't get it. He's always on my ass. He doesn't think I should get credit for my kills if the guy was going to be a suicide anyway. And today, he wants to call me the 'Mad Bomber.'"

The staff sergeant broke out into a smile. "'Mad Bomber?' Weak shit from him, but not bad. Do you know what he wanted to call Glastonary? He was trying to get all of us to call him 'Gas-Ass.'"

Despite herself, Gracie almost cracked a smile. Glastonary did have a problem with frequent and rather vile farts.

"My point is that Zach gives everybody shit. That's his style. I'm not downplaying sexual harassment or anything, so don't go running to the gunny or the LT that I'm blowing you off. But with Zach, I'm positive that's not the case. The fact that he's giving you shit means he's treating you like everyone else, male or female."

Gracie stood there, trying to process what he'd said. She wasn't 100% convinced, but she had to accept that he could be right. Thinking back, it did seem as if Zach dished out a lot of shit. She remembered him riding Eli for supposedly being in love with her.

"Look, Crow. You haven't tried to get to know anyone else in the platoon. I know you've taken Gittens under your wing, but as far at the others, you keep them at arm's length. But no one gives a shit about that. You've racked up eight kills, and you're only a corporal. That is what the platoon cares about most, and you have mad respect aimed your way. If you don't want to mix, then that's your decision.

"About Zach, maybe his including you in his smack talk is his way of trying to draw you closer into the platoon. I don't know, but I kinda get that feeling. You know, the band of brothers thing."

"I. . ." she started, then stopped, trying to gather her thoughts.

She'd left the shack angry, and when she'd seen the staff sergeant, it has seemed like a good opportunity to let it out. Now, her worldview had taken a hit, if what he'd said was true. She'd have to think about it.

"Thank you for telling me that, Staff Sergeant. I need to process all of it. Sorry for bothering you."

"That's what I'm here for, Crow. Look, I've got to run. The entire section's going to be at the brief, and I've got shit to do before that, so I'll see you then."

He turned and started to continue onto the shack while Gracie turned to go to the company CP.

Zach stuck up for me?

It was pretty difficult to believe.

"Hey, Crow!" Staff Sergeant Riopel shouted from behind her.

She turned to face him.

"You might want to dish some shit back out to him. See how well he takes it!"

"Roger that, Staff Sergeant," she acknowledged.

Gracie wasn't the queen of repartee, she realized. But given some time, she imagined she could have a few one-liners ready in her magazine when a target of opportunity presented itself.

She didn't realize that she was smiling as she made her way to the company CP.

Chapter 21
8

The peace, if it could even be called that, was rapidly breaking down. Fighting had become more intense, and the Marines had been drawn into several sustained firefights. In one firefight, ten Marines from Hotel had been WIA with four of them being casevac'd to the *Josh*. They were placed into stasis until they could be brought to an appropriate medical facility.

It could have been worse for the platoon, but Hotel's PICS platoon had come to the rescue, breaking the attack. The attackers had left eighteen bodies behind, bodies that were identified as being members of the Arm of the North, a newly-formed Svea militia.

Since then, attacks on the Marines had been stepped up. Incoming fire became more frequent, and while not fully engaging the Marines, pot-shots and IEDs in their path occurred on almost every patrol.

The fact that the bad guys hadn't really engaged the Marines was probably explained by the six PICS Marines immediately in front of Gracie. The CO had made the decision to screw the "perception of aggression" that the Federation wanted to avoid and have PICS Marines with every patrol in force. No matter how much the bosses on high might gnash their teeth, the CO had the final call on the ground. She might never make full bird[23] if the civilian power brokers had anything to say about it, but that one move cemented the battalion's rank-and-file's opinion of her.

Gracie had loved her time in a PICS. If she hadn't become a sniper, she could have easily finished out her enlistment in them. The combat suits had a size limit, so more men than women were simply too big for the suit, and overall personal strength had no bearing on fighting ability in one. The same as with a sniper,

---

[23] Full Bird: Slang for Colonel due to the rank insignia of an eagle.

fighting in a PICS equalized the difference between smaller and weaker Marines and those larger and stronger. Whether behind her Kyocera or in a PICS, it didn't matter one whit that Gracie barely tipped the scales at 40 kg.

The patrol came to a halt. Whisper Creek Road was in the middle of where much of the recent fighting had been taking place. The road was surrounded by four to six-story buildings; if there had ever actually been a Whisper Creek, it had long been paved over.

One of the PICS Marines easily kicked in the door of the six-story building on the right side of the street. Other PICS Marines were doing the same to other buildings. Gracie and Eli, along with Kierk and Oesper, joined a squad of Golf Marines as thy streamed inside the building.

The SOP[24] calls of "Clear," "Coming in right," and "Next man, stand fast" echoed as each room was cleared. There was no attempt at stealth, and there was no expectation of finding anyone. Between Marine Corps drones and the *Josh's* powerful scanners, they knew that there hadn't been anyone inside the building for at least two days. That was when the family of six, the last remaining inhabitants of the building, had left.

While the patrol might find some weapons caches, the grunts were merely camouflage. The purpose of the patrol, and that of two others in different parts of the city, was to emplace scout-sniper teams where they could observe hotspots. All the activity was designed to let the teams get into their hides without anyone noticing. The hope was that they would get lost in the commotion to any observers.

The increase in violence had another effect on the teams. The S3 had decided that two-man teams were getting to be too risky. So he decided to employ two teams together for better security. Gracie and Eli would set up their hide in one of two rooms on the north side of the building and Kierk and Oesper in one of three rooms on the south side. Besides providing mutual support should they become discovered, between them, this would give them much better coverage of the area.

---

[24] SOP: Standard Operating Procedures

Gracie and Eli fell in with one of the fire teams as they cleared each room. This wasn't merely putting up a good act. While they didn't expect to find any people, each room was checked for booby-traps as well as scanning devices and detectors.

The top three floors had been apartments, three on each side of the center corridor. These took a little longer to clear. Gracie hadn't practiced clearing for a while, but she was feeling at home as the six Marines took one side of rooms while Kierk and Oesper joined the fireteam clearing the rooms on the opposite side of the hallway. By listening to the shouts, she could gauge their progression. Moving up a floor, they started to clear the next set of three apartments.

Grace was ready to go in when the point man, Lance Corporal Wistern shouted "Coming in left," as he entered, then the completely off-the-script "Oh, shit."

Corporal Huynh, the team leader immediately shouted out, "Ignore them, Irish. Keep clearing."

Gracie was on PFC Ailiet's ass and was already entering the room when she saw the six bodies lying on the floor. She stopped dead in her tracks.

"Don't stop. Clear this room," Huynh said.

Gracie's position was merely security while the fireteam did their search and scans, so she had ample time to look at the bodies. This was obviously the family that had stayed in their home. The *Josh* hadn't picked them up because they were dead. The bodies had started to bloat, and Gracie was glad she'd had her nose filters emplaced as a precaution against booby-traps.

All six were lying side-by-side. All were face down. All had been shot in the back of the head, even the baby. All were dressed, but the mother was missing one shoe. For some reason, Gracie wondered where that one shoe was.

"Shit," Eli whispered beside her.

The father had his right arm on one of his sons. Gracie took a step forward, and she could see that whoever had executed this family had shot right through the father's hand to kill the boy.

Gracie had killed eight people, but she felt the gorge rising in her throat. With a herculean effort, she kept it down. She was not going to lose it.

"The lieutenant says leave them. Battalion's going to contact the locals to recover them. Let's keep going," Huynh said.

Gracie was somewhat in a daze as they cleared the last five apartments, two on the fifth and three on the sixth. She was glad Huynh seemed to be on top of things. She'd become a liability, and she wasn't sure why. Gracie had been in combat as a grunt, and she'd killed as a sniper, but this had hit her hard.

Snap the hell out of it, Crow!

When Huynh asked her which room she wanted to use, she had to concentrate before choosing. Her subconscious, she realized, had already selected the best room to use, so she had the choice already made.

"You're supposed to stay quiet up here," Huynh said, "until the civvies recover the dead family and get out of here. Then you can set up.

"Hell of a thing, huh? These pogos are fucking animals."

Gracie and Eli sat back against the wall to wait until the two teams were alone and they could construct their hide.

"You OK, Gittens?"

"Yeah, I'm fine. Pissed, but fine," he told her. "Who would do something like that? And a baby, too!"

"Hornet-Four, this is Hornet-Actual," the lieutenant passed on her P2P.

She reached up and keyed the mic on her ear bud.

"This is Hornet-Four."

"Are you doing OK? I've had reports that you seem a little shaken," Lieutenant Wadden said.

"I'm OK. Just a little surprised, that's all. We're just waiting until the building is clear before we construct our hide."

"Do you need to come back? I don't want you out there unless you're 100%."

"That's a negative. I'm fine. The mission is a go."

She knew the lieutenant would be watching her bios on his display. She took a couple of deep breaths, trying to calm herself down. She was fine, she knew. She'd just been a little shaken.

Evidently her bios hadn't crossed some magic red line, because he came back on the hook with, "Roger, I understand. It looks like it will be a good hour before the bodies are recovered, so just settle yourselves."

Meaning I've got an hour to get back in the game or you'll pull me.

Which was fair, she knew. The lieutenant had to make sure she was up to the job.

"Roger, understood."

War was not a pretty place. People, even civilians, died. And in the long run, executed in their home or getting caught in a bombardment made little difference. Dead was dead.

She settled in to get her warrior face back on.

Chapter 22
8

"I've got movement," Eli said seven hours after the civilian authorities had picked up the bodies of the family. "Two fingers to the right of the Barber Shop."

Gracie swung her scope to the building with a white and red-striped section of the wall that they'd designated the Barber Shop. A man was standing in front of it, doing a bad job of looking casual as he looked up and down the street. He slowly stepped back until he was leaning against the wall.

No matter what else he was up to, the man was breaking curfew. Lots of people broke curfew, and while that was worth noting, it was not in itself enough of a reason to call in the cavalry to pick him up.

With what Gracie thought was forced casualness, he reached into his pocket and pulled out a stimstick, twisted it open, and put it in his mouth, just a man getting a breath of fresh air and sucking on a stick.

My ass, Gracie thought.

"We're 342 to the front door, right?" she asked.

She was sure she was correct, but she'd developed a habit of asking Eli for ranges to the various landmarks to make sure he had them down pat.

"Yep, 342."

"Go ahead and call him in," she said.

She could have just as easily keyed her mic and called in, but with a potential target, she liked to eliminate as much distraction as possible. She even turned off her earbud except to incoming P2P calls.

"Battalion's diverting a dragonfly: ETA two minutes."

"OK. I've got our friend here. Let Kierkegaard know we've got a nibble, then keep glassing the area to make sure no one else shows up."

She watched the man as he continued to suck on his stimstick for the next five minutes. There wasn't a commercial stimstick on the market that took that long to discharge, so it was pretty evident that the guy was up to something. The question was if that something was worthy of a death sentence. He could just be waiting for his neighbor's wife to sneak out for an illicit rendezvous, after all. That would be stupid, given the fact that he was in what was for all intents and purposes a war zone, but stupidity by itself was not a crime.

Battalion hadn't weighed in. The man would have been scanned with every piece of gear the dragonfly had, which wasn't much when compared with more robust systems, but it was more than the two of them had. If he were an obvious danger, battalion would have told them.

After another five minutes, Gracie was getting bored. The man was doing nothing but standing in the shadows. She was just about to give up that he was going to do anything when he quickly slid to his left. Gracie thought he was bolting down the alley on the other side of the Barber Shop, but he reappeared in a moment pulling a bag.

"Battalion says he's got explosives," Eli said, his voice brimming with excitement.

The man looked up and down the street again, then pulled out a circular object with a cone on one side. Gracie didn't specifically recognize it, but she was sure it was a shape charge of some sort, and something like that could even take down a PICS.

"I'm taking him out," she said.

As the team leader, she had authority to engage a target she viewed as a threat to this mission. Battalion could shut her down, but they had to specify that. Nothing said meant they concurred.

The man was crouching, busy attaching the mine to the side of the building down low to the ground and pointing out to the street. She knew once armed, he'd obscure it from view with some trash or debris.

At 342 meters, 345 given where he was along the building's front, this would be an easy shot.

A child with a slingshot could drop him, she told herself.

Still, there was no hurry, so she turned to Eli to confirm the atmospherics.

Eli had the binos in his left hand, holding them up to his eyes. His right was down by his side, and he was slowly flexing the forefinger.

He's pulling the trigger!

Gracie looked back downrange, and the man was still attaching the IED. She could drop him right now. Beside her, Eli was taking shot after shot in his mind.

What the hell am I doing?

"Gittens, you've fired my Kyc," she said, more of a statement than a question.

He turned to look at her, a puzzled expression on his face as he said, "Yeah, a couple of times. Why?"

Before she could change her mind, she held up her Kyocera and said, "Time for you to earn your salary. The shot's yours."

He froze for a second, then asked, "Are you sure?"

"Unless you don't want it. If you do, our friend down there isn't going to be there forever, so you better hurry."

Without another word, he immediately grabbed her weapon and got into his sitting position. They had set up the hide just inside one of the windows, both of them on a metal workbench they'd dragged over. The window sill made a decent base for the Kyocera's bipod. Within five seconds, he had the weapon on his shoulder and was sighting in.

Gracie began to have second thoughts. Eli was twice her size, and his cheek weld and everything else was much, much different than hers. She considered taking back her weapon and telling him to use his M99. At such a short distance, he should be able to make that shot. But then again, at such a short distance, he should be able to use her weapon as well.

"That's 342 meters," she reminded him.

"Got it."

"What's your temperature?" she asked.

"I've got it. All of it."

She bit her tongue. She had to let him take the shot. She reached down to the deck and picked up her M99. If he missed and the guy bolted, she'd go full auto on him.

Hurry up and take the shot! she silently implored.

The man looked like he had the IED in place, and he looked around for the bag he'd had it in. It was just out of reach, so he stood up. . .

. . .and Eli immediately took the shot.

The man dropped as if he was poleaxed.

"Where'd I hit him?" Eli asked, his voice cracking.

"I. . .sorry, I missed it," she said realizing she'd forgotten that with him as the gunner, she was supposed to have shifted to spotter.

"But he's dead, right?"

She grabbed the binos and zoomed in. The guy was on his back, one leg bent underneath him. It was hard to tell in the darkness, but it looked like he'd been hit in the upper chest. Blood, almost black in the dim light, was beginning to flow from under him, spreading across the sidewalk. He wasn't even twitching.

"He's dead. Clean shot, Gittens."

"Woah!" he said, taking the binos from her to view his handiwork.

She turned back on her comms and said, "Hornet-Actual, target at 7643-4882 has been eliminated by Hornet-Four-Bravo. Request a collection team."

"Did you say Hornet-Four-Bravo?" the lieutenant asked.

"Affirmative. Hornet-Four-Bravo."

"Roger. Understood. Give Bravo my congrats."

"The lieutenant says congrats," she said.

"Oh man, I was so nervous! But that was righteous!"

"We're not relieved," she told him, "so since you've had your shot, how about giving me my Kyc back."

He looked slightly disappointed, but that barely dented his high as he returned her weapon.

They'd been using the Kyocera as firing it was far less likely to be noticed, and even with a dead pogo on the street, other bad guys wouldn't necessarily know of it. The kill hadn't affected their mission. The two of them settled in. They'd cover the collection team—unlike with the murdered family, it would be a Navy-Marine team for this in an attempt to gather any intel—and then finish the mission.

As the two sat side-by-side on top of the table, she reached over and patted Eli's arm.

"Good shot, HOG. You did good."

"HOG," she heard him whisper in wonderment.

Chapter 23

8

". . .other than that, nothing at all since 0430," Gracie told Kierk. "And with that, I gladly turn it over to you while we grab some Z's."

Gracie wasn't sure she liked the four-man teams. She was familiar with Eli and comfortable with him, and it was taking some getting used to Kierk and Oesper. But one advantage was that they could switch off and get some rest. The two teams had been in the hide at the top of the White Castle for 35 hours already, and that was a little long without getting some shut-eye.

The White Castle was a large, six-story building that had lost one entire corner to some sort of explosion. The two teams had taken over the opening, putting up several tarnkappes and netting to keep them out of sight. But even if others couldn't see them, they had superb fields of observation, and Gracie had been pretty sure that they'd see some action. But while Marines had been attacked twice the day before and three times during the night, nothing had been within their sector.

Gracie and Eli slowly crept backward until they were far enough back and shielded by the remaining walls to sit up.

Eli took out two Bamble Bars from his pocket, asking, "You want one?"

Bamble Bars were strictly geedunk, snacks from the tiny snack bar Top Freeman put up. Civilian geedunk was allowed back at camp, but not out in the field. The wrappers did not self-destruct as what happened with their issued rats, and for snipers in particular, their code was to leave no sign of their presence. Gracie was the NCO here, and it was up to her to enforce discipline.

Gracie thought about that for about half a second before reaching out a hand and taking the bar. She twisted the package open, took out the bar, and put the wrapper in her pocket.

Problem solved.

She took a bite, and then leaned back to decompress her brain for a few minutes before she could attempt to fall asleep. Even if they hadn't seen anything, they'd been on alert far too long to be able to simply drift off. Well, at least she couldn't, she amended as he saw Eli, head back, and already out cold. The wrapper for his Bamble Bar was in his closed fist, so she leaned forward and pulled it out, putting in her pocket with the other one.

She settled back, but while she was tired, she wasn't ready just yet to nap. She felt along her belly; the familiar build-up of pressure was just beginning. Scout-snipers couldn't leave any trace of their presence. Females had piss-snakes and everyone had piss-bags to take care of urine, but feces could be a little more problematic. The solution was to take their FIPs, the Fecal Inhibitor Protocol, but better known simply as "butt-pluggers." The required length of time determined which grade of protocol was used. The two teams were scheduled to be out for 60 hours, so they were on the "B" protocol, and now over half-way through the mission, the pressure was just beginning to build up. When they returned, they would be given the "dam breaker," the counteracting injection that would release the build-up.

Gracie hated the FIB. She hated the whole process, and she hated that it presented a danger should she get gut-shot. But it was SOP, and that was that.

She would be relieving Kierk in four hours, so if she was going to get some sleep, she needed to get on it. She took out her earbud and tried to blank her mind, and she was just drifting off when an explosion sounded in the near distance, followed almost immediately by the shock wave.

Gracie sat up, immediately on the alert.

"Where is it?" she asked Kierk as she inserted her earbud.

"Behind us," Kierk answered. "Close!"

The tac net was abuzz with chatter. Gracie's AI wasn't robust enough to gather in the transmissions and isolate what it thought were the most pertinent, so she toggled over to the Bravo Command.

Golf had been hit and hit hard. One of the platoons had been patrolling only a two streets over, and someone had brought down an entire building on them.

Firing opened up, and not with the familiar buzz of Marine Corps' 99's.

"Let's go," she shouted at Eli as she grabbed her Kyocera and slinging it over her shoulder.

Ignoring stealth, she ran through the tarnkappes to the remaining edge of the wall. With Eli on her ass, she swung herself around the edge, and dangling 50 meters above the ground, and hauled herself up to the roof. The cloud of dust two blocks away was all she needed to know.

"Cover the approach," she yelled at Kierk as she ran across the roof.

Their hide was within the edge of Barrio Blanca, which meant the streets were barely more than alleys and the buildings were either adjoining or close together. Gracie didn't even hesitate but jumped to the next building, covering the two-to-three meters with a good meter to spare. Eli landed heavily another half-a-meter past her and rolled before coming to his feet.

Firing sounded to her right, and she saw a prone man with a Rustov, three rooftops over shooting down towards where the building had gone down. Gracie stopped, and without working her firing solution, aimed low. Too low. She squeezed the trigger and the round hit the rooftop just short of the man before skipping up into his hip. He twisted in pain for a second before Gracie's adjusted second shot took him in the chest.

The task force's lone Wasp buzzed the street, its 20mm chaingun an angry buzz as it hit an adjoining building. Gracie had to trust her telltale to let the pilot know she was a friendly.

The next building was only a meter away, but a full story lower. Gracie had to slow down to make the jump, afraid that a twisted ankle could keep her from the fight. Gracie heard Eli's M99 pissing away, but she didn't stop to look. She darted to the right to see if she could get eyes on the fight. She was still a block off of Camino al Norte, the road where the building had gone down, but the adjoining two blocks were made up of a line of one-story shops. With Camino al Norte a major thoroughfare, Gracie could see the ruins of the downed building. The back half was mostly still standing, but the front had collapsed into rubble.

Marines were scattered on the ground, most firing up. Gracie had to trust that the Marine AIs' Friend-or-Foe function would be working and would block anyone from taking her under fire. One Marine had not taken cover but was standing on the rubble, digging furiously with her bare hands. Gracie could see rounds pinging on the rubble around her, and when she spasmed, Gracie knew she'd been kissed with an energy weapon of some sort. She didn't fall, though, but shook it off and kept digging.

Ignore her! Get some of the bastards off her back!

She saw movement through the window of the adjacent building. She brought up her Kyocera and scoped the window. A woman was edging up, a small grenade-looking object in her hand. She was obviously trying to stay back out of sight and out of the direct fire from the Marines below her, and she crouched down and started working the window.

Gracie pinged the window for the range. It was only 223 meters. The pogo was one story lower than Gracie, but at that close range, Gracie only had to make a minor correction. The window opened a crack, and that grew to about 15 centimeters. The woman looked to arm the grenade, and Gracie squeezed the trigger. The woman fell out of sight below the sill, and as Gracie looked for another target, there was an explosion that blew out the window, which fell in one piece to the ground below.

Oh, great! Another Mad Bomber moment, she thought.

She quickly scanned more buildings. She caught two men on a crew-served weapon. They were trying to tilt it forward without exposing themselves, and all that did was to keep them from aiming at the Marines below. If they moved forward half-a-meter, they would have the Marines in enfilade. The Golf Marines couldn't see them, but Gracie could.

Three-hundred-fourteen meters. A light wind coming up the street from her seven. Targets at the same level as she was. Fire; one down. The second man stood up, looking in horror at the piece of meat that had been his friend, making him a much easier target. Fire again; another down.

A figure started running across the roof, coming towards them. Gracie began to acquire him, but he fell, the victim to someone else.

A round blasted the low plasticrete retaining wall right in front of her, sending small pieces into her face, stinging her. Gracie ducked down and heard the whisper of darts zipping past her head.

"I got her," Eli shouted from ten meters to her left.

Gracie didn't bother to look at him. If he said he'd gotten whoever had taken her under fire, then he'd gotten her.

The Wasp came in on another run, this time perpendicular to Camino al Norte, and this time coming right at Gracie. She trusted her gear, but a Wasp is a terrifying sight when it's coming at a person. Gracie went flat as the Wasp opened up, but it was aiming at one of the floors below her. Still, she felt the building shudder as the 20 mm rounds did their work.

She knew that the Wasp could take down the building with enough fire, but there really wasn't anyplace else for her to go, so she just tried to put that possibility out of her mind.

She took another glance to the street below her. The Marine was pulling another out of the rubble. As she turned to drag him to cover, Gracie recognized her as one of the Golf Company corpsmen, Doc Neves. Gracie had thought Neves to be somewhat of a scatter-brained social butterfly, more interested in fashion and partying than anything else, but there she was risking her life to save a Marine.

Fire seemed to increase around Neves as she pulled the Marine free and started to drag him away, but Gracie didn't watch to see if she made it. From the impact of the rounds, she knew where another crew-served weapon had to be. She ran forward to the edge of the building, and there, at the corner of the building on which she'd bounced the round into her second kill, someone had an old slug-thrower that she didn't recognize. She didn't have a shot at the gunman. She raised her Kyocera, but she only had the barrel in her sights, and if she went prone, she wouldn't even have that. This had to be a standing shot, and she didn't trust her to hit a three-centimeter barrel that was recoiling with every shot.

She flipped her Kyocera around to her left shoulder. Everything felt wrong. But the weapon didn't care with what finger she used to pull the trigger. It didn't care how she looked through the Miller. If she could aim it, the weapon would respond.

She leaned out over the edge of the building. She could see more of the weapon, but not quite enough.

"Gittens, get over here!"

She knew that by now, Doc Neves had either made it or was dead, but the weapon was still a threat to the Marines. She had to take it out.

"Grab my harness and keep me from going over," she told Eli as he rushed up.

He didn't question her, but locked his hands around the side of her harness and started letting her lean out over the edge.

"Further," she said.

She didn't even think about falling. She was probably 45 kg with her gear, maybe 50, but Eli was a big, strong Marine who could bench 150 eight times. Gracie was nothing.

By the time she was out to about 60 degrees, she could see the breach assembly of the weapon sticking out of the window. Someone's hand was on the breach, supporting the weapon.

Thank goodness for the hours on the range, she thought.

Gracie had spent part of her range time on three occasions firing all her weapons left-handed. She'd taken a ration of shit from the more experienced snipers for that. What sniper would ever choose his or her weak side to fire? It didn't make sense to any of them. But because she had practiced it, Gracie had a basic concept of how the cheek weld and shooting position affected her firing picture.

She had never practiced it dangling 50 meters high, though.

Ignore that. Just concentrate. It's just like on the range.

The gun pulled back, and Gracie thought she'd lost the chance, but the tip of the muzzle was still visible, and when it jerked a few times, Gracie realized that the gunman was reloading. When it started to push out again, Gracie waited for the hand to appear.

I wish I had the Barrett, she thought as she squeezed her trigger.

The Kyocera's round was not as large as the Windmoeller's and nowhere near as massive as the Barrett's, but the weapon generated tremendous velocity. The round smashed into the handguard. Pieces of it flew into the air as the weapon fell, bouncing off the sill before slowly tumbling over to plunge to the ground below.

"OK, pull me up!" she told Eli.

"Did you get him?" he asked.

"Don't know. Got the weapon, though."

The firing started slowing down and Gracie scanned the area as quickly as she could. Within a minute, she saw a figure running over the rooftops. The ROE's for the mission were extremely restrictive. If someone was retreating, that person was not an authorized target. Gracie didn't know if the guy was running away or not. He was carrying a UKI-75, which was sometimes used as a sniper rifle, and for all Gracie knew, he was maneuvering to another FFP. She dropped him at about 550 meters just as he was getting ready to jump to another building.

Moments after she fired, the air sizzled with ionization. The air above the building with the hip-shot guy and the crew-served weapon glowed as the air molecules were excited.

The *FS Joshua Hope of Life* had spoken.

That broke the back of the attack. Anyone still left alive evidently decided that they wanted to remain that way. Gracie kept scanning the area, but she couldn't find a target.

On the street below, the Marines began to take stock of their situation. Gracie was pleased to see Doc Neves being helped out of one of the storefronts. She had the rubber-legged walk of someone with minor nerve damage, but if she weren't dead, she'd probably make it. Kinetic weapons could wound someone, and he or she could die hours or days later. With energy weapons, it was usually either KIA at the scene or WIA.

Gracie wanted to wave to her, to acknowledge that she'd been pretty gutsy down there, but the corpsman never looked up. She was somewhat surprised that she felt a little disappointed at that.

"Let's get back to the hide, Gittens," she said. "But no jumping roofs. Let's find the stairs and walk back there on the ground."

Chapter 25

13

> *. . . and who we are as Marines is nurtured by not only the traditions of our own United Federation Marines, but through the centuries of our patron Marines, going back to the forming of the Spain's Infanteria de Marina on February 27, 1537. So on this, our 398th birthday, reflect back on over a millennium of Marines, and remember that you are a part of history. By your actions, you are shaping the culture of Marines to come.*

> *Happy Birthday, Marines!*

> *Joab Ling*
> *General, United Federation Marine Corps*
> *Commandant*

Staff Sergeant Klepper's deep, resonant voice faded and hundreds of "ooh-rahs" took its place.

Almost half of the battalion was gathered in Warehouse D, one of the port's two largest and the one without cargo inside. Whether in combat or garrison, the Marines did not forget their birthday, but the "police action" (never a "war") had only gotten more intense, and the battalion XO had taken a heavily reinforced Hotel Company to create a secondary camp on the south side of the city. Other Marines were out on patrol or manning positions, so half of the battalion was most of the available Marines.

"Post the colors!" Major Cranston shouted out.

The color guard, consisting of three Marines and Doc Neves on the Navy colors, countermarched and placed the colors in the stands. Doc looked good, recovered from her tingle on Camino al

Norte. Rumor had it that she was being put up for an award, maybe even a Nova.

On order, four Marines marched forward, carrying the birthday cake on a tray between them. It looked much better than Gracie would have thought possible in a combat arena, and she wondered if Gunny Coventry had actually baked it himself or had gotten it out in town. The situation was not good out there, but life went on, and bakeries probably still baked.

The major called forward the oldest and youngest Marine to get the first pieces of cake. The sergeant major was the oldest Marine, and he graciously accepted his slice, taking a bite and nodding that it met with his approval.

"Better check it for poison," Zach whispered.

I guess the gunny got the cake out in town, Gracie thought hearing that.

"And, also per tradition, the next piece of cake goes to our youngest Marine. Private Klip Poussey was born on 9 May 367. . ."

There was a collective moan from the Marines in formation.

Three-sixty-seven? He's a baby!

". . . and enlisted in the Corps on 9 May 384. He joined the Fuzos on 12 August 384, 11 days before our current deployment.

Poussey, standing proud, accepted his piece and took a tiny bite.

They didn't really have a guest of honor. None of the rank and file knew whether that was because no one had been invited or if an invitation was made to the mayor or governor and that invitation had been refused. So the CO had stood in and given the birthday speech. Normally, the guest of honor would get the next piece of cake, but as expected, she refused. Tradition also required that as the senior Marine, she get the last piece, and that was the tradition she was going to follow.

The formations were dismissed as Gunny got his small team of assistants to start cutting up the cake. Half was saved and carted away for Hotel and those on duty, but the rest was cut and placed on several trays with Marines lining up to get their piece.

Gracie started to get in line, then told Eli to hold her place. Doc Neves was with several of her squadmates, but she looked up when Gracie approached.

"Corporal Crow, happy birthday!"

"Happy birthday to you, too. You're looking good. I didn't see a trace of a limp."

"Oh, I just got kissed a little. Doc Gnish sent me up to the *Josh*, and a couple of sessions on the ELS, and I'm good as new."

"ELS?"

"You know, the Electrolavage System."

Gracie had no idea what that was, but she shrugged it off.

"I just wanted to say that what you did was pretty ballsy. I. . .I. . ." Gracie said, suddenly feeling awkward and not sure of what to say. "Well, I just wanted to tell you that."

She started to turn away when Neves said, "I heard it was you on one of the buildings keeping the jericks off my ass."

"It wasn't just me. And your platoon was showing their fight, too."

That was true. Gracie had five confirmed kills (the guy on the crewserved was dead, but despite losing a hand to Gracie, he'd almost assuredly been killed when the *Josh* zapped the building), but five from the platoon had recorded kills, to include Staff Sergeant Riopel's 2,340-meter shot from half-way across the city. Eli recorded two kills, and he probably had more, but with his M99, verifying kills was not as easy as with any of the sniper systems.

"Maybe, but I appreciate it," Neves said, holding out her hand.

Gracie took it, then asked, "The Marine you pulled out. I know he got casevac'd, but how is he?"

"Korf's gonna make it," one of the Marines around her said. "He's back on Tarawa in regen, but that son-of-a-bitch will be back before we know it."

"Good to hear. Well, I, uh, I need to get back in line if I want to get my cake. All of you, happy birthday."

"You, too," several of them said.

"Thanks," Gracie told Eli as she slipped back into line.

Someone turned on the latest Grayson Parade, filling the warehouse with the heavy counter-beat of "I Want It," probably not the type of lyrics approved by headquarters, but the officers didn't seem to object. She found herself bobbing her head to the music.

Gracie wasn't the most social person in the galaxy, mostly by her own choice—at least that was what she told herself. But she liked the big Marine Corps gatherings. They let her be part of something bigger while mainly just observing. Back on Tarawa, all the Marine Corps Balls would be huge affairs, and she liked being part of those events, even if only peripherally. This was a far cry from those formal affairs. The Marines were in their skins, weapons slung on their backs. But in some ways, it was more real to her. The Fuzo's Patron Day celebration would be in two months, and Gracie was glad they'd be back on Tarawa for that. The pageantry of the beating with the Drum Corps always sent her blood pounding, and that couldn't be done here on Jericho. But it was somehow appropriate that the Birthday Ball was here in a combat zone. Combat was the very reason d'etre of the Marines, after all.

Some of her fellow Marines were taking the "ball" in Marine Corps Ball seriously. About 20 or 25 of them had started dancing in the middle of the warehouse.

Gracie and Eli made it to the front of the line and received their pieces of cake. Gracie took a bite and had to admit that it was pretty good, all things considered. Looking at what was left and who still hadn't been fed, she figured she could come back for a second piece later.

She'd finished and was watching the dancers, who had grown to about 50, biding her time for another piece of cake when Zach grabbed her by the arm.

"Come on, Crow. It's time to shake it!"

"Oh, no," she said, pulling back. "I don't dance."

"No choice, Corporal. It's the Birthday Ball, and it's in the regs."

"Really, I don't know how to dance."

Zach didn't look back as he pulled her to the floor.

He turned around, made a stately medieval court bow, and said, "If you can't dance, then you just get to stand and watch me. I'm a wicked good dancer."

He started into some horrible gyrations, so bad that Gracie had to laugh. Despite her intentions, the beat of the music got her slightly moving.

"See, I knew you couldn't resist when you saw my moves," Zach said before settling into something far more acceptable.

Gracie got a little more into it, hesitantly at first, then a bit more comfortably. She was almost sad when the music ended. She thanked Zach and started back for the sidelines, only to be intercepted by Possum Khalil. After Possum came Glastonary, then Kierk.

To her surprise, she found she was not only OK with it, but was also enjoying it. She looked around. With relatively few women, guys were dancing alone or with each other, but the female Marines were in high demand. Staff Sergeant Holleran, the senior female enlisted Marine was just as in demand with the SNCOs as Gracie seemed to be with her platoon. The staff sergeant caught her eye as she was looking at her, and she gave Gracie a big smile and a thumbs up.

A few Marines from other units tried to step up, but the platoon closed ranks around her, and except for a couple of times, she only danced with her fellow snipers. At one point, she was part of a fivesome, valiantly trying to keep up with the Rabbit Hop. Dave Oesper was the only one of the platoon who didn't ask her to dance, and she solved that by pulling him off the sidelines and onto the floor. She knew he was embarrassed, but his smile at the end of the dance told her he appreciated it.

The venue was hardly what anyone would have wanted, there wasn't a banquet, and no loved ones were there, but Marines were Marines, always making do with less. Gracie had been to four Marine Corps Balls, and much to her surprise, this had been the best one.

She danced for almost two hours until the music cut off and the sergeant major got on the mic and said, "Sorry to pull the plug, but all of you on the port watch, you need to get ready. We've got to let the starboard watch come in for their ball."

"That's us," Possum said.

Even with no major operation planned for the day, there were still posts to be filled, and Gracie and Eli were assigned the control tower, relieving Brick Liogeni and Lance Corporal Cable-Williams from the Bravo Section.

The Marines started to drift off to get ready. Gracie looked back at the table with the birthday cake. The starboard watch's cake was there, but all the cut pieces for the port watch were gone. She'd missed her chance to get one.

She didn't care, though. This had been one hell-of-a Birthday Ball.

Chapter 26

13

The small family looked scared out of their minds as Gracie, Eli, Kierk, and Oesper entered their front room. Three Marines stood watch over them, M99s pointed slightly to the side, but obviously at the ready.

"Sergeant Pillsbury's upstairs," one of the Marines told the four of them.

Gracie wanted to assure the family that everything would be OK, that they just needed their home for a short while. From the resigned, defeated look on the man's face, though, she didn't think he'd believe anything she'd have to say. At least the toddler was asleep in his mother's arms, blissfully unaware of the Marines who'd taken over his home.

Gracie led the other three scout-snipers up the stairway where the Hotel Company sergeant was waiting. He looked relieved to see them.

"We've cleared the home. Nothing here but the four jericks downstairs. I'm going to leave a fire team here, but I've got to marry up with the rest of my platoon."

"Anything else we should know?" Gracie asked, uncomfortable with the lack of a real brief.

Once the Marines realized the current opportunity and the plan thrown together, Pillsbury's squad had been tasked with securing the home for the sniper team. The sergeant probably felt bad enough leaving a fire team for security, but he was also anxious to get back to his platoon to get his own operations order, so Gracie let it slide. She knew her mission.

Kierk was not so accepting, though.

"That's it? That's your turnover, Sergeant?"

"That's it," the sergeant said. "If you've got any questions, you can ask Corporal Weintrub. I don't have time to sit here and hold your hands."

With that, he wheeled about, gathered up the rest of his Marines, and clumped down the stairs.

"Real professional," Kierk said.

"Nothing to do about it now, so let's prepare our FFPs," Gracie said.

Kierk was actually half-a-year senior to Gracie, but this mission came down to skill with the weapon, and Gracie was given the Barrett. As the designated primary, she was effectively in charge. Kierk didn't seem to mind, and he was following Gracie's lead.

This was a pop-up mission. It hadn't been planned. The battalion was already into its embark prep, and the advance party for 3/14 had already arrived when Intel found out about this meeting, so less than 80 minutes after the warning order, the mission was in full swing. Hotel's First Platoon had been on a routine patrol in the area, and it had quickly become the focal point of the operation. Gracie couldn't blame Sergeant Pillsbury's impatience to get back to his platoon and get his new orders.

The four Marines checked both rooms that faced their target. Gracie considered splitting the two teams up, but the tiny window in the child's bedroom was not suited for the mission, and the bigger bedroom was a corner room with three larger windows, so that became their position. Moving quickly, they slapped their lines on the walls, then hung tarnkappes facing the target and camo nets along the sides. The nets would not fool anyone specifically looking inside the home, but they served to create shadows that would make observation into the room more difficult.

The target was a squat building known as the "Hatbox," or rather, the people inside of the building. The Hatbox was a round, almost bunker-looking building, the home to one of Jericho's leading industrialists. It stood isolated on a small hill in the suburb of Theodore Manor with the nearest neighbor almost 400 meters away to the northeast. From Gracie's position to the west, the home was over 800 meters away. The running joke before the war was that he'd ruined so many competitors that he was afraid someone would try to extract revenge, so he'd built a fortress protected by open ground. Urban myth or not, the fact now remained that no police or Marine force was going to be able to approach the home without being spotted.

Henri Nilsson, the owner, was not the prime target, however. He was not the big fish. What had excited Intel, and therefore the commodore, was that the house was being used as a meeting between Mark Pyritte from Svealand and Tabitha Rinzinni of the ultra-nationalist Our Homeland Party. The Federation had been calling for meetings between the northern and the two southern continents, but not between these two groups. Pyritte led a faction from Svealand that not only advocated full independence but the seizing of about 1/3 of the eastern continent as well. Rinzinni and the OHP had long advocated draconian "purity" laws and a new constitution, only to be defeated in election after election. There was substantial evidence that Rinzinni personally ordered some of the civilian massacres that had occurred, atrocities that had killed both Svea and Tinos, in hopes of fomenting full-out war. She'd escaped arrest and had been tried and convicted by the Jericho court in absentia and sentenced to a mind-wipe and life in prison. The fact that they both were meeting had huge ramifications, and the Federation Council itself had stepped in and authorized the kill mission.

The *Josh* could level the Hatbox without a problem, but there were two roadblocks to that. The first was that there were purportedly over 150 people in the building, to include the household staff and their families. The second was that the Jericho premier, who was one of only four Jerichoites to know about the mission, wanted the house intact for intel gleaning.

Gracie checked the time. In less than ten minutes, the Federation would contact the governor of Svealand to inform her of the mission against one of the north's prominent citizens, and if the FCDC commander and some of his troops stayed with her until the operation was concluded, well, that wasn't because of a lack of trust, of course, but merely to ensure her security.

"Let's get set up," she told Kierk, then, "You two, keep working on the hide."

All four had come loaded for bear. Gracie had her Windmoeller and her M99 in addition to the Barrett. Keirk had both his Windmoeller and Kycocera in addition to his 99, and each spotter carried an additional weapon as well: Oesper had an M54 grenade launcher, and Eli an old Peacemaker that Gracie had begged from Staff Sergeant Holleran. Together with the fire team on the first floor, they made up a pretty potent force. Intel had noted increased activity in the area, which didn't necessarily mean anything significant, but with the Wasp down for pre-embark, better overkill than the opposite. The crew was trying to rush the Wasp back online, but that was a four-hour evolution, so it would probably not be available should things go south.

There was no reason to range the Hatbox. The *Josh* had it at 812 meters from her position to the center window. Atmospherics between her position and the building measured by the ship were being continually downloaded into her Miller's AI.

Gracie and Kierk dragged the bed to just short of the window through which Gracie would fire if she got the call. It was too low for her to take a prone position, and being a bed, it was soft and giving under her, not a great surface upon which to fire. But she didn't have time to search the house for something to put under her. With the Barrett resting on the edge of the window sill, she'd just have to still her body and make due. At least as with many of her shots since arriving on Jericho, the range was pretty short. Eight-hundred meters was nothing for the big gun.

Gracie glanced at the time, then got on the bed and leaned up against the footboard. She was about as tight as she could get herself. She dropped the magazine and checked the rounds. The first four were M33 CDs, the "CD" designating "counter defilade." Except for the lime green tip, which was painted on for identification purposes, it looked no different than any other round. What was inside of it was what made it special. While still in the chamber, the AI programmed it for the shot. Once fired, it was on its own, but its mission was already mapped out. The round would travel to a given point, say a window, and once past it by a programmed distance, detonate with a surprisingly powerful blast for something that small. The ECR[25] was a very respectful four meters.

The technology was basically the same as with the larger energy shells, rounds that would carry a proton or plasma beam warhead over long distances before detonating, but highly miniaturized. The Windmoeller also had the M34 CD round, which was a mini-version of the larger energy shells, but its small size meant that to have any effectiveness, it had to focus the energy into a tight beam, which meant the specific target had to be identified and located once the round entered its kill zone.

One thing that still amazed Gracie was the seven-hundred-year-old technology used to power the round's tiny brain. To keep costs down, the round was equipped with a magnetic transducer. With the round rotating, the transducer interacts with a planet's magnetic fields to generate an alternating current. This tiny amount of power was more than enough to calculate the distance traveled as well as trigger the detonation.

"Now we wait," Gracie told the other three Marines.

The Navy forward observer with the battalion had released a swarm of nano-drones, drones so tiny and so well shielded that nothing inside the house should be able to pick them up. These drones should already be on their way across the open approaches to the house, and once there, some would attach themselves to windows while others were programmed to surreptitiously worm themselves inside the building. As soon as either of the two targets was in a room that could be targeted by any of the four teams, the order to fire would be given.

As they were drawing weapons, Zach had suggested putting together a kitty on which team would get the shot. Gracie had paid the entire 100 credits for her team, and she wanted to collect.

When the Svealand governor was notified, the mission was hot. Eli and Oesper continued to make minor improvements to the hide, but she and Kierk got into a semi-position, Gracie on the bed, Kierk on a chair. After only five minutes, Gracie had to stretch out

---

[25] ECR: Effective Casualty Radius

her leg. It was going to sleep in the position that she had it, and she couldn't allow that. She stretched it out straight, knowing she could bend it back and be ready in only a few seconds.

After another four minutes, the platoon command circuit lit up, and the lieutenant passed, "New analysis indicates the windows are rated R36, not R22. I say again, R36. All primaries, chamber an M18 AP first. Use that to create an opening, then the M33."

Gracie quickly dropped the magazine, extracted the M33 round in the chamber and put it back in the mag, then took out one of her armor-piercing rounds. The M33 round could penetrate anything with an R30 and below rating. If the windows were R36, the round would probably bounce off and never penetrate the home. With the M18 AP, she could defeat and penetrate anything up to an R60 rating.

She put the armor-piercing round in the magazine, locked it in place, and then chambered it. She looked over at Kierk and raised her eyebrows. He shrugged his shoulders and looked back downrange. He'd already had the .308 M4 AP round chambered, but the smaller round fired by his Windmoeller would be pretty useless if he had to smash one of the windows now. He'd only be able to fire if someone came into the open outside the building or through a broken window.

"I don't have to tell you that you need to be quick with your second   round," the lieutenant said. "Don't hesitate."

If the shot came down to her, and she took the people in the room by surprise, then she was pretty sure they'd hesitate even just a moment before realizing what had happened and try to duck out of the way. That hesitation would be all she needed. With the Barrett's superb counter-recoil system, she knew she could get off another round in just over one second. The first round would blast the window (and the super strong molecularly-oriented crystal used in higher R-rated windows tended to shatter when finally penetrated) with the follow-on round being the CD round, the one that would kill.

Jonathan P. Brazee

Gracie calmed herself. This was an easy shot. She just had to get the round through what would be an open window. Still, a bad position or buck fever could result in a catastrophic miss.

Breathe. Easy.

"Team Shark, we've got movement," the lieutenant passed on the platoon command net. "Get ready."

"Shit," Kierk said.

"Team Shark" was the mission designation for Staff Sergeant Riopel's four-man team. He'd been given the side of the building that Intel had thought the most likely target. Gracie started to relax, waiting for either the word to the staff sergeant to fire, or if it wasn't passed on the open net, for the crack of Riopel's Barrett to reach her. The staff sergeant was a good 1200 meters away from her, but over the open ground, the big gun's report would still be plenty audible.

But nothing happened. No word, no gunshot. Gracie looked over and caught Kierk's eye. He gave a shrug, then went back to his scope.

It was almost ten minutes later when Lieutenant Wadden came back on the net with, "Team Marlin, we've got movement entering 2003. Stand by for target confirmation."

Gracie jerked back into full concentration. "Marlin" was her team's designator, and 2003 was one of her target rooms. She brought her outstretched leg back in, settled the Barrett on the window sill, and read off the data still flowing from the Josh.

"Doughbaby is in 2003; I say again, Doughbaby is in 2003. Wait for confirmation on Red Piper," the lieutenant passed.

"Doughbaby" was Rinzinni. Without consciously realizing it, Gracie reached under her blouse, and pulled out the lanyard and HOGs tooth, putting the round between her teeth. Just as mindlessly, she started caressing her trigger, getting ready to take the shot.

"We do not have Red Piper. Stand by, Marlin."

She was barely aware of Eli coming to stand beside her. The world had shrunk down to the single one-by-two-meter window 812 meters away. That was all the mattered.

"Team Marlin. Doughbaby is in the back right corner of the room from your position. Engage."

Gracie didn't hesitate. Her caress became a gentle pull, and the big gun went off. She cycled the round and fired again just as the window exploded into shards of tiny crystals that flashed in the sunlight. Her second round exploded inside the room, a small orange flash just as Gracie adjusted her aim to skip the next round just inside the right window mount. It took her three more seconds to be satisfied before she sent the round downrange.

To her surprise, a middle-aged man stumbled to the window to look out in shock. The supersonic crack of a round next to her told her that Kierk had switched to his Kyocera, and a split second later, the man fell back with a chest shot.

Gracie watched through her scope, but she couldn't see any movement. The ROEs stipulated that anyone in the room was to be taken out with the bodies to be sorted after-the-fact. However, with the Psych Team now getting ready to broadcast a call for surrender, no one else could be targeted except in defense.

"We're still on the clock," Gracie reminded the other three. "We don't have any confirmation on Red Piper yet."

If Red Piper hadn't been in the room, Gracie didn't think he'd be showing up anytime soon, at least on her side of the building. But she didn't want anyone to relax. The Barrett had a pretty loud report, and by firing it, she'd given their position away to anyone in the area. Until they and the fire team downstairs were gathered up by Hotel's First Platoon and they were back at camp, she wanted everyone on the alert.

Four speaker drones flew up to surround the Hatbox, and within moments, the psych team's announcement was blaring at them. With one speaker 700 meters from them, two at about 800, the one on the opposite side of the building 950, the words were reaching Gracie at different times, rendering them difficult to make out. She focused instead on the team's position. She had excellent fields of fire to her front. The same things that made the Hatbox secure benefited her as well, at least in that direction. She leaned out and swung her Barrett around, but she had nothing to the rear.

"Gittens, open that window there," she said, indicating the one on the side wall. "Keep an eye on the road alongside us and the homes across it."

He looked back at the door leading into their room, and she added, "We've got the Hotel fire team down there. Anyone coming in the room will have to get past them."

Eli nodded and went to the window, then said, "Hey, this one doesn't open like yours."

"Well, break it. These folks are going to submit a claim anyway, so we might as well make it worthwhile."

With a smile, he brought up the butt-plate of his 99 to hit the window when Gracie said, "Not with your weapon, Gittens. You really want to have to fire that with a broken stock?"

He looked around confused until Gracie pointed out a metal chair. He picked it up and started whaling away at the window. It managed to hold up through five hits, popping out of the frame of the sixth to fall to the ground below.

"You staying with the Kyc?" she asked Kierk.

"Yeah. I think our part's done, but I'm sticking with Flora," he said. "Besides, you've got your Windy."

Like about half of the Marines in the platoon, he'd named his two personal sniper rifles.

If Kierk were on his Windmoeller, Gracie would have stuck with the Barrett. But with him on his Kyocera, she only hesitated a second before putting the big gun down and picking up the smaller one. Kierkagaard was probably right, though, so it wouldn't make much difference. All they had to do was wait for the platoon and get back to camp, then finish up their embark and get ready to get off the planet. Still, she laid the Barrett right beside her and patted her Ruger in the holster on her thigh.

"There goes First Platoon," Kierkagaard said, pointing to Marines who had started to move into the open area leading up to the Hatbox.

Gracie grabbed her helmet and slapped it on, powering up the display. She hadn't realized that Hotel's First Platoon had been so close to them, only 200 meters to their left. She knew the op order, of course, and she knew that First Platoon would clear the building and take any surrenders, but due to the extreme compression of time, she hadn't really absorbed all the details of who was where on the ground. Second Platoon was part of the security element and was spread out from just past their position on one side and then all the way past Staff Sergeant Riopel's position. Third Platoon and Weapons were on the other side of the Hatbox. Still more than two klicks out, Golf and India were on the move to join them.

A little late for the party, Gracie thought.

The display also showed movement from the homes around the Hatbox. The civilians did not cooperate with transponders, so the numbers were far from accurate, but the movement was there.

"We've got jericks gathering. Probably coming to see the show, but still, keep alert," she said, putting her helmet back on the floor.

A line company Marine would probably get his ass kicked for taking off his helmet, but scout-snipers had a thing against them. Their excuse was that they couldn't wear them and be as accurate with their shots, and while there was a kernel of truth to that, Gracie knew that the main reason was that the helmets were uncomfortable, and no one wanted to wear them if they had an option.

Gracie glassed the Hatbox again as the Marines reached half-way to it. There was no movement in any of the windows on her side of the building. She wasn't sure how many people had died inside 2003, but that had to have broken their will. She didn't think they'd put up any resistance.

The sudden firing that broke out was proof that even if Gracie was a kick-ass sniper, she was no expert on enemy psychology.

The Marines from First Platoon hit the deck, scrambling for any semblance of cover they could find. Gracie leaned out the window, but the firing was too close to her and masked by the home next door. The boom of Riopel's Barrett from over 900 meters away was evidence that even if she couldn't see anyone, he could.

The net was alive with chatter. Firing was breaking out all along the near side of the town. Gracie threw back on her helmet and spotted from where the *Josh* detected incoming fire on the platoon. She immediately realized that she could reach any gunmen who were right under Staff Sergeant Riopel's nose.

She leaned out the window, elbows on the sill, and tried to spot a target. A long burst from an automatic weapon caught her attention, but she couldn't see the gunman. Flashes revealed the window out of which the gunman were firing, though. She dropped her Windmoeller and picked the Barrett back up. She ranged the window and accepted the atmospherics from the *Josh*—she didn't have time to do her own, and less than five seconds later, fired one of her last two M33's. With the air pressure and high humidity, she could actually see the vapor-trace of the round as it flew downrange until just before it disappeared into the window opening. She hadn't changed the settings on detonation, trusting the Miller's AI, but as soon as the round exploded inside, the firing stopped.

"We've got jericks coming out at the Hatbox," Kierk said as he fired off a shot.

Gracie swung back to the building to see a dozen men coming around the corner to take the Marines under fire. First Platoon had started to assault back into the oncoming fire, and these men were coming at them from behind. One fell, probably from one of the Team Swordfish snipers, but then the gunmen made it around the corner and were now masked by the building to Swordfish.

Gracie dropped the Barrett and picked up the Windmoeller again. Some snipers had problems making a quick mental transition between such disparate weapons, but once again, Gracie gave a small prayer of thanks to the many hours she'd spent on the range firing one weapon after the other. As before, she was lucky that the range was not particularly that far, but still, the transition could be rough.

Within moments, she was squeezing the trigger at a man hugging the wall. Since he was in front of the wall, it really couldn't give him much protection, and Gracie's shot took him in the middle of his chest. He slid down, leaving a broad brushstroke of blood behind him as Gracie shifted to the man at his feet, who was in the prone position and firing on First Platoon. Her round impacted his left shoulder, probably tearing through the chest cavity and either into the heart or destroying his lungs. From the way he simply stopped moving, Gracie would have bet it was the heart—if she'd had time to think about it.

Beside her at the next window, Kierk was putting out a steady staccato of firing, each round leaving the muzzle at well over the speed of sound, a mini-sonic boom announcing each shot. Gracie acquired another target, a middle-aged man in a bright blue shirt who was running low in the manner of a trained soldier, but he fell to someone, probably Kierk, before she could fire.

Downstairs, she could hear the burp of M99s, and she knew the Hotel fire team was engaging.

She spotted a fat guy who'd gotten up and was charging the Marines, an energy gun ionizing the air. At that range, he could simply sweep the weapon to target them. He was moving quickly for his bulk, but not quick enough as a single round hit him a little behind where Gracie had intended, but the shot probably severed his spinal cord.

"Gittens, Oesper, see what you can do to support the fire team," she shouted as she acquired another target. She fired just as he dropped to his belly, her round missing high.

"Shit!" she let out before adjusting her aim and rectifying her mistake.

And then there were no more. What had been a dozen gunmen were now simply a dozen pieces of meat. One was trying to crawl back, his legs useless, but the rest looked dead.

The Marines hadn't fared as bad, but that was only relative. Four or five Marines were motionless with two being dragged forward by their buddies. They'd reached a slight depression on the ground, part of the property's drainage system, but they were still under fire. It wouldn't be long until the jericks got some indirect fire weapons to plop on top of them. At about 100 meters out, they were too far for hand-thrown grenades to reach them, but they were also too far to simply run for the cover the buildings provided.

A bright flare of light erupted from about 15 meters short of the Marines, Gracie's Miller struggling to darken the screen. It was either a toad or the local equivalent, the super-intense incendiary grenades that could burn through anything. Someone had chucked the thing almost 85 meters, which was almost unbelievable. As it sputtered and burned, Gracie had to suppress a shudder as she imagined such a painful way to go.

The firing downstairs intensified, but Gracie had to put that out of her mind. If someone could throw a toad that far, they might be able to throw one all the way into the Marines. She leaned out again, with her Windmoeller almost up against the outside wall of the building. She knew she was exposed, but there was no help for that.

A jerick on an adjacent roof popped up to spot the Marines, then disappeared from sight. If he were an experienced soldier, he'd pop up again from a different spot. He wasn't. The turkey-peeker came back right at the same spot, swinging around an energy weapon for a shot. Gracie nailed him in the head, taking most of it off as he fell out of sight.

There was a grunt from behind her, and the sound of a body falling. She couldn't waste time looking back to see who it was. Firing was intensifying around the 15 or so surviving Marines huddled in the depression. They knew they had to get out of the kill zone, but dirt was flying as rounds impacted the edge of the depression, showering them with small clods. One Marine slapped his leg, then rolled back over and scooted farther into the depression, weapon at the ready, his uniform's bones hardening to stop the round. Still, it must have hurt like hell.

A round impacted on the side of the building, about two meters behind her, but she doubted that it was aimed at her. She started sweeping her scope, trying to pick up another target. As she swept, a momentary flash of movement caught her eye, and she immediately backtracked to see a wiry young man, more of a kid, standing on another roof, holding something small. He was on the near side of some sort of large cooling unit, so no one on Riopel's team could have seen him. He took a deep breath, and with his right arm low, he started running forward like a cricket bowler. Gracie immediately realized he was the one who'd thrown the incendiary before. She didn't have the range, but she guessed about 230 and squeezed off a shot.

She was a little off, and instead of hitting him center mass, she hit his upper arm. He spun to the ground, the "Forestall Basketball" printed on his shirt clearly visible as he fell from sight. Almost immediately, he stood up again briefly appearing in Gracie's sights before he bent over as if to pick something up. The mini-sun that burst into life at his feet was proof that Gracie was correct. He jerked back, his arm a flaming torch, before falling backward and out of sight.

Her tiny earbud AI filtered in what it thought was a relevant message.

"Two KIA, request backup now!" the team leader from downstairs was shouting into his mic. "I've got a dozen jericks trying to come in."

"Hold on," another voice responded with what she thought was the Golf Company signal. "We're five mikes out."

She could throw on her helmet and make sure, but it really didn't matter one way or the other, and she couldn't afford the time.

"Eli," she said, not turning around. "Keep on with what you're doing, but watch the door. They're about to get overrun downstairs."

"Got you," he said, as a wave of relief swept over her.

She'd known one of them had been hit, but it wasn't Eli.

She continued to scan through the Miller, looking for more customers. She knew she was focusing too close. Riopel's team had better eyes on whoever was there. She shifted to where she had a better field of view, starting from about 600 meters to her left and perpendicular out 1500 meters to the edge of the opposite side of the Hatbox. She saw five gunmen swarm over a low retaining wall on the roof next to Shark's position.

She started to enter in some quick data when a round hit the wall right by her head. She ducked back, then Riopel's voice came over the P2P.

"Sorry about that, Crow. I didn't see him until too late. He's zeroed now, though."

"You've got five coming at your direct three o'clock now, on the next building. Don't know if they want you or First Platoon," she replied. "Oh, yeah, and thanks."

One of the men made a quick peek around the edge of the roof and down towards the middle of the building. They were after Riopel's team. With Gracie spotting him, he might as well have put out flashing N-LEDs in the shape of an arrow pointing the way to him, but untrained fighters rarely considered what was out of their own sight.

The building ranged at 1,345 meters. This was getting to real sniper range, farther than grunts with M99's could successfully engage. The *Josh's* data was still streaming in, and with the active range-finder, she thought she had a lock. She squeezed the trigger, and a second-and-a-half later, she was relieved to see the gut shot that knocked the man down. She would have already been firing again, but without Eli spotting, she'd needed to see where she'd hit in order to make corrections. She'd been dead on laterally, but a little low.

Two of the others wheeled to see what had happened to their buddy, and two quick shots dropped them before the last two ducked down below the edge of the low wall.

They'd be in shock for a moment, trying to decide what to do. It wouldn't take them long to decide to get out of there, but Gracie had five, maybe ten seconds before that. She pulled back inside the window, threw down her Windmoeller, and snatched up the Barrett.

Eli was standing by the door, M99 at the ready.

"Keep them off me!" she shouted, barely noticing the Kierk was on the floor, motionless.

She leaned back out, holding the big Barrett without support. She ranged the low wall, programmed the remaining round to detonate one meter past it, and fired. She saw the round explode a meter-and-a-half high. Whether it got the two gunmen or not, she couldn't see.

"Three of five down, maybe the other two as well," she passed to Riopel.

"Thanks, Crow. Keep your head down."

In the room behind her, she heard the buzz of Eli's M99. The Barrett was too bulky to bring in quickly, she was out-of-balance leaning out so far, and her arms were already trembling. So she simply let go of the big gun. She hated to do it, and she hoped they could recover it, but with only her team encoded to let it fire, it wasn't as if anyone could pick it up and use it to fire on them.

Gracie had hooked one foot around the footboard of the bed, and she used that to pull herself back. Eli was firing on full auto, sending a deadly hail of darts out the door. He stumbled as something hit him, but didn't stop firing. Gracie tried to reach her Windmoeller, which she'd knocked to the floor in her haste to get the Barrett when Eli went down, his face a bloody mess. A grey-haired man, moving with assuredness, stepped into view, an M99 in his hands, which he used to poke Eli in the chest. The man had a military air about him, but he made a cardinal mistake of not clearing the room before looking at his trophy. Gracie pulled the Ruger from her thigh holster when he realized his mistake. His eyes got huge as he started to swing up his M99, a string of darts reaching out to her when her double tap hit him in the throat and jaw. As he dropped, Gracie charged, Ruger stretched out before her. She stepped on the gurgling man's chest, almost stumbling, as she bolted out the door, screaming at the top of her lungs.

The young kid on the other side looked up in horror as she burst out into the hall. He dropped his UKI and started to turn and run when Gracie fired another double tap into his back. He fell face first, bouncing a couple of times before sliding to a stop. He pulled in three gulping gasps of air before falling silent.

Gracie ran to the stairwell and looked down, listening for movement. She heard none. She turned back, stepping over the young kid and two more jericks that Eli had dropped. One was down hard, but still alive. Gracie ignored him and went back into the room. All three of her teammates were down. She checked the pulses of Eli and Gittens, and both were gone, but within the realm of resurrection. She didn't bother with Oesper. The top of his head was mush. There wasn't a chance of him getting zombied.

Her emotions threatened to take over, and she had to fight to keep them at bay. Tears started to form, but she brushed them away and picked up her Windmoeller. There were Marines still in trouble out there, and she had to give them support.

With her Windmoeller in hand, got on her bed and settled back into shooter-mode. There was furtive movement back along Team Shark's side. Gracie snapped off a quick shot, but her target was gone before her round impacted. She winged another man, taking him out of action. One evidently thought he or she was unobserved due to the camo hood over his or her face. Gracie couldn't see much around the face, and couldn't even tell if the person was male or female, but the hat on top of the hood pretty much framed where the face had to be. Gracie took her time to carefully aim the shot. The round took the person in the forehead, blowing off the hood. Despite that, the hamburger that was left of the person's head still didn't allow Gracie to tell much about him or her, either sex, age, or anything else for that matter.

Below her, the remnants of First Platoon were gathering themselves, and the call came out for all Marines who could support them to be ready to give them cover. Gracie still had time to register two more kills when the Marines in the platoon stood up as one, and weapons blazing, charged forward. The air crackled with ionization as the *Josh* hit the nearest section of homes, clearing the way for them. Half-a-dozen jericks popped up at the sight only to be knocked back down, three by Gracie, more by other Marines.

Over the next five minutes, Gracie was on mindless automatic, a killing machine. She acquired, fired, and acquired again. She lost track of how many jericks she dropped. A rocket of some sort hit the home, taking a good chunk of the corner with it. Somehow, Gracie wasn't touched, and now with a large section of the wall gone, she just had better fields of fire. She went prone on the floor right at the corner, targeting whomever she could spot.

She was still firing when Golf Company reached the battle, followed quickly by India. The immense firepower of two rifle companies, each with a PICS platoon, quickly broke the back of the assault.

She heard Marines enter the home, she heard them clearing each room, she heard one of them say, "That's enough, Marine. The area's secure." But it wasn't until one of them put a hand on her back that she lowered her weapon.

"Is there anyone else in here?" the sergeant asked when she finally turned to look at him.

"Four downstairs," she said, "and my three brothers here."

She looked over at Eli, still on his back just a couple of meters away, and the damn was broken. The ever-emotionless Corporal Gracie Medicine Crow broke down and cried.

FS JOSHUA HOPE OF LIFE

Chapter 27
37

"OK, you're up," Zach said as he came out of the lieutenant's wardroom.

He put a hand on her shoulder for a moment before heading down the passage back out of officer's country.

Gracie knocked on the edge of the hatch and leaned her head in. Lieutenant Wadden was sitting at a small fold-down desk between the two sets of bunks. He might have been Gracie's commander, but on a Navy ship-of-the-line, he was pretty small potatoes, and he shared the stateroom with three other lieutenants. He'd probably asked his bunkmates to give him time for his after-action debrief—it would be a little awkward to do that with someone snoring half-a-meter from them.

"Sit down, Corporal," he said, pointing at the small stool in front of his desk.

She took the seat, so low to the ground that even her knees were up high. Sergeant Glastonary, all 2.4 meters of him, must have his knees higher than his head. For a moment, the image made her smile.

"First of all, let me say that I know you're happy about Lance Corporal Gittens and Corporal Kierkagaard."

"Yes, sir, very much so."

As soon as she returned to the camp, she'd rushed to the battalion aid station, and she'd been told that both Marines had been put in stasis and were being transported to the Naval Medical Hospital on Tarawa. She'd been on pins and needles until she'd gotten back aboard the *Josh* where she'd pestered the senior chief in sickbay to the point that he'd requested his daily status update seven hours earlier than normal. To Gracie's relief, both Eli and Kierk had been evaluated and resurrected. Both were in regen, and while Eli was sure to have a lengthy rehab, he should be back to 100%. Kierk had suffered significant brain damage, right on the edge of being able to recover or not, but the doctors gave him a 65% chance of a full recovery.

Dave Oesper was confirmed KIA, though. His brain had been far too destroyed for any hope of resurrection. She'd gone into the hide the de facto commander of three other Marines. Two were in regen, and one was KIA. That didn't reflect well on her ability to lead, she knew.

The fact that she wasn't even scratched filled her with survivor's guilt. Why was she spared? If karma was real, then certainly with her butcher's toll, she should have been hit, not Oesper.

Up until the mission to take out Red Piper and Doughbaby, the battalion had suffered three KIA and five WIA, two of whom required regen back on Tarawa. During the mission, just two days before the first elements re-embarked aboard the *Josh*, the Scout-Sniper Platoon suffered three KIAs with two being resurrected, one WIA requiring casevacs and regen (Cable-Williams, who'd lost his arm just below the elbow), and three more walking wounded (Staff Sergeant Riopel, Brick Liogeni, and Suggs Rustan). All three of the walking wounded refused to be casevac'd and demanded to travel back to Tarawa with the platoon.

The platoon had suffered, but not as much as Hotel. The company had been the only one of the line companies not to have lost anyone KIA or seriously WIA up until that day, but during the operation, they suffered 18 KIAs (with seven being resurrected), nine WIAs requiring full regen, and another twelve mobile WIAs. Most of the walking wounded would still undergo regen back on Tarawa as well, but this would be done at the outpatient clinic and could last from a week or so to three or four weeks.

Gracie had to wonder if it had been worth it. Doughbaby had been killed, along with well over 150 other jericks, but when Golf moved in to clear the Hatbox, Red Piper opened the front doors of the building, welcoming the Marines. Gracie had seen the holos. Despite being arrested and turned over to the local police, he was acting as if he'd called in the battalion instead of being one of the targets.

"Well, now on to your performance. First, I'm sorry to say that NVU has not certified our numbers for you."

What?

Gracie knew that the Navy Verification Unit was the keeper of records for the Navy and Marines, but for a moment, she was at a loss.

"We submitted 35 confirmed kills for you, but they are only allowing 24. The Three knew you probably wouldn't get full credit for the shot that nailed Rinzinni, but we think they were overly strict with their count."

Oh, that's what he's talking about, she realized.

She'd been somewhat preoccupied over the last few days, and she hadn't really tallied up her kills. She knew technically she'd only get credit for Doughbaby with the CD33 round as the others would be considered collateral damage, but as to the rest, she hadn't even attempted to tally up the numbers. She knew this was odd; snipers tended to be a bit anal about that, and she was no different. It had just slipped her mind.

Now that the lieutenant had brought it up, though, her curiosity had been piqued. What hadn't NVU allowed?

"Twenty-four, huh sir?"

Twenty-four kills in one battle was an incredible number, more than most snipers had in a career. Still, 35 might have been some sort of record.

"Yes, that's all. It's not like we didn't have documentation. Between your scope-cam, all the Navy and Marine Corps drones, the *Josh*, and then the BDA, we thought we'd put together a very solid 35 kills."

"If you had that evidence, why did NVU disallow so many?" she asked.

"I don't know. I can guess, though," he said.

"What, sir?"

"Well, that leads me to the second piece of bad news. The Three already started the paperwork for you for a Silver Star."

That shocked Gracie, and she sat up straighter on the small stool.

"But immediately, it came back down with a, well, officially a *request*, to withdraw it."

"What? Why, sir," Gracie asked, confused.

"I think it's for the same reason that you didn't get all 35 kills. You see, we're not at war here."

"Tell that to Oesper's parents, sir, with all due respect."

The lieutenant didn't seem upset by her outburst and instead said, "I know. I meant to say we are not officially at war. And your kills were Federation citizens."

"Who were trying to kill Marines, sir."

"You're preaching to the choir, Corporal," he said, holding both hands out as if to stop an outburst. "But the facts are facts, and someone apparently doesn't want to advertise the fact that the Marine Corps was out there killing citizens. And it's not just you. Staff Sergeant Riopel was recommended for a BC1, and his came back the same. So in my mind, and I'm completely off-record here, I think the same high someones didn't want it known that a single sniper killed 35 citizens in one battle. Twenty-four were irrefutable, and they couldn't deny them. But the rest. . ." he trailed off.

"For the rest, if there was any way to find fault, they found it," she said.

"I'm not saying that, Corporal, and I'll deny it if it comes back to me, but you're a smart woman. I can't help it if you come to the same conclusion as, well, others might have.

"But I wanted to tell you two things. The first is that everyone knows what you did. Hotel's First Platoon is calling you their guardian angel."

She knew that. She'd been invited to sit with the survivors in the galley just two hours ago at lunch, and they'd embarrassed her with the presentation of their platoon patch. They'd given her three more, which she promised to give to Eli, Kierk, and Oesper's family.

"The second is that the CO can give meritorious promotions to lance corporal, corporal, and sergeant."

"Yes, sir. One promotion every six months."

"And that doesn't have to go any higher. She's got the authority."

"And, sir?" she asked suddenly knowing where he was going with the train of thought.

"The Three went to her, and she agreed. As of the second of next month, you'll be pinning on another stripe. Congratulations," he said, standing up and holding out a hand.

Sergeant? Me?

She'd fully expected to make sergeant, but not until next year at the earliest, and this took her by surprise. She stood up and shook his hand.

"Why, thank you, sir. Or thank the CO. . .or the Three? Who do I thank?"

He laughed and said, "We should be thanking you. What you did, that was copacetic to the max, Corporal, copacetic to the max."

Suddenly, the smile fell from her face, and she asked, "But what about Lance Corporal Gittens, sir? He and Lance Corporal Oesper?"

She'd seen enough gleaned from the various recordings to know that Oesper had simply taken a shot that destroyed his head, but Eli had stood tall, facing down four onrushing jericks to protect her back. She'd asked Gunny to make sure both of them were recognized.

"Both are receiving Purple Hearts, of course, and I think Oesper will be awarded a BC3, but for the rest, I'm not sure."

"But did you read the report? Eli stood down four of them, keeping me alive so I could cover First Platoon. Without him, I'd have been killed, and then probably more of First Platoon. He deserves something, sir!"

"I know he does, Corporal Medicine Crow. But I don't know," he said, pausing as he wrinkled his brow in thought. "Tell you what. The CO can give a commendation medal, the same as she can promote you. If it comes to that, I think we can swing that. But the regimental CO can approve a BC3. Let's see what we can swing as soon as we get back. Fair enough?"

"Yes, sir. More than fair. Thank you, sir.

He looked down at his PA, which was still lying on the small desk. "You know, looking at all of this, we've got quite a debriefing still to go, and to be honest, I've had about enough of Jericho to last me a while. Let's cut this off for now, OK?"

"Uh, sure, sir. It's your call."

"I guess it is," he said, a smile breaking out. "In that case, it's time for a command decision. I'm done for the day, and I think I need to hit the gym. Tell. . ." he said, pausing to look at his PA, "tell Corporal Khalil to go back to berthing, and tell the rest we'll finish back at Tarawa."

"Aye-aye, sir."

"And with that, we're done, at least for now. You did well, Corporal, really well. I don't have to tell you that you've found your niche, and I'm proud to be your commander. Semper fi, Marine!"

Gracie came to a position of attention.

"Semper fi to you, too, sir. And I'm proud to have you as my commander. I'd be just as proud to serve with you anytime."

She performed a credible about face in the constrained space and stepped out of the stateroom.

"The lieutenant's done for the day," she told Possum. "Head on back to berthing."

As Gracie followed him off the Bravo deck, she realized what she'd said was true. She'd be more than proud to serve with the lieutenant again, to serve with any of her platoon-mates again. For the first time in her career, she thought she truly understood what it meant at a visceral level to be brothers-in-arms.

TARAWA

Chapter 28

37

"Am I late?" Sergeant Gracie Medicine Crow asked, rushing into the room.

"No," Tiggs said, getting out of the chair to hug her and give her a peck on the cheek. "They won't start for another ten minutes, and the doctor said it could take another 15 minutes for him to come around."

Gracie had never been much of a huggy person, but that was hard to avoid with the effervescent Antigone Gittens. To her surprise, Gracie didn't mind. She was probably more surprised that she had become close friends with the young woman, someone at a polar opposite from her. Where Gracie was a hard-ass, and some said, hard-hearted Marine, one who ignored make-up and fashion, Tiggs was all gossip, the latest trends, and social interaction. Tiggs took over any group, guiding them to a common goal while they thought it was all their idea in the first place. Yet, somehow, the two had bonded while watching Eli's progress over the last two months. He was still in his regen coma, and Gracie had cut short a field exercise to make it back to be there when he came to.

At first, Gracie had felt uncomfortable around Tiggs. She had promised the woman that she'd bring Eli back, and the survivor guilt was still running strong in her. It wasn't until she'd tried to apologize to Tiggs a week after returning that the damn broke, with Gracie breaking down into tears, and Tiggs, little, bouncy Tiggs, playing the mother figure, holding Gracie until she sobbed out. And Gracie felt a huge weight lift off her shoulders. She still vowed to become a better leader, a better Marine, but the guilt had disappeared like a morning mist (mostly, at least). After that, she never brought it up again, and the two became close. Tiggs, for all her surface flightiness, had a keen, questing mind, and with only Eli's unconscious body keeping them company, they'd had some deeply intellectual conversations that went deep into the night—along with a few utterly silly ones, or even a couple that strayed into the more adult-oriented topics. For such a sweet-looking girl, Tiggs had an undeniably naughty streak that entertained Gracie to no end.

Gracie took the seat next to Tiggs as the RT, the regen tech, came in to start bringing Eli around. Lieutenant Commander O'Nial, the ward's daytime charge nurse, followed the RT, looking over the man's shoulder as if waiting for him to screw up. The nurse could be a stickler for the regs, but it was evident that she really cared for each of her patients.

"That'll do it," the RT said after stepping back from the console. "I'm giving him ten minutes."

Gracie started to feel nervous. The doctors all said that Eli's progress had been good, but no one could be sure until he was brought out of his regen coma. His body might be well on the way to healing, but was Eli still Eli?

Tiggs reached out and took Gracie's hand. She was trembling, and Gracie tried to project calmness. She knew Tiggs had to be about ready to climb out of her skin.

Five minutes later, several other nurses and corpsmen came in, followed by Commander Quillion, the head regen doc. He had a young lieutenant in tow, her white medical coat the traditional mark that she was a doctor, probably fresh out of medical school.

At ten minutes, Tiggs squeezed Gracie's hand. Gracie wasn't sure what to do, so she squeezed back. At 11 minutes, Gracie was just about to ask the doctor what was going on when Eli coughed, twice, then opened his eyes.

Tiggs jumped up from her seat and rushed to his side. Eli seemed confused and tried to focus, but when he saw Tiggs, he smiled and slowly reached out for her.

"What are you—" he started to say in a gravelly, faltering voice before coughing.

"Lance Corporal Gittens, I'm Doctor Quillion. You're back on Tarawa at the Naval Medical Center. You've been here for two months. How are you feeling?"

"Two months?" he asked, his hand firmly in Tiggs grasp.

"Yes, son. You took a couple of shots on Jericho that destroyed much of your jaw and throat, and more importantly, to your brain stem, cerebellum, and occipital lobe. That's why your vision is blurry now, and you'll have trouble speaking for a while."

Damn, pretty blunt, Gracie thought. *How about easing him into it?*

"You're still on assisted breathing, but it's time to wake you up so you can take an active part of your rehabilitation."

"Jericho? Corporal Medicine--"

"Here I am, Eli. I'm fine," Gracie said, stepping up so Eli could see her.

"Eli?" he said, a smile coming over his face.

"Well, you know. . ." she said.

After all they'd been through together, it was about time she got the ramrod out of her ass and became a little more relaxed with him.

"It's Sergeant Medicine Crow now," Tiggs said. "And Gracie's been here every day to check up on you."

Eli started to cough again, and the little box beside the bed clicked and emitted a slightly higher hum. The box had leads attached to Eli's chest, and his breathing evened out.

The doctor had been scanning readouts, but as Eli's coughing subsided, he said, "I know everyone wants to spend time with Lance Corporal Gittens, but he needs to build back up his strength. So for now, everyone except for his wife needs to leave. Lieutenant Commander O'Nial will set up a visiting schedule—Commander, use Protocol D for now, and we'll adjust it after we see how he tolerates that," he said directly to the charge nurse before addressing everyone else again, "so with that, I want everyone else except for Belling and Garcia gone as in now. You two, run a full analysis and forward it to me. Ms. Gittens, you are welcome to stay, but Lance Corporal Gittens will be drifting in and out for the rest of the day."

As if on command, Eli closed his eyes and fell asleep. Gracie had wanted to tell him that his BC3 had been approved, figuring the good news would cheer him up before she let him know about Dave Oesper, but all of that could wait. She followed everyone else out of the room.

Now that it seemed clear that Eli was going to recover, she wanted to tell Gunny Buttle that she thought her spotter should be promoted to sniper as soon as he was returned to full duty. She was comfortable with Eli, and more than that, she trusted him, but she couldn't use him as a crutch if that would retard his own development. She'd resisted being assigned a new spotter since their return, and she didn't look forward to breaking in someone new, but the Marine Corps was anything but static.

It was time to march on.

Chapter 29

37

"Damn, I'm hungry," Zach said, sniffing the air. "How long are we going to have to wait?"

"Until she gets here. She stopped off at the Wounded Warrior Battalion, so if you have any complaints, why don't you march on over there and tell General Ling?" gunny said to him.

"No, you know what I mean," Zach hurriedly corrected.

No one criticized the Wounded Warrior Battalion, nor did they resent any of the care those Marines and sailors received. Those undergoing regen and therapy were their brothers and sisters, and with increasingly better medical technology, Marines who even 20 years ago might have been permanently KIA were resurrected and joined the battalion for their rehab. There was a very real probability that many of the Marines in 2/3 were going to end up in the Wounded Warrior Battaltion at some time in their career, and it had become accepted fact that juju was at work, and by saying the wrong thing, the gods of karma would make sure you were one of the ones to end up there.

Kierk reached over and thunked Zach on the head with a closed fist. He'd just returned to the battalion two days earlier, still on light duty, but back with the platoon. With three newbies, even with Eli and Cable-Williams still in rehab, the platoon was at full strength.

Gracie stole a look at Lance Corporal Tibone Mubotono. "T-Bone" was her new spotter, and she didn't think she'd ever met such an arrogant, self-centered young man in her life. The guy could shoot the left ball off a gnat at 1000 meters, but Gracie thought he would be a liability in a hot mission.

When Gunny Buttle had told her he was assigning the young Marine to her, he'd left her with a laugh and a sarcastic "good luck." Evidently, T-Bone's reputation had preceded him. T-Bone had arrived with Tennerife Delay, the second female Marine assigned to the platoon, and initially, Gracie had been happy Delay hadn't been assigned to her. She'd been concerned at how the others would react to the "all-girl" team. In retrospect, she thought she'd much rather have dealt with that than with T-Bone. Delay might not be the marksman that he was, but she seemed to listen, and Brick Liogeni was full of praise for her potential.

An electric current flowed through the battalion, snapping Gracie's reverie. She looked up to see an oversized Marine Corps van pull up.

"It's showtime," Zach said as the lounging Marines stood and started moving towards the van.

Gracie was only about 20 meters away when Chief Warrant Officer Tamara Veal got out of the van and stretched out to her full eight.

Damn, she's big! Gracie thought.

At the parade earlier, she'd seen the gladiator when they'd done their eyes right during the pass in review, but that has been at a distance and looking through the formation. Here, in the battalion square, the gladiator not only towered over the Marines, but radiated mass—a deadly, dangerous mass. Without meaning to, Gracie took a step back.

All of the battalion were in PT gear for the picnic, and Veal was in her alphas, so Lance Corporal Dolsch, one of her old squadmates, held an oversized set of shorts and a shirt.

Gracie couldn't hear what Dolsch said to her, but she barely caught the "I'll 'ma'am' you, Fanny, but yeah, let me get changed," that the gladiator said in return.

Marines had their PAs out, snapping holos as Veal looked up and pointed to the crowd.

"About time you showed up, ma'am! We're starving here!" someone shouted as Marines broke out in laughter.

The gladiator, Dolsch, and Doc Neves, who'd been recommended for a Navy Cross (Gracie figured that saving lives was politically more palatable than killing Federation citizens, not that she resented the doc's award), started back to the CP, with Warrant

Officer Veal slapping what to her were low fives with Marines along the way.

"Hell, look at the size of her," Zach said in awe as the gladiator passed them.

"Now don't you go thinking your usual crap, Zach," Staff Sergeant Riopel said. "She'd tear you in half."

Gracie had to laugh. Zach Pure Presence had a reputation for being somewhat of a horn-dog, and the image of him trying to chat up the gladiator struck her as pretty funny.

"Well, I have to admit, I wouldn't mind trying to climb that peak," Zach said, his eyes locked on the gladiator's retreating back.

"I heard they can't get it on," Brick said.

"Hell they can't!" Zach insisted. "You saw *Queen Killer*. They had all those guys hanging around, buying them stuff and shit. And didn't Jessica have that thing with, what was his name? The guy David le Peele played?"

"In your dreams, Zach," Gracie said. "That's all Hollybolly, not real. And did Natyly Jutlin look anything like the Warrant Officer?"

Natyly Jutlin was the very curvaceous and attractive star who had played Jessica in the flick, and the Chief Warrant Officer Veal had been transformed into a fighting machine with very few of her former female characteristics left intact.

Gracie didn't actually know if a gladiator could still have sex or not. She hadn't been back in Lodge Grass when her cousin had come back to be honored by the tribe, and even if she had been there, she couldn't imagine asking her cousin anything like that.

"No, but just saying I wouldn't mind getting a little taste," he said wistfully.

"Yeah, like she would ever pick you," Brick said.

The conversation shifted to other aspects of the flick and what really went on in the gladiators' training. Indigo Glastonary had some surprising in-depth knowledge of swords and swordfighting. He was demonstrating several moves when the chief warrant officer came back out, in shorts and the shirt with the 2/3 emblem emblazoned on the chest but barefoot. Gracie guessed no one had access to size a hundred or whatever shoes.

The gladiator was escorted to where the sergeant major and CO were standing. She looked nervous to Gracie, of all things.

"Fuzos, we are here to honor one of our own, Chief Warrant Officer Tamara Veal, Gladiator for Humanity!" the sergeant major spoke into his mic.

There was a rush of ooh-rahs from the gathered Marines.

"We watched her fight on Halcon 4, where she showed the Klethos what a Marine can do, but we already knew that. We were there when the battalion was on Wyxy, when one of the SevRevs thought he could take out our command. We were there when then Lance Corporal Veal identified the SevRev and tackled his ass, keeping him from detonating his suicide bomb. And that was before she became what she is today. She was just like all of you, a Marine doing her job, and believe me, no one does that better than Marines."

There were more ooh-rahs and shouts of "Fuzos!"

"So, ma'am, I'm sure the Marines and sailors of the battalion would love to hear from you," he said, unclipping his mic and handing it to her.

The collar mic was small by design, but it completely disappeared into the gladiator's hand. She looked at it for a few seconds, shifting her weight from foot to foot.

"Thank you for your welcome," she managed to get out. "I. . .I'm glad to see some friendly faces. And some not so friendly, Staff Sergeant Abdálle. Yeah, I see you there," she said, pointing down at him.

The battalion broke out in laughter and "ooh-rahs." The staff sergeant had a reputation for being a real hard-ass, but he smiled and raised his hand in acknowledgment.

"I've followed your deployment on Jericho, and I have to say, I'm proud of you, all of you. I just found out that my friend, Doc Neves, is up for a Navy Cross, and I'm, well, I'm bursting with pride at that. I just wish I'd been with you in person instead of just in spirit."

Again "ooh-rahs" interrupted her.

"I'm detached from the Corps right now. But there are eight of us serving as gladiators, and we remember our roots. And my roots, where I feel at home, is with Second Battalion, Third Marines! Fuzos!"

The battalion, Gracie included, erupted into chants of "Fuzos, Fuzos!" The battalion had a long and storied history, and now it had absorbed more glory by sending one of its own to be a gladiator.

The chief warrant officer handed the mic back to the sergeant major. She waved to the still chanting crowd, then let herself be led to the serving tables.

"About time," Zach said. "My belly's touching my backbone."

"Maybe you should hit the gym more then," Gracie said. "Get some muscle built up."

Gracie was too short to see much through the Marines, so she just let herself flow along with the other sergeants to their position in the chow line.

When she heard the gladiator shout, "Where are those privates?" she stood on her tiptoes as she tried to see what was going on.

"What's she doing?" she asked.

Indigo Glastonary, who was over two meters tall, had a much better view, and he said, "She's doing the serving, her and the CO."

The CO was always the last to be served, and she'd often done the serving at functions like this, but Chief Warrant Officer Veal was the guest of honor, so Gracie was surprised that she was serving as well.

With the entire battalion and some additional friends of the gladiator at the picnic, the line moved slowly. The gladiator was speaking to each Marine as well, which further slowed things down. Gracie wondered how long she would keep serving, but 25 minutes later, when the sergeants reached the front, she was still at it.

Gracie was the fifth sergeant in the line, and when she held out her plate for a scoop of the macaroni salad, she was surprised that Chief Warrant Officer Veal recognized her.

"Corporal Medicine Crow, it's good to see you!"

"It's Sergeant Medicine Crow now, ma'am. I was promoted last year."

"Oh. Well, congratulations! I never bought you that drink, you know, the one for saving my ass on Wyxy. We waited half the night for you, and then after that, you know, I had to leave."

"Yes, Ma'am, I didn't make it. But don't worry, you don't owe me anything. You took on that SevRev suicider. I wasn't in any danger myself."

"Well, you still saved my ass, and I'm grateful for that."

"Sergeant Medicine Crow was one of our best snipers on Jericho," the CO said from beside the gladiator where she was handing out dinner rolls.

"It doesn't surprise me," the gladiator said.

"Thank you, ma'am," Gracie said once more before starting to step to her right to get her dinner roll, then hesitating.

She looked back at the gladiator, who had stopped scooping out another spoonful of mac salad to see why she'd stopped.

Gracie wasn't sure why she'd bothered to stop, but she decided to plunge in with, "Uh, ma'am, have you met Chief Warrant Officer Falcon Coups?"

"Of course, I have. There are only eight Marines serving as gladiators, you know. Why, do you know her?"

"Yes, ma'am. She's my cousin," the sergeant said before turning and holding her tray out to the CO.

Why the hell did I have to say that? She doesn't need me to suck up to her, she scolded herself.

"Really?" Zach asked as soon as they passed through the line, plates laden with grub. "Falcon Coups is your cousin?"

"Yeah," she said as she looked for a place to sit down and eat.

"How come you never bothered to mention that little tidbit to any of us?"

"I didn't think it's important. I don't think it is. So how about keeping quiet about it, OK?"

"OK, if that's how you want it. But other people heard, so I bet it goes around."

Most of the gladiators were well known to the public, especially those who'd been braided by winning in the ring, and with the Marines love of all things pertaining to unit loyalty, brotherhood, and the culture of semper fi, everyone in the Corps knew each and every gladiator.

It wasn't as if there was a surplus of the Apsaalooké in the Corps, not that anyone would recognize their name for themselves. There were 21 current members of the tribe serving on active duty in the Marines (along with 12 in the Navy and 32 in the FCDC), a small number, but a high percentage considering the overall population of the nation. Every Marine would know that her cousin was from Earth, an American, and a Crow. Gracie was from Earth, and American, and a Crow. Heck even her last name had "Crow" in it. If no one could connect the dots, then that wasn't her problem, and she rather liked it that way.

Sergeant Gracie Medicine Crow wanted to be known as the best sniper in Marine Corps history, not as the cousin to a gladiator.

Chapter 30

32

With a sigh, Gracie got out of the beat up easy chair someone had scrounged and put in the platoon briefing room.

"Have you decided what you're going to do?" Zach asked.

Gracie glared at him, but he didn't seem to have a joke or insult on his lips. He seemed genuinely interested. Glastonary and Manny Chun turned to look as well. All four of them had hidden out in the briefing room. Gracie, because she had her meeting with the major, and the other three simply because they could, and slacking off was something that soldiers had done ever since there were soldiers to do it.

"No, not yet."

"You're going to be seeing Major Cranston in ten minutes, and you haven't decided?"

"No, I said I don't know yet," she snapped.

Zach seemed to take it in stride, not taking umbrage, and he said, "I can walk over there with you, if you want. It's your call, but sometimes it helps to talk it out."

Gracie waited for the punchline, but the sergeant seemed earnest.

That's a miracle. He's actually being nice.

"No, it's OK. I'll handle it."

She turned to leave the briefing room, and Manny shouted out "Good luck, Gracie!"

She had she'd been suspicious of everyone when she'd first joined the platoon. A couple of experiences while with Echo 3/12 that had gone over the line—one in particular with her platoon sergeant who'd taken a more intimate interest in her than protocol (or Marine regulations) allowed—and that had resulted in her erecting the wall she kept between other Marines and her, a wall that allowed for professional interaction, but very openly kept out social interaction. With this platoon, though, that wall had slowly begun to crumble. She was still reserved, but starting with Eli, and even with jerks like Zach, she realized that not every man in the world was trying to get into her panties, and her platoon mates seemed to care about her not only as a fellow scout-sniper, but as a brother-in-arms. She was sure that any one of them would have her back no matter what turned up. And no matter what she told the major, no matter her decision, they would support her.

She walked past the company headquarters, still deep in thought. She usually made decisions quickly with very little equivocation, but this time, she had gone back and forth as she considered her options.

Lost in her thoughts, she almost missed the brand new second lieutenant who had just exited the company CP.

"Oh, sorry, sir," she said, snapping a belated salute.

The lieutenant could have been an ass about it, but he saluted back with a calm, "No problem, Sergeant, but keep alert."

The lieutenant took a left on the sidewalk while Gracie continued in the opposite direction. After about ten steps, she stopped and looked at the retreating back of the lieutenant. Some butter bars might have gotten upset with her, some would have reacted like this one had. Officers ran the gamut from assholes to nice guys with everything in between—just like enlisted Marines. And neither end of the spectrum had an advantage in being a good leader. That was something that couldn't be pigeon-holed. Gracie thought Lieutenant Wadden was a great leader, and she would follow him anywhere. On the other end of the personality spectrum, her Echo Company commander in 3/12, Captain Jerez, could be extremely demanding and swore like a drunken sailor, but he was also a superb leader. When Gracie had hesitantly reported her platoon sergeant to her lieutenant, Captain Jerez had taken swift and severe action, not the least was firing the staff sergeant from his position. Wadden and Jerez were almost polar opposites, but they were alike in that their Marines would do anything for them.

Gracie was feeling comfortable with her platoon mates, and she was sure they respected her as a sniper, but did she have it in her to develop the same sort of loyalty and dedication. Did she even want that?

She turned into the battalion CP, her mind still warring with itself. She knew what she wanted, but was that a mistake? Was she shirking from a challenge?

She checked her PA; she had two more minutes.

"Sergeant Medicine Crow, how're you doing?" Staff Sergeant Holleran asked as she exited the S4 office and spotted Gracie. "I've got a new Model W in yesterday, all sitting pretty in its case. Maybe you should come down and pop her cherry. Of course, I'd have to go with you, you know, to make sure you don't break her."

Gracie had to laugh. She'd gotten close to the staff sergeant after returning from Jericho, and she even called her Megan when they were alone. The Model W was the latest and greatest Barrett, and it would be pretty fun to see what the weapon could do. That was one of the benefits of having a friend who ran the armory: she now had a pretty free reign in the place.

She hadn't told Megan about her present predicament, though. Megan was an onwards-and-upwards kind of woman, and Gracie knew what she would want her to do.

"Sounds good, staff sergeant. Give me shout tonight and I'll let you know when I can break off tomorrow."

Megan gave her arm a pat as she walked past and said, "Will do. We've got Fox coming in around 1600, so if they can get their shit in line, I can probably break free at 1900. I'll give you a call."

"Is that you, Sergeant Medicine Crow?" Major Cranston shouted from inside his office. He poked his head out a moment later and said, "I thought I heard you. Come on in."

Gracie followed him in, getting ready to center herself on his desk, but he moved to the side instead, taking a seat on his couch and motioning for her to sit on the couch kitty-corner to his.

Oh, it's going to be the casual touch, she thought. *I think I'd rather keep this formal.*

"So, Sergeant, I hope you thought long and hard about this," the major said, skipping any small talk.

"Yes, sir, I have."

"Good, good. So what's it going to be?"

"Sir," she started, then stopped to take in a deep breath of air. "I really appreciate this, and I can't tell you how much. You've given so much support to the platoon, and now this? I'm really, really grateful."

"I'm not liking where I think this is going, Sergeant," the major said, a frown beginning to turn down the corners of his mouth.

Oh, crap! He's going to be pissed.

"I. . .it's not that I don't think. . .I mean to say, sir, I really appreciate it, but I think I have to turn it down."

There, it's out, she thought as she felt a huge weight lift off her shoulders.

The major suddenly started studying his fingers while Gracie waited for the explosion.

"Is it the academics, Sergeant? I know the Academy is demanding, but I've seen your transcripts. You went to a tough school, and your grades were good. I know you can make it there."

"Oh, no sir, it's not that."

"Then what is it? You do know that only 20 Marines get into the full program each year. And you are cleared to take one of those spots."

"I know, sir. And I'm honored that you think I deserve one of those seats. But the fact of the matter is. . ."

Just spit it out, Crow!

". . .the fact of the matter is that I don't want to be an officer."

The look on the major's face was almost comical, like a little boy who'd just been told there was no Santa Claus. Gracie would have smiled had she not been in such a tense situation.

"I. . . I don't understand, Sergeant Medicine Crow. Why not?"

"No disrespect, sir. I don't hate officers. But I don't want to do what officers have to do. I've watched Lieutenant Wadden, sir. I've seen the look on his face when he sends us out on missions. He wants to go. It's in his blood. But he can't because he's the platoon commander, and it's our job to do the actual fighting, not his."

"Well, maybe, but that's because he's the Scout-Sniper Platoon commander. If he were still with a rifle platoon, he'd be in the fight. And when he's a company commander, hell, that's the best job in the Marines," he said, his eyes lighting up when he said "company commander."

"I know, sir, but the lieutenant, he's a sniper at heart. He became an officer because he was a good sniper, just like you're offering me. And I'm the same. I've got being a sniper in my blood, and I don't want to give that up. And if I honestly evaluate myself, being totally blunt, I'm a helluva sniper, but without any false modesty, at best, I might be an adequate officer, and for me, adequate doesn't cut it. I need to be the best, and I can be that doing what I'm doing now."

The major sat back, looking stunned. Gracie knew he must have been thinking this was a no-brainer for her. And it was a no-brainer, just not the way he thought it would be. Gracie also knew that he'd be personally disappointed. He'd taken ownership of the platoon, and with how the platoon had performed so well on Jericho. To have one of his snipers get into the Academy would have been a feather in his cap as well.

The major seemed to be getting his thoughts in order, and it took a few moments before he said, "I understand, Sergeant, believe me I understand. Right now, sitting in back of this desk, I miss my time as a company commander. But if I stick with it and do my best, maybe I can get command of a battalion someday. And if I think back far enough, you know, to the Old Corps," he said with a laugh, "when I was a corporal and a fire team leader, I thought it couldn't get any better than that. But it did, and I can't describe the personal satisfaction I've felt as a commander.

"So do this for me. The CO's gone for the day, and I won't tell her your decision until morning. Think about it. Call your family. I think one of your people is a major, right? Major Watts, right? Why don't you give him a call and see what he says? I can authorize the comms with battalion."

Holy Heavens! He's done his homework on me, Gracie thought, feeling things were getting a little creepy.

Major Franklin Watts was of the Apsaalooké, but he wasn't from Lodge Grass. Gracie knew who he was, and she'd seen him before, but they weren't close, and she wouldn't feel comfortable calling him up out of the blue.

"So I'm not taking your refusal as a done deal. Take the night, and let me know in the morning."

He stood up, hand outstretched as he asked, "Deal?"

Gracie looked at the hand for only a moment before she took it and said, "Deal."

"OK, good. I'll wait to hear from you in the morning."

As Gracie left the S3's office, she felt 100 kilos lighter. She'd agreed with the major to wait until morning, but she knew in her heart she'd made the right decision.

Being an officer was in no way a declaration of superiority. It was simply a different position to be filled as the unit completed its missions. A platoon commander was no "better" than a rifleman, who was no better than a tank driver, who was no better than a cook, who was no better than a sniper, who was no better than a platoon commander, bringing the circle to a close. Just as a finger is no better than a toe but part of what makes the body work, all those Marines are the parts that make the Marine Corps work. Without them, without all of them, the Corps would fall apart.

Gracie was a scout-sniper and a damn good one. She enjoyed the work, and she knew this was how she could make the best contribution to the Corps. This was where she belonged.

She was whistling as she left the CP. She turned right instead of left, though. She was going to go to the armory before returning to the platoon to tell the others her decision. She had a sudden desire to take a look at the Model W first.

Heck, she was a sniper, and weapons were in her blood.

Chapter 31

33

"So, you're out of here, huh, Sergeant?" Corporal Estiville asked, scanning her orders.

"Yeah, sure am. I've got a 1500 shuttle to catch; then I'm gone."

"You heading out to. . ." the corporal said, pausing to look at his readout, "the *Juneau*?"

"No. I'll pick up the battalion when they debark. Right now, I'm going home for some leave. First time in four years."

The corporal looked back at her records again, then asked, "Lodge Grass? On Earth? Where's that?"

"In Montana," she answered, then added, "In the United States," when the confused look stayed on the corporal's face.

"Ah, the United States. In Hollybolly, right?"

Gracie stared in shock at the corporal.

"The United States isn't in Hollybolly."

"But that's where they make all the flicks, right? I watch them all the time."

"Uh, you do know that there is not one 'Hollybolly' place. The 'Holly' is from Hollywood, in the US, in California. The 'bolly' is from Bollywood, in Mumbai. That's in India."

"Yeah, where they make all the flicks."

"They don't make them right there. It's just a generic term for the industry," Gracie said, wondering how the corporal had such a lack of knowledge.

The corporal shrugged and handed Gracie back her orders.

"Well, anyway, have a good leave back home. You're good to go."

Gracie tried not to shake her head as she left admin. Her mood brightened as she headed for the front hatch. It wasn't that she'd had a bad time with the Fuzos. It had been good. But it was time, she figured, to move on and see new things.

She took the corner into the main passage, and suddenly, she slowed down. She'd been in the passage many times, and after her welcome into the battalion almost four years ago, she'd never looked at the plaques on the wall. It was only now that she was leaving that she suddenly became curious. She checked the time. She could afford to spend a few minutes here and still get to the chow hall to eat before leaving for the spaceport.

The Fuzos were noted as one of the most storied battalions in the Corps. It had the third most battle streamers of any battalion, and its Marines and sailors had shone. Nine of them had been awarded the Federation Nova-—five of them posthumously. There had been eight Marines go on to serve as commandant, nine as Sergeant Major of the Marine Corps. One corpsman, Styles Wu, had gone on to earn his commission, rise to the Chief of Naval Operations, and finally ascend to the Chairman of the Federation Council. Along with General Lysander, that meant two in the battalion had risen to the highest position in the Federation.

The personal plaques were around the corner at the entrance to the CP. The plaque closest to the front hatch was also the newest one. It shone in bright burnished copper. Although Gracie knew who it was for, she still had to read it. It was hung in honor of Tamara Veal, Chief Warrant Officer and Gladiator.

"That was quite some fight," a voice said from in behind her.

Gracie turned to see Staff Sergeant Riopel standing there.

"Yeah, it was," Gracie said, turning back around.

"And you helped put her there."

Gracie shrugged, but she agreed. If she hadn't zeroed that SevRev, he'd probably have blown himself up, taking Veal with him. No one had mentioned that in a long time, but it felt good that the Staff Sergeant had mentioned it. He hadn't forgotten.

"They're making a flick out of it, you know," she said.

"Yeah, I heard. So who's going to play you? Diedre St. Billings?"

Dierde was the latest overly-developed celebrity who seemed to be a celeb simply because, well, because someone decided she should be. Her first foray into flicks had been a disaster, and she was now somewhat of a standing joke.

"Fuck you, Staff Sergeant. With all due respect, of course," she said. "I'm thinking I'm going to call the producers up and tell them I'm going to play myself. I'm going to be a star. I don't think anyone could capture my absolute gloriousness."

The staff sergeant laughed, and then said, "You might have something there. So, are you going to the chow hall? I'll walk you there."

"You can walk me, but I'm sort of meeting Zach there."

"I just said I'm walking you there, not eating with you. We staff sergeants can't mingle with the riffraff, you know," he said with an affected air of 18th Century high-society.

"OK, let's go then," Gracie said, reaching out to gently touch Tamara Veal's relief as she stepped off.

BOOK 2

Jonathan P. Brazee

KULISHA

Chapter 32
62

Gunnery Sergeant Gracie Medicine Crow glassed the gentle slope stretching out 1,500 meters before her. The slope was full of depressions and terrain features, which along with the vegetation, offered plenty of places for concealment.

She checked off the most logical FFPs. If they were the most logical, then no sniper should select them, but not all snipers were that smart. Successful snipers were, but Gracie had cut short the careers—and lives—of more than a few enemy snipers who had not been as accomplished as her in their craft.

She examined each spot, then applied a trick she'd learned of shifting her gaze a meter or so, then relaxing her eyes. Sometimes, her peripheral vision could pick up something out of whack when her direct vision couldn't. Her first counter-sniper kill had come that way during the Gerryland Incursion when the enemy sniper was using his version of the Federation tarnkappe. Looking directly at it, the light-bending camouflage had worked, but by looking slightly to the side, the very minor border between the artificial and the natural had caught her attention, and she registered the kill.

That didn't work here, though. She picked up nothing. She shifted to her secondary positions. Personally, she would never have selected these positions, either, given the terrain. They were still too obvious. She saw nothing at the first, but as she was shifting to the second, something caught her attention. She swung back, not quite sure what she'd seen, only that her subconscious alarm had gone off. It took almost half a minute, but there it was. One stalk of grass was bent to the left when the surrounding grass was either upright or leaning right. Someone or something had passed by. It could have been a few days ago, and it could have been something as innocuous as a bird perching on it, but Gracie's instincts screamed at her that it had been a person and very recently. She examined the terrain and the angle of the bent grass, and she was sure that it was a sniper and to where he or she was stalking. She zoomed out slightly, and then settled in to wait.

It took almost five minutes, but an entire bush along the route she'd identified momentarily shook. Gracie immediately zoomed in, but there wasn't any sign of a person there. It didn't matter. Bushes just don't decide to shake like that.

"Jed, I've got something, 30 meters to your left and back maybe 20," she passed on the comms.

"Roger that," the sergeant said as he started to move to his left.

"OK, that's far enough. Now back up," Gracie told him.

She watched him back-step until he reached the offending bush, then said, "Stop. Now two steps to your left. Now one step back."

"Here?"

"Bingo."

The sergeant held up his three-meter gotcha stick over his head, but instead of bringing it down stretched to its fullest extension, he reversed it, and as if planting the Federation flag on a new planet, brought it straight down. From where it hit the ground, just below Gracie's view, a ghillied Marine arose, defeat evident in his posture. Or her posture, as the case might be. As the Marine pulled back her hood, Gracie identified her.

"You get another one?" Top Riopel asked from where he sat beside her.

"Yeah. Corporal Franzetti."

"Franzetti? Shit, I thought she was a lock," the top said. "You going to let anyone pass today?"

"I'm not 'letting' anyone. It's up to them if they pass or fail."

"Roger that. But we've got to get snipers out to the battalions, and we can't do that if you fail each candidate."

"But we can by sending unqualified snipers out there who are going to get zeroed their first time out, Top?"

This was an ongoing argument between the two. Top Riopel thought that seasoning in the field was acceptable for all those except the obvious failures. He called it Darwinian Selection. If they survived, they'd be effective scout-snipers. Gracie thought that each sniper sent out to the field already had to prove that they were effective.

The two SNCOs were actually quite close despite this difference of opinion. Along with Major Wadden and Staff Sergeant Suggs Rustan, the old 2/3 platoon mates made up four of the sniper school's staff of 22 Marines. Add in Sergeant Kathy Albert and Staff Sergeant Brice Fa'amoe who'd also done tours with 2/3, the school had a very evident Fuzos feel to it.

"Well, we've got 12 more out there and more than two hours left. Let's see if anyone can make it through."

"Roger that," Gracie said as she started glassing the range again.

She didn't have ill will for any of the candidates, and she hoped all of the rest of them would succeed today, but no one was getting a free pass. If they wanted to graduate and become scout-snipers, they had to earn it.

Chapter 33

62

"You wanted to see me, sir?" Gracie asked, poking her head inside Major Wadden's office.

"Yes, Gunny. Please, come in," the major said, holding out a hand to indicate she should take a seat. "How did it go today?"

Is he backing Riopel? she wondered. *Master Guns Frielander must have already given him the numbers, so why's he asking me?*

"Four passed, sir."

"Four out of twelve. Not so good."

"There's still Wednesday, sir. We'll see how many learned from today."

"Yes, I guess we will. Hopefully, more will make it, and I can keep the colonel off my ass."

He said that matter-of-factly, and Gracie did not get the feeling that there were any undertones in his wording. Not that she thought he'd really compromise his standards. The major was probably at his terminal rank. He'd been stuck in the scout-sniper community too long. An enlisted Marine could make a career in the sub-field, but not an officer. Other than his second lieutenant billet as a rifle platoon commander, the major had been with the sniper community for the rest of his officer career, and that was pretty much career suicide. Because of this, and because of his nature, he was not apt to bow to pressure from above when he thought that would compromise the mission.

"But that's my problem, I guess, and that's what I get paid the big credits, right? And I didn't call you in to discuss our latest class of candidates."

Gracie looked at him expectantly.

"I've got set of orders that just came in. They're sending you TAD back to Tarawa for duty to parts unknown—well, I mean wherever you're going from there isn't mentioned other than 'additional duty off-planet.'"

Gracie sat back, puzzled at what he'd just said. She'd only been with the school for a little less than four months, so it seemed odd that she'd be getting any orders, whether TAD or permanent. After 205-2 graduated, she was slated to become the SNCOIC[26] of 205-4, something to which she was really looking forward.

"I've gone ahead and pulled them on the S-Screen for you."

That was a telling comment. If they were on the secure S-Screen, the orders were too classified to be sent to her PA, even with the PAs Gen 2 factorization module installed.

He handed her his screen, which she read, becoming even more confused.

CLASS: TOP SECRET

From: Director of Marine Corps Personnel
To: Gunnery Sergeant Gracie F. Medicine Crow, UFMC, EN3762178

Subj: Temporary Additional Duty Orders

1. *You are hereby temporarily relieved of your current duties and ordered to report to the Director of Marines Corps Personnel at Headquarters, United Federation Marine Corps, Tarawa, NLT 0800 local 13 June 409, for further duty off-planet.*

Forrester Truong
Lieutenant General, UFMC
Director of Marine Corps Personnel

CLASS: TOP SECRET
FULL DELETE AFTER READING

---

[26] SNCOIC: Staff Noncommissioned Officer in Charge

There's nothing there! she thought before looking up at the major in confusion.

"Yes, my feeling exactly," the major said, obviously reading the expression on her face. "And sorry, I don't know anything more to tell you. But if you looked at the header string, these are TBA orders, To Be Accepted. It's your choice on whether you want to implement them or not."

He took back the S-Screen and then made a show of hitting the delete button, starting the complicated process of completely eliminating any trace that the message had ever existed.

"But how can I decide if I don't know what they're for?" she asked. "And I'm taking 205-4 next week."

"Orders like this don't come lightly. Someone has a very specific mission for you. And don't worry about getting a class. We'll get you the first one forming up after your return."

"Sorry, sir. I'm just confused. Why me?"

"Why you? It's not because of your winning smile, Gunny. It's probably because you have more kills over the last eight years than any other Marine, I'd be guessing. Probably since you were the Inner Forces Corps NCO of the year in 404. Probably because everyone in the Corps knows you are the best sniper we've got on active duty. Without going too far out on a limb, I'd say the Corps needs someone with your skill level for a particular mission."

She wondered what mission that could be, but her mind was blank.

"Do you think I should take it, sir?"

"That's your call, Gunny. I'd have to consider, though, that you were selected because someone thought you were the right fit for the mission, and if you turn it down, the next person, someone slightly less-qualified, will have to step up to the plate. But that's just me, and I'm pretty much a desk jockey."

There was a hint of longing in his voice, and Gracie raised her eyes to really look at him. She immediately knew that he'd jump at the chance. He'd been a not-too-shabby sniper in his day, with 12 confirmed kills as a corporal and sergeant before accepting his commission. Since then, once back into the scout-sniper community, he'd been relegated to supporting Marines like Gracie, to enable them to do their mission. For someone like Major Wadden, that had to eat at him.

For the thousandth time, Gracie was grateful that she'd turned down her own chance to earn a commission. She was a doer, not a director. And because she was a doer, she'd never doubted that she'd accept these orders. If the Marine Corps wanted her to do something different, then she was not going to argue. She'd hesitated not because she needed to think about it, but only because she wanted to know what she'd be doing. But even if it weren't some sort of super-secret, high-speed-low-drag mission, even if it were only to perform in some sort of dog-and-pony show for a visiting VIP, she'd do what she was ordered. That's what Marines did, after all.

"Of course, I'll accept, sir. I'm not in the habit of turning down orders."

"I know that, Gunny, and I knew you'd accept."

"But how will I get there? You just sent my orders to their component electrons."

"There's a board convening to select the Commandant's Enlisted Advisory Council, and you've just been nominated."

"Oh, God save me," she blurted out.

The CEAC was a group of about a dozen Marines, from corporal to first sergeant or master sergeant, E-4 to E-8, who advised the commandant mostly on matters concerning the enlisted Marines, but also on all issues pertaining to the Corps. The members served for two years at HQMC.

"Oh, you won't get selected. Too headstrong, I'm thinking will be the reason. But you've got orders to get interviewed. After that, I imagine the General Truong can get you to where you need to be."

"OK, sir. I guess that makes sense. When do I leave?"

The major looked at his PA, then said, "You'll be on the 2000 shuttle, so you've got four hours. I think I'd get ready about now if I were you. Uniform is Alphas. Anything else you'll need for the mission will be provided later."

Four hours? Thanks for the huge lead time, she thought, quickly standing up.

"Well, sir, I've got a lot to do and not much time to do it, so I'd better get cracking."

She came to a quick position of attention and started to perform her about face when the major said, "Do good out there, Gracie. But I know you will."

She hesitated. She had known the major for going on nine years now, and to the best of her recollection, that was the first time he'd ever called her by her first name.

"I will, sir. Don't worry about that."

She stepped out of the office, then glanced at her PA. She'd have to really push it if she was going to make the shuttle. Gracie had a huge smile on her face as she made her way to the admin shop to pick up her orders. As much as she'd looked forward to becoming the next class' SNCOIC, nothing beat being in the field for real, and she knew she'd be in the thick of things soon.

TARAWA

Chapter 34
62

Gracie strode up the flower-lined walk and rang the bell of the small duplex. A second later, she heard a screech inside and a "She's here!" There was the sound of thundering feet, then the doorknob turned back and forth a few times. She tried to keep a straight face as a "Mom! I got it," came from inside. It took a few moments, but the front door ponderously opened to the bright eyes of a six-year-old Daphne Gittens.

"Auntie Gracie! You're here!" the little girl said as she launched herself into Gracie's arms.

"Daphne! What did I tell you? Give your Auntie Gracie a chance to come inside," Tiggs said. "Oh, it's good to see you, she added, leaning in to kiss Gracie's cheek. It's been too long."

With Daphne perched on her hip, Gracie entered the small home. The smell of something delicious filled the air, and Gracie's mouth started to water.

"How's the little man?" she asked Tiggs, nodding to the bassinet where Eli Junior lay sleeping.

"He's a brat!" interjected Daphne.

"Daphne Ann Gittens, that's no way to speak about your brother!" Tiggs scolded.

"But he is, mamma! He threw up on you today."

"Well, sometimes babies do that," Tiggs said. "You did it, too. Many times."

"Did not!"

"Oh, yes, you most certainly did young lady!"

"Well, if I did, it's OK 'cause my spit-up is sweet like a rose," she said, the imp in the girl showing through the innocent-looking facade.

Gracie couldn't hold it in, and she broke out into laughter.

"Oh, please, don't encourage the girl, Gracie. I don't know where she gets this."

"Not from her father," Gracie said, "so that leaves who?"

"You're probably right," Tiggs said, tousling her daughter's hair. "There might be a bit of me in her."

"Daddy says I'm all you!" Daphne said.

"Well, *All-me*, let your auntie sit down and catch her breath, OK?"

Gracie took a seat on the couch with Daphne welded to her side while Gracie, hostess extraordinaire, brought her a glass of fresh lemonade with a sprig of mint in it. Knowing Tiggs, she'd squeezed the lemons by hand and grew the mint in a small garden. Gracie would probably have problems simply asking a fabricator to make lemonade. For the thousandth time, she wondered how such opposites could be such close friends.

"I wish you could have given us some warning. I didn't have time to make a special dinner and just had to throw something together."

Gracie took a long, lingering sniff. If this was how something "thrown together" smelled, then she wondered what a "special" dinner would smell like.

"Sorry about that. This came up at the last minute. I literally had four hours to get packed and on the shuttle."

"Well, Eli will be here in about an hour. The platoon just came in from six days in the field."

The two friends, with only intermittent interruptions from Daphne, started to catch up with each other's lives. They hadn't seen each other for over a year, and there was quite a bit to cover. At one point, Eli Junior woke up crying, and without missing a beat in her re-telling of Daphne's recital, she reached into the bassinet, picked him, up, and pulling down on the collar of her blouse, put him to her breast.

Gracie was mesmerized by the sight, and inexorably, she felt a tingle in her nipples. Gracie wasn't the mothering type, at least not now, so she was surprised that her body had reacted to what was a very natural sight.

Tiggs noticed her attention had slipped, and misreading the meaning of that, stopped her story to say, "I'm so sorry about Zach."

Even six months after the fact, Gracie felt a small stab of pain in her chest. She and Zach hadn't really been a thing, at least as others assumed they were. They had mutual respect for each other, and despite him being a 180 from what she admired in a man, they had kindled a small degree of a romantic relationship. Part of it was that they understood each other's world, and part of it was that once she opened up to him, Zach could make her laugh. And if they found comfort in each other's company, then why not?

But Zach had been killed 189 days ago on Epsilon Erdi, the Double E, when a primitive chemical rocket had shot down the Stork in which he was riding. Eighteen Marines were killed, the only ones to die on the mission.

Gracie hadn't loved Zach in the Hollybolly sense of the word, and both of them knew that Gracie was not going to settle down until after she retired from the Corps. But the pain she'd felt when she'd found out had been as real as any other pain she'd ever felt—and Gracie had sworn that she would never again make the mistake of getting too close to anyone else while she was still in the Corps. Her Ice Bitch nickname had gradually shifted to the Ice Queen, but even ice could melt, and she didn't want to suffer like that again.

"Thanks, Tiggs," she said.

"Is there, I mean, I know it might be a little soon, but is there anyone else?" Tiggs asked.

"Naw. And there won't be. There'll be plenty of time for that after I retire. I might want to get one just like him for myself," she said, pointing at Eli Junior.

"Or like me," Daphne whispered.

Their chat thankfully slipped back to more mundane matters, interrupted a few times while Tiggs checked the dinner. It was almost an hour later when the front door opened, and Eli came in, covered in six days' worth of Tarawa's burnt orange clay.

"Daddy! Auntie Gracie's here," Daphne shouted, running to him and hugging his leg.

"Honey, be careful! Daddy's pretty dirty," he said, trying to keep her away from the rest of him.

"I should say so," Gracie said, pointing at the clumps of clay on his boots. "TA 15?" she asked, remembering the clay in that training area.

"TA 23, at Wilson. Good to see you, Gracie."

"Oh, no, you don't, Eli. Into the garage with you!" Tiggs said, coming into the room. "Daphne, don't you be getting any of that on you!"

"OK, OK, I'm going. I just wanted to see if Grace was here yet," he said as he went back out the door. "Grace, meet me in the garage."

Gracie rolled her eyes, a more of a snort than a laugh escaping from her. It was rather funny for her to see Staff Sergeant Eli Gittens, all 2.3 meters of him, being controlled by the tiny Tiggs.

"Come one," Daphne said, pulling Gracie by the arm to the inside garage door.

It took two of her little hands to turn the knob, but she managed it and pushed the door open just as the outer door was rising. A moment later, Eli walked in, trailing little clods of clay as he stepped.

The garage was full of boxes, stacked almost to the ceiling.

"I thought a garage was for a hover, not boxes," Gracie said.

"You know how it is," Eli said as he started to slip off his boots.

Gracie didn't know how it was, however. Since enlisting in the Corps, all her personal possessions would fit into two seabags and a mount-out box. It made things much easier.

Eli dropped his trou, then stepped out of them. He used his right foot to hold them out to Daphne, and she held her nose while taking and dumping them in a clothes hamper.

"Thanks for not going commando there, platoon sergeant," Gracie said.

"Kinda got out of the habit once someone came into the family," he said, tilting his head at Daphne.

"So, you still living large as a ground pounder?" she asked him. "No itching to get back to a scout-sniper platoon?"

"Living large and loving it," Eli said. "I've got a kick-ass platoon, my LT's staying out of my hair, and things are looking good for gunny next year."

Eli has stayed with 2/3's Scout Sniper Platoon for only three months after coming back on active duty. He'd picked up E4 and gotten orders to NCO School. After graduating, Eli had gone to 3/9, but to a rifle platoon, not the sniper platoon, and he had stayed a grunt ever since. Where Gracie loved the act of being a sniper, Eli loved the act of being a leader, and from everything Gracie had been able to find out, he was excelling at it. Still, she couldn't help but give him shit about it whenever she could.

"I'm still a HOG, Gunnery Sergeant, but I've seen the light. I'm a ground-pounding, snake-eating, grunt, and damned proud of it."

"Damn! Damn!" Daphne said.

"Now you've done it!" Gracie said, trying to stifle a laugh.

"Daphne, honey. Why don't you go help your mother, OK?" Eli asked as he bent down to her level.

The little girl gave her father a kiss on the cheek, then obediently trundled back into the house.

"It's like I've got to speak a foreign language when I'm home," Eli said as he stepped up to a shop sink alongside the near wall of the garage.

"The life of a married man."

Eli looked around for a towel, and seeing none, simply shook out his hands, sending droplets flying over the boxes.

"The CEAC? You?" he asked her.

"I know. I'm probably not the right fit, but I got nominated, so I'm here."

"Well, I guess you could go into the interview picking your nose and farting. I've heard they frown on that sort of stuff at headquarters."

"Yeah, right. No, I'm here, so I'll give it a shot. But they probably won't select me."

"It's your life, and I don't have to add better you than me."

"Eli, you coming?" Tiggs shouted from inside the home.

"Let's get back in. I've got to put on a different shirt, and yeah, a pair of pants. You don't have to remind me. But after dinner and we get Daphne to bed, and maybe before Eli Junior wakes up, let's sit down and talk. There's a lot to catch up on."

"And sorry about Gunny Pure Pleasance. I was shocked when I heard the news."

"Yeah, me, too," Gracie agreed.

She followed Eli back in the home, and as he bolted up the stairs to get something else on, she took a seat at the table while Tiggs brought out some sort of seafood pasta. The aroma rising from it was amazing.

Gracie didn't know what tomorrow would bring, but for tonight, she would relax with friends, and that was something pretty hard to beat.

Chapter 35

62

Gracie looked into the retinal scan on the bulkhead, which confirmed she was who she was supposed to be, and the hatch slid open on a whisper of air. Gracie stepped inside—and was surprised to see quite a few familiar faces, including one Staff Sergeant Tibone Mubotono.

"Ah, the Ice Queen," T-Bone said as he leaned back in his chair. "I should have known you'd be invited to the party."

"Gracie, good to see you again," Shaan Ganesh said, standing up to shake her hand.

"Good to see you again, Shaan. Dutch, Brooke, Spig, Cezar: happy to see you too," she said, nodding at a few of the Marines in the room. "Anyone know why we're here?"

"What, no love for your old spotter?" T-bone asked with a laugh.

"Good to see you, too, T-Bone," she said, trying to keep her voice neutral.

She'd never gotten along well with her old spotter. He'd been just too full of himself, and he'd never seemed willing to follow her lead. They'd survived two missions together before she'd received orders to 2/6, and she'd fervently hoped that would be the last time they'd be in the same unit. It looked like that wish was not going to be kept.

T-Bone was not incompetent with a weapon in his hand, and Gracie had to grudgingly admit that he was probably a better marksman than she was, but there was more to being a sniper than being able to hit the target, and T-Bone's rash personality left him open to mistakes—at least in her opinion. Still, he'd racked up a very respectable 28 kills, which was three more than Gracie had over the same period of time.

"No, none of us knows yet, but looking at who's here, it's got to be a high-priority mission," a pleasant-looking Marine said as he stood up to offer his hand. "Staff Sergeant Carlito Rapa."

"You're Bomba?" she asked, surprised.

"Guilty as charged," he said with a warm laugh.

This is the Grey Death? she wondered.

Gracie had spent her entire career with the Inner Forces and Rapa had been with the Outer Forces, so while she'd heard of him before, and she'd even seen him on the holo when he'd received his Navy Cross, she'd never met him. In person, he looked like an accountant—no, like a chaplain, the kind of guy with whom she'd lay out her problems. This was the sniper who'd tallied 52 kills in two days on Florin-3 despite losing three teammates, having half of his body paralyzed, and having a couple of hundred of Baron Keister's men trying to flush him out.

"Well, good to finally meet you, Bomba," Gracie said, impressed.

"Likewise."

She caught a glimpse of T-Bone, studiously ignoring the mutual fan fest going on a meter from him, but with a slightly disgusted look on his face.

What? Little baby T-Bone doesn't like not being the center of attention? she thought, holding back a smile.

She took a seat between Bomba (it was the press that named him "The Grey Death." His Marine nick had long been "Bomba") and Shaan. Over the next few minutes, several more Marines came in, including Sergeant Tennerife Delay and Gunnery Sergeant Manny Chun.

"Four Fuzo snipers?" T-Bone announced to the room. "They must really want the best."

"Eat me, Mubotono," Spig McConnaughy said.

Gracie looked around the briefing room. There were 16 of them there, 16 of who were probably among the most accomplished snipers in the Corps. Whatever was up, it was big. She and Manny were the only two gunnies. The Corps had some incredibly accomplished E8s and E9s, so if the two of them were the oldest and most senior snipers present, then wherever they were being sent was probably going to be physically taxing.

When the hatch swished open again, Gracie looked up to see who else was joining them, then jumped to attention when she saw it wasn't another sniper but a full bird and a captain. The colonel waved them all back to their seats as he went to the head of the table and sat.

"I'm Colonel Soeryadjaya, and I want to thank all of you for coming. This is Captain Lysander," he said as the captain raised one hand in acknowledgment.

Captain Lysander? Captain Esther Lysander, as in the daughter of General and Chairman Ryck Lysander? Gracie wondered, staring at the captain for a moment before deciding, *It is her!*

". . . you scan your acceptance, pass it to the next person," the colonel was saying.

Gracie snapped back to the present. The colonel had handed a small PA to Dutch, who was sitting to the colonel's right. Dutch took his time to read it, then held it up to his right eye. A moment later, he lowered it and passed it to the Marine next to him, a sergeant whose name Gracie hadn't caught yet. No one said a word while this was happening. Gracie took the time to steal a few more glances at Captain Lysander. She had a pretty strong rep in the Corps, but Gracie didn't know much about her other than her pedigree.

It took a while, but the PA made its way down the table to Gracie. She picked it up and read it through. It was assigning her a temporary and mission-specific TS-4 security clearance, which was sobering. As with all snipers, Gracie had a TS-1, so a T-4 was almost scary.

What the heck have I gotten myself into?

Most of the statement was generic, just that once she scanned her acceptance, she was bound by the provisions of the clearance and that breaking them had all sorts of drastic and dire consequences. That was all legalese to her, and she had no problem with any of it. She hit the accept, then held the PA to her eye for the scan. The light turned green, signaling its acceptance, and Gracie passed it to Bomba.

It took a full 20 minutes for the PA to make it around the table, all of that time in silence. The colonel simply leaned back and stared at the bulkhead above Gracie's head. That is until the PA made it back to him. He quickly snapped back to life and checked the readout, then turned to the gathered Marines.

"Now that we've got that out of the way, it's time to get to the meat of this. Are any of you familiar with Kepler 9813-B?" he asked. "No? It's been mentioned in the newslines a few times lately."

There were only about a gazillion Keplers, Gracie knew. Even before interstellar travel, the Kepler mission, which started in 2009, Old Reckoning, with the original Kepler satellite, cataloged hundreds of thousands of stars and planets. Most of the viable planets in human's interstellar neighborhood were subsequently renamed and colonized. The unusable worlds and stars were the ones that still kept the original Kepler designation to this day. If this planet still had a Kepler number, it couldn't have been very important to humanity, so Gracie wasn't sure why she should know about it.

"OK, then, let me give you a little background," the colonel went on, turning to start the holo projector in the middle of the table.

A dark blue star appeared over the table, with several planets orbiting it. The scale was off, though, Gracie thought. Either those planets were huge, or the star was too small.

"This is Kepler 9813," he said, as the projector momentarily bathed the star in a bright emerald light. "It's an ultra-cool dwarf."

Ah, so that's why it's so small, Gracie thought as she put her elbows on the table and leaned in.

"And this is Kepler 9813-B," he said as one of the three planets was highlighted. "The planet's claim to fame has been its lifeforms, which look somewhat similar to fungus on Earth."

He switched the view on the table display to an expanse of what looked like nothing more than rotting oyster mushrooms. They looked disgusting, and Gracie's stomach churned and their very "alienness."

"No terraforming, sir?" Bomba asked.

There had to be hundreds of planets with some type of life, although until mankind ran into the Capys and then the Klethos, none of that life had been much beyond simple multicellular structures. There were only a handful of planets that had anything as developed as a tree analog. So mankind did what they do, and planets were terraformed, making them into good little models of Earth.

"Not worth it, Staff Sergeant Rapa. As you can see," the colonel said, switching back the display, "9813-B is tidally locked. Kepler 9813's gravity is so powerful that the gravitational gradient creates a synchronous rotation in the planet. That means, the same side of the planet always faces its sun."

Ah, like Earth's moon.

"This is not that rare of an occurrence, but usually, planets like this are blasted with too much solar radiation to allow for life. However, because Kepler 9813 is an ultra-cool dwarf, the radiation that hits the planet is in the habitable zone, but only along the rim between the day side and the night side."

"Oh, like *Ribbon World*," Shaan said.

The colonel stole a quick glance at the captain, his eyebrows twitching, and Gracie thought that this wasn't the first time they'd heard that.

"*Ribbon World* is a figment of some Hollybolly writer's imagination," he said in a slightly condescending tone as if talking to a child. "The idea might make for an interesting setting, but the practicality isn't there. Yes, the trope has been alive in scifi books and flicks for centuries, but there is a reason why no tidally locked planet has ever been terraformed.

"Oh, sorry, let me get off my soapbox. The bottom line is that the planet has not been terraformed, nor will it be. You can't survive on the planet. There are only traces of oxygen, but don't worry about that. Before you could suffocate, the hydrogen cyanide would kill you."

He smiled at his little joke, one Gracie was sure he'd told before. However, what he said was, well, alarming. Humans couldn't survive on the planet, and now it looked like they had some sort of mission there? What, to shoot rotting fungus?

"So why am I telling you all of this? Well, there has been a pretty big break-through. The Allied Biologicals lab, testing some old samples, discovered that one of the lifeforms has a biological structure that can be a huge benefit to humans, for everything from cellular atrophy to regen."

That caught Gracie's attention. It was standard dogma that Earth-life and all other xenolife were incompatible. If you planted an Earth tree on a planet with alien life, the tree acted as poison, clearing an area around it in which no native life would grow. And despite the similarities in body structure between humans, capys, and Klethos, that was merely parallel evolution. None of the three known intelligent lifeforms were biologically compatible. And while the capys could eat Earth crops, the reverse wasn't true, nor could Klethos and humans exchange food without breaking it down first into its component atoms and restructuring it.

But if what the colonel said was true, then the enormous potential for maybe profit first, and human benefit second, would render the planet into prime real estate, and the galaxy was full of squatters.

"Allied Biologicals, with assistance from the Federation government, has unofficially established a research center on the planet's surface."

That must have cost a mint! Gracie thought.

"The UAM[27] has not been notified."

That was not surprising. All new research that can possibly affect humankind was supposed to be reported to the UAM and a license issued. Supposedly, this type of thing was too big to be left under the control of any one government.

"However, the Brotherhood has just filed with the UAM that Sectors 334 through 338 are actually their territory. The Brotherhood has long held that 338 was historically theirs, but

---

[27] UAM: The United Assembly of Man, the overarching central human government. While not 100% binding, it never-the-less represents over 95% of humanity.

they've never pushed forward on it until now. And coincidently, Kepler 9813 is in Sector 336.

"And to further muddy the waters, we have reason to believe that at least one commercial entity has been poking around. Some equipment vital to the mission has mysteriously broken down, and the signs are pointing to sabotage."

It was becoming clear what was happening. But Gracie wasn't sure why they were being brought together. Just stick a battalion of FCDC around the research station and be done with it.

"So why not send in the FCDC?" he asked as if he'd read Gracie's mind. "The problem is that if we send in the troops, we're essentially opening up a Pandora's Box. We're announcing to the galaxy what we're doing, and we need more time to develop the potential before we do that. Sending the FCDC, or a Marine battalion, will require a response in kind from the Brotherhood, and we don't want war."

"So you send us in unofficially to protect the research station from the unofficial Brotherhood personnel and the unofficial corporate personnel, and no one raises a fuss, right Colonel?" Gracie asked. "There's nothing really happening, after all."

"You got it in one, Gunny. That's about the long and short of it.

"And with that, I'm going to turn it over to Captain Lysander, who will be the mission commander. She'll give you your initial brief now on what you have to do to get ready, then you'll receive more on the ship. You embark in seven hours, so I suggest you pay attention. Captain?"

He stood, waving everyone else down as they started to rise as well, then nodded and left the room. Captain Lysander waited until the hatch shut behind him before speaking.

"As the colonel said, I'm Captain Lysander, and I'll be commanding this mission.

"First, I'm sorry to say, all of you have failed your interview for the CEAC."

There was a low-level of chuckling as the Marines heard that. Gracie guessed that the others had also been given the same excuse to come to Tarawa.

"But as the colonel said, we embark in seven hours, and we've got a lot to cover, so let's get down to it."

Gracie leaned forward to listen in. She'd never fought in the vacuum of space, much less on a planet hostile to human life, and she wanted as much info as possible. But even if the environment was different, she was a sniper, and she'd do what snipers do.

FS PORTOLUMA BAY

Chapter 36
62

The *Porto* fell out of bubble space some 900,000,000 kilometers from Kepler 9813-B. The ship was running silent in full stealth mode, drifting silently and trying to pierce the shielding of any other ship that might be in the system.

The *Porto* was a schooner, a new class of small, stealthy ships with more surveillance and stealth capabilities than arms. With her Kylefelter meson cannon and Clovis launchers, she packed a punch, but she didn't have much ship-to-surface capability, and her ability to transport troops was limited. She didn't have room for a Stork, just two small shuttles and a duck egg launcher. She was an excellent platform for snooping and pooping among the stars, and she was a good recon or SEAL insertion vehicle, but she was outclassed as a ship-of-the-line. If there was a Brotherhood man-o-war in-system, the captain wanted to know about her before her counterpart on the other ship knew about the *Porto*.

Gracie looked over at the captain, a young Lieutenant Commander, slumped so casually in his captain's chair. He had to be wired, but he exuded confidence and calm.

Gracie was one of two Marines on the bridge. Captain Lysander, as the mission commander, sat in a small fold-down seat to the side of the bridge. Gracie was the senior enlisted Marine on board, but she was on the bridge because Senior Chief Watkins, the *Porto's* COB, the Chief of the Boat, had adopted Gracie and invited her to watch with him as they entered the system.

The senior chief was from the Kumeyaay Band outside San Diego in the US, and as a fellow American and fellow First People, he considered Gracie as a long lost cousin. The Kumeyaays had one of the largest gambling empires on Earth, and they didn't follow too many of the old traditions, but blood was blood, and he'd taken Gracie under his wing. Gracie wasn't even too sure why the master chief had joined the Navy. The Kumeyaays didn't have a warrior ethos, and no one from the extended Watkins clan wanted for money, but he'd done well in the service. He and Gracie were the same age, and he was already a rank ahead of her and the COB of a ship-of-the-line.

"Ears, got anything?" the captain asked.

Gracie thought all the nicknames in the Navy were kind of funny. "Ears" was an earnest lieutenant (jg) who monitored the surveillance. "Boats" was the CWO2 d'Alto, the bosun. "George" was the junior ensign aboard the ship (and in this crew, the only ensign, so she was also the "Bull Ensign," the senior ensign on board). Gracie still wasn't sure how that worked out. "Cheng" was the chief engineer, and "Skipper" was the ship's captain (she'd already known that one).

"Negative, sir. All quiet."

"Guns, stand down the cannon, but keep the missile tubes ready," the skipper ordered before turning to Captain Lysander and saying, "We'll just sit quiet for an hour or so to see if our arrival was noticed. If there's nothing, we'll start moving in until the POC; then it's your call."

Captain Lysander was the mission commander, but the Marines, the FCDC platoon, and the replacement lab personnel were all onboard the *Porto*, and as such, under Lieutenant Commander Chacon's control during the passage. Once the ship reached the Passage of Command, an assigned distance from the planet, command would shift to Captain Lysander, and the skipper, even if senior to the Marine, would fall back to a subordinate position.

Chief Watkins pointed at Gracie's coffee cup and raised a questioning eyebrow. Gracie handed it over, and the chief refilled it from his thermos. Gracie thought most sailors would take their coffee intravenously if they could. Still, it was a good brew.

Gracie leaned back against the bulkhead, blowing on the now full cup to cool it down from scalding to merely blistering. Things were pretty Spartan at the research lab, according to the briefs, and she knew she wouldn't be getting real coffee there, so Gracie was determined to enjoy it while she could.

"Sir! We've got comms going out. Putting it on the speakers now," "Comms," a first class petty officer said.

". . .on't know how much longer we can hold out."

"Who is that, and why are we just now hearing it?" the skipper shouted.

"That's Alpha-Three, sir, the research station. I've only just now got through the protocol for booting in-system comms."

"Any identification on who is attacking?" another voice asked.

"That's Goby Station responding to Alpha-Three," Comms said without being asked.

Goby Station was the nearest naval facility, but that didn't mean it was close.

"Fuck! I think they just broke through!" a panicked voice said. "You've got to help us!"

"Ears, what's going on?"

"I'm picking up the same broadcast, but not much else. I don't know who's attacking them."

"Captain, how long to get my team down to their position?" Captain Lysander asked.

The skipper looked at Boats who shrugged and said, "As fast as we could? Maybe eight hours. That's using the shuttle, not the duck eggs. Add another ten hours if you want to use those."

"We need help now! You've got to get here! I can hear them outside the door!" the operator from Alpha-Three said.

"Wait one," Goby Station passed.

"I can't wait!"

"We can't make it," Captain Lysander said. "They're lost. But maybe there's something we can do."

"I'm all ears," the skipper said.

"First, if we initiate comms with them, can anyone trace us?"

"Depends on what kind, ma'am," Comms said. "On a direct beam, not likely, but possibly."

"I don't mean that. On the hadron comms."

The *Porto* had five hadron communicators, each tied to a different command. They did not act as standard comms. What was sent on one system was recreated on any of the other linked systems without actually transmitting anything. Other than message torps which entered bubble space, this was the only current method of galaxy-wide instantaneous communications. On populated worlds, there were enough official and commercial nodes so that a message was sent from one node in a system to another node in the target system, then normal comms forwarded the message from the node to the end user.

On a world like 9813B, there were no systems, so the first ship in left a satellite which was linked to another back in more frequented space. The *Porto* could send a direct message to the research station, but that almost certainly be picked up by any ship in the system. What they were hearing now was the rebroadcast from the system node as the poor saps at the station cried out for help.

"Well, we could use the hadrons back to PEM302, then have it re-routed here and sent out under standard comms."

"And whoever is out there won't be able to pick us up?"

"No, ma'am."

"Captain, send a message to them to hold on, and we'll be there in two days."

"But we can get you there sooner than that."

"Yes, sir. But we can't get there in time. Those unfortunate souls are lost," Captain Lysander said, tilting her head to the speakers from which the cries for help were still pouring. "We can't save them, but maybe we can flush out who're the attackers."

"Ah, I get it. Pass that, and then sit here and see who bites."

"Yes, sir."

The skipper seemed to think about it for only a moment, then he grabbed a stylus and started scribbling on his PA.

He hit the send with a flourish and said, "Pass that over the hadrons via NF3, Greg, and make sure it comes back over the node in the open."

"Aye-aye, sir."

Gracie heard the sound of an explosion over the speakers. It was muffled, but it made the situation on the planet clear. She could see Comms, or Greg, as the skipper had called him, speaking, but she couldn't hear him.

A few moments later, the speakers broke with "K9813B Alpha Three, this is the *FS Admiral Miguel Posov*. We are on our way, ETA 40.32 hours. Hold on the best you can."

"I can't hold on that long!"

"Understand your situation. Get into your panic room and wait. Do not attempt to resist or secure property. God be with you."

"Do they even have a panic room?" Gracie asked Chief Watkins, who shook his head no.

Even without a real panic room, Gracie realized that by passing the message like that, the skipper might be giving an excuse to the attackers to simply take the research and not seek out and murder the staff.

"The *Posov*, sir?" Captain Lysander asked.

"Might as well make it something with a little more punch than we have. And I know she's out cruising right now. We sent that out through Third Fleet, and they'll tell the *Posov* to keep low for the next 40 hours."

With the message sent, it was time to wait to see if anyone took the bait and reacted. It didn't take long.

Less than two minutes had passed when Ears said, "I've got an anomaly, sir. Probably a shielded ship moving closer to the planet."

"Brotherhood?" the skipper asked.

"I'm running the probabilities on that, but I don't think so. Looks commercial, probably Yantos-made, possibly GE."

The skipper raised his eyebrows for a moment, probably in relief, Gracie figured. A Brotherhood ship would not only be better armed, starting a ship battle with a supposedly peaceful ally was not something done lightly. A corporate vessel was a much easier target, from warfighting, political, and legal standpoints.

"Sir," Captain Lysander asked, "Are your lifeboats shielded?"

"No," Boats answered for the skipper. "That sort of defeats the purpose of a life boat in being seen. Our rekis are shielded, though."

"You have rekis? I didn't see them on the manifest."

"I don't think they were originally part of the TE, but we've had them as long as I've been aboard. They're in C24. I can have them assembled in an hour."

"So they're the R version?" Captain Lysander asked.

"That's affirm."

"Captain, I take it that you want to take your Marines and seize that ship out there?" the skipper asked.

"Yes, sir. I'm assuming you don't want to break your own shielding by firing at the vessel, and I know the Federation doesn't want any of the research to get out of the system. We don't know what's being uploaded, but all the samples will need to be lifted off the surface.

"And there's another thing. If we're going to have to clear out the bad guys, I'd rather they didn't have any support the ship there can provide. I want them cut off."

Gracie could almost see the skipper's thoughts shift on his face and he considered the idea. She would have thought, though, that this would be Captain Lysander's call, but evidently the protocol that helped the Marines and the Navy function as a team still had command with Lieutenant Commander Chacon.

"Any more information, Ears?" he asked.

"Their shielding is pretty good, but I'm getting enough gravitational disturbances to know they're out there, and it looks like they're heading to take up a position along a standard ascent profile for the station."

"How long to reach a launch point for the rekis, given full stealth?" the captain asked the navigator.

"About six hours, sir. Anything faster, and we'll start to lose stealth. If we launch the rekis, though, sir, and if there's a Brotherhood ship out there, she'll see the sleds," she said.

"She'll know something is out there, like I know we've got something out there, but she won't know exactly what," Ears said. "She won't know they're Federation rekis."

The captain chewed his lower lip as he processed all this for a few moments before making his decision, saying, "Nav, bring her in.

"And Captain Lysander, what's your plan?"

Chapter 37

62

The reki slowly floated out the hatch of the darkened hangar. The *Porto* was only 20 klicks from the target ship, so despite the high-tech shielding, they were close enough so that any break in simple light-discipline could give their position away. The target ship, which had been visually identified as a Yantos Executive III, one of the most common corporate ships in the Galaxy, was conducting recovery ops, her hangar bay open to space, and while the ship's sensors should be blind to the *Porto*, any of the EVA crew could simply look over and see a stray light.

Gracie was both excited and nervous. She was a gunnery sergeant with almost 24 years in the Corps, but this was her first space-borne operation since boot camp. She felt exposed in the eight-man space sled. The R-version was heavily shielded, both from shipborne surveillance and with a space version of a tarnkappe, which essentially bent light waves around the sled, from visual means. Unlike with a tarnkappe, though, something as low-tech as two tiny pinhole cameras allowed the Navy coxswain and the Marines full visuals to the front.

Gracie was the section commander of the Marines on the first reki. Her job was to secure the hangar entry, then hold it while Captain Lysander, in the second reki, took the ship itself. As part of that mission, Gracie was carrying her Windmoeller as well as her M99. T-bone, who was in Gracie's section, had been royally miffed that he wasn't the designated sniper, but when Gracie had asked him when his last simulation in null-G had been, the staff sergeant had admitted it had been back at sniper school. Gracie had tried to contain the satisfaction she'd felt when he said that. If it had been more recent, she'd have had to give him the mission, much as it would have galled her. But her simulations last year had her quals up-to-date, so she was justified in her decision.

Shooting in zero-G was in most ways easier than on a planet. In deep space, there were few if any forces that acted upon the round once it left the barrel. With the scope switched to zero-G mode, it was as simple as point and shoot, keeping a tight body position. If the shooter was not anchored, the recoil could impart a slight angular rotation, but it wasn't like the Hollybolly flicks where firing sent the shooter spectacularly flying backward. A round might mass 13 grams while a gunman in an EVA suit might mass 200 kilos, so while the force imparted on both would be the same, how it affected each would be different. In orbit, the round would be affected by the planetary gravitational pull, which would try and keep the round itself in orbit. However, while that was much more difficult to calculate as the force changed as the round's distance from the surface changed, the effects were generally less than those on the planet's surface.

What might create difficulties in the situation facing them was that to keep the hangar bay doors open, Gracie might have to take out anyone going for the emergency close switch, which would be well inside the hangar near the main entrance into the ship proper. If Gracie took a shot, the round would initially travel through zero-G, but as it crossed into the ship's hangar, it would be affected by the ship's artificial gravity. Scope AIs had a notoriously hard time calculating a firing solution across such an interface. No Federation scope AI, at least, had the ability to measure gravity from a distance, and whether a ship was under ½ G or 1 G could make a huge difference achieving a kill or a miss.

Gracie turned to look at the breaching chamber clamped to the back of the reki. If the crew of the ship got the hangar doors closed, Gracie's Marines would have to use it to breach the ship if they could. This was essentially the same piece of gear that Marines had used unchanged from 200 years ago. It would work, she knew— if the ship hung around and let them. If the ship took off, the *Porto* would follow and blast it into its component atoms before it could enter bubble space, leaving the assault team to float around until the ship returned. Rekis were fine for space, but they could not land on a planet.

The reki was on silent running, but knowing how long an Executive III was, Gracie's EVA AI could calculate the closing distance. Gracie felt her nerves rise. As a sniper, Gracie was used to long stalks where the key was to remain concealed. Sitting in open space, with just the reki structure under her butt, was unnerving. The closer they got to the target ship, the more she felt exposed. At 2000 meters, she felt the crew had to see them coming in.

"Over there, to the right of the shuttle. The red emergency button," the coxswain passed on the wire.

To keep emissions to a minimum, each Marine and the coxswain were wired into the frame of the sled. They could communicate without fear of anyone picking up a signal. That would end as soon as they left the reki, but for the moment, the old-tech was superior for the situation.

"Got it," Gracie said, noting the emergency hangar doors closing switch.

She tried to get a feel for how deep hangar bay was. The ship was not particularly large, and the hangar took up almost ¼ of the round vessel. Gracie figured that the switch was 25 meters inside the hull. Looking at how the crew moved about inside the ship, she thought it was set at about ½ G.

There was one more major force that would affect the bullet's trajectory. There was both an electrostatic boundary and an atmospheric boundary between open space and the hangar. Either one could seriously affect the round. Like a reentry vehicle skipping off the atmosphere and heading back into space, so too could a round skip right off the boundary, especially if the angle was too oblique. Even at a better angle, the boundary could alter the shot enough to cause a miss. This was another area where the scope AIs were weak and why continual practice and re-qualifications were necessary. Once again, sniping almost became more art than math.

The key was to get as perpendicular as possible, and the coxswain was doing a pretty good job at that. The captain and the second reki, not having to worry about the same kind of shooting, would come in at a shallower, less exposed angle.

"Can you orient this thing so we've got the same aspect at the hangar?" she asked the coxswain.

At the moment, the hangar's "up" was at Gracie's seven o'clock. She'd fired at different aspects in the simulators, but she'd done better when both she and her target had the same aspect.

The coxswain complied, and within a few moments, the ship seemed to rotate to match Gracie's up. She knew that was a trick her brain was performing to match what her eyes were seeing and what her middle ear was feeling.

Gracie kept her crosshairs just off the red emergency switch. The distance to the open hangar door didn't really matter to her firing solution, so she didn't have to adjust her point of aim.

"That's it!" she shouted at about 700 meters out as the crew suddenly leaped into action. "Drop the screen."

The reki had pretty sophisticated counter-surveillance, but it was still little more than an open sleigh, and it was not infallible. They'd been picked up.

The coxswain cut the display, giving Gracie a clear shot forward as he goosed up the speed. Gracie kept her crosshairs locked, shifting slightly as they surged forward.

There! Got you!

A crewman inside the hangar, in the typical green overalls of cargo crew, bolted for the emergency switch. Gracie had to wait while he ran behind the parked shuttle, but as he emerged and reached for the switch, she squeezed the trigger.

Without air in the barrel, the round was at least twice as fast, and it took only a split second to reach the ship, pierce the hangar bay's atmosphere, and hit the man center mass. He dropped like a stone; whether KIA or not, Gracie didn't bother to check. He wouldn't be hitting the switch either way, and that was all that mattered.

Standing just behind her, three of her Marines opened up with their M99's spraying the hangar. A young woman with bright turquoise hair ducked under the parked shuttle, then crab-walked to the bulkhead with the switch. As soon as she emerged from under the shuttle, her bright hair a nice target, Gracie took her down with a shot to the side of the head.

Gracie's alarms screamed out, getting close to redlining. Someone had them under fire. Energy weapons didn't dissipate in space, so they were receiving the full force of the weapon, but the EVA suits, while less-than-perfect against kinetics, were much better protection against energy weapons. They couldn't hold up forever, though, and the Marines had to neutralize the incoming fire.

"Find the gunners" she shouted over the comms.

If there had been any doubt by lurking forces in the system, that put them to rest. Gracie's comms would go out to anyone out there, and even if they couldn't decipher the encrypted words, the fact that something was passed would be noted. The section was not under comms silence, but still, Gracie hated to take that step.

She glassed the hangar, trying to find the source as her display reached 70% and her face shield started pulsing with the red warning light. She couldn't see anyone firing, and there wasn't much of any place to hide in the hangar.

If they're not inside, they must be outside. She shifted to the shuttle, which was by now only about 150 meters away, and her scope immediately caught the energy bloom of three weapons. The only way the scope could pick them up was if they were pointed at her, so these were the culprits.

"On the shuttle. One by the front, two in the cargo bay!"

She threw out the adjustments she'd mentally attached to her sight picture and simply aimed center mass at the figure just to the front of the shuttle. The instant her crosshairs were on the person, she squeezed the trigger, and a moment later, her round hit, and the person went limp, arms, spreading out. She started to shift to the other two, but the three Marines behind her and Bomba, who was in the third row, left side, had riddled the two with their M99's 8mm darts.

Whoever they were, their EVA suits were no better than the Federation's suits against kinetics. They offered no resistance to the high-speed darts. Unlike the gunner at the front of the shuttle, who had perfectly spherical globs of blood trailing away from him, the EVA suits of the second two immediately sealed up the punctures, so there was no sign that they'd been hit other than the fact that they were not moving.

The coxswain, Petty Officer Third Class Sahadi, had kept to his task even while they had been under fire. The reki pierced the hangar curtain, jerking as gravity's fingers pulled at them. He landed the reki with a bounce, and Gracie and her seven Marines bolted off to clear the hangar. Gracie stumbled and fell to one knee as her body adjusted from Zero G to gravity, but with only about ½ G in the hangar, she wasn't much at risk of hurting herself like that.

Gracie's position was near the main entrance to the ship, and she ran around the parked shuttle. Just as she reached the front, the pilot's hatch opened, and a body fell out. Gracie stumbled over the figure and fell flat on her face. As she spun, she saw the woman, try to struggle to her feet, a Victor 2mm in her hand. Gracie had her M99, and she could have dropped the woman, but something stopped her. She lunged forward, wrapping her arms around the woman's legs. Almost crawling up her back, wrenched the snub-nosed handgun out of her hands and stuck her face into the woman's short blonde locks, shouting over her externals for the woman to freeze.

To her surprise, the woman did just that.

"Gunny, you OK?" Shaan Ganesh asked, running up.

"Yeah. I do believe this is one of the shuttle pilots."

Shaan hauled the woman off the deck, and Gracie saw the frightened face of someone who looked no older than a high-school student. She had pilot wings on her overalls, though, so she couldn't really be that young.

"Sit still and you won't be hurt," she told the pilot, sliding the Victor into her thigh cargo pouch. "Understand?"

The girl nodded, not looking like she believed her.

Damned baby, Gracie thought. *Either that or I'm getting old.*

She looked around the hangar. T-Bone came out of the back of the shuttle and gave her a thumbs up.

"Falcon One, we are secure," she passed on the net.

"Roger that. We're 30 seconds out," the captain said.

Almost to the second, the captain's reki touched down on the hangar deck. The eight Marines jumped off and bounded up to the entrance. Sergeant Lester Piccolo, the junior Marine in the detachment, set a small breaching device against the lock, and ten seconds later, it erupted in a glorious display of purple, yellow, and blue sparks that reached out to fall slowly to the deck. Piccolo kicked the hatch, and it swung open. Within moments, the captain's assault team had disappeared into the bowels of the ship.

Gracie set three of her team to cover the hatch, then had two watch out the hangar doors. Surprisingly, in addition to the pilot, there were five living crew, and only one of them was a WIA with a dart through the meaty part of his bicep. Two of the prisoners were in still buttoned up in their EVA suits, and Gracie ordered them to take off their helmets. She wanted to be able to see their faces.

Once the helmets were off, Gracie was pretty sure they posed no threat to them. They were frightened, and more than that, cowed. Gracie had to think that despite the situation, they hadn't thought they'd face Federation Marines, and that had broken their spirit—that and the fact that there were eleven dead bodies of their comrades being laid out on the deck beside them.

Some of them, she was sure, had at least seen the dead technicians at the research station even if they hadn't participated in the killing, and that had to be going through their minds at the moment. There was a good reason for that. The chief of the station's replacement crew had demanded that there be no survivors. Luckily for these six, though, the captain and the skipper both had said that even if these were civilians, they would be treated as EPWs. It wasn't up to the military to pass judgment, after all. They'd leave that to the courts.

Fifteen minutes later, the assault team declared the ship secure. Without a casualty, the Marines had seized a ship in space, one that would give up its secrets once the FCDC sleuths got through with it.

It had been a good day's worth of work.

KEPLER 9813-B

Chapter 38
65

By the time the Marines landed at the research station, the corporate raiders (they still hadn't identified themselves yet, not that they'd be able to hold back once the interrogators had them in their less-than-tender hands) still on the planet had abandoned the station. Sixteen dead Federation citizens were stacked in the living quarters, but three were found in a state of shock, but alive and huddled together in a storage closet. Evidently, the captain's "panic room" message had an effect, essentially removing the need to eliminate them.

Captain Lysander tried to ask them what had occurred, but the three were almost incoherent, and having hidden themselves, they hadn't observed much. The captain put them on the shuttle back to the ship and after the team had secured the building and the immediate area, approved the replacement team's transfer to the planet's surface.

The research station was designed for 30. With 16 in the research team, 17 Marines, and eight FCDC station guards, the station's life-support systems would be taxed. With the Marine's HED 2s, each Marine could technically survive for a week or more outside of the station, but that would be an onerous drain on their energy and alertness. The Hazardous Environment Deployment System 2 was not the full monty System 3 that was in effect a mini-PICS, but it still covered the entire body with both a laminated polymer "skin" and an electrostatically maintained layer of breathable air around the Marine, the "bubble," which worked in much the same way as the curtains Gracie had used on Wyxy. CO_2

was vented through a one-way charged vortex located at the small of the back, and O2 cylinders under extreme pressure fed in just enough oxygen to maintain bodily functions. A cylinder was good for about 14 hours, depending on body size and exertion, and switching them out could be done in seconds.

Gracie hated the System 2 skin layer. It felt like some Grade C Hollybolly horror flick, with the semi-intelligent glob invading her body. It made her feel claustrophobic in the way it intimately hugged her body, leaving only her mouth, nostrils, and eyes uncovered. The less said about the tubes that automatically wormed their way into her anus and urethra the better. She shuddered each time the tubes invaded her body with what seemed like intelligent design. She knew it was better to have them, which allowed bodily waste to pass through two additional charged vortex valves that could be opened than to let the waste build up between her body and the polymer skin, but she didn't have to like the insertion process.

Once the new research team and the FCDC Installation Security team arrived, the *Porto* moved further from the planet, but close enough to scan the surface as well as the entire system. Ghost readings were pretty good indications that others were lurking as well, probably two commercial-type ships and at least one military-grade ship, most likely Brotherhood. Scans on the surface were illuminating. There was a group of humans located about 2,000 klicks north of the Federation station. They were heavily shielded, but not well enough to evade the Porto's scans. The Intel officer aboard the ship gave it an 86% probability that they were a mid-level corporate pirate group, hoping to grab a few discoveries and run back to the parent company where whatever they found could be exploited. The Marines would most likely be tasked with rounding them up, but as they posed no real physical threat, that would only occur once the Federation station was secure.

Security was the Marine's highest priority at the moment. While the new research team tried to make sense of what was at the station and what had been found on the shuttle, the FCDC IS team was setting up a hi-sec entrance to the station, and the Marines were about to go on an orientation patrol. They had to see the lay of the land if they were going to be able to defend it, much less go on the offense.

The first patrol might be for orientation, but some of the corporate mercs who'd killed Federation citizens were still out there. Just because they'd run didn't mean they would not bite again if given the opportunity.

Chapter 39

65

Gracie stepped around a "squashed toilet," the name she'd given to one of the varieties of fungal-looking, well, plants, would be the closest analog, that blocked her path, and "plants" seemed more benign that "nightmare mushrooms." Her HED 2 kept out any potential smell, but from her visual cues, she could imagine a foul, rotting stench assaulting her nose.

Gracie was not a happy camper. None of them were, she thought, but she knew she pretty much hated this planet. The vegetation gave her the creeps, with the various purples, mauves, and indigoes that seemed to be prevalent. As a kid, Gracie had ridden her old Bombardier over the wide-open plains of eastern Montana, and she'd loved her family's trips to the green forests of the mountains further west into Oregon and Washington. This place was a polar opposite and seemed diseased and nasty, an abomination of nature. Brushing up against the plants sent her skin crawling, even if they never actually touched her skin. It was her imagination running wild, she knew, projecting smells and textures to the planet's vegetation, but she couldn't help what she felt, and she didn't look forward to having possibly to do a stalk through them.

A breezed picked up, and the flaps and fronds moved as if animated. The movement any time the wind blew would help the Marines if they did have to stalk, but it also made picking out an enemy sniper far more challenging.

In *Ribbon World*, the planet had been a very static, very meteorologically calm place. Kepler 9813-B was nothing like the Hollybolly planet. Convection currents kept winds fairly robust from the night side to the day side of the planet. The facts that the winds could reach upwards of 100 KPH was probably a reason that the soft-tissued plants tended to be low and ground-hugging. The tallest growth they'd seen so far was a thin stalk that extended about two meters high from a wider and lower base.

As their presence on the planet was no secret, the *Porto* had deployed some scanning drones over the station and surrounding area, and the Marines had sent out their own dragonflies. Gracie was constantly checking her readouts to see if any of those had picked up anything within range. The readouts were quiet at the moment, but that was not a guarantee that there was no one out there. Other forces had shielding that could defeat the Federation scanners.

As the leader of the patrol, she focused more on her readouts than in the surrounding area, something that was totally against her sniper training. She knew she had to trust her Marines to keep their eyes open, but that was very difficult for her. She thought she'd been a decent grunt before becoming a scout/sniper, but as she considered it, back as a PFC or lance corporal, she had a specific task to do, and she didn't have to monitor the "big picture." As a sniper, even as a SNCO, while she had to take a leadership role back in garrison, out in the field, her mission was just as tightly focused as when a lance coolie, no different from any other sniper regardless of rank. She had a specific job to do then. This leading a patrol, with all the other factors involved, was much more challenging and stressful to her.

Up ahead, a small ridge slanted off to the right. The ridge would offer eyes on the station. At 4,600 meters from the station, that was a pretty long shot for a gunman, but it was well within range of indirect fire weapons and more than a few crew-served weapons. Gracie touched her wrist screen, using her finger as a stylus, and adjusted the patrol route to climb the ridge. JC, Staff Sergeant Cezar Constaninescu, was on point, and he dutifully changed direction to follow the new route.

Gracie had served with JC twice before, and it had only been aboard the *Porto* that she found out his "JC" nickname was not from his initials, but from a boot camp label as "Julius Caesar." Master Guns Masterson's admonition to know her Marines had come back to her when she found out. She'd been making an effort to follow that since then, but sometimes, it seemed as if her personality reasserted itself.

"We've got signs here," JC passed on the patrol circuit as he reached the crest of the ridge. "I'd say two people."

Several of the plants on the planet were easily bruised, and a dark liquid beaded where they were touched, a liquid that could burn naked skin. As there weren't any multi-cellular mobile organisms on the planet, this seemed like an odd evolutionary trait, but it was fortuitous for the Marines.

Gracie called the patrol to a halt and then moved forward to where JC was waiting. He pointed down, and it was unmistakable. Gracie could see the outline of two bodies, then a trail as they left the area. She crouched where the outlines were, and she had a clear view of the station.

The plant fluid was reabsorbed within a couple of hours, basically sucked back into the body of the plant, so whoever had been observing them had been there somewhat recently. Gracie felt a slight shiver as realized they'd probably observed her patrol.

She looked back along the observers' exit trail. She contemplated tracking them down, but this was supposed to be a simple recon patrol, and they were due back in less than two hours.

Gracie reported the sign, and the captain said she'd ask the *Porto* to see if they could follow the tracks.

"Bomba, you and T-Bone set up half a dozen seisos. I want this ridge covered so if our friends come back, we'll know it."

Gracie and the rest of the patrol set up a hasty security while the two staff sergeants emplaced the tiny sensors. With a battery life of two months, that should be enough. At least Gracie hoped they'd be off the planet within that time frame.

But the fact that someone had put eyes on the station was a pretty strong indication that whomever else was on the planet was not going to simply abdicate to the Federation. Gracie knew that things could get ugly, and get ugly fast.

Chapter 40
65

Despite Gracie's misgivings, the next five days were quiet. That was five days standard, not local. Kepler 9813-B had no rotation, so no day and night. The station was located in what could be described as early evening, where the light was still bright enough to be useful and the temperature was moderate.

The *Porto* had lost the trail of the two observers on the ridge, but Gracie felt as if there were eyes on them. She was getting antsy just sitting in the station and going out on local patrols once a day. The Marines had been broken down into two sections, port and starboard, with Manny Chun taking the starboard and Gracie the port. Only one patrol was out at a time, and so that left too much time just sitting in the overcrowded station. The science types were busy trying to make sense of what was left in the station and getting their work back on track while the IS team, also broken down into two watches, provided security inside and immediately outside the station.

Gracie leaned back and gave her scalp a good scratching while she watched to see how Verry Onkle was going to react when she found out she wasn't getting the position of chief of mission. Verry was as stereotypical a bimbo as could be portrayed, but she was Gracie's secret vice. The Alliance-made series about their Explorer Corps was too far-fetched to be taken seriously, and just about everyone in the show was sleeping or trying to sleep with everyone else, but Gracie still enjoyed it. She knew there were only five more episodes left in the season, and she was contemplating giving in to Tennerife and just binge watching the rest instead of doling out one episode per day. She knew the guys might revolt if she decided to binge watch. Dutch was the only male to join Gracie and Tennerife in avidly following the drama—and he took a lot of grief for that from the others.

Of course, anyone could watch what they wanted on their PA, but the station only had one full-sized display, and watching a show was one way to be together without driving each other batty in such confined quarters.

She checked the time. This episode would be over in 12 minutes. Maybe she'd play one more before opening it up to the rest of the section.

The benefits of being a gunny! I get to decide what we watch, at least until the geeks got off duty, she told herself.

The "geeks" were a dedicated group, though, and they pretty much kept their noses into their work. One of them had told Gracie how much Allied Biologicals was paying them, and with that kind of money, Gracie would probably do the same thing. For the 180 days they were scheduled to be at the station, they'd each make more than Gracie had made so far during her entire career.

Gracie turned her attention back to Verry when the alarms went off, a raucous blaring accompanied by revolving red lights placed high on the bulkheads of each space. Gracie was up before she knew it, rushing for her helmet. The captain had ordered them to remain in their powered-down HED 2s unless in the autojets showering, which was the only time they could get out of them. With the alarm, the helmets were slapped on and the HEDs powered up. There wouldn't be waste tubes inserted for an emergency donning, but still, Gracie didn't normally like the constricting feel of the field closing in over her. In this case, adrenaline overcame any discomfort as she passed to the captain, who was out with the starboard section, what was happening.

The entire area surrounding the station was under surveillance, and despite Gracie's instinct to rush out to the rescue, she stopped at the viewscreens. On the backside of the main building, two of the IS team were rushing to another, who was down. The downed guard's bios showed he was alive, but in pain and shock. Gracie pulled up a window on the screen, and sent the recording back a minute, focusing on the downed guard. Immediately, he was back up and slowly walking his post. He came to the end and turned around. He paused for a second, and just as he started to move again, he fell to the ground, clutching his knee.

Gracie immediately knew it had been a sniper. And snipers were known to wound one person, then pick off the others who came to that person's aid.

"First Team, out with me. Take cover and keep your eyes peeled. Second, cover the entrance," she told her Marines.

She'd earlier broken down the port section into two teams. She was the team leader for First, Bomba for Second.

Within ten seconds, First Team was cycling out the main lock at the front of the main building. They'd be out of the line of fire from whomever had taken down the IS guard, but as soon as they cleared the corner, they'd be fair game—that was unless there was someone else out there on their side of the station.

Gracie was half-expecting being taken under fire as they exited, but nothing happened as they rushed to the left. Gracie halted them while they still had cover, and she was just about to move them forward when the three IS guards, two dragging the third who was writhing in pain, came around the corner.

Shaan and Dutch jumped forward to assist, and within another 20 seconds, they were back in the entrance and cycling. Gracie stared at the downed guard. The kinetic round had destroyed the knee. One of the IS guards kept telling the injured man that he was lucky, the sniper had missed a lethal shot. It hadn't been luck, Gracie knew.

Unlike the Marines, the IS guards wore the much less expensive environmental exposure suits. Like any other suit that could be worn in space, it has a self-sealing feature, so despite the damage to the knee, the suit had closed off the leg to the rest of him. His knee was gone, and he'd been exposed to 9813's atmosphere, but none of that would be fatal. Gracie wanted to get feedback from any of the sensors to determine from where the shot had been fired, but she knew that this was the act of a skilled sniper. He or she hadn't wanted to kill the man. Wounding him would take more resources to get him off-planet and back to regen, but that was secondary, Gracie thought. The shot was simply intended as a message, and whoever was sending that message didn't have to kill to do that.

Someone wanted the Federation off the planet, and the gloves had come off.

Chapter 41
65

"Farouk was my trooper, Captain, and with all due respect, you need to track down the megbast who shot him and zero the bastard," Sergeant First Class Enrico Juarez shouted, standing up and placing both fists on the table as if to emphasize his point.

The First Sergeant was the IS team commander, and he'd been steaming since his man had been shot. Farouk had been treated almost two hours ago by Dr. Williams, the Allied Biological geek who had an MD as well as multiple Ph.Ds. and served as an over-qualified corpsman, and he'd been zip-locked and put into stasis until he could be CASEVAC'd.

Gracie could tell that Captain Lysander was losing patience with the sergeant first class, but she was still maintaining her composure—for how long, however, Gracie couldn't guess.

"As I informed you, Sergeant, the CASREP has been transmitted, and we're awaiting further orders. This station was not designed as a combat outpost, as you well understand, and until we have our orders, and until we have a little better idea of what we have out there, we're staying put," the captain said.

"So we just let the meg shoot us with no response?"

"No response yet, Sergeant—*yet.*"

Gracie was vaguely aware of the FCDC cultural hierarchy. The IS branch was low man on the totem pole, being little more than federal jimmylegs, guards for Federation installations, embassies, government offices, and anywhere else where access was controlled. At one point in history, they had guarded Navy and Marine bases until the Navy essentially fired them, almost immediately followed by the Marines. Gracie figured that the sergeant first class might have chaffed at this during his career, and perhaps he pictured himself joining the Marines in direct combat action, gaining a little street cred. To be fair, though, it could just be anger at losing one of his men. From their short time together, Gracie thought the team commander was very protective of his troopers. He'd taken a shine to Gracie, too, giving her one of their nifty FCDC multitools.

Gracie didn't like to huddle inside the station, either, but she understood the hesitation of those on high who were controlling the op. Captain Lysander might be the mission commander, but she wasn't allowed a free rein. With the various players on the planet, proven and assumed, consequences of any action had to be considered.

Not that someone else hasn't already jumped over the line in the sand, Gracie thought. *First the raid, and now the sniper.*

Until Farouk was CASEVAC'd and the fragments in his knee analyzed, no one would know for sure what weapon had been used to take him down. The *Porto* had found the round's trace: it had been fired from 1,616 meters out from a spot indistinguishable from any other location surrounding the station.

Hitting a target's knee at that range was a feat of skill, but not an impossible one. Gracie was sure she could make the shot nine times out of ten, so the difficulty of the shot was not an indication of whom the sniper might be. There were enough trained snipers who left the various services in order to cash in on corporate gigs that any company could hire someone quite skilled. And if the Brotherhood was on the planet, as Intel thought, their sniper training program was very, very good.

But the *Porto* calculated that there was an 82% probability that the round was a .3005—which was the Brotherhood round of choice for their sniper teams. The fact that the round fractured upon impact was also indicative that it could be Brotherhood.

"Indicative" did not mean conclusive, however. Any weapon used by a government of man could be obtained, legally or illegally, by the corporate world.

If the enemy sniper was Brotherhood, then Gracie knew that higher-ups would be taking into consideration in what an aggressive act against that sniper could result—which Gracie, in typical Marine fashion, thought was utter bullshit. Whoever that was had already taken the first step, not the Marines, and if that person was

Brotherhood or not, he or she, or whoever had issued the orders, had to take responsibility for any subsequent actions.

Still, a good scout-sniper preferred to know the lay of the land before going out on a mission. Sun Tzu said, "Know your enemy and know yourself, and you can fight a hundred battles without disaster." That might have been first uttered more than two thousand years ago, but that didn't make it any less accurate today, and if the OK to engage was given, Gracie would like to know just who they faced.

Chapter 42

65

"Captain, we've got a hit on the seisos on Calcutta," Dutch said, turning from the console.

The seven Marines who had just sat down at the small dining table to eat turned around as one, then stood, leaving their food to gather around the makeshift command post, which was little more than a folding table shoved up against the bulkhead in the galley/common room. The Allied Biological team had insisted that the "muscle," as they referred to the Marines and IS team, didn't get in their way in the lab, so the Marines and FCDC had set up tables, making the common room even more crowded. The FCDC table hosted monitors that displayed the 22 cams they had emplaced both inside and outside the station, while the Marines' had the main comms with the ship as well as the feeds from their various scanners.

The dragonflies had been almost useless. Several of the drones had disappeared, failing to obey commands to return to the station, and the others usually showed nothing but static when a signal was even received. Gracie thought it was ironic that with all the high-tech equipment they had deployed, it was the simple, extremely old-tech seisos, which recorded the vibration of footsteps, that was giving them a hit. "Calcutta" was the ridge where Gracie had led her patrol that first day.

"Can we tell how many?" the captain asked Dutch, who had the watch while half of the Marines ate.

"Looks like three, but the AI puts that at a 54% prob."

The captain switched her throat mic, the flashing green light on the ship's comm station evidence that she was on the hook with the *Porto*.

After a few moments, she turned to the others and said, "They don't have anything concrete, but they're pretty sure there's something there. They just can't tell us what."

Having great gear meant nothing if the other side could jam or spoof it. The *Porto* was a pretty impressive piece of Federation equipment, but their opponents, be they Brotherhood or corporate, evidently had the equipment to render the *Porto* blind to them.

"So what do we do, Captain?" Manny Chun asked.

Captain Lysander hesitated only a moment before answering, "I'm taking this as a potential threat to the station's safety. As such, it is my call, and my call is that we're going to get visuals on them, and if I still deem them a threat, we're going to take them out."

There was a chorus of "ooh-rahs" from the rest as the Marines expressed their joy at finally being able to do something.

"Specialist Khan, please get Sergeant First Class Juarez," the captain told the FCDC on watch.

"And since Calcutta was in the port section's AO, Gunny Medicine Crow, your team's got it. Sorry about that, Gunny Chun."

Manny's face fell while Bomba punched Gracie's arm in excitement.

"But I'm going with you, Gunny," the captain told Gracie. "To give weapons free in case our comms are being jammed."

That put a little damper on things, but Gracie knew the captain was right. Only she had the authority to authorize action on her own, and only for self-defense. If she couldn't communicate with Gracie, she couldn't give the order to open fire.

The mission was essentially an immediate action drill that had been briefed ad nauseam. Eight minutes after receiving the seisos hit, the port section was exiting the station at the lab door, the IS team was on full alert and with four troopers outside the station, and the starboard team was suited up and ready to act as the quick reaction force.

Gracie took her team back away from Calcutta, using the station itself to keep them out of a direct line of sight for anyone on the ridge. After retreating 30 meters, the team reached a low depression that ran at a 70-degree angle away from Calcutta. It took them farther away from their target, but it allowed them to move quickly and unobserved by line-of-sight. With Bomba leading at a controlled jog, they quickly covered the 150 meters to where a fissure bisected the depression, a fissure that led to within a few hundred meters of the ridge.

Gracie never intended to approach that closely, though. She didn't have to. All she had to do was get eyes on the target and within range of any of the team's weapons. The place to do that was on a wrinkle at the fissure's lip, a weird formation where the ground puckered up a ten or twelve meters as if some cosmic deity had a little extra material when making the planet and just left it there without smoothing it out.

The bottom of the fissure was a little rough, so the going was slow. Gracie was very aware of the fact that they had mined the fissure with more seisos, and if they had, whoever was out there might have as well. Someone with ill intentions could be tracking them as they moved, ready to blast caps at them as soon as they emerged.

It took nine minutes to reach the wrinkle, 21 minutes since the initial alarm. That was good time, really good time, but it was also more than enough time for anyone setting up on the ridge to take the station under fire. Four FCDC troopers were continuing their security sweeps, in full view of anyone on the ridge. Gracie knew that Juarez, with the rest of his team ready but hidden from view, had to be having a conniption, knowing that he had four troopers sitting ducks as they projected an all-is-normal appearance to any watchers.

The wrinkle was not particularly large, and Gracie did not want to bring up the entire team. She had previously designated the three best marksmen to crawl out of the fissure and edge to where they could get eyes on the ridge: Bomba, T-Bone, and herself. She nodded to the captain, then along with the other two, pulled herself out of the fissure and started to low-crawl up the wrinkle. Gracie had dreaded crawling through the planet's vegetation, but with her eyes on the mission, she compartmentalized her disgust and ignored it. It wasn't as if this was some herculean stalk, though. Fifteen meters later, she was peering under the leaf of a plant which looked like nothing more than an oversized and droopy magenta oyster mushroom.

She pulled up her Zeises and started glassing the ridge, all in passive mode. She had the urge to laz the range, but with all the surveillance and counter-surveillance going on, she thought the laser would light up like the LED signs on Vegas to whatever sensors were trained on the area. She knew the range, anyway. From the center of the wrinkle to the high-point on the ridge was 2,108 meters. She could adjust on that if need be.

She immediately caught sight of something out of place, something big and bulky. It took a moment for her eyes to be able to make some sense of what she was seeing. Whatever it was, it was camouflaged with something akin to a Federation tarnkappe. But as with the tarnkappe, it worked best from a head-on aspect. By taking the route she'd chosen, the three Marines were at closer to a 120-degree aspect, which was more than enough to be able to see an outline of sorts.

Then there was movement. A body, also camouflaged, was exposed for the briefest of an instant right beside the larger piece of gear. The movement ceased, and the body was invisible to her. But that didn't matter. She knew where the person was.

"I've got a weapons system, probably energy, and one person at two fingers to the left of the apex," Gracie whispered.

"Roger that. I've got another, one to the left and one back," Bomba said.

The three Marines were ready to take action if an attack looked imminent, but Gracie held off. She wanted to be sure they had everyone. After another five minutes, the three agreed that there were three personnel on the ridge and one weapon. From the size and general outline, it was probably an energy weapon. The range from Calcutta to the station was too far for personal energy weapons. The Marines might not be able to breathe Kepler 9813 B's atmosphere, but it was still atmosphere, and that would dissipate energy beams. So if whoever was out there was going to use it, it had to pack a pretty powerful punch.

"Bomba, scoot back and tell the captain. Then come on back, but bring Shaan with you."

"Tibone, keep your Barrett trained on whatever kind of gun that is. If you see anything moving around it, take the shot," she told T-Bone. "But until then, hold on. I want the gunman, too."

She waited a moment, and despite her best intentions, she had to ask, "You've got your environmentals loaded, right?"

"No, Gunny. I decided I'd keep the scope set for Rio Tinto," he said, naming one of the Federation's heavy planets. "Makes it more challenging, you know."

Gracie let his sarcasm slide. She might not like the guy, but she trusted his shooting skills.

As she lay on the ground, she felt the lump of the Victor 2mm she'd taken off the pilot back on their ship. Gracie would deny that she was superstitious to her dying breath, but she did feel more comfortable with talismans around her. She knew her hog's tooth was draped around her neck, but in her HED 2's, she couldn't very well pull it out and put it between her teeth as she liked to do with each shot. The Victor, as small as it was, still had the heft and size to be felt as she lay on it.

Gracie wasn't sure why she had such a fascination with the Victor. It really wasn't that effective of a weapon. She'd jokingly told Bomba that she'd kept it because stealing an enemy's weapon was one of the four tasks a Crow warrior had to accomplish to become a War Chief. This had then led to a long discussion on the background of the Apsaalooké, but in reality, she just felt good with it in her possession.

Three minutes later, Bomba returned with Shaan, and more importantly, with the captain's OK to open fire. The fact that there was an energy weapon of some kind there was the deciding factor. Gracie knew the captain was probably dying down in the fissure, and she'd considered having Bomba bring her too, but the more Marines on the wrinkle, the more chance that they'd be spotted. Whoever was on that ridge had to know about the wrinkle and had to know it could be used as an FFP.

Gracie assigned the targets. Bomba and Shaan, armed with their Kyoceras, and Gracie, armed with her Windmoeller, would target the three individuals. T-Bone, with the Barrett, would try and take out the weapon. Gracie knew that T-Bone was not happy about not getting a kill, but the targets were predicated on the capabilities of each of their weapons.

All four Marines took a prone position, bipods deployed. No one would fire until each Marine was locked into his or her target, so they could be there for a while, and the bipods would take up the strain of their weapons.

Gracie caught a break as her target, the person beside the weapon, moved almost immediately, and Gracie had him. Whoever it was had little ability to stay still. He or she had moved three more times before Bomba said he had his target. Then they had to wait for Shaan. After eight more minutes, Gracie was about to give up on the third target, thinking he might have left the ridge. Even with a bipod, it was difficult to remain locked on a target. Her eyes were beginning to water, and she had to rapidly blink several times to clear them.

"I've got him," Shaan finally said to Gracie's relief.

"Everyone still locked on?" she asked.

At their affirmation, she said, "On my count of three, engage. One. . .two. . .three!"

On three, she smoothly squeezed the trigger. Shaan's and T-Bone's shots rang out simultaneously, followed by Bomba's and Gracie's an instant later. The crack as Bomba's and Shaan's darts broke the sound barrier sounded weird in the planet's atmosphere, but the unique environmentals had been calculated and entered into the firing solution. Over 2,100 meters was no easy shot with the smaller weapons, but each round flew true. Gracie saw her round impact on her target, destroying the integrity of whatever camouflage the man was wearing. His right hand moved a few centimeters as if trying to reach his chest before falling still.

T-Bone fired five shots, one after the other. One the fourth, a small explosion erupted from the side of the weapon. Gracie didn't see his final shot as she was quickly scanning the ridge for any movement of someone they hadn't spotted. There wasn't any.

The four Marines continued to scan for another minute before she told Shaan to get the captain. She continued to look for any signs of the enemy until the captain flopped down beside her.

"Three dead and the weapon probably put out of action. No sign of anyone else," she reported as the captain glassed the ridge.

She evidently didn't see anything either.

She brought down the glasses and said, "Good job, Gunny. I'm sending Delay back now."

Sergeant Delay had been designated the messenger. With comms continually blocked, it was back to the same way the Roman legions had to communicate over distances. Gracie didn't feel great about sending Tennerife alone like that, but they'd just cleared the route, and the captain wanted as many hands available to provide an overwatch.

"Bomba, take your team to Bravo now," Liege told the staff sergeant. "But remember, we haven't cleared any farther up the fissure."

"I'll remember," he said with a bemused tone.

He acted like he might have something else to say, but he kept it to himself and went to get his two Marines. Gracie wanted them farther up the fissure, closer to the ridge, and able to cover more of the area behind it.

As Manny took the starboard section straight up the gut, so to speak, to the ridge for the battle assessment, Gracie's section provided cover. She half-expected Manny to come under fire, but nothing happened. His section moved slowly over the rough terrain, and as they came abreast of the wrinkle, the captain changed her plans and jogged the 700 meters to join them.

When the Marines reached the ridge, they conducted a pretty thorough search. Bullpup took the cover off the weapon, and Gracie couldn't help but be impressed. She didn't recognize the model, but the engineering was unmistakable. That nasty piece of work almost assuredly had more than enough power to cause a serious hurt to the station and everyone in it.

The weapon was too big to haul back, so Manny placed something on it, and five seconds later, Gracie's binos had to struggle to dim the small star that suddenly blossomed into life. It took the toad all of 20 seconds to reduce a good part of the weapon to slag.

A few moments later, Manny turned to Gracie's direction and gave a half-assed salute. He gathered up his section and started on the way back to the station. Gracie waited until Bomba and his team reached her before she took her Marines back.

Whether the dead men on the ridge were actually going to take the station under fire or not would never be known. But what was known was that if you posed a credible threat to Marines, you were going to pay the price.

Chapter 43
66

"I never thought I'd say this, but I'm glad to be out among the fungus," Gracie told Bomba.

"You and me both. I'm about ready to commence some serious violence on the geeks."

Since the takedown of the team on Calcutta, things had been pretty quiet on Kepler 9813-B—outside of the station, that was. Inside was another story. Evidently there was a small rebellion among some of the junior scientists, and the infighting was constant. Gracie couldn't catch all of the technical gobbledygook, but it seemed that three of the scientists had issues with the direction of their research and the reports being passed up. Dr. Tantou, the chief of mission, had been very vocal about asserting his authority, and just an hour ago, he'd gotten into a pushing match with Dr. Verone, shoving her onto the common room table and knocking the captain's lunch onto the deck. Aside from the fact that Tantou might have been doing the captain a favor, considering how vile the meals were becoming, Captain Lysander was not a happy camper, and she jumped up and shoved the larger civilian up against the bulkhead. In no uncertain terms, she told the chief of mission that no one, and that included him, was to exert physical force on anyone else.

Gracie had been shocked by Tantou's action, but then she had to smother a laugh when the captain forbade the use of physical force while manhandling the chief of staff. After that, the tension refused to dissipate, though, and even grew stronger.

The Port Section was off duty, not that the Marines were actively patrolling at the moment, but off-duty in the station, unless released into the sweet embrace of sleep, was far worse than being on-duty, which was boring enough. With the simmering looks going back and forth, Gracie was about to scream out her frustration, so exercising better judgment, she'd grabbed Bomba and headed out. They didn't have a destination—just getting out of the station for an hour was what she needed.

They told Bullpup and Dylan, who along with PFC Grissom from the IS Team were manning the small security station they'd all constructed the week before, their general route and then strode off into the other-worldly vegetation.

Without a real mission, they should have remained inside the station, but things had been very quiet lately, even to the point that all jamming of comms had ceased. The consensus was that the "other side" had given up trying to disrupt the Federation mission. They'd still be out there doing their own thing, but it seemed as if they were willing to live-and-let-live. Dr. Tantou had been trying to push Captain Lysander to take offensive action against whoever was out there, but until she received such orders, the captain merely nodded her head before promptly ignoring anything further from him.

With full comms, Gracie didn't think she was taking an unreasonable risk, whereas if she'd remained inside, there was a pretty good probability that she was going to go bat-shit on someone. Taking the lesser threat to the integrity of the mission, she'd opted to go outside, ostensibly to check on the sensors in the fissure. Besides, Bomba was pretty good company. Gracie had always respected the Marine's professional accomplishments, but now that she'd worked with him, she plain out liked him as a person. Her last close male friend, one who'd moved past her inner guard, had been Zach, who was the complete opposite of her. Bomba, who was much more similar to her, was quickly becoming more than a mere teammate. How far that might go, Gracie didn't know, but for the moment, she enjoyed his company.

"You'd think they could all agree on something, at least. I mean, this is pure science, right? It either is or it isn't," Gracie passed on the P2P as she skirted a slimy-looking mauve fan. "This thing here is either a sick-looking attempt at a plant, or it's got something in its cells that can help humans. Yes or no."

"They certainly don't think so," Bomba said. "The Three Amigos seem to think their esteemed leader's got his head so far up his ass that he can't recognize what the data indicates."

"Fuck them and fuck this planet," Gracie said, more to herself than to Bomba.

"Why Gunny! I've never heard you resort to such language," Bomba said with a laugh.

"Well, fuck you, too!" she said, her mood brightening.

Bomba's good spirits had a way of rubbing off on her.

They reached the fissure and started moving up it, mindlessly wanding each sensor to make sure it was functioning. They were almost on autopilot as they chatted. Bomba had recently become interested in Gracie's life as a member of the Crow nation. First Peoples, except for Hawaiians and other Pacific Islanders, had not emigrated off-planet in huge numbers. To Gracie's knowledge, there were no planets, other than the Hipao Confederation worlds, where First Peoples made up a majority. From the Arctic Ocean to Tierra de Fuego, most First Peoples had remained on earth, close to their ancestral lands. For the Apsaalooké, that meant Montana in the USA. Gracie knew her nation's history, how they'd originally developed into a separate people in Ohio before being pushed first to Manitoba and finally to Montana. Hundreds of years had created strong roots, and Ohio and Manitoba were merely academic footnotes in history. Gracie's roots were in the plains of Montana, on the banks of the Greasy Grass.

Because too few First Peoples had emigrated, much of what others knew, or thought they knew, came from Hollybolly flicks. Much of it fell into the category of the Noble Savage, which was rather far from the truth. Gracie had to convince Bomba that they were just like anyone else, with good and bad, with noble and cretin. She wasn't sure he quite accepted that. Whenever he could, he got her to start telling him about life as a Crow, and when she did, there was just the slightest bit of awe reflecting from his eyes.

Still, he was an easy ear, and she didn't mind it. If she elevated her people a bit, glossing over some of the low points, she didn't think he'd complain.

"Have you two centered yourselves?" the captain passed on the P2P.

Their checking the sensors had been an obvious ruse, but still, Gracie felt a twinge of guilt.

"Yes, ma'am. We're fine."

"Good to hear. But as long as you're out there—and the only ones out there, I might add--I want you to check something out for me. The *Porto* picked up an anomaly at 28987-68822. Take a look, and keep your feeds live. I'm getting the rest of Port ready as the QRF, but I'm not sending them out unless needed."

"Roger that!" Gracie passed, suddenly feeling excited as she entered the position on her display.

The tribal historian Gracie disappeared in a flash as the scout-sniper Gracie snapped into place

The *Porto* was a long, long ways out in the system, and at such distances, her scanners and sensors were not as effective as had she been in orbit. They'd picked up an anomaly, as the captain had said, about 1200 clicks to their right. What the anomaly was, Gracie couldn't guess. The ship's crew didn't know, which is why it was an anomaly, after all. It could be something significant, or it could be something completely natural and benign.

The captain obviously wasn't too alarmed, or she wouldn't have sent the two of them for a look-see, but being Marines, they had to assume the worst. They were in full tactical mode as they clambered out of the fissure and started on a course to the position. Bomba had the point, but with only two of them, Gracie was two paces to his left and two behind. She had her M99 at the ready, and her Kyocera was slung over her back.

This wasn't a low-crawl stalk, but still, they moved cautiously and methodically, taking a solid 40 minutes to cover the 1200 meters. Along the way, they spotted nothing out of the ordinary, but the wind from the night-side was brisk, and the vegetation was in constant movement. Someone could have been lying in wait just off their approach and easily remained unseen.

They were less than ten meters from the position before Bomba pointed. It took a bit of mental gymnastics before her brain could register what she was seeing, but once it clicked into place, she knew that something, about two meters long, was covered with a camo-sheet. The sheet was doing an excellent job of mimicking the background, but she could pick up the outline.

The two Marines walked to about a meter away and looked up and down its length, making sure that the feedback to the station picked up everything.

"Can you tell what it is?" the captain asked.

"No, only that it doesn't belong here. It's manmade; that's for sure."

"Can you see any security?" she asked.

Gracie had been thinking the same thing, wondering if whatever it was had been boobytrapped to discourage anyone messing with it. She wished she had a better scanner than the standard HED 2 system.

"No, nothing. Can the *Porto* sense anything?"

"That's a negative. They don't. . .wait one; they're sending something now," the captain said before starting again a moment later, "With the feed, they think there might be a power source under the camo, but no combustibles."

"They think? Just great," she said, making sure to toggle that so only Bomba could hear her.

"Stand back," she told Bomba again, this time with the captain on the circuit as well.

She took four steps back, looking for a rock. She didn't want to dig around under the vegetation, but luckily, she found a two-kg one where she could easily pick it up. She hefted it a couple of time, then let it fly. It struck the object with a solid thunk before bouncing away.

Nothing blew up, so Gracie took that as a win.

"Nice tech, Gunny," the captain said. "But I'm afraid we want a little more effective data."

Gracie looked at Bomba and rolled her eyes.

What now? she wondered.

Then a glimmer of an idea hit her. She stepped up to the object again, motioning Bomba to stay back. Each HED 2 had numerous tie-down straps that connected to bands around various sections of the wearer's body. Gracie pulled out the right hip strap, extended it to its full two meters. She carefully attached the end clamp on the corner of the camo-sheet, then crept back until the strap was almost taut. She lay down, and before she could give herself a real reason not to take such a stupid risk, she gave into her curiosity and pulled the strap. The camo-sheet fell off, revealing. . .

"It's a friggin Palomino!" Gracie shouted, jumping to her feet.

As a kid back at home, Gracie had roamed the prairies for miles on her Bombardier Calgary-3. It had been a sturdy workhorse, and she'd loved the freedom it gave her. The hoverbike could get her into and out of trouble as she willed.

The WCD Palomino that stood proudly before her was more than a few rungs up the ladder than her poor Calgary-3. The Palomino was a rich boy's toy, but not a slouch when considering performance. It was sleek, fast, could go over almost any terrain, and very, very sexy.

This one almost looked right off the shelf. Some Palominos were the standard tan and gold, but others had the camo-pattern that supposedly meant the owners actually took them into rough country and not just down to the local BestMart. They were made in the Alliance of Free States, and with the tariff, they were even more of a status symbol on Earth and, she assumed, the rest of the Federation.

There was a small box attached to the handlebars, which the captain was now telling her the *Porto* identified it as a standard, if illegal in most of human space, masking system.

"Pretty machine," Bomba said as they stood looking at it.

"That's about a year's worth of a staff sergeant's pay," Gracie told him.

"Well, someone left it here, someone who's out there right now," he said, looking around.

Which was, of course, correct. Someone had driven it there for a purpose, and the only purpose that could be was to put eyes on the station at the least. And Gracie and Bomba had not been stealthy in reaching the bike, so. . .

Gracie felt an immediate itch between her shoulder blades. She instantly knew that someone had eyes on them. She could feel the crosshairs centered on her chest.

She lunged for the bike, jumping on the seat.

"Get on," she shouted.

She hit the starter, which not surprisingly, failed to work. But even if Gracie had only seen a Palomino once before, she knew about them, and like all hoverbikes, they had a law enforcement override. Marines didn't have those overrides, but FCDC troopers did, and Gracie just happened to have one.

She grabbed the multitool Juarez and given her from her belt, whipped out the override, and hit the start once more. Expecting to feel a round explode into her at any instant, she gave a sigh of relief as the motor purred to life.

"Hold on," she shouted over her shoulder as she gunned the bike.

As the bike leaped forward, Bomba almost fell off, and he clutched at Gracie to keep on. One hand went around her waist; the other grabbed her left breast—which through the HED 2 hardly constituted copping a feel, but it was immediately released and his hand lowered to her belly.

Gracie grinned, but she wasn't sure if that was because she knew despite the urgency of the situation, nice-guy Bomba had been embarrassed, and she'd give him some serious grief later, or simply because the Palomino was such a fine machine. Probably a bit of both.

They shot forward, the bike reading the ground, making the ride as smooth as if on a highway. Gracie swerved a hard right, telling herself she was throwing off anyone trying to acquire them as a target, but reveling in the bike's pure power and responsiveness. She swerved back to the left as Bombay squeezed her tight.

They were only about 1500 meters from the station, and the Palomino took less than a minute to make the trip. Over rough ground, that was pretty amazing, all the more so that Gracie wasn't even used to the feel of the bike. Gracie wasn't done yet—she didn't want to be done.

"We're coming in hot!" she passed on the open circuit to let the IS team and the two snipers on duty know they were inbound.

She roared around the station, leaning hard to make the turn as fast and as tight as she could. Bomba finally lost his grip and tumbled off the back. Without his weight, the bike surged forward, and Gracie almost lost it. Regretfully, she brought the bike to a halt, and with a pat on the fuel cell tank, swung her legs off it.

Bomba limped up, rubbing his ass and with a rueful smile on his face.

"Someone's going to have a long walk back," he said. "Now I'm sort of wishing it had been me doing the walking."

"Oh, you loved it, Staff Sergeant. You know that," she said.

"Yeah, I guess I did. Take away that gracious fall back there, and that was a pretty hellacious ride. Do you think we were being targeted?"

"If this was my ride, I'd target anyone trying to steal it, so yeah, I think we could have been."

"Uh, Gunnery Sergeant Medicine Crow, if you'd like to leave your toy and come on inside, we need to have a few words," Captain Lysander passed on the net.

"Wow. Sucks to be you, Gunny," Bomba said.

"Comes with the territory," she responded. "How about you push this baby up to the security post while I go attend to the captain. Tell them to shoot anyone who tries to come and take it."

Gracie's heart was racing, and she felt on top of the world. She had a royal ass-chewing coming, but it had been worth it.

What was the captain going to do? Shave her head and send her to some poisonous ribbon world?

Chapter 44

66

It took two days, but the captain finally relented. Since no one came a'knocking at the station's front hatch claiming ownership, the Palomino was reported as "abandoned property under Federation jurisdiction." She instituted some pretty stringent guidelines: two riders at all times, and never exceeding 1,000 meters from the station, which put a pretty big crimp in the monster bike's capabilities, but it was better than nothing. Within another day, everyone in the station, Marine, FCDC, and geek alike, had taken a test ride. Captain Lysander had at first demurred, but even she couldn't resist, and when she and Gracie came back from their ride, her face had been flushed with excitement.

With the tension inside the station and the lack of action outside of it, the Palomino had been a nice morale-boosting break, something that lasted all of five days when they received a mission order. Any action was better than no action, but this was not the type of mission that excited anyone.

They had known from shortly after landing on the planet that there was another installation of some sort 2,000 klicks to their planetary north. It didn't take a genius to figure out that was probably a clandestine research station, probably corporate, but possibly from a foreign government. The Marines' mission was to protect the Federation station, however, not to arrest any interlopers—at least that was what their mission had been. Mission creep had reared its ugly head, and they were now supposed to shut down that other installation and arrest whoever was there.

Technically, the Marines could not arrest anyone. The restrictions concerning *posse comitatus* and the military were a long accepted and vital component to the conduct of the Navy and Marines. But the FCDC was not military despite being organized and run like an army, and it had the power of arrest and detainment.

So for this mission, a five-man IS team would be the focus of the mission with the Marines providing security in case those being arrested took offense to that. Sergeant First Class Juarez was about beside himself with excitement, giving Captain Lysander what could be construed as orders, orders she studiously ignored. The troopers were there to make the actual arrests, but she was not going to give up any authority to a fuckdick sergeant first class.

The *Porto* had come back into a far planet orbit to launch one of her two shuttles. Two thousand klicks were just too far to travel overland, even if they had ground vehicles. As they waited for the shuttle to land, Gracie conducted a final inspection of her Marines. All of the scout-snipers were hard-charging, highly motivated and accomplished devil dogs, but as with many elite units, they tended to slack off a bit when tasked with straight-leg infantry missions. At least, that was what Gracie had experienced in her career. Every one of them was an infantry Marine and had served as such, but even for Tennerife, who had been a sniper for the least amount of time, it had been four years since she'd served as a regular grunt.

"You know this is because of AB," Saanvi Veer said, sipping her tea as she watched Gracie inspect Bomba.

Gracie looked up at the scientist, wondering what she meant.

Dr. Veer must have recognized the questioning look, so she added, "Whoever is out there must be reaching a breakthrough, so the AB board wants them stopped. We're at loggerheads here, and they can't allow someone else to push ahead of us."

Gracie wrinkled her eyebrows and looked back at Bomba, who merely shrugged. Allied Biologicals had pull, to be sure. The mere fact that the Marines were supporting the science mission was proof of that. But Gracie had assumed that "AB," as the geeks referred to their employer, was merely a tool being used by the Federation. She never considered that the tool might be wielding the power. She had to admit, though, that what the good doctor was saying made sense.

Corporate power within the Federation structure had diminished following the Evolution, but Gracie wasn't naïve enough to believe it had been curtailed. Money talks, as the saying went, a truism that had affected governments going back to Mesopotamia.

"Don't let yourself become lackeys," Saanvi said before turning and heading back to the lab.

Gracie frowned as she completed her inspection. She didn't think they were lackeys. They were United Federation Marines, after all. But if this mission was merely to squash competition, did Veer have a point? Were they really just corporate jimmylegs in Federation uniforms?

She didn't like that train of thought and was grateful when the shuttle landed a few minutes later. She focused on the mission itself, not on the reasoning behind it.

The mission itself was anti-climatic. There was no resistance at from the Jindal-Fergusson crew, who readily admitted working for the giant conglomerate. The 15 lab rats were all Confederation citizens, but Jindal-Fergusson was a galaxy-wide company, with offices and assets within the Federation. If—when—they were found guilty of trespassing, corporate espionage, and whatever else the Justice Department threw at them, the Federation would be able to easily take action against them.

Dr. Tantou and his sidekick Dr. Polonov had accompanied the mission as well, and while SFC Juarez and his team processed the prisoners, they two geeks went through the J-F lab, confiscating data discs, papers, equipment, and more than a few samples.

Gracie's Marines conducted a thorough search of the installation, which was smaller than their own station, but big enough to house quite a bit of gear. Shaan found a closet that served as an armory, and as Gracie and Captain Lysander examined the cache, complete with small arms and longer-range weapons, including a 15 mega-joule hadron beam projector similar to the weapon destroyed on Calcutta, Gracie kept thinking that none of the prisoners had that mercenary air about them. She was pretty sure that there were some operators roaming around who had not been arrested in the sweep.

She felt better when all of the weapons were loaded aboard the shuttle along with the prisoners and everything else confiscated. As the shuttle pilot lifted off to return them to the station and to take the prisoners up to the ship, she wondered who'd been left behind, and what those people might do now that their employers were gone.

Chapter 45
66

Two days after the capture of the J-F lab, the captain and Manny Chun led another raid on a small installation 500 klicks to the south and just at the twilight line at the edge of eternal night. The three bodies there had suicided with brain wipes just minutes before the Marines and the IS team broke into their small, shielded shelter—there'd be no chance of a resurrection for any of them. Some of their equipment was Brotherhood, but not enough to make a declarative statement as to their origin one way or the other. Their DNA was scanned and forwarded, but if they were from the Brotherhood PHM or another high-level security organization, there would be no record in any public data base that they ever existed.

The aggressive nature of their recent efforts bothered Gracie. This was not a war zone, at least officially. And Saanvi Veer's words had begun to weigh heavily in her thoughts. Gracie did not join the Marines to bolster some company's bottom line but to protect Federation citizens. She bit her tongue, though, and said nothing. In such close quarters, discord could quickly escalate into a bad situation.

She did discuss the situation with Bomba, however, and she was relieved that his feelings and thoughts reflected hers. At least she wasn't alone.

The two of them were in the bunkroom, sitting across from each other, knees almost touching in the cramped quarters, discussing whether there would be pushback to their recent actions when that question was answered. The alarms went off as an explosion rocked the station. The two Marines pulled on the ever-present masks hanging from their belts and dashed out into the common room.

Smoke was pouring from the lab, and the geeks were stumbling out. Two of the idiots didn't even have their masks, and

Tennerife was helping one of the coughing scientists with an emergency hood. Gracie almost tackled the second geek, pulling him to the wall and throwing another hood over his head.

The red flashing light switched to yellow as the klaxon shifted to a slightly more tolerable chiming.

"Is there anyone else in there?" she asked Dr. Tantou, who looked dazed.

He did a quick headcount, then shook his head no.

"I want all of you in full enviro-suits," she told him. "Now."

"Dutch, get a hold of the captain, then stay here with the g. . .science team. Tibone, take Shaan, Tenner, and those three," she said, pointing to three IS team troopers who had rushed in, "and get weaponed up. This could be a diversion. If it is, weapons free.

"Bomba, JC, and Spig, full HED 2s. We need to assess the damage."

Several of the scientists sat down in shock, but the Marines and the troopers rushed to comply.

"I can't raise the captain," Dutch said.

"Keep trying."

Within a minute, Gracie and the three other Marines were opening the lab door. The yellow light indicated that there was no longer an active breach, but still, Gracie was relieved when there wasn't a rush of air in or out of the lab.

The main lab was full of smoke that hung about eye-level, but there didn't seem to be much in the way of damage. Flickering lights in the bio-cell were a good indication that the main damage was in there.

Weapons drawn, the four, using their best room-to-room techniques, entered the room. It was a mess. Debris littered the deck, but what caught their eyes was the meter-wide gap in the walls. Light from Kepler 9813 streamed into the room. The warning light remained a steady yellow—the room had been contaminated, but the breach had self-sealed.

"Gracie, look at this," Bomba said, toeing a fin assembly that lay up against some cabinets.

The four-finned, ten-centimeter-long assembly told the story. Someone had hit the station with the rocket, blowing a hole in the wall of the bio-cell and exploding inside. The station's damage control system had almost immediately covered the breach with its life-support field.

Gracie didn't recognize the make of the rocket, but comparing it with Federation munitions, it probably had a range of 12 klicks or so.

"Gunny, I finally got through to the captain. They're inbound, and she says Alert Condition Alpha but to stay in place until she gets back," Dutch passed over the circuit.

Gracie and Bomba had just been discussing that the reaction might be to their rounding up other installations. She guessed she had that answer now.

Chapter 46
66

"I've got it at 4,565 meters," Dutch told Gracie.

> *Shit. That's too far.*

The station had been hit five more times since the first rocket strike. The lab itself had been abandoned, and everyone while in the station was in the common room and suited up 100% of the time. The captain had tried to get the geeks off the planet, but that request had been denied. Whether that was an Allied Biologicals or Federation call, Gracie didn't know.

The *Porto* was still out in the far reaches of the system somewhere. The captain had requested she take a synchronous orbit overhead to be able to provide her superior fire support, but once again, that request was turned down. At least Gracie understood the reasoning behind that. It had become more apparent that there was another man-of-war in the system, probably Brotherhood, and any ship taking station over the planet opened herself up to a pretty significant risk.

The captain had immediately sent out her scout-sniper teams in a cordon around the station, but they'd had little effect. The incoming was fired from eight or nine kilometers out, and with the captain keeping the teams no further than three klicks from the station, the ranges were just too great. Both T-Bone and Brooke had tried to engage targets at almost five klicks, but without effect.

Now, Dutch and Gracie had activity, but out of range. Three men were manhandling a launcher up a small slope. They were in bulky suits, which was impeding their progress, but within five minutes, ten at the most, they should be in position to fire at the station.

Gracie wasn't sure how they'd arrived in the area. She couldn't see any signs of a vehicle, and if they had one, she didn't think they'd be physically pushing the launcher up the slope.

Jonathan P. Brazee

"Call T-bone and see if he's got eyes on them," she told Dutch.

She only half-listened in while she kept her Miller on the targets. Her finger ached to squeeze the trigger, but she knew that would be a mistake.

"That's a negative, Gunny. They can't even see the bad guys."

There goes that option.

The Barrett could throw a round that far, even out to about six klicks, but without much in the way of accuracy. Tiny inconsistencies in the round, coupled with simple chaos theory, made hitting a target at such distances all but impossible. Barretts had been at the leading edge of range for kinetic small arms for the last five or six hundred years, and the W series was the best Barrett yet, but no matter improvements in the weapons, distance was still a cruel master. The current record was an amazing 4,188-meter shot taken by Staff Guard Master Henriks Smith of the New Budapest Army, a record that had stood for almost 49 years.

Gracie contemplated making a quick stalk, trying to close the distance. There was a depression about a klick in front of her, and at 3,500 meters, she might be able to take them out. But she'd almost have to run across the intervening distance, an open terrain which wouldn't give her much in the way of cover.

"You might as well take the shot, Gunny," Dutch said.

"It's too far."

"If you don't hit them, at least you might make them abandon their position."

"Only to pop up somewhere else."

"Sure, Gunny, but if we don't do anything, they're sure-as-shit gonna fire a couple of them bad boys at the station. Eventually, one of them is gonna seeing-eye it into the common room, and we'll have dead geeks to clean up."

He was right, she knew. Her mind started churning with a firing solution. Forty-five-hundred meters just wasn't programmed into the scope's AI. Bullet drop and all the other factors were magnified as the round slowed down. Then again, without planetary rotation, firing on Kepler 9813 B was easier in some aspects. Wind might gust, but it was generally from one main direction to another, nightside to dayside. She started feeling a little excited as she thought about it. Forty-five-sixty-five. That would be a feather in her cap.

"What's the longest you've done?"

"What, on a live target? Three-seven-oh-three. On Duluth 3," she said.

"No, I mean any shot. Like on a range. I know you, and I know you've tried."

Of course, I've tried. All snipers had tried.

"On Tarawa. Halstone Impact Area, range 612. I hit a stationary target at 4,245 meters."

"So this isn't much more than that," Dutch said matter-of-factly as if pointing out the obvious.

"Yes it is, and that was with a stationary target and known variables. And it took me three shots to walk it in. In case you haven't noticed, those are walking targets out there."

But Gracie had already decided. She was going to take the shot.

"Not walking fast, pushing that thing," Dutch said.

Gracie switched her scope AI to manual and started entering data. She threw out Coriolis and rotational drift, but kept in spin drift, backing off a bit as the round's rotation would slow down. That could introduce some wobble, which would make the drop even greater as it got closer to the targets. The factors affecting the trajectory banged around inside her brain pan, and in the end, she applied a hefty amount of Kentucky windage.

"You've got your wish, Sergeant. I'm taking the shot."

"I knew it," Dutch said, excitement in his voice. "I knew you couldn't resist."

"You just keep your eyes peeled and give me any corrections."

Her hand automatically went to her throat to pull out her Hog's Tooth. Being in her HED 2 nixed that, and Gracie frowned. She knew she didn't need it, but just as her famous ancestor War Chief Joe Medicine Crow went into battle during WWII with a sacred eagle feather under his helmet, she would have felt a lot better with the tooth in her mouth.

You have it Crow. Just around your neck. Same thing.

She selected the lead man, the one pulling the launcher as her target. If she managed to get him, maybe the launcher would roll back and crush the other two pushing it. She put the crosshairs directly on his shoulder, then led him by about half a meter. If she'd calculated correctly, the round would impact about five seconds later, taking him down.

Easy peasy.

"You ready?" she asked Dutch, not taking her eyes off her scope.

"Good to go."

Gracie took in a deep breath, then let half of it out, willing her pulse to slow down. She slowly squeezed the trigger, and was almost surprised when the round went off. The big gun kicked against her shoulder, and when Gracie re-acquired the sight picture, the round hadn't even covered half of the distance, its vapor trail mapping the trace. It might have been something in the planet's atmosphere, or it might have been Gracie's hyped senses, but she thought it was the most vivid vapor trail she'd ever seen—and it immediately let her know she was going to miss.

"Left one, up four," Dutch said from beside her. "Meters."

Four meters high was a huge miss, even considering the range. She'd given too much weight to the drop, and she'd ruined her chance of a kill.

Except she hadn't.

When the round hit high on the slope, almost at the top, a puff of dirt marking the spot, the lead man jerked to a stop, then looked around. The two pushing the launcher ran it up his legs, and he turned back to yell something at them. Gracie figured he was telling them they were under fire, but after a moment, he put the strap around his shoulders and started pulling the launcher again.

"I don't fucking believe it," Dutch said in wonderment. "They're still at it."

Gracie couldn't believe it, either. She'd be diving for cover if someone was firing at them.

"Adjusting," she said.

Down four, not so much lead. Easy, easy, squeeeeeze. . .

The round went off, and as she picked up the vapor trail, a thrill ran through her. She might have pulled off the impossible. The trail rose, then started the graceful curve back to her target.

But she missed again.

"Low, half a meter, right one," Dutch said.

She'd hit just below the man and a step back, under the launcher.

This time, the man jumped, stopped, and looked back. He pointed right where the round had hit, his posture looking like he was questioning them. One of the pushers stepped around from the back of the launcher and looked to where the first guy was pointing.

Gracie hastily cycled another round. She was going to nail one of them before they could run, and if not that, she'd try and take the launcher out of action.

"Amazing," Dutch said.

Gracie was trying to rush the shot, so it took a second to register. They weren't running. The pusher reached down to finger about where the round impacted, then stood up and shrugged. He stepped back into position, and once again, they started back up the hill.

"Un-fricken-believable," Gracie muttered.

A wave of calm swept over her. She felt destined. The yobos up there had been given every opportunity to get the hell out of Dodge, and if they refused the invitation being presented to them on a golden platter, who was she to let them off the hook?

Without over-thinking things, she let instinct take over, adjusted her sight picture slightly up and slightly forward. She squeezed the trigger, felt the kick against her shoulder, and was already cycling the next round when her target spun around and fell to the ground.

"Hit!" Dutch screamed. "A mother-fucking hit!"

The nearest pusher, the one who'd come forward to examine where her second round had impacted, had just looked up, giving Gracie a full countenance, when her round hit him square in the chest. It looked almost as if the top half of his torso had come off as he flopped over backward, falling on the third man, who looked up in horror and confusion.

That look lasted for only a second as he took off like a Montana jackrabbit, bounding directly down the slope, not taking the same path as they'd been pushing the launcher. Gracie snapped off two rounds at him, but she wasn't even sure she'd come close. He disappeared from sight, running too well to have been hit.

Gracie brushed off the minor disappointment, her mind numb with what she'd just done.

Dutch was on his back, legs kicking the air in excitement like an overturned cockroach.

"Oh my sweet Glynis, I've never seen shooting like that!" he said, rolling over to slap Gracie on the shoulder. "Copacetic to the max, Gunny! To the max!"

Gracie wasn't done, though.

"Back on your glasses," she said.

Slowly and methodically, she fired five more rounds, three of them hitting the launcher. It looked pretty slagged, and after seeing Dutch's begging puppy-dog eyes, she let him take four shots of his own. The last one could have possibly come within a meter of the launcher, but spotting through his glasses, she told him it was a direct hit.

"Report it in," she told Dutch.

Act like you've been there before, she kept telling herself as the excited Dutch threatened to envelop her with his enthusiasm.

Still, it was pretty difficult. She was walking on air. Four-thousand-five-hundred-and-sixty-five meters. That was a helluva shot!

Chapter 47

68

Deledriay and Lum each held an arm of the limp body of Vicky Espinoza as they dragged her in through the front hatch. Vicky was face up, her head, or what was left of it, hanging down, leaving a trail of blood and brain matter dripping onto the white deck. It took Gracie only a single look to know this was a kill shot. Vicky was gone for good with no chance at a resurrection. Juarez rushed to help, cradling his trooper's head tenderly as they laid her on the table.

"No POO,[28] but I've got an azimuth of 290," Dutch said, back on the sensor array.

The mission was limited with regard to their sensors. With the *Porto* so far out, she wasn't much help, and most of the Marine's organic sensors had either failed, been jammed, or knocked out. The *Porto* had left three of their Eagle Eyes in orbit, but other than locating some installations, the surveillance satellites had been surprisingly ineffectual. Gracie thought they were lucky that one of their remaining dragonflies had managed to pick up the trace of the round that had ended Corporal Espinoza's life.

Captain Lysander stood over Dutch, looking at the map taped up on the bulkhead. She reached up and ran her finger along a rough 290 degrees azimuth away from the station.

"Right there, that's where I would be," she said, pointing at a slight rise about 1700 meters away.

That would be the textbook firing position, Gracie agreed—which was why she disagreed with the captain. She was pretty sure whoever had taken the shot was a skilled sniper, and someone that skilled wouldn't be following Sniper Firing Positions 101.

---

[28] POO: Point of Origin

Jonathan P. Brazee

"Captain!" Sergeant First Class Juarez shouted out from where he was standing over Espinoza's body. "What are you going to do about this?"

His face was red, and he was breathing heavily. Shaan and Spig each took a step closer to the captain as if they thought Juarez was going to attack her.

Captain Lysander slowly turned to look at the IS Team leader, then simply said, "We're going to kill the bastard."

Chapter 48

68

Twenty minutes later, eight teams slid out the escape hatch on the southeast side of the building. The shot that had killed Corporal Espinoza had come from the other side of the station, so this gave them a chance to get out and under cover while unseen—provided there were not more than one of them, or that the sniper had not moved quickly to another vantage point. All 16 Marines, though, made it out and into the vegetation. Each team had its own corridor in which to move, and two teams were to take overwatch positions close to the station, but other than that, the other six teams were on their own.

Gracie was ready for a long stalk. She didn't know where the opposing sniper was or if he was even still in the area, but it was going to take a while to find out.

She and Dutch were basically going up the gut. They had to circle around the station, then start forward. If the enemy sniper were still in his position, then she and Dutch would be the most exposed. The slightest mistake and they'd be spotted.

The foundation upon which the station sat gave them a degree of cover, so the two were able to scoot around fairly quickly until they were abreast of the main building. Then Gracie signaled Dutch that it was low-crawl time. She adjusted her elbow and knee pads, and the two commenced their stalk. She knew that for the next 120 meters, their stalk would be relatively easy. The ground was covered with the toilet seats, whose broad fans completely concealed the ground. Unless they got too high or rubbed up against any of the central stalks, they should remain out of sight of any observer. After that, things would get more problematic, and she'd decide what to do then.

The two Marines had barely moved forward ten meters when the muffled report of a shot reached them under the toilet seats.

Gracie froze, adjusting the contrast of her display to see what had happened.

Hell! Brooke's hit!

Brooke and Rez were on the other side of the station, not even into their stalk yet. They shouldn't be visible to anyone from their position, but Brooke was hit in the leg. Gracie waited for a moment to see if her avatar was going to gray out, but it mercifully stayed a light blue. Unlike the bulkier enviro suits the troopers wore, the HED 2s did not have the same degree of ability to close off breaches, and as they were designed for hazardous environments, if the damage done was great enough, the suites attempted to save the life of the wearer by killing him or her. The theory was that exposure in a toxic environment could be more damaging and decrease the likelihood of a successful resurrection and regeneration, so stopping all bodily functions kept the poisons from contaminating the body.

That was all well and good in theory, but even without further complications and not considering whatever damage a body had sustained, resurrection still had a 3% failure rate just from the process itself. It was better never to die in the first place.

"Francisco, get Mahmout back to the station. The rest of you, keep your friggin' heads down!" the captain passed on the command circuit.

Gracie looked back and caught Dutch's eyes. He shrugged, and the two started moving forward again. Gracie didn't know what mistake Brooke had made, but she was lucky only to be hit in the leg.

It was easy to get into a mind-numbing routine: reach out with her arms and one knee, pull and push forward, repeat as needed. But any routine became dangerous. She had to keep her mind sharp.

Another shot rang out, but no one was hit. For a sniper who had shown skill in Espinoza's head shot, he had now racked up a hit in a leg and a miss. Maybe the head shot had been luck. That gave Gracie a little more confidence—not enough to relax or take chances, but still, it was a welcomed thought.

That warm and fuzzy came crashing down when the report of a third shot reached them. This time, the avatar when immediately gray. It was Spig McConnaughy.

"Spig's dead!" T-Bone passed. "Head shot! I don't think he can be brought back! We're still under cover, and there's no way we were spotted!"

"All teams halt!" the captain passed. "Freeze in place."

Gracie and Dutch had only moved forward 60 meters or so. They were still under the heavy fans of the toilet bowls, so she knew they were out of visuals. At a sudden suspicion, she toggled her display, then looked at Dutch. His HED 2 matched the ambient temperature perfectly, and he was putting out no electronic emissions.

"Check my temp," she told him.

A few moments later, he gave her a thumbs up, and she let herself relax as she realized they were not giving off a temperature gradient. So she was surprised when a round pierced the toilet bowls to hit the dirt between Dutch and her. She immediately rolled to her right, stopping on her back just short of a particularly large plant. Dutch had rolled left and was on his stomach, hugging the dirt. He looked over to her with not quite fright, but certainly concern in his eyes.

"Stay still," she mouthed at him.

One of them must have touched one of the plants, making it move, and the enemy sniper was probing the brush by fire. If she could only look forward, she might be able to spot him as he fired again.

She was looking at Dutch when the next round tore into his back at shoulder level. He didn't make a sound as his avatar grayed out.

"All teams, immediate retrograde to the station. Do not continue!" the captain passed.

"Bullshit, Captain! I'm going to get that asshole," T-Bone passed, anger flaring in his voice.

"That's a negative, Staff Sergeant Mubotono. You will return to the station."

"We can't back down!"

"That's an order. Return to the station!"

Gracie didn't listen to see what T-Bone would say. She scooted over to grab Dutch's harness and started to drag him back, expecting to feel the hot touch of a round at any moment. But it didn't come for her. It came for Bullpup Kneffer; it came for Marc Piccolo, but not for her. Twenty minutes later, she was struggling to dash to the entrance. Spec Potter ran out to help her with Dutch, and between them, they got him back inside the station.

It was a shocked group of Marines that straggled in. Two of them were WIA. Three were KIA, with Spig almost certainly beyond resurrection. Dr. Williams thought Dutch would make it, but with his spine shattered, he'd have a long, long time in regen, and spines were tricky about reaching a full recovery.

"What happened?" Bomba asked Gracie as they watched Dr. Williams send Dutch into stasis.

Gracie wasn't sure what had happened, but she relayed to him the details the best that she could. She was trying to figure out what had given them away.

"Gunny Chun, Gunny Medicine Crow, to me," the captain said once the dead and wounded were tended.

"What the hell happened out there?" she asked them, her eyes blazing.

"Whoever it is, he knew where we were," Gracie said. "We were out of sight, and I just checked Dutch for a temperature gradient right before he engaged us."

"Then how the hell could he spot you? You must have made a mistake!"

"CO_2, ma'am. I think it was CO_2," Bomba said, breaking into the conversation.

"What?"

"Gunny Medicine Crow said she was on her back, but Dutch was on his stomach, so why did he get targeted and not her? I think it's because our CO_2 waste vents are here," he said, reaching his arm around to point at the small vortex valve at the small of his back. "We're pumping out CO_2 with every breath. We're recovering some of that O_2 with the splitter unit on our back, of course, but not all of it, and that excess gets vented."

"And here on this planet, with its screwed-up atmosphere, that would stand out like a neon plume, if you have the right kind of scanner. I think he might be right, Captain," Manny said.

The captain furrowed her brow as she digested that, then seemed to accept the statement.

"If that's true, then how do we deal with it? It's not like we can go out without our HEDs, and even if we could, we're still breathing out CO_2."

"The IS Team's suits don't vent," Manny said.

"You want to do a stalk in those?" Gracie asked him.

"Well, no, but what other options do we have?"

"The emergency hoods don't vent, either, but those would be almost as bad to fight in. And they've got limited comms," the captain said.

"Maybe I've got an answer, ma'am," Bomba said. "But I'd need a bit of time to work it out. Can you give me 30 minutes?"

The captain looked at the two gunnies, who offered nothing, so she said, "You've got them."

Bomba took his leave, then grabbed JC and pulled him into the supply closet.

"I hope he's got something," the captain remarked.

"We could always cut and run, you know, call in the shuttle," Manny hesitantly offered.

"Marines don't run," the captain said automatically before softening her tone, "but if we can't figure this out, we might have to consider it. I'm not going to get everyone killed for some bio-patent."

Gracie knew how hard that was for an officer to say. This wasn't the old Federation, where officers who surrendered were executed, but it would be a career-ending move, and even being the daughter of the late great General Lysander wouldn't be enough to save her.

Gracie stepped back to check on the wounded. Dr. Williams had things well in hand and had done the most that could be done for them here at the station.

"Someone knows his shit, huh, Gunny?" Shaan quietly asked her as they both watched him finish up with Bill.

Gracie knew he was referring to the sniper, not the doctor.

"Just like we do."

"Do you think he could be a Memitim?" he asked with a concerned tone.

"What makes you think that?" she asked, turning to look at the sergeant with a frown.

"You know, like how he, how he, you know, without seeing where any of us were."

The Memitim were the shadowy enforcers of the will of the Brotherhood First Brother. Supposedly part sniper, part ninja, part assassin, they were culturally popular threads of the human tapestry, even if Gracie was sure that the flick-makers and novelists were exaggerating their capabilities. They were supposedly quite skilled, but so were Federation snipers.

According to ancient Abrahamic lore, the memitim were a type of angel who killed those who had fallen out of the protection of their guardian angels. They were God's enforcers. Gracie didn't buy the almost supernatural aspects some people projected onto the modern Memitim, but that didn't mean she discounted their abilities. If that was a Memitim out there, then Bomba's CO_2 theory held more sway with her than any of their fictional abilities.

"It doesn't matter who he—or she—is. We're Marines, and people fear us, too—and for good reason."

T-Bone' ears perked up when he heard the word "Memitim."

"You think it might be one of them?" he asked Gracie.

"Could be. Or maybe not. Don't care much one way or the other."

Gracie did care, but only with regards to knowing her enemy. If that was one of the Brotherhood's best out there, she needed to know that to face him. But she didn't want to start something that could sap the will of any of them, so she refused to react overtly to the possibility.

"Have you ever faced a Memitim?" he persisted.

"Yeah, right. In all the Federation-Brotherhood wars over the last 25 years, sure."

The fact that the Federation and the Brotherhood had never been officially at war in their histories seemed to fly her sarcasm right over his head.

"So the great Gunnery Sergeant Gracie Crow, the holder of the record for the longest kill in history now, hasn't managed that feat," he said, his eyes alight with, what, a challenge? "And if I did, if I zeroed one, what would you say?"

"Look, Staff Sergeant Mubotono," she said, putting a little steel in her voice, "this is not a competition. If you nail that guy out there, I'll shake your hand and congratulate you. But remember, we're a team, and we work as a team."

"Oh, sure, Gunny. A team. But every team has a captain," he said before stalking off.

"What's got him all riled?" Shaan asked.

Gracie was tempted to chase T-Bone down and ask him the same thing, but there were more important things on her mind, so she let him go. Instead, she went to the supply closet and opened the door.

"What the heck?" she asked as she took in the sight of Bomba kneeling in front of JC.

The scene took her by surprise, and for an instant, she thought she'd broken in on a rather disappointing intimate moment before her mind registered that both were still in their HED 2s, and Bomba was wrapping duct tape around JC's waist. Hanging from just above JC's butt was a lump of something now covered with the same silver tape.

Bomba looked up with a smile and said, "I think it might work!"

"What in Mother Earth are you doing?" she asked, perplexed.

"The scrubbers. For the air in the station. We've got a year's supply here. I'm just hooking them into JC's ass and using the duct tape to make sure it stays there. There's some leakage, sure, but I think most of the CO_2 is making it into the scrubbers."

"Not to mention if I fart!" JC said. "I think it scrubs rotten eggs, too."

"I told you, that's not in the same place. The CO_2 is coming out of this little vent that takes it through the bubble. Your farts, they're still inside of your suit, especially since I had to kind of tape over that other vent to make the scrubbers vent."

JC rolled his eyes at Gracie and tried, unsuccessfully, to smother a laugh that Bomba didn't seem to notice.

"Do you think it'll work?" she asked Bomba.

"Yeah, I think so. We'll want to test it, first, but yeah."

Gracie waited until Bomba was satisfied, then she followed the two Marines out and back to the common room. Despite the bodies in stasis, despite their losses, the gathered Marines, troopers, and even Dr. Williams broke out into laughs. Even Gracie joined in. JC had to waddle slightly when he walked, and he looked like a baby who'd taken a dump in his diapers.

The captain stifled a smile as she asked Bomba to explain his contraption, and when he was done, she'd agreed they had to test it. One of the geeks ran into the lab for a piece of testing equipment, assuring the captain that it would pick out CO_2.

The captain, the two gunnies, Bomba, T-Bone, Rez, and of course JC, exited the station from the same southwest side hatch. The captain motioned for JC to take a few steps away and then aimed the small scanner at him.

"Jump up and down," she passed to him.

He did a few jumps, then dropped to his belly and jumped back up.

"Not bad," she said on the open circuit. A little leakage, but minimal. I think this might work. OK, everyone back inside."

With the news that the CO_2 was masked, the captain ordered everyone to get their own "fart catcher," as JC was insisting they call it, installed. And the first one would be hers.

"I'm going out with you," she said, and both gunnies raised their eyebrows at that.

"Look, we're missing too many of us. I can work out ranges and environmentals. I can be a spotter."

"So can I, Captain," Biming Lum said. "Let me go, too. I don't have an HED, but I don't need one of those fart-catchers, either."

She only hesitated a moment before nodding at the trooper.

"If he's going, so am I," Sergeant First Class Juarez said.

"No, you're not. I need to you here in command. If anything happens to us out there, I need you to call in the shuttle and get off the planet."

The IS Team leader seemed to be about to argue, but when the captain said "command," that seemed to immediately mollify him.

Bomba became the group armorer, personally taping each one of them up. It took an hour, but after Juarez had taped the last one on him, they were ready to go.

The captain called them in to go over the plan once more. It hadn't changed much, but with people missing, there had to be adjustments. She was going to take the place of Dutch and be Gracie's spotter, Lum was going to be Rez' spotter, and the both of them were going to hang back and provide overwatch. Without a spotter, T-Bone would take the Barrett and stay back as well, ready to engage if he saw anything.

"Get a last drink and a bite to eat if you want," the captain said. "Don't forget to take a shit, too. With the duct tape on our asses, better to do it now since we don't have any FIBs."

Bomba had said he thought that if really needed, the duct tape could be rolled up a bit far enough to uncover the anal vent, but the captain was right. Better to do it now than out in the field.

It took almost 45 minutes to get everyone fed, through the station's two heads, and through their weapons checks, but finally, everyone was ready. Manny took a head count as everyone moved to the exit.

"Who am I missing?" he asked. "I'm down one."

Gracie looked around counting heads when Shaan said, "It's T-Bone."

"Check the other rooms," she said as the captain powered up her suit, bringing up her display.

"Shit!" the captain said. "He's out there already."

Gracie powered up as well, and there, some 400 meters from the station, T-Bone's blue avatar shone brightly.

"Staff Sergeant Mubotono, what are you doing?" the captain sent on the command circuit.

There was no answer.

"Tibone, you're in some deep shit. Hold up," Gracie passed on the P2P.

"Sorry Gunny. You don't get all the fun. I'm the best man for the job, and you know it. And I don't need 15 minions scrambling around messing things up. It's me and him, like it should be. When I zero him, everyone will know I'm the best sniper in the Corps, not some lucky PC asswipe like you."

His circuit cut out, and Gracie couldn't raise him again.

The captain was still trying to raise him until Gracie cut in on the P2P.

"He's not going to respond," she said. "He's on a mission to prove he's the best."

The captain erupted with a string of obscenities before saying, "He'd better hope that sniper nails him because I'll have his ass if he survives."

Then, powering down her suit for a moment, she said, "Mubotono's already on his way. And so are we. Mount up."

With the now familiar zing of bubble fields powering up, the thirteen Marines and one trooper moved to the hatch and exited the station. Gracie didn't like the fart-catcher. With Spig gone, she was the smallest of the Marines, and the duct tape and scrubbers felt like she had a large cat clinging to her ass. It affected her gait. She was essentially going to take the same route as before, so without hesitation, she began to crawl where the scrubber was less of a constriction and more of merely an extra weight. T-Bone was up ahead of her, and part of her wanted to crawl up there and beat some sense into his head. But anger created mistakes, and mistakes could cost her and the captain their lives. She had to purge T-Bone out of her mind.

She kept waiting to hear a shot ring out, and it wasn't until she'd reached the same distance she'd had when Dutch had been hit that she began to acknowledge that either the enemy sniper had left the scene or that Bomba's fart-catchers actually worked.

Twenty minutes later, the toilet bowl canopy began to thin out. She'd have to slow down now as the two of them would be much more exposed. The HED 2s had decent camouflage capabilities with the same syntho-chromatophores that gave the Marines' skins and bones their ability. It was good, but not great. Any trained sniper should be able to spot them if they made a mistake.

On the plus side, she'd begin to have her own fields of fire, and it was possible that she could spot her target. She started scanning with her Miller, but still motioned for the captain to move up and use her glasses to search the area ahead. She hoped that one of them could catch a sign, any sign of the enemy.

When the shot rang out, she almost jumped before realizing it was a Barrett, and it was ahead of her. It had to be T-Bone. She was still going to kill the guy when all of this was over, but she hoped he'd succeeded. She waited vainly for him to come back on the net, full of his braggadocio style while he boasted how great of a sniper he was. The net remained silent.

Now, what? she wondered. *Do we wait? Do we go confirm a kill?*

She was just about to displace forward when T-Bone fired again.

*You'd better have got—*she started before a single, sharper report rang out.

Immediately, T-Bone's avatar went gray. An instant later, three more shots rang out, almost in unison, from two Windmoellers and a Kyocera. Gracie hadn't been in a position to see any sign of the sniper, but at least three of her fellow snipers had. Gracie felt a surge of relief. With three acquiring him at once, surely he'd been taken out.

"I didn't see anything," the captain said. "Did you?"

"That's a negative, but somebody did."

"Report," the captain passed on the net.

"Saw the shot and took my own. Probable hit," Rez said.

"Not so sure I was on target," Dylan Tash passed. "Took a snap shot when I thought I saw something."

"Same here. I'm sure we both spotted him, but I don't know if I hit him," Bomba said.

"What now?" Captain Lysander asked Gracie. "I've never thought about what you guys do if you can't confirm the kill."

"Depends, ma'am. Usually, we don't do anything unless we're ordered to do the BDA."

"We've got one dragonfly still operable. I'm going to get the coordinates from Staff Sergeant Francisco and have it fly in for a look-see."

Gracie liked to keep her display relatively clean. She already hated being in the confining HED 2s, so the less she had to clutter up her vision, the better. But she toggled over to surveillance and hooked into the dragonfly's transmission. The little drone's visuals were surprisingly clear, and its track took it right over her position. She couldn't pick herself or the captain out on the display, which was as it should be. She risked a glance up, but she couldn't see the drone as it flew over.

The coordinates of where Rez had fired were now superimposed on the display, and Gracie was trying to make out anything on the ground when another shot rang out, and a second later, the drone's feed disappeared.

He shot the drone out of the sky?

Gracie wasn't sure she could do that, and as a professional, she had to be impressed. As a Marine, though, she could feel a fire rising from deep inside of her, increasing her need to destroy her opponent.

"I guess I missed," Rez passed.

I guess so.

"Did anyone pick up anything?" Gracie asked, hoping someone had spotted the shot that had taken down the drone.

The silence on the net was deafening.

Finally, the captain said, "The Eagle Eye trace shows 175 degrees."

Gracie popped up the last position of the drone, then backtracked at 355 degrees. Either Rez had been pretty far off from where he'd spotted the round that had taken T-Bone out, there was more than one sniper, or he'd moved like lightening to get to a new position, all without being spotted. She wished she knew the answer, but she suspected that it had to be that Rez had never actually seen the target.

She wanted to be sure, if she could, so she did a quick map study, and something caught her attention. She flipped the aspect to 3D, and a pattern became clear. There was a series of slight dips in the landscape, more like ripples of ancient waves on prehistoric sea beds. Covered with plant life, they were not obvious. But the terrain was there. If the area had been prepped, it could be possible for someone to move quickly and out of sight. It wouldn't be easy, but it would be possible.

The HED display was hardly the best available, and it could be unwieldy. It took her several tries, but she was finally able to highlight the ripples using her ocular stylus. She sent that out to everyone.

"I think our target is using this to maneuver. Manny, I want you to shift left, then using Delhi as cover, get up and haul ass to an FFP in the vicinity of 22455-67395."

She suddenly realized that with the captain there, she wasn't in command, and she gave her a quick glance.

The captain nodded, so she continued, "Everyone else, get into a good FFP, then stay put until Manny's in position. Manny, you and Riko keep your eyes peeled. If I'm right, you're going to have clear enfilade if the target tries to move between positions."

"Roger that. We're on our way."

"Now we wait," Gracie told the captain.

Chapter 49
68

"Hauling ass" was relative. For snipers on a stalk, it was still a pretty slow process, all the more so when the target was also hunting them. It was almost thirteen hours before Manny and Riko travelled the 1900 meters to their new position. Gracie had managed a good solid two hours of peering through her Miller before she had to start trading off with the captain, twenty minutes on, twenty minutes off.

When Manny reported they were ready, it was a relief to be back on the move again. And they had to move. They all were the bait. It was extremely unlikely that 12 Marines could move in on someone who obviously had mad skills without being spotted, so Gracie's plan essentially meant that she was offering up one of them to be shot at in order for Manny to take his shot.

It's not going to be me, she thought before feeling guilty about thinking that.

If it weren't her, it would be one of her fellow Marines. Whoever made a mistake would become the target.

Gracie eased past her temporary hide and slowly crept forward, the captain right behind her. She'd been apprehensive with the captain with her. The woman had never attended scout-sniper school, after all, but she wasn't doing a bad job, Gracie had to admit. And if she made a mistake that drew the enemy sniper's attention, well, that was the luck of the draw.

There was a slight depression five meters to Gracie's right, but it was not deep enough to give complete cover, so Gracie ignored it. If she could pull up relief maps, so could anyone else, and that meant they'd be aware of the depression. If it didn't offer full cover, Gracie wasn't going to use it.

As she crept forward, her thoughts drifted to the fart-catcher taped to her butt. Bomba hadn't said how long the two scrubbers would last, but she'd begun to worry about that as she waited for

Manny to get into position. Surely they would last long enough to complete the mission, she thought, but now, as she crawled, her butt felt vulnerable.

Her senses were on full alert. She'd much rather have been stationary in her hide, waiting for the other sniper to make a mistake, but they had to flush him out, and that was only going to happen by closing in on him. Gracie kept expecting to hear the report of a shot reach out to her, but silence reigned. Either the Marines were being extremely skilled in their stalk, or the enemy sniper was being patient, maybe waiting until he had more of them picked out before firing.

It was almost three hours later, while Gracie and the captain were only 400 meters from the rise, that the expected shot was taken. Immediately, Shaan's avatar grayed out, and another shot was fired. JC's avatar, right next to Shaan's, went light blue.

"Get ready, Manny!" Gracie passed needlessly.

And nothing happened.

Was this all for nothing? Gracie wondered, anxiety flooding her.

She was sure her plan had failed when a single, very much welcomed crack of a Windmoeller reached her from Manny's direction.

"Target down," Manny passed.

"Give me a feed," the captain demanded.

Manny opened up his Miller's feed, recycled fifteen seconds, and the image of a figure in some sort of ghillie appeared, a breathing system over his mouth and nose and hunched low as he ran along one of the ripples Gracie had spotted. With the magnification, Gracie could see the man's face as he looked toward his left, the direction to where the Marines would be—all those except for Manny and Riko, that is.

Manny fired just as the man turned to him, his face seeming to realize that something was wrong. Too late. He looked like he was starting to dive to his right when Manny's round took him right in the middle of the chest. The ghillie evidently didn't conceal any armor as the man fell back, both legs bent beneath him. He tried to rise, and one leg flopped out before he went still.

"Any sign of anyone else?" the captain asked him.

"That's a negative. It was just him."

"Just him" had cost the Marines and FCDC at least two non-resurrectable KIAs, three more KIAs, and three WIAs. Against trained Marine snipers, that was more than Gracie would have thought possible. She stared at the image of the man, wondering just who he was.

"We need to recover the body," the captain said. "We've got to find out who he is. Staff Sergeant Carlito, you and Sergeant Delay are the closest. You're up."

"Keep your head down, Bomba," Gracie told the staff sergeant on the P2P. "We don't know for a fact that there isn't anyone else around."

She maneuvered to her right until she had a better view of the rise, but her attention kept drifting back to the avatars of her last two snipers, other than her, in the Port Section. Five of her section were down, KIA or WIA. Her stomach felt sour, and for a moment, she thought she'd have to rip off the duct tape as her gut spasmed. Gracie had dealt a lot of death in her career, but she hadn't experienced it very often, and never to this degree. She tried to will the two other Marines forward without incident. She didn't think she could lose anyone else and still function.

Bomba and Tenner were cautiously moving forward, weapons at the ready, and as they reached the foot of the rise, Gracie began to hope that all was well.

Which of course, meant it wasn't.

Two quick shots rang out, and Gracie lifted herself to her elbows to get a better view. Bomba and Tenner were hitting the deck, scrambling for cover, and Gracie let out a sigh of relief—before she saw that both Manny and Riko's avatars had grayed.

"No!" she shouted as she dropped back down to her belly.

*Where the hell. . .*she started before her mind started going into overdrive.

Sitting in her last hide for thirteen hours, she'd reviewed the terrain over and over, plotting possible FFPs, plotting routes. The area was embedded in her mind, and suddenly, as if the curtain was removed revealing the Oz, she knew exactly where the enemy sniper was, and more than that, where she had to be to engage him. Furthermore, while Bomba and Tenner were momentarily safe, when the gunman moved to his alternate position just a handful of meters away, he'd have the two Marines dead to rights in an untenable position.

She marked a position on the map, then sent it to the captain.

"Captain, right now, put everything you have on that spot with the M99. Everything!"

Captain Lysander had been carrying a Kyocera, but that was more in case Gracie wanted it. She was also armed with her personal M99. At full combat load, she had over 4,000 of the small but deadly 8mm darts. And at only 400 meters away, she should be able to shred the area.

To Gracie' surprise, the captain rose to one knee, completely exposing herself, before opening fire. If the enemy sniper had been watching their position, the captain would have been cut down before she could fire, but the gods of battle were watching over her, and the captain was blazing away like some Hollybolly hero.

Gracie didn't need to be watching her like some awestruck schoolgirl. She jumped to her feet and took off, the fart-catcher bouncing on her butt and threatening to throw her off stride. She'd considered juking and dodging to throw anyone targeting her off, but she thought speed was of an essence, and she had to cover over 100 meters, in full gear and over uneven terrain. It was an all-out sprint.

An M99 was a quiet weapon, and once Gracie had covered 20 meters, she couldn't hear the captain firing. She couldn't help herself, though, from glancing up to the captain's target. Pieces of fungal-plants were flying into the air as the high-velocity darts struck, their tiny fins spreading out as the points felt resistance. Gracie was positive that the enemy sniper was at the point—if they were lucky, the captain had already taken him out. If they weren't as blessed by the gods of war, then at least she was keeping his head down.

She hadn't zeroed him, though. While Gracie was still 30 or 40 meters from her goal, a shot echoed from above her. On her display, the captain's avatar flickered light blue, then back to bright blue, then back to light blue again. Gracie didn't bother to try and figure out what that meant, but a glance back up showed that there weren't darts impacting anymore.

Shit! she thought as she tried to redouble her speed.

Gracie was completely in the open, and the sniper couldn't miss seeing her. She probably had two seconds at the most before he targeted her. Her short legs churning, she surged the last few meters, diving over the tiny fault-line as the expected sound of the shot reached her.

Gracie landed hard, knocking the breath out of her, and it took a moment for her to realize she hadn't been hit.

Take that! she thought, deliriously happy that she was still alive, and more than that, in a position that put her and her opponent on almost an equal footing.

He still had the high ground, but he couldn't move without exposing himself.

"Captain, are you all-right?" she passed on the P2P as she caught her breath.

"I. . . I think I'm hit."

She thinks she's hit? Is she or isn't she? Gracie wondered, confused as to the captain's response.

She'd figure that out later, but for the moment, she passed, "Stay down. Don't become a target."

To Bomba, she passed, "You're in a bad position. He's going to ignore you now while he attends to me, but you've got to move in case he gets me. Try and slide over another 50 meters to your northeast. You two might be able to get some cover and concealment there."

"Roger," Bomba passed.

Gracie could hear the concern in his voice, but he didn't bother to try and talk her out of anything, and that was somehow more comforting than if he'd done that. He was relying on her abilities as a Marine sniper to defeat their opponent.

His confidence fanned her own, bringing it back to life. She'd take this asshole on. She'd bought Bomba and Tenner more time, if nothing else. The enemy sniper could read terrain just as well as Gracie could, he certainly realized he was in an exposed position, and he knew Gracie was his biggest threat. Anyone else could wait.

Gracie quickly passed to the two remaining Starboard teams to keep alert. Neither team was in a position to help her, but they could be if Gracie were taken out and the sniper made a mistake in moving to engage Bomba.

With the others briefed, she had to address the situation at hand. Gracie was on a natural platform, some 25 meters long, and protected by a 70 cm high lip. The platform was mostly rocky, but it had some vegetation scattered across it. On top of the lip, the plant growth was thick, providing excellent concealment.

Three-hundred-and-twenty meters away, the enemy sniper was prone along one of the ripples. He had excellent cover from the front, towards the station, but from Gracie's position, he would be exposed if he retreated down the ripple, he'd be exposed if he tried to climb up and over the crest, and he'd be extremely exposed and an easy target if he tried to come down the slope. He was a good 20 meters higher than Gracie. The only way to avoid her would be to move forward through his previous position, the one that the captain had just shredded.

Shit! Gracie thought.

While she was collecting her thoughts, she could very well have been doing that, slipping to the front and then moving to a different FFP.

She turned towards her belly and eased her Windmoeller forward until the Miller had a line to the position. She couldn't see anything. Either the sniper was already gone, or he hadn't thought of that yet. She was just about to ease back when the breeze picked up, and the tattered growth started to sway—all except for one of the purple balls. It remained almost motionless. The purple balls tended to move in the slightest breeze, so something was holding it back. She couldn't see the base of the ball because of the top of the ripple.

Gracie aimed as low as she could on the ball and fired a single round, just clearing the ripple and blasting the ball into a purple mess. She caught the briefest movement as something scurried back down. She couldn't make anything out, but after seeing the ghillie on Manny's feed, that didn't surprise her.

She knew she hadn't hit him, but she hoped that would discourage him from trying that again.

She checked her display. Bomba and Tenner had almost reached their destination. In another few minutes, they'd have ginned up a better position. She felt relieved, but that was not good enough. Gracie had to take out the threat that loomed over all of them.

Trying to remain as motionless as possible, Gracie started scanning the ripple. It wouldn't take much for her to be able to spot him. This wasn't some sniper versus sniper exercise, where two snipers were let loose in a large training area. Gracie knew where he was, and he knew where she was. At 350 meters, the tiniest mistake could reveal an exact position.

To lessen that chance, Gracie was not traversing her weapon—she was letting the scope do the scanning. If she spotted something, then she'd bring the weapon to bear.

And that was almost a fatal mistake. The Miller's small AI flicked through and highlighted possible unnatural shapes or odd movements, the majority being false positives. The flickering almost became part of the background noise, and when it hit yet one more, it took a moment for Gracie to recognize it as the muzzle of an otherwise hidden weapon. Her Windmoeller was not in position to fire upon it, and Gracie ducked back down a split-second before the ground where she'd just been erupted in a mini-volcano.

Think, Crow! she admonished herself. *Don't rely on tech! Think like a sniper!*

Her heart racing, she shifted her position. That had been a close call. She ran a finger over the muzzle of her Windmoeller, checking to make sure her frac-tape was still on. She wondered if the enemy sniper didn't use something like frac-tape or if he did, if it had fallen off. Either way, she was still alive and kicking because his muzzled had been visible.

Gracie didn't know how she'd been spotted, and wondered if it had been her scope. She wished she'd had a truthteller with her. She could set that up offset from her position. If it was spotted, the worst her opponent could do would be to take it out, and in doing so, reveal his position.

Unfortunately, she didn't have one with her. She might as well wish for a Wasp to strafe the other sniper or the *Porto* to be overhead and send down one of its ground support beams. Still, the idea of a remote kept tickling at the back of her mind. If there was only some way to get the enemy to focus on someplace she wasn't, and then even engage it, Gracie could end this right here and now. How to do that, though, was the real question.

As she eased forward, again, her mind started listing what she had with her. A Windmoeller sniper rifle with Miller scope. Her M99. The tiny Victor handgun she still kept with her. Her sniper kit. A fart-catcher hanging off her butt. A Hwa Win combat knife.

The fart-catcher came back to her mind. What if she could make it disgorge CO_2 instead of absorbing it? Was the other sniper still monitoring for it?

Curious, she edged back down under cover, then undid enough of the duct tape so that she could worry one of the two cylinders loose, quickly taping the remaining one back up. She realized that if the sniper was still monitoring CO_2, she'd just given up her position, but unless he had a CD round, she was still safe for the moment.

That thought made her pause, but as no counter defilade round came blasting her way to explode a meter over her head, she shrugged and went back to examining the cylinder. She quickly realized that she couldn't do much with it. The air that came in was pressurized from her HED 2, not the cylinder. When it was disconnected, there wasn't any air movement at all.

She set the scrubber down, ready to abandon that line of thought when a thoroughly disgusting idea hit her. She wanted to reject it out of hand, but unfortunately, she thought it could work. She looked over her shoulder back towards the sniper on the hill, wondering if she should just go mano-y-mano, like in the flicks, but he'd proven to be a worthy and skilled opponent. Gracie knew she was good, but she was not T-Bone. Her ego was not going to let her ignore any potential advantage.

With a sigh, Gracie flicked off the automatic kill option on her HED 2. If she got hit bad enough, then maybe the planet she hated would finish the job on her. She didn't think she really needed to turn off the option, but it would suck if half-way through this, she'd be KIA.

She took out her Hwa Win and checked the blade. Short and triangular, the blade wasn't standard issue but had been a favorite among Marines for a hundred years.

How am I going to do this? she thought, wishing she had someone else to help her.

But there wasn't anyone else, so she carefully reached under her ass, like she was wiping herself, and slit the polymer undersuit around the anal valve, then the urinary valve. After that, it was surprisingly easy to pull them out, the tubes attached to them following in trace.

Gracie stared at the two tubes, holding them gingerly. Luckily, she hadn't used the anal tube, but still. . .

The tubes were standard bio-tubing. They could be compacted down to a small cylinder about 5 centimeters long or stretched out to almost a meter in length. Gracie unwrapped more of the duct tape, then she used it to connect the two tubes. The urinary tube had a smaller diameter, so she stuck one end inside the larger tube, then hoped the duct tape made a good enough seal.

She checked the time. She'd been there for almost 15 minutes. The enemy sniper knew there were other Marines still in the fight, and he couldn't take too long to take Gracie out if he wanted to either escape or fight on, so Gracie had to work quickly if she was going to retain the initiative.

Looking at her weapons, her thoughts went back and forth several times before she reluctantly chose the Windmoeller. With one more piece of duct tape, she attached one end of the tube to the stock of the weapon.

She knew she had let a bit of CO2 escape when she'd pulled the scrubber, so this was a logical position, but it might be under too intense scrutiny for the same reason. So keeping low, Gracie crawled to a spot 10 meters away. It took her almost two minutes to ease her Windmoeller into position. She breathed a sigh of relief when it was in place and she hadn't eaten a round while emplacing it.

This was only half of the equation. Gracie had to get into a good firing position as well. She wanted to simply move to her left, but the pseudo-plants got in the way. She ended up having to almost weave the tube between the stalks, taking five minutes to set up two meters away from her Windmoeller. She wished it was farther away, but that was all the tubes she'd had inserted into her.

Gracie brought up her M99. It didn't have the angles that her Windmoeller had, angles designed to minimize being spotted, nor the trac tape that disguised the muzzle. . .

Crap! I should have taken that off the Windy and put it on the 99, she thought. *Too late now.*

No angles and no trac tape on the M99, but it would have to do. She put it on the ground, then slid over it, just as she'd done back on her final stalk back at Scout-Sniper school so many years ago.

It's been a long time just to come back full circle, she thought.

She peered through the various fans, balls, and stalks that served as plants, shifting her position until she had a good view of the ripple.

OK, this is it, she thought, bringing up the end of the tube, piercing the bubble, and placing it into her mouth.

She couldn't remember which end of the tube this was, whether it had been attached to the valve or had been inside of her, and she preferred not to think about it as took a deep breath, then exhaled through the tube. She didn't know how much air she needed to make it through, so she breathed twice more, her eyes peeled for any sign of the enemy.

And there was nothing. She knew the other sniper was there, watching, but he hadn't taken the bait. Gracie took another breath and blew through the tube. Still nothing.

Maybe he needed more. She gently pulled on the tube, and two meters away, the tip of her Windmoeller twitched—and almost immediately, a shot rang out. The Windmoeller was hit and flew up and back. Three-hundred-and-fifty meters away, Gracie spotted the sniper. She'd been looking at the position for the last few minutes, seeing nothing. As soon as he fired, though, his shape was evident to Gracie's trained eye.

Gracie grabbed her M99, pulling it forward in one smooth movement—just as the other sniper seemed to realize it was a trap and started to swing his weapon to take Gracie under fire. As the gunman turned, he became a she, her face clear above the breathing mask.

He or she didn't matter, and Gracie fired her M99 on full auto, sending the hyper-velocity darts over the intervening distance. The enemy sniper managed to snap off one shot, which still came distressingly close to Gracie, but that was all as the little darts shredded her body. Gracie kept firing as the sniper fell forward over the edge of the ripple, her body sliding down the slope and leaving a bright red trail that contrasted with the dull pastels of the planet.

Chapter 50
69

Two days after the shootout, Gracie stood back as the new Mei Shan scientists took over the lab. Unbeknownst to any of them, the giant multi-galactic corporation had bought out Allied Biologicals' share in the bio-rights to the planet. The Mei Shan Group was headquartered on the independent (and tax haven) world of Du Pierre 4, but Mei Shan Plastics, Inc, was incorporated on Hiapo, and therefore as a Federation company, qualified under Federation law for the purchase—this despite the fact that as far as Gracie could pull up on the interweb, the company had nothing to do with biological research.

The AB team seemed in great spirits, happy to get off the planet and secure in the knowledge that there would be hefty bonuses thrown their way. Dr. Tantou seemed the happiest, and if Gracie could read him, relieved.

Dr. Williams was the only one of the team working. He was assisting the *Porto* doctor preparing for the transport of the popsicles, the eleven bodies in stasis, back up to the *Porto* and the Mei Shan transport. The troopers and the enemy snipers were going to the Mei Shan ship, but by unspoken demand, the Marines were going to the Navy ship. The brotherhood between the Marines and the Navy created a trust that wasn't always there with other organizations, and the Marines always preferred Navy medicine. Lieutenant Commander Chacon had tried to send the shuttle down to pick up the popsicles right after the battle, but he'd been ordered to stand down until the Mei Shan ship arrived in system.

With the buyout, secrecy was no longer a factor, and the Marines expected to be recalled soon. Mei Shan had their own security teams, so the IS Team was being lifted off today, and the Marines, while still at the station, were somewhat redundant. And the Marines were down to eight effectives. The captain was one of those effectives, even if she was still limping. When she'd got up to fire her M99, she'd given Gracie the cover to run to her position, but the sniper had simply shifted her position and fired at the captain, hitting her in the fart-catcher. One of the scrubbers had stopped the round, but it had been forced into her hip and butt cheek, leaving a nasty mass of bruised flesh. A couple of hours under local regen on the *Porto* would go a long way in starting the healing process, but the captain would not leave while she had Marines still on the planet.

Eight effectives meant nine Marines were down. Gracie shifted her gaze to the line of popsicles. Dr. Wiliams gave six of them fairly good prognosis. Riko could possibly be resurrected in the *Porto's* sick bay. He'd been shot in the side, not doing much damage but destroying the integrity of his HED 2, so the suit had shut him down as per protocol. It was well within the ship's capabilities to zap his heart back and heal the relatively minor wound. The rest would probably go back to one of the Naval hospitals before being resurrected. Dutch faced a long and painful regen, but he should be able to make it. Spig and Farouk were the only two confirmed fatalities, and T-Bone was on the borderline. All told, the Marines and the IS Team were pretty lucky to escape as lightly as they did.

Only it didn't feel light to Gracie. Including her, there were only three left from her section.

Ready to load first were the causes of her losses. Two mystery people who had chosen to attack them. The man was a good candidate for resurrection, but the woman Gracie killed was not. They wouldn't even try. They'd take her DNA and search for a match, but Gracie knew they wouldn't find anything. Hollybolly took liberties with science all the time, but their favorite trope of DNA manipulation to give someone a new identity was more of a fact than fiction. Whoever these two were, from a DNA aspect, they were no longer the same two people as when they were born.

"Don't keep dwelling on it," Bomba said, coming up and leaning an arm on his shoulder.

"Too many lost," she said.

"And there'd be more if you hadn't gone warrior queen out there. You saved our asses, including my mother's favorite son's ass, and for that, she'll be eternally grateful."

"Your mother will be grateful?" Gracie asked as a soft chuckle escaped her.

"Sure. Well, maybe me, too. I'm fond of that ass, too, and I'd have hated to see it get shot off.

"Even if you looked like a penguin doing it," he added.

She turned, knocking his arm off her shoulder and leveling a wicked punch right under his ribcage.

"I did not!" she protested, before breaking out into laughter.

And it felt good to let loose.

She had looked like a penguin, she knew. One of the Eagle Eyes had captured her run to her position, the fart-catcher banging on her legs, keeping her strides short—buzz-saw quick, but short. Even watching the recording, she kept expecting to see herself cut down.

"OK, we're ready for them," a petty officer said, coming into the station.

"That's us," Bomba said, powering up his suit.

Gracie followed him, and along with the rest of the Marines, the captain included, they carried each Marine outside and loaded them into the shuttle. The loadmaster strapped each one down and motioned for the next. In a ziplock, material restraints were preferred over locking beams as there had been occasional instances of locking beams interfering with what were essentially only temporary containers. On the ship, they'd be transferred to sturdier units.

When Manny was loaded, Gracie lingered a moment, reaching out to touch the ziplock. She could see his shape inside, but no details. Dr. Williams had been confident that he'd make a full recovery. He'd looked pretty bad, his chest a mass of hamburger, so she'd been relieved to hear that.

As she started down the ramp to go back to the station, she had to get out of the way of Rez and Hamilton as they pushed the Palomino up the ramp and into the shuttle.

"Hey, what're you doing with Isá?" she asked, watching the beautiful machine disappear into the cargo bay.

"Orders," Bomba said. "The Intel types want to get their hands on it."

Gracie understood that, but still, it hurt. She'd even gone so far as to name the bike Isá, which meant "Arrow" in Crow. She wasn't the type to name inanimate objects, but this time, it seemed appropriate.

The serial number had already been sent on, which came back as "no such number" from WCD, no surprise. Gracie didn't know what else Intel could find out, and even if she expected to leave the planet soon, she hated to see the bike go.

She turned to get off the shuttle. The eight remaining Marines stayed outside until the shuttle lifted off, watching until the shuttle's flare was lost from site.

"I don't know how much longer we're going to be here," the captain said. "But we might as well make the best of it."

Gracie was the last to turn and follow the rest inside.

FS PORTOLUMA BAY

Chapter 51
69

The Marines were taken off the planet nine days later, but not how Gracie had expected. It had been obvious by the second day after Mei Shan had taken over that something was wrong. The Marines were spending most of their time in the common room when they weren't leading the Mei Shan security on lay-of-the-land patrols, and the arguments arising from within the lab were hard to miss. At one point, Captain Lysander started to open the door to find out what was going on when a short, broad-shouldered guard blocked her way, apologizing, but obviously determined to keep her out. The captain was still the mission commander, but after a few moments, she just shrugged her shoulders and sat down. It was obvious that even a captain could catch short-timer's disease.

On the third day, a construction team came down from the ship to start enlarging the camp, something to which the Marines were looking forward. Having their own berthing and head would be nice. That construction came to an immediate halt three days later after one of the corporate bigwigs came down to the station and locked himself and his retinue in the lab with the scientists for five hours. When he came out, he was not looking happy. Three hours later, the construction crew was picked up and lifted off-planet.

No one was talking to the Marines or the Navy. Lieutenant Commander Chacon knew no more than the Marines. The captain ended up not even asking anymore and immersing herself in a century-old holo series, and taking her cue, the rest of the Marines took their packs off with a resounding thud. There wasn't even a facade of providing any security.

On the ninth day, the captain was recalled to the ship, and by now, even the scientists were done with whatever scientists do. Most of them were not even from the Federation, but one was a fellow American from Baltimore, and he and Gracie had some lengthy discussions on the NFL, something that bored most of her fellow Marines. Gracie was a Portland Sockeye fan, but Steve was a diehard Ravens fan, a club that went back almost to the very origins of the game.

"Gunnery Sergeant Medicine Crow, I have a message for you," one of the unfailingly polite security team members said.

Gracie hadn't even bothered to learn any of their names, so she gave him a generic thanks and took the headset.

"Gunny, you've got 90 minutes to pack up and get ready to leave," the captain said.

"Ninety? That's not enough time, ma'am. The weapons are still in the racks."

The two of them had actually discussed packing them out, but a Marine without access to a weapon was useless, and as long as they were on a planet that had proved to be hostile, they keep the weapons handy.

"I had to fight to get that. They wanted an hour."

"What's up, ma'am?"

"I'll tell you when you get up here. Go to it."

They managed to be ready, barely, when the *Porto's* shuttle touched down. The weapons may not have been packed per regulations, but they were all accounted for, and that was the big thing. Gracie's seabag was not as neat as she usually kept it, and as far as the captain's, that was better left unsaid. Rez had simply stuffed everything he could find in the bag whether it was known to be the captain's or not.

With the ship in orbit, the flight took 35 minutes. Gracie felt a wave of relief as she stepped onto the hangar deck. Captain Lysander met them and told her to leave the gear with the Navy for now and to get her people cleaned up. She'd meet them in the officer's mess in an hour. Gracie passed the word, and five minutes later, was standing blessedly under the hot needles of the shower. Shipboard showers were hardly optimal, but she thought it was the best one she'd ever had. If she never got into a HED 2 again, that would be too soon.

Before going down to the planet's surface, they'd each left a clean uniform and sundries in a Navy laundry bag. The bag, with her name stenciled on the outside, was waiting for her on her rack. Being naked was a wondrous feeling, but pulling on a clean panties and bra, followed by a uniform that didn't try to climb into every pore and opening on her body was sublime. She'd mist-showered at the station, of course, and she'd been out of her polymer HED 2 skins while doing that, but even within the confines of a Navy ship, this was oh so much better.

She checked her PA, then gave her short hair a quick brush and left berthing, heading to officers' country and the wardroom. The *Porto* might be small, but it still followed the traditional layout of all Navy ships.

She wasn't the last one in the Wardroom, but almost. Two minutes after she arrived, the captain and the ship's skipper came in. They came to attention, then sat back down to hear what the captain had to say.

"That was not the easiest mission I've had," she started. "And I'm sure you can all say the same thing. We've lost one of us for sure, and that could end up being two. Seven more are going into regen—well, maybe not Sergeant Rikoman, but you know what I mean.

"But no matter what, we upheld the honor of the Corps. We got hit, but we hit back.

"That's not why I called you here, though. We'll write our after-action reports. I'll conduct your exit interviews. But that will start after we get a good Navy meal and some sleep in a real rack. Right now, I wanted to let you know just what the heck has happened."

Almost as one, seven Marines leaned forward to hear what she had to say.

The captain took a deep breath, looked at the ship's skipper, and then turned back to the Marines.

"As you know, Mei Shan bought the bio-rights to whatever Allied Biologicals had on the planet. How that worked, I don't know, and it's not important. What is important is that the planet is a bust. That is, what is on it is a bust. There is no known biological gold mine."

"What?" Gracie muttered.

If there's nothing there, why were we dragged here to protect the station? And why were other people there trying to steal the secret?

The captain held out both hand, palms down, to quell the murmurs.

"Whether there was ever any potential, we don't know yet. What is pretty clear, though, is that Allied Biological knew pretty early on that the line of research was a dead end. That might have been after the initial word had been leaked, or it could have been a scam from the beginning."

"Scam?" Tenner asked.

"Yes, a scam. We are now sure that from the time we arrived, the planet was a dry well. There was scientific interest, both as a ribbon world and because of its life forms, but nothing there is of benefit to man."

"No medical miracle?" Gracie asked. "No cure for the Brick?"

"None at all. Which should have been obvious. Have we ever discovered organics on any planet that we can make use of? The capys can eat earth products, but have we found anything we could use? We were all pulled in by the promise, an empty promise."

"And that's what all the arguing was about. Tantou, and I bet Polonov, they knew all along. But the others, they weren't in the loop, and when their experiments were going south, they started to see the light," Bomba said.

"Yes, it seems that way. And Allied Biologicals needed to keep the facade going."

"Until they could sell the rights!" Gracie said, a curtain falling from her eyes.

"You got it in one, Gunny. We sure that's exactly what happened."

"What about everybody else?" Gracie asked. "Why were we getting hit if what was there was worthless."

"That probably wasn't known initially. It looks like it was coming out, though. The station we took? Their research had pretty much uncovered it."

"Is it true that AB pushed that raid?" Bomba asked in disgust.

"Yes," Lieutenant Commander Chacon said. "Too late, though."

"What about the attacks on us?" Gracie asked, afraid that whatever the captain said would only confirm the vague thoughts beginning to coalesce in her mind.

The captain looked at the skipper, who nodded. He was back to being the mission commander now that they were off the planet, and it was evidently his call to reveal whatever the captain was going to say next.

"Sources," she began, and Gracie could almost hear the quote marks in her voice as she said the word, "indicate that the indirect fire attacks were made at the behest of Allied Biologicals. They wanted to push a sense of urgency into the bidding process."

"If others are desperate enough to hit Marines and FCDC, then whatever was being guarded had to be pretty valuable," Gracie said bitterly.

The captain didn't respond, which was all Gracie needed. She felt anger boil to the surface. Saanvi Veer had told her not to be a lackey, and that was exactly what she'd been. What they'd all been. She'd killed people for who? For a fucking company, just to increase the price on a scam. She wanted to kill again, but not the minions. She wanted to clear out the Allied Biological board of directors, starting with the chairman and working her way down.

"What about the Brotherhood? Were they here?" Bomba asked.

"Almost certainly," the skipper said.

"Were those Memitim that the two gunnies zeroed?"

"Probably. We'll never know for sure, though," the captain said.

"So we get into a sniper match with Brotherhood Memitim, and what, we just ignore it?" Gracie asked.

"They won't admit it, and to be frank, neither will the Federation. You won't mention it again, once we leave this wardroom."

"That's bullshit, ma'am," Tenner said, finally opening her mouth. "They killed Spig. Dead. No resurrection."

"That's right, they did. And Gunny Medicine Crow killed one of them. Dead. No resurrection.

"Look, I know you're all upset. The Brotherhood is never going to come clean on this. They don't want anyone to know they were taken in. And the Federation isn't going to force the issue."

"Why not, ma'am?" Tenner asked.

"Because it's not worth a war. No single Marine is. Not Spig, not anyone else. No, according to the records, Spig was killed in the line of duty in action against criminal elements."

"So what's going to happen? I mean to AB? Mei Shan, they're one of the biggest corporations in the world," Rez asked. "They're not going to stand by and let some two-bit company take them like that."

"They probably will. Whatever they paid for the rights, that's peanuts compared to the damage they'd suffer if it were known that they'd allowed themselves to be taken. If I had to guess, I'd say they'll keep the research station open, always on the brink of making a breakthrough. Eventually, it can be closed down on a cost-benefit basis."

Gracie sat quietly seething. She didn't say anything else, barely listening while the captain went on for another five minutes, closing with the "keep your lips sealed stricture." She told them the consequences of breaking security, then had them all retinally scan their understanding.

Gracie almost refused, but she realized the scan was only a formality. Acknowledging understanding or not wouldn't matter if she broke security.

"May I speak with you privately, ma'am?" she asked as the others filed out of the wardroom.

The captain agreed, and Gracie followed her to her stateroom. The captain closed the hatch, then pointed to the fold-down stool in its slot in the bulkhead. Gracie didn't take it but remained standing.

"Captain, all of this is so much bullshit, I don't know where to start."

"You think I don't know that, Gunny? You don't think I'm royally pissed?"

"I killed for them, ma'am. I killed three people, not to protect the Federation, but so the Allied Biological CEO can buy a blue Lambo to match his red one. In my book, that's murder. You don't have that on your hands, ma'am, with all due respect."

The captain's eyes hardened, and in a dangerous tone, she said, "Because you pulled the trigger, you think that makes you more liable? I'm the one who order you into the fight. I'm the one who ordered Marines to kill and die. I'm sorry Gunnery Sergeant, but you don't have a flying fuck of an idea on how heavily that weighs on a commander's shoulders. You were obeying orders. I *gave* them!"

Gracie seemed oblivious to the captain's tone, and she said, "You should know, of all people. Your father led the Evolution, so we could escape the yoke of corporations, yet now you seem to be surrendering to them. How can you do that, you of all people?"

Captain Esther Lysander stared at Gracie for a moment before she slowly stood up, towering over the shorter woman. Her eyes dance with fire.

"How dare you, Gunnery Sergeant! You don't know the first thing about my father, what he believed in, what he fought for, what he died for! He believed in the Federation, all of it. And that includes the corporations. He did what he did to save the Federation, and some of what he did was horrible. He killed 11,000 people on Watershed. Men, women and children. How the fucking hell do you think he felt about that? He was devastated, but without a doubt, he'd sacrifice another 11,000 in a bleeding second if that was what it would take to save the Federation. Eleven-thousand more innocent souls.

"Let me tell you this, Gunnery Sergeant! If you try and bring my father into this to shame me because you don't have a clue as to what sacrifice means, I will fucking crush you like a cockroach," she said, her nostrils flaring.

Gracie stood up to the captain. She knew she might have crossed the line, but she didn't care.

"With all due respect, ma'am, I've 22 years in, so I've got my validation. I can resign today, and there's nothing you can do about it. You can write me up, you can court martial me, but when I'm 70, I get my retirement one way or the other."

A validation was nowhere near as valuable as a regular retirement. With eight more years, she could retire and begin to draw full retirement pay and benefits. With only a validated service records, she'd have to wait until she was 70, and both the pay and benefits would be far less. No one was stupid enough to leave the service after 22 years unless they had something sweet already lined up, but Gracie was angry, and she felt used.

The captain stared at her, and with a visible effort, gained control.

"If that is your wish, Gunnery Sergeant, so be it. Head down to personnel and fill out your resignation. I'll approve it and forward it out today.

"You're dismissed."

Gracie almost said something, probably something she'd regret, but she came to attention, performed her best about face, and marched out of the captain's stateroom.

EARTH
CROW NATION, MONTANA, UNITED STATES OF AMERICA

Epilogue
144

Gracie pulled to a smooth stop under the broad new-oak overlooking Greasy Creek, cutting the power. She'd never tire of Isá. The machine was beautiful, and as she flew across the plains, she felt freer than she'd had in a long, long time.

She'd been extremely surprised to find the Palomino waiting for her when she'd returned home. Surprised and touched. When Rez and Hamilton had pushed it into the shuttle, it was not under orders to send it to Intel. They'd just done it, unwilling to leave it to the Mei Shan crew. They hadn't told Gracie a thing about it—she couldn't be held liable for what she didn't know. Somehow, they'd gotten the bike back to Tarawa, then back to Earth where it sat in her parent's garage waiting for her. When her parents reminded her that it was there after she got back home, they didn't understand the tears that flowed down her cheeks.

Still sitting on the bike, she looked up into the massive branches of the tree. Once, there had been hundreds of the trees along the creek, part of a soil conservation project. Two hundred years ago, most had been cut down as non-native (and non-natural) species. The massive tree was one of only a handful that had survived the purge, and it had been a major reason she'd bought the plot. Gracie felt at home in the wide-open plains, but the tree gave the plot a more homey feel.

She looked over to where the foundation had been laid. It looked small and bare, but she knew that once the house was erected, it would be a pretty good-sized home. The support beams were scheduled to arrive next Wednesday, and once they were snapped into place, the rest of the components would quickly follow. In two weeks, Gracie was hoping to move in to her first, and hopefully last, home.

She checked her watch, noted the time, and powered up Isá. She had to get a move on. She turned and started to the dirt track that served as the temporary driveway, but stopped before going 50 meters. Looking over her shoulder, a wicked grin came over her face.

Go for it! she told herself.

She turned Isá around once more, sat for a second, then gunned the bike, the G-force shoving her back into the seat. Within seconds, she was at 80 KPH and approaching the creek's high banks. Just before the front repeller cleared the edge, she hit the powerboost, and the bike literally jumped into the air.

Sunlight flashed on the slow-moving water as bike and woman flew over. Gracie landed with a thud on the far side, back repeller fishtailing before she brought the bike under control. This was one of the many Coups girls' properties, but Gracie didn't think the young woman would mind if she used it as a shortcut to the main road.

Ten short minutes later, Gracie was pulling into her parent's front yard. A strange hover was in the drive, and Gracie got off her bike and hurried to the enclosed porch.

"Gracie, your friends are here," her mother said, but Gracie was already rushing to get a hug from Tiggs Gittens.

"I'm so glad you could make it," Gracie said. "It means so much to me. All this way, too."

"Don't fret, sista. We've been planning to see the Mother Planet for a long time. Let the little ones visit our roots."

"Little ones?" Gracie said with a laugh. "Not so little to me! Henri, come give your Auntie Grace a hug," she said to the gangly young man standing behind his mother.

"What are you, two-point-three?" she asked him.

"Two-point-three-five," he said with a smile as he allowed Gracie to pull him in. "Eli's only two-point-three," he added.

"But Eli's got 20 kilos on you," she said, pinching Henri's ribs.

"Junior's just been made a team leader with 3/13," Sergeant Major Eli Gittens, said, coming out of the front door, a leading a small girl by the hand. "Electra, say hello to your Aunt Grace."

"Hello," the little girl said, moving half behind her dad's leg.

Gracie hadn't seen the Gittens family for almost two years, and little Electra probably didn't remember much about her."

"Eli Junior's a fire team leader? What, they're letting children run the Corps now?" Gracie said with a smile.

"I know. I can't believe how old he's gotten, how old all of the kids have gotten," Eli said.

"Where are—"

"Persephone and Jared are down running by the creek, trying to catch frogs or something," Tiggs said. "Jared wants to know if he can ride a horse before we head off to Los Angeles."

"I told him we don't have any horses," her mother said, a worried look on her face. "Maybe if we talk to Jerry, he'd let us head over this afternoon?"

"Oh, no trouble," Tiggs insisted. "We've got seven stops on this trip, and with Cairo the last, he also wants a holo of him on a camel."

Gracie didn't know how to ride a horse—the only one she wanted was her Isá. But how could she retain her title of favorite auntie unless she could ask Jerry Not Afraid if the kids could ride around on one of his horses? Besides, after this morning, Jerry would have a hard time saying no.

"And how is Daphne?" Gracie asked Tiggs.

"Doing fine. She's back from maternal leave, kicking butt and taking names, from what Bill says. She was going stir crazy, sure that the commission was going to fold without her guiding hand."

"Sounds like her," Gracie said with a laugh.

"She wishes she could be here, too, but you know, her duties. . ."

"I understand. I'm just amazed you came. When I invited you, I never thought you'd come half-way across the Federation to be here."

"How could we miss it, Grace? We owe you. I owe you," Eli said.

"Gracie, I don't want to be a mom, but don't you think you better get ready? Time's running short," her mother said, wringing her hands.

"Oh, sure. If you want to gather up Jared and Persephone" Gracie told Eli and Tiggs, "you can head on into Lodge Grass. There'll be food after, and mingling of course, but later in the afternoon, we'll see about rounding up a few horses."

Gracie received a hug from each of them, including Electra, then went inside her parent's home. Her sister Dana was in the kitchen, placing pemmican on a large platter. Gracie knew that Dana had spent days making it, and the thought touched her. Any fabricator on the reservation could make it, but Dana had wanted to do it the old way.

Gracie went upstairs and into her old room. She had some good Montana dirt on her face, so she took a quick Navy shower, then came out and stood over her bed where her dress blues had been laid out.

Her emotions surged as she looked at the uniform. There, on the bed, was her career. There wasn't much on her chest, comparatively speaking. Her highest medal was her BC3. Gracie had been in the shit more times than she could remember, and she'd been in some intense fights, but not much of that translated into awards. Part of that was because her missions were often classified, but part of that was, she thought, because even if the Marine Corps' mission was to close with and destroy the enemy, some people were not as comfortable with what she had been. She'd been the handmaiden of death, reaching out and touching those who she felt should die. And for the straight-leg grunt, the fact that she could reach out 4,000 meters to dish out death seemed almost unfair to some. She didn't know how that was different from arty or air Marines, but the fact was that snipers, even if every kill they made statistically saved the lives of three Marines, were rarely decorated.

She'd built a reputation, and she'd even had somewhat of a cult following, but her chest was pretty bare, the distinguished shooter badges hanging under her two rows of ribbons the only indication of anything out of the ordinary.

But on her sleeve, the chevrons of a Marine Master Gunnery Sergeant and the ten service hashmarks looked good. Her arms were so short that the chevrons and hashmarks almost filled the entire sleeve. Together, they told the story of a long and successful career—one that had almost ended prematurely. She picked up her PA and scrolled the many congratulatory messages she'd received on her retirement, going down to the L's and punching it up.

Master Gunnery Sergeant Medicine Crow,

It is with pleasure that I offer my congratulations on your upcoming retirement. It has been an honor serving with you, and I wish you the best in the next phase of your life.

Esther Lysander
Lieutenant Colonel
United Federation Marine Corps

It was short and sweet, but Gracie owed the colonel a debt of gratitude. Back on the *Portoluma Bay*, eight years earlier, Gracie had submitted her resignation in a fit of anger. The next day, she'd come to her senses, but she knew it was too late. It wasn't until Captain Lysander asked on Tarawa just before she'd been detached if she still wanted her to forward the resignation that Gracie realized she'd been given a second chance.

Captain Lysander had not only held onto the resignation, but she'd given Gracie a sterling fitrep with a recommendation for early selection to master sergeant. Because of that, a month-and-a-half ago, Gracie had become Master Gunnery Sergeant (Retired) Gracie Medicine Crow, with the pay and benefits of a full retirement.

Get going, Crow. You'll have a long time to contemplate your memories!

For the first time since her retirement ceremony, Gracie slipped on her uniform. It felt like coming home. She buttoned it up and looked in the mirror.

I still look kicking!

Time was getting short, so with one last brush of her hair, which for the first time since her enlistment was reaching over her collar, she left the bedroom and headed downstairs.

The house was empty—everyone was already in town. Gracie hurried out, swung her legs over Isá, and took off into town. It was a short trip, maybe five minutes, before she was pulling in front of the field office of the tribal council. She was shocked at the size of the crowd who broke into applause as she parked and got off the bike.

There were only 22,000 registered members of the Crow Nation, but there had to be double that number of people there. A Marine chief warrant officer and his team came up to shake her hand only to be shouldered out by the governor's support staff and more than a few news teams. Gracie didn't realize this was that big of a thing.

Dana barged through the different groups and rescued her, pulling her by the hand into the field office.

Gracie spotted Eli and Tiggs by the front door—and another familiar face, and she pulled Dana to a stop.

"Sergeant Major, I'm surprised to see you here," she stammered out.

"You invited me, didn't you?" Sergeant Major (Ret) Megan Holleran said, her hand out to shake.

Gracie had sent out about fifty invitations to the ceremony, but that was mostly as a courtesy. Federation Space stretched out a long way, and coming all the way to Earth wasn't something she could have expected. But here was the sergeant major, her Marine Corps Emblem pinned to the collar of her dress.

"Gracie, we have to go," Dana said, pulling on her sister's hand.

"Megan, we'll talk after the ceremony, OK?" she said as she was pulled inside the building.

Darrel Old Coyote, the tribal council chairman, stepped up to shake her hand.

"Quite a crowd out there, huh, Gracie?" he said. "I don't know if you've met the governor, so let me introduce you. Governor Wiederhof, Gracie Medicine Crow. Gracie, the governor."

Gracie shook the governor's hand. She'd seen her on the news before, but this was the first time she'd seen the five-term governor in person (which wasn't surprising as she had spent almost all of the governor's time in office off-planet).

"It's a great pleasure to meet you, Master Gunnery Sergeant," the governor said, a huge smile on her face.

Gracie murmured something back that she hoped sounded intelligent. The woman had a force of personality, and Gracie understood how she'd been elected and re-elected five times now.

Darrel escorted Gracie, Dana, and the governor to a small waiting room where her mother, father, and older brother were sipping tea. He then slipped out for a few minutes while the governor skillfully directed the small talk, even getting Gracie's usually taciturn father into telling a humorous story involving an eight-year-old Gracie and a baby skunk.

Everyone was laughing, even a red-faced Gracie, when the chairman stuck his head back in the door and said, "It's time, Gracie."

To the governor, he said, "And as I told you before, Madame Governor, the ceremony itself is only for Apsaalooké. My assistant, Bryan, will sit with you in the meantime."

"I know, Darrel. No worries. I'll be waiting here."

Gracie and her family stood up, shook the governor's hand once more, then followed Darrel to the back of the field office and out the rear door. There, in the parking lot, a huge bison-skin tent had been erected. The Crow had raised bison for hundreds of years, but Gracie was shocked at the size of the tent. It had to have taken hundreds of skins.

A roped-off area was to the right. Camcorders from the governor's office, the Marine Corps, and news outlets were behind the rope busily recording. As the chairman had told the governor, the ceremony was closed to outsiders, and that included camcorders. This was as close as they were going to get to the actual ceremony.

Jonathan P. Brazee

Gracie's family entered the tent first, followed by the governor, while she stood outside the entrance flap, waiting.

"Gracie Medicine Crow, enter," a voice called out from inside. Gracie took a deep breath and stepped forward.

****

Forty-five minutes later, Gracie pushed open the bison-skin flap and stepped back out into the late-morning sunlight. The edge of the flap knocked the eagle headdress she was wearing askew, and conscious of the press, she quickly straightened it up.

There was a smattering of applause as she stood there, waiting for her family and the council to step out. Gracie nodded once, and then feeling self-conscious, tried to look dignified until Darrel took her by the arm and escorted her and her family back up into the field office while the other 300 or so attendees filed around the side of the building to reach the front were the mass of people were waiting.

The governor was waiting outside the room where she'd been left.

"Congratulations," she said to Gracie, then "You must be so proud of her" to her parents.

Gracie was aware of a chant growing outside, and to her utter amazement, it was "Gracie, Gracie!"

"Well," the governor said with a laugh. "Maybe I need to take lessons from you. I can't think of anytime recently that I've had people chanting my name."

Darrel escorted Gracie and the governor out the front doors, her family in trace, when the crowd roared at her appearance. Gracie tried to wave, and her headdress started to slip again, and she had to reach up to right it.

Gracie stopped short of the podium along with the governor, and Darrel took his place, testing the mic by taping it.

"Apsaalooké, friends of the nation, and of course, our honored guest Governor Bianca Wiederhof of the great state of Montana, *sho'daache!*"

The crowd erupted into cheers at his greeting. He had to wait until it died down to continue.

"It's a great day, right? We've been blessed in our land and our people, and we're here to celebrate one of our own. I can smell the food cooking, and my stomach's growling, so please after we're done gabbing up here, I invite all of you to share in our hospitality. I'd like to thank all our volunteers for fixing up the grub, and a special thanks goes to Peter Yellowtail from WWY Ranch for providing all the bison burgers. Peter, you out there? I bet you're having second thoughts about that now when you see how many people showed up!

"We've got the Moon Troupe, our fine young teen traditional dancers, we've got our own Slate Axe—not the most traditional singers," he said as the crowd laughed.

Slate Axe was a chemo-rock band that had gathered a pretty good following in the northwest, and they were decidedly not traditional.

"We're here, of course for our honoree," he said, sweeping a hand back to indicate Gracie, "but for all of you out there who might not know much about us, here's a chance to get to know us a little better.

"But enough of that. First, I'd like to introduce to you. . .hell, I don't need to introduce her to you. If you don't know Governor Wiederhof by now, you must be living under a rock! I give you, the governor of Montana!" he said, giving her the podium.

"Master Gunnery Sergeant Medicine Crown, people of the Crow Nation, fellow Montanans, and welcomed guests to the Big Sky country, *Ka-hay!*"

The governor actually had the pronunciation of "hello" down pretty well, Gracie noted.

"This is a great day for the Apsaalooké and a great day for all Montanans. One of our daughters has distinguished herself in the service to tribe, state, country, and Federation . . ."

Jonathan P. Brazee

Gracie's PA vibrated with the pattern of a personal message. She wondered who it was and looked back at the governor, trying to look attentive. The vibration continued, and she kept ignoring it, but curiosity was driving her crazy. Very few people had the number, and most of them were here. Finally, as the governor spoke on, Gracie slid the PA out of her pocket and took a quick look. A smile broke out on her face as she saw the message.

Gracie,

If I got the times right, you've had the ceremony by now. Please accept my congratulations. I wish I were there, but you know the Big Suck. My only question to you is when I do see you next, do I have to bow to your eminence?

Bomba

Gracie slid the PA back into her pocket. Sergeant Major Carlito Rapa was on the Navy's annual show-the-flag tour, giving dog-and-ponies while the Federation both showed its strength and tried to woo good will. The training was pretty much worthless, but the libo could be great, and being the Marine Corps battalion attached to the show fleet was considered a reward for the previous year's performance. Bomba was a big part of his battalion's rise to excellence, and his name was being bandied about for bigger and better things. Only Gracie knew that as soon as he hit 30 years in another eleven months, he was retiring, and his first stop was going to be a small ranch house under a new-oak tree on the banks of Greasy Creek.

Gracie didn't know how long he was going to stay. Both of them had the unspoken realization that this was a test run. They respected each other, they liked each other, and there was a little love thrown in. But brotherly love in uniform didn't necessarily translate into romantic love once out of it. Bomba was raised a city boy, and the quiet life of the Montana prairies might not suit him.

It suited Gracie, though. And her people followed a matriarchal line. Men moved in with women, not the other way

296

around. She'd welcome Bomba into her life, but without expectations. If it worked, it would. If not, well life still had opportunities that might come her way.

A round of clapping broke through her reverie. The governor was done, and Darrel was back at the podium.

"And now, the reason we're all here, and I have to tell you, from the bottom of my tired heart, that I am truly honored to be here today. I was there at the Agency 24 years ago when we bestowed upon our own Gladiator, Chief Warrant Officer Falcon Coups, also a Federation Marine, the title of honorary chief. I didn't think then I'd ever be so proud, but I have to tell you folks, I'm about bursting at my seams now.

"For those of you who don't know what happened, Master Gunnery Sergeant Gracie Medicine Crow retired almost two months ago from the Marine Corps and came home. We Apsaalooké, we're a warrior people—well, some of us are," he said, patting his rather large beer belly.

"And we are a people of tradition, so I asked Gracie to come up to the Agency and tell our chief historian her story. It turns out, Gracie had quite a story to tell. After her first tour, she became a Marine Corps sniper, and during her career, she recorded 144 kills, more than any other Marine in the last 50 years. One of those was at 4,565 meters, the longest shot ever recorded. She can't tell me what it was about, but I saw the certificate. Go ahead, look it up on Guinness. This girl can shoot."

Gracie's record looked to be lost three years ago when a Confed sniper got a reported kill at 4,567 meters. That record lasted all of three days before the Guinness keepers of all that is holy went over three different satellite feeds, adjusting the distance to 4,564 meters. So by one meter, Gracie was still the record holder. She knew the record would fall. The new Daewoo VT-50 was supposed to put the Barrett to shame, but until some hard-charger reached out farther than she had, she was still the top dog.

"Here, listen to me go on. Well, to cut to the chase, Wendy Davis, our historian, she came to me and said that something had happened, something that hadn't in over 500 years. If we used a little imaginative interpretation—Governor, you know we can be more than a little imaginative to get what we want," he said as the governor laughed and raised her hand and gave an exaggerated nod, "and we had a unique situation.

"So we brought in the executive branch, we brought in the judicial branch, and what we came up with was the vote that went to the general council three weeks ago.

"To all the rest of you standing here, what we asked was if the old warrior task of stealing a horse could be changed to stealing a 'mode of transportation.' Now, unless you're trying to sneak a ride on one of Jerry Not Afraid's herd, there aren't too many chances to steal a horse anymore."

Several planetary militias did have mounted troops, Gracie knew, but she'd never brought that up.

"Once again, I keep drifting, so back on track. Well, the vote came in 87% in favor. With that, well, we had a winner.

"From when we rode the plains, at war with most of our neighbor First Peoples—sorry about that, Hank" he said, pointing back to one of the men behind Gracie. "That's Hank Gladstone, my good friend and counterpart with the Blackfoot Nation.

"Anyway, where was I? Oh, yeah. From back then, there were four tasks a warrior had to perform in order to become a war chief. First, he had to touch a live enemy warrior, second, he had to disarm an enemy warrior, third, he had to lead a successful war party, and fourth, get ready for this, he had to steal an enemy horse. The last Crow war chief to do this was over five hundred years ago, and get this, his name was Joseph Medicine Crow, who served in the US Army in Europe during World War Two. Joseph Medicine Crow. Gracie Medicine Crow.? See a pattern here?

"Oh, and listen. Many of you here in Lodge Grass have seen Gracie tooling around in that sweet WCD superbike of hers. Do you know what model that is? Yep! It's the Palomino! And that's what Gracie stole! She really did steal a horse!"

Not many of the crowd seemed to have realized that before then, and the laughter was loud and boisterous.

"Well, my wife keeps telling me I talk too much, and the one we came to honor is standing behind me now," he said before turning around.

"Gracie, I was truly honored to conduct our ceremony today, and I'm sure our friends here would love it if you would share a few words."

Gracie was suddenly nervous. She'd never been much of a public speaker. She reached into her blouse and pulled out a sweat-stained and tattered piece of polychord that hung around her neck and kissed the Hog's Tooth that was attached to it.

"Ladies and gentlemen, I present to you, the first Apsaalooké War Chief in over 500 years, Master Gunnery Sergeant Gracie Medicine Crow!"

Jonathan P. Brazee

Thanks for reading Sniper. I hope you enjoyed it. As always, I welcome a review on Amazon, Goodreads, or any other outlet.

If you would like updates on new books releases, news, or special offers, please consider signing up for my mailing list. Your email will not be sold, rented, or in any other way disseminated. If you are interested, please sign up at the link below:

http://eepurl.com/bnFSHH

Other Books by Jonathan Brazee

Women of the United Federation Marines
Gladiator
Sniper
Corpsman

The Return of the Marines Trilogy
The Few
The Proud
The Marines

The Al Anbar Chronicles: First Marine Expeditionary Force--Iraq
Prisoner of Fallujah
Combat Corpsman
Sniper

Jonathan P. Brazee

The United Federation Marine Corps
Recruit
Sergeant
Lieutenant
Captain
Major
Lieutenant Colonel
Colonel
Commandant

Rebel
(Set in the UFMC universe.)

<u>Werewolf of Marines</u>
Werewolf of Marines: Semper Lycanus
Werewolf of Marines: Patria Lycanus
Werewolf of Marines: Pax Lycanus

To The Shores of Tripoli

Wererat

Darwin's Quest: The Search for the Ultimate Survivor

Venus: A Paleolithic Short Story

<u>Non-Fiction</u>

Exercise for a Longer Life

<u>Author Website</u>
http://www.jonathanbrazee.com

302

Made in United States
North Haven, CT
19 March 2023

34285625R00167